LIFE IN L.A.

LIFE IN L.A.

STORIES FROM
LANGUAGE ARTS CLASS
BY 131 SIXTH-GRADE STUDENTS OF
BERKSHIRE MIDDLE SCHOOL

Edited by

Daniel Fisher
Deana Straub

CONTENTS

8:15

9:15

9:15 (continued)

10:15

10:15 (continued)

11:15

11:15 (continued)

1:20

2:20

TO THE AUTHORS

You ought to be in pictures.
Your editors are proud of the work you have done and
know this is just the beginning of great things to come.
Your future's so bright, you've got to wear shades.

8:15

ALL-STAR

ALL-STAR, *by **Will Kostello**, is a story about a kid from New York and his journey to get in the NBA.*

Clang! It was the sound of the ball hitting the crooked metal rim. The street courts in New York aren't in the best shape. My best friend, Malcolm, took another shot. *Swish!* The ball went in the net.

"I think that's enough for today," said Malcolm.

"You're right," I said. We took our ball and left the court.

The air was cold in the winter of New York. Winter is the most important season for most of the people of New York. Why? Because it's basketball season. My high school, Brooklyn Academy, is one of the best in the state. We've won back to back championships the last ten years. I am the star starting shooting guard and average fifty points per game. Malcolm is the starting small forward. We are undefeated this season heading into the state championship.

While I was thinking about how we're going to win the championship, a man came up to us. He was wearing a suit and tie.

"Hello, my name is Jack Johnson," the man said. "So, I was just wondering, how old are you?"

"We're both sixteen," I said.

"Perfect!" the man replied. "I come to all your high school games."

"And..." I replied hesitantly.

"I want you, Brent Jones, to play for the New York Knicks."

Malcolm and I stood there stunned.

"What do you mean play for the New York Knicks?" I asked.

"I am the scout for the Knicks. I have not seen anyone play like you play. I've been to all your high school games."

"I'm not that good," I told the man.

"Are you kidding me?" the scout began. "You average fifty points a game!"

"I don't know," I replied nervously. "I don't think I'm ready."

"Well, here is a folder with all the information. If you change your mind give me a ring," the scout was gone in a flash.

When I arrived home, I told my mom about my conversation with the scout. "No, no, no," my mom said. "You are too young to play in the NBA."

"But, all of the greats came out of high school, like Kobe, Dwight, and..." I began.

"You are not ready," she interrupted.

"Just talk to dad about it," and I handed her the papers. I went to my room. Our apartment is as big as a high school restroom. So if I joined the NBA, I would get money to move my parents to a bigger apartment, or maybe even a house! I just wish they will say yes. Little did I know that tomorrow would be the best day of my life. I fell asleep.

The next morning, I heard the best news from my parents. They told me that I could play for the Knicks. I was exploding with joy! But, that wasn't all of the news. They also found out that I have an eight million dollar contract for one year. My first game was tonight.

"What?" I exclaimed. "Don't I have a practice or something?"

"No, they think you're ready enough, so you don't have to practice."

The school day was over in a snap. The game was at 7:00 p.m. against the Pacers. I was escorted by a bus to the stadium. When I arrived, I was greeted by the one and only, Carmelo Anthony! I was in the presence of one of the greatest basketball players alive! I was in shock. He greeted me and offered to show me around before the game. We walked for about fifteen minutes. When we got to my locker, my jersey was waiting for me: I was number one.

I was in the locker room prepping for the game with my teammates. It was finally game time. We did our team huddle and the announcers called us out one by one, they called Carmelo. I knew that was next.

"Ladies and gentlemen! Welcome our newest player, Brent Jones!"

The crowd erupted in cheers. That's the exact moment that I knew all my hard work had finally paid off.

THE CAMPING TRIP

In a galaxy far, far away... actually, it was in my backyard. Well, anyway, my brother and I have to use teamwork and trust to build a tent before nightfall. Luckily, we have the help of our dad in **THE CAMPING TRIP**, *by **Mya Waple**.*

My three-year-old brother, Liam, and I were out in our backyard playing baseball with an old, yellow plastic bat he got for his birthday when he turned one. The huge dent in the bat was made from his 'homerun' over the fence. After baseball, he wanted to play football. He doesn't have a real football, so we used a small red and blue foam football. This football is in pretty good shape considering the way he plays with it. After football, Liam and I laid down on the grass and looked at the clouds above us. The clouds to the East were white, puffy, cotton ball clouds you see in the movies. The clouds to the West didn't look very promising. They were misty, dark gray clouds that Liam calls stormy clouds.

"I hope it doesn't rain!" I say to Bubby, which is my brother's nickname.

"What's rayne?" Liam asks. I tell him that is when all the water falls down from the sky and we have to go inside or we'll get all wet.

"Ooh! raaiiinn!" he shouts.

A few minutes later, after a serious game of football, my dad walks out into the yard and opens up the garage.

"Hey Dad!" I shouted from across the yard. "What are you doing?"

"You'll see," he replied as he slid into the garage.

A minute later, Dad walks out with a strange looking box and a handful of rods. He set the box on the ground and starts to take out a red piece of fabric with slots on the side.

Finally, Dad said, "We're going backyard camping!"

Now I could clearly see that the red looking fabric was a tent, and the rods were the things that hold it up. I had never really gone on a backyard camping trip before. At least it sounded fun.

My Dad set up the tent very quickly.

"Have you done this before?" I ask with curiosity.

"Yes," he replied. "I set this tent up on a camping trip with Uncle Joe."

My brother jumps right in to help and ruins the whole tent! I told Liam that it was nice of him to try to help, but he had to be more careful. He said okay and helped put the tent back together.

It was almost finished except for the last rod. Where is the last rod? Oh, no! We're ONE SHORT! What were we going to do! We didn't have a replacement for the lost pole. We looked everywhere. We even looked in the garage under a lot of rusty tools and inflated basketballs.

When we gave up looking and were about to put the tent away, my brother walks up to me and hits me in the back! But, it wasn't with his hand. Liam started laughing and I turned around to look at him. In his hand was the black metal rod. I asked him where he found it and he said it was in the box! I felt kind of stupid and a little confused, but at least someone found it.

So, Dad finished putting the tent together. It was not a very large tent and had a couple of holes in the ceiling, but it was good enough for me and Liam. After it was done, we filled up the tent with pillows, blankets and lots of snacks to eat.

It was about 5:30 p.m. by the time we finished setting up and we were exhausted. Liam was still full of energy, as usual! We took off our shoes and started to relax, but then Liam jumped on my back! He was laughing so hard, I could see tears in his eyes. Our dad took him off my back and started to tickle him. He was laughing even harder now! By the time our tickle fight, pillow fight and snack war was over, it was already 8:30 p.m.! By that time, all of us were tired; even Liam. We all started to relax and doze off to sleep.

"What a surprise! Dad fell asleep first," I whisper to my brother. "No way!"

My brother started to laugh as I did a very realistic impression of our dad sleeping.

"He snores too loud!" Liam said with his serious voice. We both laughed.

Liam was the next one to fall asleep. He slept with his blanket covering his face and cracker crumbs all over him. I was the only one awake in that old, worn out tent and it started to grow on me. I thought about what had happened on its adventures: how it got its rips and tears, and how its red started to fade to brown. I looked at the holes in the ceiling and tried to count the stars. As I did, my boredom took over my eyes, and I was the last one to fall asleep.

Everything about this day was great. In fact, it was better than I could've imagined. Let's just hope it doesn't rain!

THE CAR CRASH

THE CAR CRASH, by *Kaitlyn Moore*, is the story of a young girl who was in a very severe car crash. Does she get hurt? Will she survive? Will she ever be the same?

Riley is a fun loving eight-year-old girl who has always wanted to ride horses. Riley was planning to be a professional horseback rider. Riley lived in a small town called Bakersfield. They called it Bakersfield because all the best wheat for baking was grown in Bakersfield.

One Saturday morning, Riley and her mom were driving to the bakery down the street when something tragic happened! There was a big car accident and Riley was severely hurt. Riley was too young for anything this terrible to happen to her. She had been in the hospital for almost three weeks now.

A young lady brought her some ice cream. Riley had always loved ice cream!

"Thank you," Riley replied. Riley ate the ice cream. She can only speak and move the top part of her body. It was a miracle that she survived everything: they said this was the smallest thing that could have happened.

Once Riley had healed from her injuries and was comfortable using her wheelchair, she was allowed to go home. When they arrived home the weirdest thing happened. Riley tried to stand up, and she did slowly! She leaned down, put her hands on the floor and pushed herself into a handstand! She realized she could do amazing things even with her wheelchair.

The next morning, her mom had amazing news. She signed Riley up for horseback riding! Riley had always loved horses and wanted to ride them. Riley was so happy to hear the news. Mom said, "You also get your own horse that you can name."

All night long, Riley had been thinking of names for her horse: Brownie, Flop, Gem, Cat, Hot Dog...! She was so excited. Actually, she was just joking around with those names. She would find the best name in the whole world for her very own horse!

They were finally on their way to Orchard Farm. Riley was so excited to meet her new horse. They pulled up to the farm entrance and a young lady greeted them, "Hello, are you here to pet the horses?"

"Um, no, I'm here to ride my horse," Riley said in a soft voice.

"Oh," said the lady in surprise. Riley's mom explained that even though Riley was in a wheelchair, she could still do everything that anyone else could do, if she just believed that she can.

Riley met a brown horse with beautiful eyes. "I think her name should be Sparkles," Riley announced.

"That's a nice name," said her mother. The lady gently helped Riley get on the horse. Riley straightened her back and pulled on the reins, and Sparkles slowly walked out of the barn into the fields. Riley was too excited to even think about being scared. Sparkles winked at Riley, almost like they had a secret code. I think Riley had found her passion. Riley loved Sparkles and never wanted to leave her. She planned to visit Sparkles every day.

It's amazing that Riley could do these things even though she was in a wheelchair. Never underestimate someone who believes in their abilities. She could do anything that you and I could do; just maybe not in the same way.

COLOR DAZE CHEATER

The saying goes "cheaters never win," but Sean believes he can. In **COLOR DAZE CHEATER** by *Ethan Lulkin*, you will discover how Sean breaks the rules. Will he win? Or, will he lose?

"Wake up, everybody; it's time!" the counselors screamed in the middle of the night.

That was the call to tell the campers that it was time for Color Daze. Color Daze is a three-day competition between the Black team and the Red team. In the oldest cabin, the Mohawk cabin, everybody was ready and had been waiting for this event the whole year. This will be their last year of Color Daze.

Everybody got out of their beds and walked outside. Half of the camp was wearing black, half of the camp was wearing red. The two colors identified what team they were on. Black team won the last several times, but Sean wasn't going to let them win this year.

Sean had dark hair and was very tan; he was on the Red team. His plan was to cheat through Color Daze. It had never been attempted because it's nearly impossible, but he had a plan. He was thinking it over as they were walking to the Color Daze campfire to choose the captain. For his plan to work, he could not be the captain.

All of the boys were at the humongous campfire that stood way over their heads. They were lined up and waiting to find out who the captains were going to be this year. To be chosen, you had to have a whistle put around your neck. Sean wasn't chosen, but his best friends were. On the Black team, good friends of his were chosen, Nick and Eli. On Sean's Red team, his best friends, Josh and Pedro, were chosen. This was perfect for Sean because his best friend, Josh, could help with some of the plans. Tomorrow the plan will take place, Sean thought to himself.

"We're table setting today," the counselors said early in the morning. "So, get up and head to the kitchen. We need to set the tables before breakfast."

Luckily, the Black team was table setting, so Sean had some time to get his plan started. He got out of his bed and tiptoed out the door. From that point, he sprinted to a shed where no one would see him. He then stuck his hand under the shed to get his folder which had all his plans. He got out his first plan. He put the rest of his folder away and got ready to put it in action. It was very simple, but very helpful.

He went through the woods to get to Bob's Lodge, a tall structure where the teams made their songs last night. He found the Black team's songs in a crate which was locked. That made it a little harder, but he had a Plan B. He filled up a water bottle and then dumped all of the water in the crate. He did this multiple times. He also put some on the floor to make it look like he tripped. That would hold them back on learning their cheers and songs for songfest which is a big part in Color Daze. Also, if anything else is in there, it will be ruined. He might get lucky, but most likely not.

"Everybody, start heading up to the kitchen for breakfast!" the megaphone roared.

"Oh man," Sean thought to himself. I have to get back. So he sprinted through the woods, tripped over branches, got hit by a rope, and got scratched by some more branches. He got to his cabin with a red face. He snuck through the back door and slipped on some red clothes. He then stayed back with the captains so he wouldn't look too suspicious.

"Can I make the Capture the Flag plans?" Sean asked.

The captains turned around and started whispering, "Sure, but it better be a good plan." Pedro was not happy.

He needed to figure out the Black team's plan to make his own plan work. So, tonight, he was going to sneak in the office to find the Black team's plans for capture the flag. But first, he had the whole day to make more plans to win Color Daze.

The day started off with Sports of All Ages. He had a plan for this. He asked past Red team members, who were counselors, to rig the sports games. He even bribed them just to win. So, when the first game started, he would hope they would do what he wanted.

It was time for soccer, his first game. He nodded to the ref, and he nodded back. This plan had to work. He took control of the soccer team, making a plan to let him be on defense and be in front of the ball at same time. It was kind of confusing, but their team destroyed the Black team. He won by cleating all of Black team's players and also slide tackling them, which is illegal. But the referees let him cheat. "It's going to be a good Color Daze," thought Sean.

At the end of the day, he found out that their team won every sport, but the ball throw, which is impossible to cheat on. They had their final meeting as a team for the night and then went up to the mess hall for dinner. This was the time for his plan to steal their Capture the Flag plans.

"Hey, how are those plans going?" It was Pedro.

"They're going good," Sean replied.

"Let's meet at ten tonight, and then see how you are doing," then Pedro left.

This was going to be hard. He was going to have to get the other teams plans first before he could write his own. He will have to get his plans the hard way, but it will be faster.

He ran to the office then walked around the walls to the garage of the office, and then, crawled through a tiny hole to get inside. He stood up to see vibrant blues, vivid yellows, and dark reds. There was about a million cases of Gatorade in front of him. He opened a door. It was not very good security, and everything was unlocked. He sprinted to a room, ran in and found a key on the left side of the room. He looked around to find a folder with a lock on it. On the cover it said, 'Black Team Capture the Flag Plans'.

Sean opened the folder and found some paper to make a plan to go against the Black team. Sean finished the entire plan before 9:00 p.m. without being caught. At 10:00 p.m., Pedro and Josh met Sean at some picnic benches. Pedro and Sean were shocked to see he finished the plans: everything thought out and ready.

The next day, when they did some more sports in the morning, they won almost everything from his bribery. Then at night, they won Capture the Flag because they got in every weak spot on the Black team's defense. They won 5-0.

They also won Song Fest because the Black team still didn't finish rewriting the songs from the water spill. All that Sean had planned had worked so far. He just need this last one to work to be positive that he would win. For this last plan, he needed help.

He went to ask Josh for help to win Burn that Rope. Burn that Rope is a relay throughout the whole camp grounds. The finishing event is building a fire to burn a rope. Sean told him everything about how he was cheating to win. Josh was shocked to hear that he wasn't actually winning, and that his best friend, Sean, was cheating. He was about to report him, but he smirked and said, "Fine, I will do it."

The plan was on.

Sean was about to put his plan to work when the camp owner brought him to the side, and whispered into his ear, "Why did you cheat?"

The camp owner then took him to the campfire and disqualified him from his final plan for Burn that Rope. Josh must have reported him. Red team ended up winning Burn that Rope anyway. They were going to announce the winner, which had to be Red team. They stopped him too late.

An announcement boomed over the campfire, "It has been a long, hard Color Daze and now it is time to decide the winner. The winner of Color Daze is..." he held up a banner that said 'Red Team' in black letters.

Everybody on the Red team went crazy. It sounded like lions were roaring all around you. The Red team was so happy; some of the campers were even in tears.

"But, because of cheating, the Black team has won!"

The cheering on the Red team side stopped and the Black team started cheering. Josh had done the right thing and cannot accept winning because of cheating.

THE ESCAPE

When a boy named Justin is just eleven years old, his whole life turns around. A plan needs to succeed, or he will never escape his worst nightmare in **THE ESCAPE**, *by* **Michael Potocsky.**

Every year, one is chosen from each state to live inside the walls. This year, I was chosen. No one has ever returned from the city inside the walls.

On the day I was chosen, I was in shock. I never thought that I would even be chosen. Out of the 700,000 people in Michigan, I had to be chosen. They do this every six months to decrease the population.

On the bus ride to my death, I was seated next to two boys. Everyone was chained into their seats. I started to talk to a few other boys. Both of them looked about my age. "Hi," I whispered.

"Hi," both boys responded.

"My name is Justin."

The boys exchanged looks, and then said their names in return. One boy was named Daniel, and the second was named Ethan. Both of them were also eleven years old. Daniel had brown hair and blue eyes. Ethan also had brown hair, but hazel eyes. Daniel was from Nashville, Tennessee. Ethan was from Seattle, Washington. After we finished talking, I fell into a deep sleep. I dreamed of what dying would be like.

I was very scared. I never was so worried about death until now. After a long but not really peaceful sleep, I was at the site. It was a five hour ride, but we were finally here. My heart was pumping very hard now. While approaching the bus door, I thought through my life memories. I would miss my parents, siblings, relatives, and most importantly, my friends. I don't know if they would kill us right away. Would it be painful? Will they poison us? I have lots of questions to be answered.

The door opened, and I walked onto the wet grass. I was instructed to walk through the gate. After walking through, I glanced at the tall structure. The walls are at least 50 feet tall. I entered and was fascinated by the remains, but also scared of the next steps of my life.

There was a guy who took us into the walls. There were a lot of rooms. The guy closed the doors instantly, and I was locked inside. With no way to get out, there was nothing I could do. I could be dead in seconds, minutes, hours, days, weeks, months, years, etc. My life was coming to a close.

The man started speaking, "Hi! I am Winston Harrington." I gave a little chuckle. "Excuse me? Why are you laughing?" he demanded of me. I was getting stared at from every direction.

I eventually spoke up, "Um, your name is kind of funny."

He snickered. I wasn't sure why he was laughing. I just exclaimed that his name was funny. He spoke loudly, "I was kidding! That isn't my real name. I just like to go by this fake name." Then he took us to a room: a room full of hot lava. Everyone glanced at the lava. Is this how we were going to die?

Winston announced in a high-pitched voice, "You are not going to die!" I was shocked that he just said that, but I was relieved. He told us that we would have to live here, though, and there was a chance of dying. He described where everyone would live. Boys were in their own dorms and the girls were in their dorms, but in an opposite hallway.

I walked to my own dorm. I was instructed to go to it and get settled. We would have school for five hours a day. For a couple of days, I adjusted to my new home. Winston said there is only one way to escape the walls, but no one ever had escaped. I don't know if this will be a good lifestyle. I would figure out if I even wanted to escape later.

On my third day at my new home, something happened. It was something really bad. Someone from outside the walls had spotted someone inside the walls alive. We are going to be under a massive lockdown. Sirens were going off loudly. I ran to a safe place. I heard glass shatter, a loud scream, a lot of loud screams. I had to get out of the closet where I was hiding.

I started to climb up one of the walls. Gunshots fired, one aimed for me. I somehow found my grip on the solid wall. I climbed the 50-foot wall, until a bullet went right by my ear. My foot slipped, and I was hanging by only my hands. If I fell, I would die. I was able to keep climbing as more shots were fired. I lost my footing several times, but I managed to get to the top. Now I faced another problem: climbing down the wall. It was another 50 feet down. I started descending. I had to be careful with my footing. All of the people were on the other side of the wall. I was safe as long as I climbed down the wall without falling.

After making it to the bottom, I saw someone familiar. Ethan had made it out as well. After a light jog over to him, we started sprinting for the forest. The forest was kind of big. But I didn't think this was an ordinary forest. I was pretty sure this was a rain forest. This was bad. Tigers live in some rain forests. I had never thought about seeing a tiger. I couldn't go back to the walls. I had to risk my life getting through the rain forest, and I had to do it fast.

Gunshots were still going off in the distance. A bridge stood in the distance. Ethan and I made it to the other side of the bridge easily. I had some survival gear in my backpack that I grabbed when I heard the sirens back inside the walls.

We slept on the hard, cold ground. I was so uncomfortable. I finally fell asleep after a long period of time. I woke up when the sun gleamed into my eyes. Ethan was also awake. We got up and started walking to a nearby cabin. A cabin? Why was there a cabin in the middle of nowhere?

We walked over to it and slowly approached the old, wooden door. There was a window, and we peeked inside: I couldn't see anyone. The door was unlocked, so we walked right in. I glanced around the room: stove, pots, tables, chairs, couch, beds, and a lot more.

I closely looked at the electric fire place as it was warm. I turned it off and then touched the glass covering it. It fell over. I felt the back of the fireplace, and it opened. It looked like a passage. I walked in and called back for Ethan. Ethan followed me into the tunnel. It was dark, but some sunlight sank in.

We walked and walked and walked, until I saw something. Sunlight beamed into the passageway. We might have just discovered a way out! In fact, the passage had taken us back to Michigan.

Ethan said, "I have to go to the airport. I need to buy a plane ticket to get back to Seattle."

"Okay," I replied.

"Is this your house?" Ethan asked.

"Yes!" I exclaimed. We sprinted to the garage, typed in a code, sprinted straight to the door, and ran into the house.

"Justin!" my mom yelled as she gave me a great big hug. "How did you get back?"

I simply replied, "We just escaped a nightmare."

EVEN THOUGH MY MIND IS CRAZY: IT'S STILL MY MIND

Can your own brain deceive you? Shay Emerald deals with her bizarre and mysterious brain every day in **EVEN THOUGH MY MIND IS CRAZY: IT'S STILL MY MIND,** *by Saarah Fattouh.*

It happens every morning, every afternoon, every evening, and every night. I'm constantly reminded that I'm different. Sometimes, surprisingly, I forget until the female nurse comes in to my room. She always comes with a bottle of water in one hand and antipsychotics in the other. "It's time to take your medicine Shay," she grumbles.

I remember: I'm not normal. My life wasn't always like this. I never thought I was crazy. I still don't think I am, but when I was 13, I was diagnosed with Dissociative Identity Disorder, also known as Multiple Personality Disorder.

My parents thought my imaginary friend, Ton Laer, was just a phase. That it would die out as fast as my love for Barbies. That I wouldn't play hide-and-seek with her or pretend to brush her hair. But my mom found me in the middle of night, standing in the snowy street, making a gesture that looked like I was holding someone's hand. My lips where blue and cracked. The veins in my hands where obviously cold, bulging out, and even more blue than my lips had been at that moment. Everything I've been told, all the stories I've heard about how I lost my mind: I don't want to believe it, but what choice do I have? I just can't trust myself to make decisions.

"You know they're just saying those things just to get in your head," Ton Laer remarks in a snooty voice.

"Oh, so I guess the medicine they give me is just candy?" I snap back. "That they are all playing some huge joke on me."

"Pretty much," I get thrown back at me with a giggle.

"Not everything is a joke, Ton. I just need to accept the fact that I'm sick and I always will…" I begin until I get cut off.

"Don't say that! Don't ever say that! You're not sick," Ton Laer said in a pained voice.

"Then what am I?" I whisper silently.

"An unfinished puzzle."

"How did you get in here anyway?"

"I have my ways," she says in her snooty voice once again.

Never, in my whole life, have I ever been left in so much suspense just by someone saying "I have my ways."

"That's not the answer I was looking for, but I know you're not going to tell me. So, I'm not going to bother," I conclude. That same night, I was given my usual Benadryl. But not a part of the routine was being woken up at 3:00 A.M. by Ton.

"No time to sleep! Look what I found in your mailbox from the hospital," Ton Laer shoved a pamphlet in front of my face.

"What?" I question as I start to breathe heavily.

"They left a little note for your parents," she hands me the note.

> *Dear Emerald family,*
> *We had a spot open up at the hospital and now we have a room for your lovely daughter, Shay Emerald.*

I look back up and I am unable to speak. Ton isn't there anymore. She must have left.

I walk downstairs slowly, so I won't make any noise, and surely, Ton is there. Her eyes are closed; she is weeping, banging on the coffee table with her closed fist.

"What are you doing?" I question as I yank her hand.

My parents run down the stairs at the wrong time. "Shay!" my mom shouts. "Why are you hitting the table?".

"What? I'm...no...no, it wasn't me! It was Ton. It was Ton," I have tears running down my face. I'm losing my breath with every word that I say. This just isn't real.

"Shay, I'm sorry," my mom begins. "I can't. I've tried to help you to the best of my ability, but there's only so much we can do as parents for a sick child. I think we've reached our limit." She pulls the pamphlet out from under the newspaper on the coffee table. Without any regret, she explains to me how this was a great hospital and they would take care of me.

Even though she didn't bring it up earlier or even ask for my permission, I knew I was going to the hospital, and soon.

The next morning, I find myself getting into my parents' car with a suitcase. I was zoned out, and my face had a distraught expression. Now I know that I'm not stronger than this disease that slowly infects my body. And it won't stop infecting me until this thing...is me.

Ton Lear smiles.

"What do you want, you monster?" I scream.

"Nothing. I just have a question this time."

"You're going to get in my head like you always do!"

"No, I just want to know," Ton Lear begins, "if you could trade your brain with a super healthy one, and not be crazy, would you?"

"Even though my mind is crazy, it's still my mind," I simply reply.

"You're lying to yourself, Shay," Ton Lear continues. "I see it in your eyes and I know you don't want to go to this hospital. Just admit that you hate your crazy brain and I will leave, forever!"

"Yup, you're right. I dislike my brain, but I can't abandon it just because it has abandoned me."

We arrive at the hospital at 9:47 A.M. My parents sign me in and walk me to my room. They give me a hug and leave me in the hands of a female nurse with firm eyes and long hair. She explains the schedule to me, but my mind is 100,000 miles away and I have no clue what she's saying. I just nod my head and smile.

I ended up staying in the hospital for two months. It was until October 5, 2015, the night Ton went away. She left no trace of her existence, no trace at all. There were no letters, no goodbye, no nothing. I almost feel sad even though she was a burden on my life. I do kind of miss her. She was my friend, my best friend, my sister; and now she's gone forever.

The next night I go home. My dad grabs my one, heavy bag from my luxurious suite and we leave. I look out the window for the whole ride home. My mother tries to start a conversation with me, but I have no interest in talking to either of my parents. The rest of the ride is so silent, in an eerie kind of way. I impatiently sit still until we got home.

My parents are still driving up the driveway when I get out of the car. I slam the door and run to my room. Once I see my colorless room, I sprint toward it and face-plant on a pillow. Feeling tired, I slowly drift off. My eyes become heavier as I tune out the world, and then, sleep.

Finally, for once in my life, the thing I call Ton Laer, could now be called **noT reaL**.

FIREFIGHTERS IN MY HOUSE

FIREFIGHTERS IN MY HOUSE, by *Sloane Goldberg, is an interesting traumatic event that included middle-of-the-night worries. Make sure to read this exciting mystery, with tons of twists and turns.*

*B*eep, Beep, Beep.
    What's that sound? It was the piercing sound of the house alarm at approximately 10:37 P.M. I awoke frightened; thinking that someone broke into my house. I immediately felt butterflies settling in my stomach.

"Mom!" I shriek loudly. "Mom!" My frantic mother was already wide awake from her sleep. Does she even know what happened?

First things first, we inspect the house. No burglars were in sight. We were so scared while the alarm rang and rang. My mom decided to call 911. The firefighters arrived quickly at our doorstep in just 15-20 minutes. As all firefighters do, they make a grand entrance with horns blaring and lights glaring. It is freezing cold outside and raining. This is the worst night ever!

A firefighter knocks on the door, and I am shivering cold. I feel as if my knee caps are going to fall off. As we open the door, we look down to discover a cryptic note on the porch that reads, "Remove your tree or else!" I look outside and spot teenagers having a campfire, despite the freezing rain outside. I know I could be overreacting, but I couldn't help but wonder if they planted the note.

The two firefighters step inside the house with feet bigger than Bigfoot. They are tall, strong, and manly. They ask questions about what happened and what caused the alarm to go off. My mom and I look at each other and remain as quiet as crickets. Finally, we respond, "We don't know. That's the reason you're here!"

The firefighters proceed to inspect the house. Apparently, it wasn't the alarm that caused all of the issues; it was the smoke detector. We should have known all along! Our smoke detector is five feet away from the kitchen and, when we cook smoke comes out of the pan. Once that happens, excess smoke gets stuck in the smoke detector. It is that process that triggers the smoke detector to go off!

A firefighter advised us not to touch it for the rest of the night, and, if we listen, it should not go off again. Just as my mom and I cuddle up in her bed to watch a movie, it goes off again. Instead of calling the firefighters back, we just wait to see if it stops, and it doesn't. My mom attempts to fix the alarm, but really has no clue what she is doing, but she fixes it. How? I have absolutely no clue! My mom has never fixed anything like that in her whole, entire life.

I still hear creaking in my house and the ringing sound from the alarm is stuck in my head. I shrivel up like a prune in my bed, but cannot manage to even close my eyes. I can't take it anymore. I am so scared, and I beg my mom to go sleep at my grandma's house.

After half an hour of tears, we pack our clothes, toiletries, and flashlights and head to my grandma's house. My mom decides it is the best idea to go sleep there. As we are preparing to leave, I suddenly have an intense craving for pizza! I ask my mom if there are any nearby pizza places that are still open. She searches online for the nearest pizza place and discovers Jet's Pizza is right on the way to my grandmas! Perfect! We jump in the car and I glance at the clock; it's 12:30 A.M.

My mom and I dash into the pizza shop and order a small, round pizza. We wait ten minutes in the sketchy pizza shop. We talk about how West Bloomfield looks mysterious and dark at this time of night! The pizza is ready and we are approximately two minutes away from my grandma's house. We sprint to the car and, after the longest two minutes of my life, we are there.

We walk up the creaky stairs quiet as two mice, and I try to find my room in the dark. I am so tired; all I want to do is fall asleep. My mom almost tripped down the stairs! I almost broke a lamp! All that my mom and I want to do is sleep! But, I sit on my bed and eat my hot, delicious pizza. Now, I think it's time to shut my eyes and go to sleep. But, I can't fall asleep. It's impossible to do after this emotional evening.

I am up until 5:00 A.M. excessively worrying until, finally, my eyes are forced to shut. I think to myself that I totally forgot that I had to go to school soon! I didn't do my homework or anything to get ready for school.

I panic and yell, "Mom, wake up! I have school!"

She replies back, "Calm down! You don't have to go to school today: it's Saturday!"

Last night felt like a whirlwind. Finally, I can go to sleep.

THE FUTURISTIC MENACE

What would a future criminal be like? Billy, Joe, and Pablo find out while facing the most dangerous criminal of the future. How will they stop the criminal? Find out in **THE FUTURISTIC MENACE**, *by **Joshua Prabhu.***

It was always a normal, yet exciting, day in the futuristic city, Drone. Billy, Joe and Pablo were living their daily lives. They all worked in a factory making weapons for the military like weapons, machinery and much more!

One day, Billy, Joe and Pablo received a special order to make 20,000 mechanical parts and a 100,000 fuel cells. They were astounded by the order and they only had a day to do it! They got to work right away and they never stopped working! Pablo wanted to know who sent them this order and the factory said they didn't know. Pablo was curious and told his friends that they should keep it for a while. Then, he or she would get angry enough to come here and get the order themselves. Joe and Billy agreed and they waited for about two days for the person, who made the order, to come to the factory.

This person finally arrived on the third day and he was extremely frustrated. He went up to the front door and started kicking it until the guards came and tried to stop him. Unfortunately, he had weaponry that was unknown and so powerful that it wiped out all of the guards in one shot! Billy, Joe and Pablo were very frightened of the menace, and they were so afraid that they called the police and the military.

The police and the military arrived in seconds thanks to the new system of transportation which is teleportation. The menace was aware of the military and the police, so he started his mysterious weapon. Just when it looked like he was about to start fire, he just randomly threw his weapon to the ground and the weapon broke. The military and the police were very confused about his action, so they put their weapons down. As soon as the weapons were down, the menace got a small weapon from his pocket and wiped out most of the military and the police! The remaining military and police were so scared of the new menace that they retreated.

Then, the menace noticed Billy, Joe and Pablo peeking out the window and he knew that they saw everything. Billy, Joe and Pablo saw that he was aware of their presence so they started to run for their lives. The menace saw them running and instead of chasing them he just teleported away! They hid for about an hour until they knew he was gone. They had to figure out how to stop him before he caused many more catastrophes.

They went back to their houses and they all called each other to discuss of what to do about the new menace.

"Maybe we should make weapons for ourselves to stop him," Billy suggested.

Joe responded, "How about we just ignore this and move on with our daily lives?"

"If we ignore this, he could go to extreme measures like taking over the world or even destroying the world!" Pablo exclaimed.

Billy answered, "Pablo is right and we should start making weapons right now!"

"Fine, I'll do it," Joe responded.

"We'll each make our own weapons that suit us best," Pablo concluded. They all agreed and started to make the weapons. They also said that they should make the weapons in about a day.

The very next day, they all had their weapons finished and they were ready to find the new menace. But, they forgot one thing that was very important to do before they set out to stop him; to know where he actually lives and his name. Billy remembered to do just that!

Billy, Joe and Pablo were looking at the computer to find anything about the menace. They looked on CNN to see there was a news report about him. There actually was a report, but they got no information whatsoever. They had to do something that would be very illegal: they had to hack into his profile! They hacked into his profile and they found everything about him. His name was Bob. They found out that he was wanted around the entire galaxy! They also found out where he lived.

Billy demanded, "Joe, get a piece of paper!"

Joe asked, "Why?"

Billy exclaimed, "We're going to jot down the address and stop this guy once and for all!"

They noted the address and set out to find and stop the menace. They went to the exact address location, but they found nothing.

"There must be a secret lever or button around here," Pablo suggested.

Billy responded, "Good idea, let's check the area." They checked the area, but they still couldn't find anything."

Pablo said, "That library shelf looks very suspicious."

"Let's check it out," Joe demanded.

Billy suggested, "It could be a trap!"

Joe concluded, "Then I'll check it out." He went to the shelf and found a secret button. When he pressed it, the ground started to lower under him. Billy and Pablo got on it and they thought that it would lower to the lair.

They couldn't be more right and there was Bob, the menace, right in front of them. They got their weapons ready and, when they were about to charge toward him, he turned around and they started to fly in midair!

"Right now, I'm holding you with my latest invention called, The Levitation Watch," Bob said.

Billy, Joe and Pablo tried to fight back, but they just couldn't! Bob let them down and exclaimed, "If you move even a muscle, I will activate my laser that will destroy your city, Drone, once and for all!"

Billy found a way to stop the laser from working. He found a device on the floor which read, 'Electricity Destroyer'. He knew that this might shut down the laser and they would have a chance to stop Bob once and for all.

Billy quickly threw the device and it shut down the laser. Bob was very frustrated with what just happened and he got out his gun which he had used against the military. He started firing! Billy, Joe and Pablo took cover and they started firing right back. It was an intense battle when Billy threw a capture device at Bob and he was inside the device. They had finally defeated this evil menace. They took him to the police station where the menace would spend his whole life between bars.

Billy, Joe and Pablo each received an invite from the mayor about joining the army of Drone. They all thought it would be an honor to be part of the army, so they accepted the invite. They were excited to start their new lives and whatever menace tried to destroy Drone, or even the world, they would be ready for it.

GOING TO CAMP

GOING TO CAMP, *by **Marley Wolf**, is an exciting story about the day that Marley leaves for camp. Read to find out if the departure from her family is easy or a total mess.*

Saying goodbye to my family and friends is hard, but going to camp is worth it. Every year, I go to camp for one month. Today, I will be making my way to Cheboygan, Michigan with all of my best camp friends and my brother. I know I will be forced to say goodbye to my parents for a month, but I know I will be seeing them again soon enough.

I felt my mom tickling my back and I turned my body over toward her and pulled my covers up. "Hi," I said faintly.

She smiled, "I am going to miss you, Marley." Her blonde hair dangling over my face as she started talking again. "But I know you're going to have so much fun, and the days will go by in a flash." Then she snapped, "Now it's time to get up and get dressed!" She got up and turned on my lights.

My Walden sweatshirt and black Nike shorts were spread out on my desk. I quickly threw them on and laced up my white low top Converse. My carry-on bag was hanging on my brown leather chair right next to my desk. I grabbed the heavy, colorful, bag and hung it around my right shoulder. I said goodbye to my room, and headed downstairs. I was super anxious: being super excited and nervous all at the same time is normal when going to camp. Departing for a while is the hard part, but, when you get to your destination, you know you will forget all about home.

When I went downstairs, my favorite breakfast appeared on the kitchen table; scrambled eggs, crunchy rye toast, and fresh fruit. I sat down quickly and grabbed a slice of toast, a couple of eggs, and I pulled my bowl of fruit closer to me.

"Thank you so much for breakfast, Mom and Dad," I said thankfully. My brother, Dylan, sat right next to me pounding the great tasting food down his body. He was going to camp with me too. I was really sad to leave my family, but I couldn't wait to arrive at the best place of my life.

"Twenty more minutes!" My mom screamed from her room. I heard her voice ringing throughout the house and decided to go say my last goodbye to my red fawn, Shar-Pei dog, Chewy. I ran all of the way up the flight of stairs and skipped to my brother's room where my dog usually laid down.

"Hi, Chewy," I greeted calmly. His tail started wagging back and forth, and his little eyes were getting watery. I bent down to meet Chewy on his level. I gave him a kiss on his doggy cheek, and his slobbery tongue licked my forehead. I knew he could tell when someone was leaving: when the duffels come out and when we are stuck in our room debating on what we should wear. I grabbed his paw humbly gave him one more kiss and went downstairs.

Time was running out, and nerves started kicking into place. I cleared my place at the table and realized it was my last at-home meal for a month. My mom came downstairs in a lulu lemon sweatshirt and studio pant leggings. I put my carry-on bag into the trunk, and speed-walked back into the house.

"Everyone, gather into the kitchen!" My dad demanded. As I came into the house, I shut the caramel wooden colored door and made my way into the kitchen.

"Why did you ask us to all come in here, Dad?" my brother asked curiously.

"Well, your mom and I wanted to give you guys something special before we sent you guys off to camp."

I was so excited that, in my head, I was thinking; *what could it be? Is it a new carry-on? Sweatshirts, maybe sweatpants? More Stationary?* My mom pulled something out of our kitchen cabinets. There was one blue bag with green wrapping paper, which I assumed was Dylan's. And, there was a purple bag, with blue wrapping paper which I immediately guessed was mine.

"Here you go," my mom said as she distributed the bags. I didn't know if I should open it now or at camp. I decided it would be more fun to open it at camp.

"Mom and Dad?" I started. "Can I please open it at camp? I'll send you a thank you letter about it!" My parents said that was okay and my dad went outside to pack the trunk. In the trunk there were four duffel bags which took up all of the space.

"It's time for everyone to get in the car!" my Dad ordered. Dylan and I walked out of the house, not even bothering to say goodbye to anything. We were just so happy to leave that we couldn't bare thinking about what was behind us. Only what's in front.

I hopped in the car, and went on my phone for the very last time. I had to sign off all social media, and then I texted my entire group of friends.

"Marley, spend time with us. Please get off your phone," both of my parents whined.

"I was just about to," I argued right back. I turned off my phone and put it in the glove compartment.

"Are you guys excited?" my mom asked in anticipation. "You have been looking forward to this time all year!" Dylan and I nodded our heads. I was so exited, but at the same time a little anxious and resistant.

Ten minutes later, after what felt like a long car-ride full of butterflies and excitement, we arrived at the high school where we were to depart from the real world. As I got out of the car, there were tons of guys and girls directing parents where to park and stand, and guys unloading bags from cars, and loading them into U-Haul trucks.

My whole family got out of the car. My dad went to go help the guys take our bags and my mom stayed with us. My dad finished loading the last bag and made his way toward the three of us.

"Ready to go on the bus?" my dad asked. My brother and I nodded, and our whole family walked together.

"Ten minutes until the bus departs!" I heard a random voice scream.

"It's time for us to go," I said emotionally to my mom and dad. They hugged me and my brother and told us to have a great time. They would write to us every day and miss us tons.

I walked one step onto the bus and realized I was about to have the best camp experience ever.

THE MIRACLE SOCKS

In **THE MIRACLE SOCKS**, *by* **Trey Lipsey,** *a boy named Jackson finds magic socks before the big football game. Can he lead his team to victory, or will he fail?*

The 20...the 10... the—click, clack, pow!

"Jackson Williams tackled at the five yard line to lose the game. The Falcons advance to the finals while the Tigers go home. What a game!"

As we shake the other team's hands, all the players make fun of me for losing the game. I feel miserable. On the car ride home, my parents say I did well. I don't respond. Instead I sit there in the car, in silence.

We finally get home, and I run straight to my room. I sit on my bed, and I think about the game. I sit there for the rest of the night, and eventually I fall asleep.

When I woke up, I go to the living room and turn on the television to watch ESPN, a show about sports. On the headline, it says the Falcons used illegal players in the game and that the Tigers are back in the playoffs. I couldn't believe my eyes! I started screaming, and I ran to my mom's room to tell her the news.

When my football coach got the news, he sent an email out to our team saying we had practice tomorrow. I invite my friends, Zack and Jake, over to play catch with the football outside. Zack threw a terrible pass to me, and it landed in the trash, so we had to go dig it out. In the trash, we saw these glowing socks. We decided to pick them out of the trash and put them in the washer and dryer.

Once the socks were clean, I tried them on, and we went out to play catch again. I threw the ball at Jake. *WHAM!* The ball nails him right in the chest. I threw the ball so fast Jake couldn't even see it.

The rest of the week went by fast, and we were soon headed to the championship. With my new socks, I discovered that I could run faster and no one could tackle me. The championship game is tomorrow.

I wake up early the next morning, eat breakfast, and head to the field. Our team does the warm -up, and then it is time to start the game against the Eastside Panthers. The first play of the game, I score a touchdown. The crowd went crazy, and our team felt really excited. We kicked the extra point and made it. The score was 7-0.

We kick the ball to the Eastside Panthers, and they return the kick. As I'm running down the field, trying to tackle the returner, I notice that the returner doesn't see me. That means I can lay down a huge hit. As I get closer to the returner, I lower my shoulder. *BOOM!* I hit the dude so hard that his helmet flew off and the medics had to come on the field and take him to the hospital. It turns out that I broke his collar bone.

We start the second quarter on defense, and the Eastside Panthers are on the thirty-yard line. Coach keeps me out to give me a breather. The Eastside Panthers hike the ball, and the quarterback throws a deep pass to the wide receiver. He catches it for a seventy-yard touchdown!,

I think in my head, "Oh, no!" The Eastside Panthers kick the extra point and the score is now 7-7. The coach keeps me out for the return, and Jake returns the kickoff for forty-five yards! I come on the field, and the coach calls a screen pass to me. A screen pass is when the lineman purposely doesn't block the defense. So, when the quarterback throws the ball to me, the linemen run to me and block whoever tries and tackle me.

I run for a fifty-yard touchdown, and the Eastside Panthers are fierce. The touchdown was at the end of the quarter, so we get to go to halftime happy and pumped up. We kick the extra point and the quarter ends. We head to the locker rooms, and the coach tells us that we have to do a better job on defense. The coach hands us all oranges so we can stay energized, and we head back to the field to start the third quarter.

We kick the ball off to the Eastside Panthers, and they run for a twenty-five yard return. The next play, they hand the ball off to their running back, and he is tackled at the line of scrimmage. It's second down now, and the Eastside Panthers decide to pass. They throw a slant route to the man Zack is supposed to guard, and Zack misses his tackle. The Eastside Panthers run for a touchdown. I start to get nervous once again. The score is 14-14, and the quarter is ending quickly. They kick the ball off to us, and I return the kick. I see an open lane to run through, and I take it. I break a tackle, and the next thing I notice, I'm off to the races! I'm running down the sideline for a fifty-five yard touchdown on the kickoff.

The quarter ends, and we get a pep talk by the coach as we start the fourth quarter. We kick the ball off, and I get the tackle. The Eastside Panthers' offense takes the field. They run a running back toss where the quarterback pitches the ball to the running back. I run to the running back. *Click, clack, pow!* I tackle him. I get up and start walking, and I notice my socks. They're ripped! I run to the sideline and start to cry.

The next play, the Eastside Panthers score, and I become furious for some odd reason. The clock is winding down: there are 0:35 seconds left and we have the ball on the twenty-five yard line. The score is 21-21.

Our coach decides to run a screen to me again. This time, it doesn't work, and I get stuffed at the twenty-six yard line. It was now second down with 0:20 left. Coach calls a slant route to me, and I run my route. I get wide open, and the quarterback has a perfect throw to me, and...I drop the ball! My team looked confused because, with the socks, I never drop the ball! The coach calls a wheel route, and this could be the last play of the game. I hear the quarterback say, "Hike!" and I run my route. Two guys are covering me this time. The quarterback passes it to me, and I jump as high as I can, and I catch it! I run for the touchdown and win the game even without the socks!

We did it! We shake the other team's hands, and they told me good job this time. We got our trophy and went home. My mom gave me a great big hug and told me that I did a great job. Today was awesome. Now it's time to get ready for baseball season!

THE MYSTERIOUS SWAMP MONSTER

THE MYSTERIOUS SWAMP MONSTER, by *Joshua Sherman, is an exciting story about a swamp monster at a summer camp. It is up to a supervisor and the counselors to save the camp from the monster.*

It was always a normal day, yet exciting, day except when Billy and Pablo bullied Bob. The camp supervisor, Nachos, didn't know that Bill and Pablo were even bullying Bob. And, Bill, Pablo, and Bob didn't know that there was a swamp monster watching Bill and Pablo's every move.

One day, Bob was all beaten up and sore from Bill and Pablo: he could barely walk. He went to the swamp to get away from Bill and Pablo because he was super tired and he didn't want to get up today. He was so scared to tell the supervisor, Nachos, that he was getting bullied by Bill and Pablo. It would have to go on until camp is over.

The swamp monster wanted to get Bob, so he could turn him into a swamp monster just like him. Then, Bob could get Bill and Pablo for bulling him. The swamp monster hid in the swamp and when Bob came to relax at the swamp, the swamp monster got him. The swamp monster had to wait until Billy and Pablo made Bob faint or did something else to him.

Bob went to the swamp again to relax and to stay away from Bill and Pablo. But this time, he got beaten up by the swamp monster. He realized that the swamp monster was using all the things Bill and Pablo used to bully him. He fainted and the swamp monster took him into the swamp and that was the end of Bob.

Then, one by one, every camper started disappearing. The supervisor noticed a track leading to the swamp and, out of nowhere, he saw a swamp monster coming for him. He ran as fast as he could to warn all the counselors to go home. But, when the counselors were getting ready to go home, the swamp monster and Swamp Bob stopped them and all the counselors also became a swamp monster. The supervisor ran as fast as he could to get away from the swamp monster and his army. He thought that they were in the swamp because he saw heads earlier when he saw the swamp monster.

He went to the swamp and he saw little swamp monsters and the counselors heads coming toward him and he recognized Bob's voice. Bob yelled, "Help me from the swamp monsters spell!"

Bob also helped Bill and Pablo from the horrible spell that the swamp monster put on every camper at the camp. Bill, Pablo, Bob and Nachos tried to free all of the campers, but it was useless.

Bob finally said, "We should close the camp for right now until everything is back to normal." Nachos agreed with Bob. The camp needed to close until they could get it back to normal again.

They closed the camp down and went back to the swamp. They tried to help the campers and the counselors to snap out of the spell that the swamp monster put on them. It took all day, but they finally did it. They saved the campers and killed the swamp monster.

The campers even stayed far away from the camp area just in case there was another swamp monster. Later that day Bill and Pablo said, "We are sorry for bullying you with our pranks."

Bob replied, "It's okay, just don't do it again." And they became best friends.

When the parents arrived, there was no one around because they were hiding in the other camping area. The parents didn't realize there even was another camping area. The supervisor, Nachos, and Bill, Pablo, and Bob went back to the swamp area to make sure the swamp monster was gone. Then they were able to help reunite the campers with their parents. All the parents and kids were so excited to see each other. Everyone looked forward to camping next summer; without the swamp monster.

THE NEW SPECIES

When is the last time you heard about a new species? Jessica finds something interesting in **THE NEW SPECIES,** *by **Taegen Lemberg**.*

It was beautiful, sunny day in the forest. Jessica was looking forward to enjoying the day, so she went for a walk. She ended up finding lots of nature and animals! She brought her journal, which she takes everywhere she goes. She wrote about the cool things she saw and all about her day in the forest.

"What is that creature called? I've never seen it before," she said.

There was a really cool animal. It looked like a mix of snake/polar bear/unicorn. He didn't seem mean. So, I drew a picture of it and brought it home. I fed it some of my neighbor's dog food. I named my new pet, Bob.

Bob was a mean pet: he wasn't nice to me at all. He would always bite and scratch me even when I wasn't even looking at him. He also wasn't a good pet because he would always jump on the table and eat my dinner. I didn't like him anymore. He had sharp teeth, so he would scare me whenever he growled. Whenever he would scare me, I would let him run outside just to see if he would run away.

I was hoping he would run away because he was so mean and I had to find a way to get rid of him! He would only be nice to my neighbors, but not me! He was my pet and he was supposed to be nice to me!

"Woof, woof!" barked Bob.

"STOP!" Jessica yelled at Bob, but Bob didn't stop barking.

I didn't expect him to be so mean when I brought him home. I expected him to be innocent and a nice pet to have in the house. So, the next day, I ran with him on the leash in the forest to take him back where he was found. He wouldn't be able to keep on hurting me. Once I found the spot, I took the leash off of him and ran away as fast as possible. He couldn't chase after me and hurt me.

When I arrived home, I locked all of the doors and the windows. That crazy animal wouldn't be able to get into the house just in case he followed me home! I was so scared. I started thinking that the snake/polar bear/unicorn was going to get in and hurt me because he might have remembered where my house was and how he could get to it.

The next day, my mom drove me to the pet store to look for a new dog. I found one that I absolutely loved.

"This dog is my favorite!" I yelled. The workers told me that her name was Fluffy and we brought her home with us that day.

I woke up the next morning and I was okay and my new dog was waiting for me to play. I was so glad for not getting hurt! I kept her name of Fluffy! Fluffy is so fluffy!

She was nice to me unlike Bob was. I was happy with my new dog! I think she likes me!

I always go outside and play with her! Sometimes I get scared when Fluffy and I walk on the same path as Bob.

I'm scared that Bob will come back and hurt us. The only thing I kept saying in my head is... what if, what if, what if? So, I told my mom and she said I would be okay and she will always protect me. I wasn't scared anymore and my family and I were all safe from Bob. We loved our new pet, Fluffy!

THE PORTAL OF PONIES

What would it be like to be a pony? What would happen to your clothes? Would you be able to do magic? Cassia finds out in **THE PORTAL OF PONIES**, *by **Nathalie Morgan**.*

The sunrise came up over the horizon as Cassia pushed her hair out of her eyes. She looked up at her alarm clock, and freaked out when she saw the time. It was 10:03 a.m. "Oh no," Cassia yelped as she remembered that she was supposed to hang out with her fellow Pony sisters at the mall. They had agreed to meet at the fountain at 10:35 a.m. Cassia was going to be late! She grabbed her leather jacket, her cars keys, her phone, and some cash.

She pulled out of her driveway and quickly put on her nametag (in case there were any new members of the club) that read, "Hello, my name is: Cassia Bellister." As quickly as she ran out the door, Cassia was at the mall. And she was just in time; it was 10:29 a.m. "Perfect!" Cassia thought to herself. As her heels clicked along the pavement, she found herself at the fountain. It was 10:35 a.m., but no one was there.

Cassia circled the fountain twice. Then, someone with black as night leather gloves covered her mouth and dragged her into a dark, scary room. She started crying and screaming for her life. Then she was blindfolded. When the blindfold was removed, three figures were visible. The figures wore green and gray cloaks. They started to whisper to Cassia, saying, "I'm sorry it had to be you, but this might be a nightmare coming true."

Then the tallest figure reluctantly spoke, "Hello Cassia. What you are about to experience is very painful." Then Cassia was shoved into a glowing portal. She started to scream: tears streaming down her red cheeks.

Cassia woke up with four faces staring at her. "Am I crazy?" Cassia wondered. "Am I really seeing four ponies?"

"What is she, Princess?" asked Twilight Shimmer, thirsty for knowledge.

"I believe that she is a human turned into an alicorn as I have never seen her before. That must be it," Celestial responded.

"Wait, I'm a pony?" Cassia gasped, surprised.

"How do you know about ponies?" Lunar questioned, flipping her purple, indigo, and black mane over her shoulder.

Slowly, but surely, Cassia explained that magical ponies were in a television show and she was a big fan. Lunar then led her to a big comfy room with lots of windows and a huge soft bed that looked like it was fit for a queen.

The room was filled with books. Cassia picked one up and started to read. It was about an alicorn named Starry Night. She was said to come from a far away land that had no magic. Cassia was tired and she wanted to go to bed, but her curiosity got the best of her. She saw a mirror and wanted to see her alicorn self.

When she came up to the mirror, she gasped and said, "I'm Starry Night." Cassia knew this because her nametag read, "Hello, my name is: Starry Night." Her mane was flowing and shimmering in the pale light. It was blue and had streaks of purple in it. Her coat was a dark blue, almost a black color. Her side had a mark on it. It was a blue star with a comet behind it. She yelled for the ponies.

"Yes, Starry Night?" they replied in unison.

"That's just it! You called me Starry Night. But, my real name is Cassia Bellister. I was shoved into a portal, and now I'm in a legend. I'm just really confused," Cassia breathed in and out, dazed.

"Oh, you are Starry Night: The Warrior Princess that was said to come when we need you most," Twilight Shimmer said excitedly.

"We really do need you right away," Cadenci explained. "Queen Crystalliess has posed a threat again to our land and she has returned to extract our magic. She plans to attack soon."

"Then, let's battle!" Cassia exclaimed.

A cackle rang out through the air. It was Queen Crystalliess. She grabbed Cassia and flew off. Then, a swoosh of air blew Cassia into a pit where she found the portal.

There was a loud voice that rang out, "The portal will close in ten, nine, eight..." Cassia had to choose between her true home and her dream one. But, unfortunately she didn't have time to choose.

Queen Crystalliess pushed her into the portal. Cassia woke up, dripping like a wet rag. What a crazy dream, she thought. Her? Cassia? A pony fan girl? Why would a superhero fan dream about ponies?

She got out of bed and noticed in the mirror what looked like a bruise in the shape of a comet behind a star. But, it was a dream, wasn't it?

A SMALL GIRL WITH A BIG DREAM

Renae is a regular girl, but when her mom tells her something, her life changes. Find out how she deals with these changes in **A SMALL GIRL WITH A BIG DREAM***, by* **Ryann Tolbert.**

I found out that I'm adopted. I'm Renae: a normal fourteen-year-old girl who goes to school, enjoys singing, and spending time with my mom, Stacey. This is the story of how I found out that I was adopted and how my dreams were quickly becoming a reality.

"Hey Renae, are you coming to school or not?" Rashanda asked.

"Yeah, of course she is!" said Rashelle.

"I think I can speak for myself," I said. "And, yes, I am going to school."

"Well, let's go then," said Rashelle.

When I arrived at school, it felt a little different. Usually, I would go to my locker, talk to my friends on my way to class, and eat lunch with my friends. Today, on my way to my locker, everyone said 'hey' and the guys started flirting with me. This went on for the whole day. I just ignored it because I knew that this special attention wouldn't last long and I would soon go back to my ordinary routine.

When I arrived home, I told my mom about my weird day. My mom said, "You need to see this." Right there on the television, there was a picture of me. I was so confused about why my picture was on the news.

"I have to tell you something Renae," my mom continued. "You're adopted. That's why you got all that special attention at school. Your picture was on the news this morning."

"Then, if I'm adopted, who are my real parents?" asked Renae.

"I don't know!" said my mom. "They wouldn't show them on the news, it was just your picture."

"Well, then," I said angrily. "I'm going to find my birth parents and you can't stop me because you're not my mom."

As I slammed the door in Stacey's face, she ran outside and yelled, "If you come in the house and continued to live with me, I will help you find your birth parents!"

"Only if you promise," I said.

"I promise," said Stacey.

"Fine!" I yelled.

We went inside and Stacey called the foster home while I went online. We did this for hours, days, and even, weeks. Finally, someone called and asked if they could see their daughter.

We went and met the person who we talked to on the phone and it turned out that it was Brian Star, the biggest music producer in the world, and his wife, LaShelle Star. I was in shock that I almost fainted.

"Wait. Are you my parents?" I asked.

"Yes, we are Renae," said LaShelle.

I went to my new home and it was like a hotel. Seriously, I even had a private butler! Once I settled in, we went to the studio where my mom and dad worked.

My dad asked, "Do you want to try a song?"

I said, "Yes! I would love to." I went in the sound booth and recorded a song that I wrote from my journal.

"I think we found our new recording artist!" said my dad.

I said, "Really? I always wanted to be a singer!"

My parents replied, "Now your dreams are finally coming true!" As I squealed for joy, I went home and started writing in my journal. I still wonder why my parents gave me up.

A TWIST IN TIME

When a girl makes a quick decision, she ends a soccer player's career in one, single moment. In **A TWIST IN TIME** *by* ***Jonah Liss***, *see how she makes things right.*

It was another ordinary, dull day at Petoskey Middle School. Blake and Mya had just left bus #34. They didn't know it yet, but the day was going to be full of excitement.

Blake and Mya were seventh grade twins who both attended Petoskey Middle School in Washington. Most people couldn't even tell they were twins or even relatives at all! Blake had blonde hair with blue eyes and was medium height, with a quiet personality. Mya was the opposite. She was small with brown hair and eyes and was very outgoing. They were both twelve years old, with an August birthday.

As another dull day at school came to an end, the sun was shining tremendously bright on this Thursday. Blake darted home in a hurry, while Mya slowly took her time.

She paused and gazed at the sight of the blossoming trees. She looked down at the bright green grass and saw a four-leaf clover. Mya slowly reached down trying to pick up the clover without touching any of the poison ivy growing around it. She grasped the clover tightly in her hand and whispered, "I wish I could control time." Just as she had expected, nothing happened.

Mya walked home to their small, white house. The school year was almost over and it was the beginning of summer. There was a slight breeze that made the grass flow around beautifully. Mya walked up to their house, grasped the door knob and yanked it open.

"Mya, is that you?" Blake shouted across the house.

"Yes," blurted Mya.

Mya slowly walked up the creaking steps to her upstairs bedroom. She grabbed the door knob and twisted it open. She took a baseball from her black desk and slowly tossed it up and down. Mya didn't even know how to throw a baseball the right way. She peered out her window and saw Luke Johnston, their next door neighbor, playing soccer. Luke was twelve years old and also went to Petoskey Middle School.

Mya attempted to toss the baseball on her bed so she could run out and play soccer with Luke. But, the ball hit the window right behind her bed. Shards of glass flew everywhere and some even fell to the outside from her upstairs room and the glass and the baseball hit Luke in the leg.

Luke fell to the ground, helplessly lying down on the grass. Blake was watching the Washington Wizards basketball game downstairs when he heard the accident. Blake sprinted to Luke who couldn't talk because the pain hurt too much.

Blake rang the doorbell at Luke's house to try to get Luke's parents to come out. The door flew open and Mr. Johnston ran over to Blake. Blake tried to explain the accident to the best of his ability, but he wasn't even sure what had happened. Mrs. Johnston started the car and they quickly drove Luke to the hospital. Blake went back inside his house.

"Did you see what happened to Luke?" Blake asked Mya.

Mya was crying. "I accidently threw the baseball at the window and I think the shards hit Luke," she admitted in tears.

Blake yelled, "What! Do you realize what you did? His dreams were about to come true. He was to play on the school soccer team as a starter!"

"I know! I messed up. I am really sorry!" exclaimed Mya in tears.

Blake questioned Mya some more, "How did the baseball hit him, weren't you inside?"

"I broke the window," she whispered.

Mya ran out of the house before Blake said anything else and ran to where she had dropped the four-leaf clover. After searching for a few frantic minutes, she found the clover. She thought about what to do with it for a while. The only thing she wanted in the whole entire world was for Luke to not be hurt and to erase the mistake she had made. Guilt was the worst feeling in the world and it was crossing through Mya's thoughts. It made her feel like a bad person, but she wasn't. As time flew by, it seemed like there was no possible way to change the mistake.

Mya sat on a tree trunk between her bus stop and her house and eyed her amazing surroundings. She noticed a clock sitting next to a couple flowers.

The clock looked like a normal clock. Mya turned the hands randomly to 7:30 a.m. and suddenly she was brushing her teeth in her bathroom like she did every morning. She looked outside and it was bright. With the clock still in her hand she turned it to 3:30 p.m.; the time when she got off the bus.

Mya and Blake were walking home from their bus stop. Blake ran ahead and Mya slowly followed with the clock hidden in her backpack. Mya went up to her room and placed the clock in a drawer in her dresser. Mya decided not to move the clock anytime soon.

Mya looked out her window and saw Luke playing soccer. She ran and joined Luke in the soccer game. Mya learned a valuable lesson: you can never be too careful. It was an amusing game, and, of course, Luke won again!

VANISH

A normal day in the life of a class of sixth graders turns into the strangest day of their lives. What goes wrong? Find out in **VANISH**, *by* **Jacob Schwartz**.

It was only the fourth day of school at Palm Oaks Middle School and the kids were already having the time of their life as a sixth grader. There were great teachers who taught them a lot and the students were well behaved.

One day, the kids were having fun playing at recess. Four...three....two...one... the school bell bursts out ringing and signals that recess is over and it's time for fifth hour. Mrs. Cloom was the teacher for fifth hour Social Studies. The students had been working on a big project for two weeks, but they were supposed to be finished today after long, hard, work. The students were concentrating extremely hard, rushing to get their work done first.

Suddenly, there was a strange noise outside and everyone rushed to the window. They were surprised to see a school bus in the school parking lot. Was it time to go home already? Everyone turned to look at the clock, but when they turned back around, the teacher and fourteen other students were gone. Everyone was talking at the same time, what had happened to them? Where had they gone?

They decided to go to the office to tell the principal of this incident. The halls were eerily empty and so was the office when they got there. The students checked every room in the school, but no one was there. The students started to panic, but then they realized, being students, how foolish they were to be worried about this; no teachers meant no learning. No learning meant no school. And, no school meant they could make the school their hideout and do anything they wanted!

All of the eleven students that were left in the whole school almost demolished the school entirely. They sprayed the walls inside and outside with graffiti, left cracked and broken windows, and ate up all the food in the cafeteria. They even went through the teachers desks and found some really personal stuff!

One of the students decided that the celebration needed to be bigger, so they ran to the Supply Store five miles away, not stopping for cars or stop signs, causing more havoc all over town. They decided their party would be in the Party Center in Full Moon County. The students were disappointed to see that there was already a party going on inside. To their surprise, they ran inside to see that the ones that were having the party were none other than every person from Palm Oaks Middle School!

"Hey everyone!" called their Science Teacher, Mr. Nat. "Where have you been, and why are you breaking in to the school party?"

"School Party?!" the students cried in astonishment.

"But, but, we thought something had happened to you guys. We thought you had been kidnapped!" cried Vicky.

"We had been kidnapped," chuckled Mrs. Mirp. "We were kidnapped onto a party bus by Mr. Polto (who was the school principal), driven 15 minutes from Palm Oaks to here, and had a party for the last day before school camp!"

The eleven students who had missed out on the party all sighed in disappointment.

"You kids missed the whole party. That's too bad for you. Let's go back to the school," Mr. Polto exclaimed. "Remember to pack your things for Camp on Monday!"

The kids cheered in excitement. The kids that were left behind were utterly terrified. What would everyone think when they came back to a school that was completely demolished?

Fifteen minutes later, everyone gasped when they saw the school. Who did this? When did it happen? How did it happen? Is it dangerous to go inside? These questions were swirling around everyone's heads but eventually they got in. They searched the school and found a painting of the principal falling into a volcano. They all gasped. The students stared at it while everyone was wondering. The students turned around to see all the teachers that used to be gone once again. But this time, they knew where they had gone to investigate this; the police station.

They must have taken the naughty students to the police to investigate the destruction. One of the students concluded that the teachers were Ninjas, and that they could disappear without the slightest sound. Another student suggested that the teachers were birds and could fly away very quietly. One other student argued that the teachers were secret agents and could slip away quickly and without a sound. No one knew what really happened.

The students waited and waited for hours, playing on their phones, playing board games, doing everything to entertain themselves, but the teachers never returned. Five days later, the whole incident, and everything they had learned in school completely vanished out of the students' minds.

THE WHITE VAN

When two siblings just wanted to go on a bike ride, they find out how terrifying it could be. In **THE WHITE VAN** *by **Alyssa Durrell**, two siblings find out the dangers lurking in the white van.*

Alex and Alison were twin siblings who were twelve-years-old. When they got home from school, no one was home. They decided to go on a bike ride because they were bored. They only wanted to go down the street, so that, when their parents got home, they wouldn't find out that they were gone.

They got out their bikes and started down the street, but things didn't seem right. It seemed like they were being followed. They looked behind them, but they didn't see anybody. Right after that, a white van came zooming past and they could hear creepy voices coming from the van. Suddenly, they got really scared.

They were so close to turning back, but then Alex turned toward Alison and laughed, "Ha, ha! It was just a joke. Stop being a baby!"

Alison was still scared, but Alex persuaded her to go on. A couple of blocks down the street, they thought everything was fine, but the van came back. This time the van didn't pass; it kept following them. They turned down the next street and the van was still right behind them. Alison and Alex looked at each other like it was time to get back home, so they pedaled faster and faster trying to get away. But the van kept following them.

They thought the van was going to run them over, but it didn't. It just kept getting closer and closer. Alex was riding his bike so fast that it spun out of control and he fell.

"Alex!" Alison screamed. "Get up, get up!" She had tears in her eyes.

She tried to help him up, but she was too weak. So, she sat down beside her brother and closed her eyes to surrender. The last thing she heard was a van door opening.

Alex woke up in a dark, tiny room with a small food bowl and a small drinking bowl. Alison was right beside him, but she was still sleeping.

"Alison, wake up!" Alex whispered.

"What happened?" Alison replied dizzily.

"I don't really know!" moaned Alex.

There were no windows, doors, or pretty much anything that they could escape from except for a vent that was almost impossible to reach. They heard voices just like the ones from the van. All of a sudden, the voices would stop for a second, but then they came back. The twins didn't really know what to do and they were tired, so they went back to sleep.

When they woke up they saw a man standing over them; a very weird, creepy man. The man didn't say anything: he just picked them up by the collars of their shirts and kept dragging them. Alex and Alison tried to fight him but the man was too strong.

He dropped them in a different room which was slightly bigger. This time there was a door and a lower vent that they could easily reach. It's like they wanted the twins to get out. They thought that they must be tricking them, but they tried it anyway. They climbed into the vent and crawled until they couldn't crawl anymore. While they were crawling around in the vent, it suddenly gave in and they fell through! This time they were in a different room that was glowing white. It was so bright that they couldn't see anything.

"Alex, what's happening?"

He replied, "I don't know, Alison."

The twins couldn't do anything but close their eyes. They closed their eyes and hoped that they would wake up in a different room or even better, at home.

When they opened their eyes, they were outside somewhere that they didn't recognize. There were a lot of houses surrounding them, but the twins thought that it could be a trick or a trap. The twins stood up and walked toward the houses slowly and steadily trying to make sure that this wasn't a trick. They were also scared and all they wanted to do was to get back home.

The twins went toward a random house and knocked on the door, and an older woman opened the door and asked what was going on.

"Can you please help us?" Alison cried.

"We've been kidnapped!" Alex remarked. "Can you call the police?"

The old woman had a worried look on her face and invited us to sit down. She gave us warm milk and cookies. She picked up the phone and called the police telling them about our situation. She told us to sit back and relax until the police arrived.

The next thing they knew, they heard sirens and they looked out the window. There was a police car, a fire truck, and an ambulance. They all came in the door and took Alex and Alison out of the house and into a car.

The twins filed in the car and suddenly felt sleepy like they were being gassed. The next thing they remember they were waking up in their own house. Everything was back to normal, but still, no one was home. It was all just a dream, or was it?

9:15

AN ADVENTURE THROUGH THE DOOR

In a world with human-sized bubbles you can float in and mythical creatures that try to kill you, two teenage twins stand together. In **AN ADVENTURE THROUGH THE DOOR** *by* **Samuel Sundberg***, the twins find that the saying "curiosity killed the cat" is also true for human boys.*

One summer day in July, Jam got up from bed and went to go wake up Ham, who sleeps in the attic. Surprisingly, Ham was up and staring at a mysterious door in the middle of the room connected to nothing else.

"Should we look at it or should we leave it alone?" said Ham.

"I think we should just leave it alone in case something bad happens," said Jam.

Later that day, Ham went to the attic to go to bed, and the door was still there. It felt like it wanted him to go through it. "I wonder what this thing does?" he said to himself.

Curious, he opened the door and stepped through it, screaming for his life as all the particles of his body spread apart. Jam heard the screaming and went into the door after him.

In the middle of traveling through the door, they met the ghost knight, Sir Sunchips. He was hairy and was 146 years old. He told them, "I have brought you here to fulfill your destiny to be knights. I tried before and died in the process. You will face many challenges along the way. I didn't even get past the first one. You have come from a line of knights. In order to keep that lineage alive, you must become knights yourselves."

Right after that, they landed on their backs in a forest of pines.

"This is so far away from home, I already feel homesick," said Ham.

Sir Sunchips gave them iron armor for protection and a flaming sword to fight with. He told them, "You have to go through the forest, cross the bridge to the city of clouds, and ride the bubble to the castle."

They started off on their journey back home when suddenly an ice tiger blocked their way on the bridge. He shot an ice ball at their feet, hoping it would make them stand still, but they dodged it by dancing.

Ham started across the bridge to distract the tiger, and Jam sliced the tiger in half from the back with his sword.

"We are going to die if this is the easiest," said Jam.

They then traveled on across the bridge to the city of clouds (or Cloud City). In the city, a robot handed them free bubble rides to the castle. They went into a bubble and floated off into the distance. They pondered, "What are we going to have to slay next?"

Inside the bubble they felt safe, but outside a flying fire phoenix appeared and shot a fireball at them. Their armor blocked its shot from them, but the bubble popped!

"Well, there it is," said Ham sarcastically while falling.

Flying down toward the phoenix in a spiral motion with their swords pointing down, Ham and Jam struck the fire phoenix right through its body, killing it. They fell to the stairs of clouds leading up to the giant castle with blood all over them.

"Hmm... that was too easy," said Jam.

Sir Sunchips was there. "You have proven that you are worthy knights, and therefore I will give myself to you," Sir Sunchips said. He gave himself up so that they could have invincibility to protect themselves against the poison-breathing dragon.

They rushed for the door and encountered the dragon, which seemed like he was expecting their presence. It had seven heads and seven tails. One by one, Ham and Jam sliced off each head and tail only to find that two heads and two tails grew back in their places.

Ham thought quickly, "Maybe it has a weak spot?"

He looked near the spot on the dragon where all of the heads came together. If they could stab the dragon there, it would keep the heads from growing back.

He yelled to Jam, "Go for where the heads meet!"

They both raised up their swords once more and slayed the dragon, feeling that Sir Sunchips was giving them tremendous strength with no struggle at all. With the dragon lifeless on the ground, they ran to the door and went through it, not looking back. As they were going through the door, all of their armor and swords disintegrated into particles. They had landed back in their world.

"I thought that was fun," said Ham.

"So did I, '" said Jam.

"That was the coolest Saturday in the world," said Ham.

Then Jam said, "How about a snack?"

"I'm feeling Sun Chips!" said Ham.

AN ARGUMENT FOR CHANGE

A young man wants more from life than a nine-to-five job. In **AN ARGUMENT FOR CHANGE** *by* ***Brandon Martinez-Eaddy,*** *he goes searching for it.*

Today is the day David Feldman's life is about to change. It is the day everything about him would change.

David walks into his office building thinking of quitting his job. David sits down at his cubicle fighting with himself over quitting his job. He thinks and he thinks so much it interferes with his work. When he finally works up the courage to walk to his boss's office he says, "I am quitting my job to fulfill a life of happiness."

David and his boss even get into an argument about it. By the end of the argument David has no job, his boss is all riled up, and all of his coworkers are witnesses to it.

After David has packed all of his things into a box he walks to his car with pride for quitting his job. David starts the car and drives off. He turns a final corner to the street his house is on.

David gets inside of his house and calls his friend Patrick, who is happy for him and says they should celebrate. They throw around a few ideas like a movie or dinner. Then David says, "We should go skydiving."

All you can hear is crickets on the other end of the line.

At first Patrick isn't too sure, but by the next day Patrick will be convinced.

David and Patrick are on the plane getting ready to jump. The guide counts down "3... 2... jump!"

When David and Patrick jump it's like nothing they've seen before. It's exhilarating.

Once they reach a certain altitude, they open their parachutes while preparing for a safe landing.

When David and Patrick land they can't stop talking about it. They also talk about going to another country.

A few weeks later they are driven to a hotel with fancy sculptures. They are astounded.

Just like that they were hooked on these trips. The bills started to pile up to thousands in credit card debt. Soon enough David owes the bank 560,000 dollars. They foreclose on his home and repossess his car. The only place he could live was with Patrick, with no job and most importantly no money.

All because of an argument.

THE BIRTHDAY PARTY

What happens when a birthday party becomes an adventure of a lifetime? The story **THE BIRTHDAY PARTY**, *written by* **Jack Green**, *is an adventure that Jack and his friends will never forget.*

Finally, I heard the announcement. "Next laser tag starts in 3...2...1...." I am so ready; I am so ready....

The field is a large room with a very high ceiling in the shape of a rectangle. In the center of the room there were many small walls that are useful to hide behind or use for a sneak attack.

As soon as the teams entered, the laser beams began. They were coming from every direction. It was hard to see and even harder to see my own teammates. I raced around trying to avoid being hit, because after you are hit several times, your laser gun needs several seconds to reboot. You are a really easy target when this happens.

After what seemed to be a very long time, but was really only a few minutes, I made it to their base. I was hit many times on the way, but I finally made it! Shooting the opponent's base gets you extra points, and I was ready to score a few. The base is small, so hitting it is difficult. Slowly, I aimed, and then fired! I did it! Then, as I ran back to my own base to protect it, I spotted someone shooting at it. I paused, took a deep breath, and then fired at my opponent.

"Got 'em!" I yelled to my teammates in excitement.

Wow, this is my best game ever, I thought. *This time I will get first place!* Over the loudspeaker, I heard "Game ends in 10... 9...."

Run! Run! That was my only thought. Sprinting across the larger room, I saw the exit door slowly closing.

"3...2...1...," came the announcement.

I jumped for the door, but I was too slow. It closed in my face. How would I get out? A few others had also missed escaping, so together we set out to find our way out.

"How do we get out of here?" I asked my friends Michael, Vivi and Nora.

"I don't know!" they all replied together.

Then, I saw a huge portal, like a very small door, on our left. Then there was another one on the right.

"Where do those go?" Vivi asked.

"Ahhh!" Michael screamed.

"What happened?" I yelled back.

Just then, a weird creature appeared out of nowhere. It looked like an alien with a big face that looked like a rotten apple.

The alien reached out and pushed me to the side!

"I wonder what they want," I asked my friends

Then, we heard a strange scream that sounded like a zombie. The creatures were heading right for the big door that led to the arcade.

"It's trying to get into the arcade! I think they are trying to invade the Earth!" Nora yelled.

Now, another person screamed. It was Vivi. She was on the ground. I ran to help her up, and an alien-zombie ran up behind me. It pushed me away and ran straight for the door. That was when we noticed them coming out of all the small portals that filled the room. All the aliens that got out were piled at the door to the arcade trying to pry it open. We were all really scared. I accidentally shot my laser gun and hit one of the many portals in the room. It slammed shut.

"That's it! We have to shoot all the portals so they close. Then, the creatures will stop getting in!" They were sprinting now, making their way to the door. "Shoot on 3!" I screamed at all my friends.

"1...2...3...shoot!" I yelled.

From the back, I felt a shove. I went through one of the still-open portals and found myself on a very weird planet. Everywhere I looked, I saw aliens with flying cars. It looked just like the moon with many craters. It was almost exactly like what I have seen on Google Earth. However, there were no planets around.

I was all alone. As the aliens came closer, I could see their faces. They were so ugly! I mean, have you ever seen a rotten apple up close? It's not a pretty sight. There must have been hundreds of them. The planet just looked like a rock floating in space. Then I saw an alien looking at me.

He made a zombie-like sound, and all of a sudden they were running toward the portal.

Quickly, I jumped through one of the open portals and shot it. It closed, and I was safe.

"Phew, we escaped the aliens," Nora said.

I heard a loudspeaker say, "Next laser tag starts in 3...2...1...."

"Wait for me!" I shouted.

"Where were you?" they all said.

"I'll tell you later," I replied.

We sprinted out the door as fast as we could. We saw the door slowly shut. This time our dives were successful.

THE CHANGING PATH OF LIFE

Join Janet in **THE CHANGING PATH OF LIFE** by *Ethan Darnall*. These fast changes in events keep you on the edge finding how her life has changed dramatically.

My name's Janet. I have two American parents who both moved to China with their parents when they were kids. But when their parents moved home, they were old enough to stay. They got attached to China and didn't want to leave, so they stayed and got married.

* * *

"Mom! I don't want to go to bed this early!" I whine. "I want to stay up and wait for Dad to get home."

"Dad said that he won't get home until like one in the morning. It's a school night!" Mom says, clearly getting grumpy. So instead of arguing and making my mom mad, I go upstairs and go straight to bed. I still should tell you that I'm an only child and have two regular, boring parents. There's not much to know about except that I'm sixteen, my dad works at a donut shop, and my mom works at a school. Although this day may not sound important, it is, trust me.

I walk down the stairs to get breakfast. I see my mom in the kitchen with something in her fist and her eyes wide open. I ask, "You okay? You look like you had too many coffees."

"Yeah I'm fine! Nothing wrong here!" she said on the verge of gibberish, it was so fast.

I think, *Don't people act like this only when they are trying to hold in a secret?* "Mom, what's in your hand? Tell me the truth."

Then Mom comes to her senses and says, "I found this note in my bed, and it says that Dad will be going on a mission to find out who the killer of the Chinese ruler is."

"What! How is this possible! I expect more of my own parents! I thought you said you would never lie! I should have never trusted you! You disgust me! How am I ever supposed to ever trust you again! I am practically speechless over how little I can trust you now! You know what? I don't care... because we have a bigger problem. Dad is probably going to die out there! I have to save him," I said.

"Honey, he knows what he's doing. I don't want you going out there," my mom claims pridefully. And she thinks I actually will listen to her.

*   *   *

I have a plan. It is the middle of the night. I sneak upstairs and carefully grab the keys off my mom's desk.

Sneaking through the doorway, I almost let the door slam but quickly save it. Then I drive to my dad's current hotel. I had to guess what hotel he was at. I guessed and looked for him in all of the hotels near the crime scene.

"UGGH! You weren't supposed to know about this, Janet! I've got a dangerous but high-paying mission, and we are falling behind on our mortgage. Without this mission, we will be homeless!" says my dad.

"But Dad, I can't risk letting you die! I'll be too depressed to do anything or go anywhere! I want to do this with you," I say.

"No, final answer," says my dad. He punches numbers into his phone. "Yes please, I would like to order a police escort, please," he says to the police officer on the phone. But that's only what he thinks will happen.

*   *   *

Now, to keep anyone from finding out it was me, I will come back to the place of murder and kill off the detective. I'll rent the hotel next to the crime scene and be ready to surprise attack them, the assassin plans out.

*   *   *

I knew this would happen, so when he was talking to me and banging his head on the wall, I rigged his phone secretly. When the police see where the call is coming from, it will show a place in New Jersey. The camp where my parents sent me for the summer that taught me code-breaking *really* helped out.

I follow him to the scene of the crime. But my dad is being so casual that I gradually start being less careful and follow him right into the room of the crime. To make the long story short, the guards catch me and ask my dad if he knows this person.

"WHY ARE YOU HERE!" my dad yells.

*   *   *

While the guards are making a ruckus about it, the assassin thinks, *Now's my time!*

*   *   *

Crack! Crack! Crack! Crack! Crack! I see all the guards drop dead. But we realize a guard has thrown his knife, which hits the assassin on the side of the face like a slap as he reloads.

He drops most of his bullets, and they scatter everywhere. Without time to pick them up, he puts his last bullet in and shoots my dad.

"NO! This is all my fault! Why was I so ignorant to have followed you here! NO! NO! NO!"

I grab cuffs off of a guard, put them on the assassin's ankles and wrists, and then dial 911. It is only like an instant before a team of heavily-armed vehicles and men armed with assault rifles show up and take him into custody.

Even though I may be scarred for life, I am extremely sad about our loss, I will never forgive myself, and I am mad over my ignorance, this family is stronger than you'd imagine.

CONQUEST OF FREEDOM

In a world where an alien civilization rules with an iron fist, two kids must find a way to rebel and overthrow the aliens. Adventure will come in **CONQUEST OF FREEDOM**, *by **John Hermann**.*

It was the year 3412, exactly twelve years since the aliens arrived and twelve since the invasion. This all started when Jane's careless brother, Joe, made a random crop circle. He didn't know that it meant things to the aliens that are too terrible to say.

It was a good thing it wasn't in their cornfield because it all happened so fast they hardly had time to comprehend it. First, laser beams came out of the sky and zapped almost everything they touched. Whatever they touched got all alien-like. People turned to aliens, and the same thing happened with the animals. Plants were crystallized, and homes were destroyed.

Then alien warriors came down from their starships and did even more damage.

When everything stopped, most of the cities were in ruin. The ships were in the atmosphere waiting to attack again.

Now Jane and Joe were walking past a cornfield. It was their old one before they went on the run. Lightning and thunder came, but no rain. Something was blocking it. Little did they know was it was an alien warship in stealth mode.

Lightning struck in the middle of the cornfield. Jane's instincts were telling her to run away, but something was forcing her to go in the field.

When they got to the area where the lightning struck, they couldn't believe what they were seeing. There was a ghostly figure before them. The figure said, "Greetings, I am the guide spirit. Wherever disaster strikes, I'm summoned. I have a great deal of power. I —"

"If you are summoned whenever disaster strikes, why didn't you come during the invasion?" interrupted Jane.

"I was in hyper-sleep and was not able to wake up. Only now have I been able to wake up because a pounding sensation broke me out of hyper-sleep."

"What was the pounding sensation?" asked Jane.

"It was the disaster signal that was implanted into my brain."

Suddenly an alien warship came down from the clouds. "I will demonstrate my powers that I mentioned earlier," the guide spirit said. The ship blew up, and the shockwave was tremendous. The light was super-bright, and there was ringing in Jane's ears. The last words she heard were from Joe as he shouted, "Jane? Jane! Get up! Help me! Help!" Then she passed out.

Jane woke up in a strange room. She was on a bed made out of super-soft material. The guide spirit was tending to her wounds when a man walked into the room. The man said, "That will be all, Joane," and the guide spirit disappeared. The man sat down on the bed and said, "Hello, Jane. My name is Captain Ryan. I am the leader of the resistance."

"Where have you been hiding all of these years?" asked Jane.

"We have been in our base of operations in the middle of Antarctica." Captain Ryan explained how the resistance is just a few survivors of the invasion, and they have cured some people who were turned into aliens.

When she got better, Jane's training began.

It had been about a week since Joe's capture. All that time, he had to do forced labor, eat terrible food, and suffer mistreatment.

When he was in his cell, the whole place vibrated. There was an explosion, and the final battle began.

Humans charged in with the guide spirit leading the way. The guide spirit teleported quickly while the humans clashed with aliens. Aliens were vigorous on the attack while humans were agile and took them off guard. Joe found that one of the cell door bars was loose and charged through the door.

The alien king attacked with ultimate tech cannons. The aliens seemed to be winning, when all of a sudden other alien prisoners, who had escaped, came and fought alongside the humans. While the aliens were taken off guard, Jane was able to sneak past the fighters and take out the alien king. When the aliens saw that their king was defeated, they had no other choice but to retreat.

The humans won. They threw a huge party they called Freedom Day. Then Joe said, "Why did the —"

"— aliens keep you alive?" finished the guide spirit. "Well, it turns out that you and your sister are part alien and part human," the guide spirit said.

CUPCAKE ADVENTURES

When a girl was stuck in a cupcake land, it involved portals and bright skies. In **CUPCAKE ADVENTURES** *by* ***Chloe Motley****, you'll hear all that and more.*

My name is Julie Baker, and I had a major problem. I was stuck in a land—a cupcake land! Here's how it happened.

I was walking through the woods when I saw this bright place. I wanted to see what it was because I had never seen that part of the woods.

When I got a clear look at the place, I saw that the whole place was made of cupcakes. There were cupcake houses and cupcake-topper trees. The sky was pink, and the roads were purple. It was a sugar paradise.

I saw that I was looking through a portal, so I stepped into it. It transferred me to the bright place. I looked back and saw that there were no more woods, only cupcakes.

There were a lot of people. One came up to me and said, "Hi, my name is April."

"My name is Julie," I said.

Then two more girls came up to me and said hi. April said, "These are my cousins, Brooklyn and Beth." I showed them where I came from. I also told them what had happened. They said they could help find my way out.

We went to April's house. She said she had a map and some food that we could use. There was a portal on the map to go home. I asked why they didn't go home, and they said it's because they learned to love Cupcake Land.

Once we were on our journey I was excited. I wanted to tell everyone what happened. But April told me not to. She said we had to keep it a secret. Halfway to the portal, Beth got hungry, and so did we, so we ate cupcakes.

Once we got to the portal everyone was pretty excited, but I realized I wanted to take Beth, April, and Brooklyn with me. When I told them, they agreed. They said that they do miss their family. So we stepped in the portal together.

I asked my mom if they could stay with us because she thought they were friends from school. But they said they didn't need to because the people in Cupcake Land have homes. So they got their family back, and I got new friends.

DISNEY WORLD HORROR

In the daylight, it's a destination for family fun. But everything changes after hours in **DISNEY WORLD HORROR** *by* ***Adam Rhen.***

People say that Disney World is the happiest place on Earth. That wasn't the case the night my friend Liam and I went. In fact, it turned out to be the deadliest place on Earth.

We had spent the day walking around the Magic Kingdom. It was humid out, and kids with their parents were getting ready to go home. Over the loudspeaker we heard a voice say, "The park will be closing in twenty minutes, so please start exiting the park."

Liam smiled and said, "We should take one last ride on Splash Mountain!" I told Liam that we shouldn't. The park was closing, and we needed to leave. Liam said, "Come on, Malcolm, just one last time?" I caved and agreed to go, so we ran as fast as we could over to the ride.

From behind us we heard a weird voice say, "The park is closing; you two have to leave!" We turned around, and there was Mickey Mouse.

"But we just—"

Mickey interrupted Liam and told us just to go ahead.

It was weird because no one else was on the ride, not even the person controlling the ride. We got on anyway, and it started moving.

It took us to the part with the frog on an alligator. It was right by a house that was made out of a tree stump and surrounded by lily pads. The lights on the ride started to flicker and then went off. "What's going on?" Liam said, frightened.

I replied with, "A magic genie did it, and he is going to grant us three wishes."

Liam looked surprised, "Really?"

I gave Liam a goofy look. "Um no, of course not!"

We turned around, and there was a frog behind us holding a guitar. I said to Liam, "Where did that frog come from?"

The frog took one big jump and landed near us. In a deep voice it said, "It's time, it's time, it's time to die."

We both freaked out, jumped out of the log ride, and ran as fast as we could.

While we were running, I turned around to see if the frog was behind us, and *BAM*, the frog hit me in the face with his guitar. I fell on the ground with blood all over my head. "It's time, it's time, it's time for you to die," the frog said to us again.

"Come on, Malcolm, we have to go!" yelled Liam.

When we left we went to the gift shop to hide, but the door was locked. Liam punched the window out and reached in and unlocked the door. The alarm was beeping when we ran in. "We have to hide, Malcolm. They are coming for us."

I looked around the room for a weapon to use, when I found a sword that looked like the one that Jack Sparrow used when he was fighting Davey Jones. Liam looked confused. "You are going to kill them with a plastic sword?"

I said back to Liam, "If the robots came to life, maybe the swords will, too. " We looked down and the swords were real. "We have to climb the fence to get out of here," I said to Liam.

We both grabbed a sword and walked toward the exit. We made it to the fence and started to climb when we heard from behind us, "It's time, it's time, it's time for you to die." We jumped off the fence and ran at the robot, swinging the sword left and right, and jammed it right into the frog. The robot frog fell down to the ground and slowly faded, saying, "It's time, it's time, it's time for you to d...," and shut down and died.

We both stood up, grabbed our swords, threw them over the fence, and climbed to the other side. I picked up my sword and looked closely at it. "Look, Liam, the swords are plastic again." He grabbed his sword, and his was plastic, too.

All of a sudden a bright spotlight hit us. We both hit the ground in fear when we heard the voice on the other side of the light. "It's time, it's time, it's time for you to get in the van!"

Liam and I looked at one another, confused. Liam's mom said again, "I said it's time to get in the van. I have been waiting for you guys for an hour!" Liam and I laughed, got up off the ground, and left the park.

ELEVATORS GOING DOWN IN HISTORY

A girl's day at the aquarium turns into her worst nightmare. In **ELEVATORS GOING DOWN IN HISTORY** *by **Ava Stasinski**, will she regret her choice to face her fears that day?*

We all have some fear that we want to face. My fear was clearly elevators. It all took place in the summer of 2011 in a parking structure elevator. That day I just wanted to face my fear, but clearly that just didn't happen and made my fear go down in history.

My family and I were heading for Newport Aquarium in Kentucky. We parked our car in the parking structure and walked over to the elevators available. I was somewhat scared because I didn't really enjoy elevators that much, but that was the only option to get down to the aquarium. Just the feeling of being in an elevator is scary. I feel very claustrophobic, close together, and uncomfortable with the motion of the elevator.

The elevator opened up, and right in front of me were a ton of people. There were moms, dads, grandparents, and a bunch of kids. The elevator was jam-packed. Our family stepped in, and I had that feeling of being congested. It was extremely hot in there! I pressed the button on the elevator feeling skeptical about being with this many people in an elevator. As soon as I pressed it, we started going until I heard a loud snap....

The elevator just officially broke down. We were stuck with lots of people in a tight, congested area. I was freaking out, but still trying to keep it together. Also it smelled really bad in the elevator. It kind of smelled like mold and stinky chemical products. I looked around and saw other families and their kids being worried and not knowing what to do! Other family's kids look worried and scared wondering what had happened. My brother Blake was super-scared and thought that we could never get out!

After a few minutes someone decided to say, "You know what? This elevator isn't going to move itself. We need to press the emergency button." So he stepped forward and pressed the button.

A few seconds passed with no answer. Then all of a sudden we heard a man telling us that they will come and help us get up. That was huge relief. Kids started feeling happier now knowing that it would all be okay. Everyone waited anxiously to be let out!

About seven minutes later we heard someone telling us not to panic, and we will be let out very soon. We could hear the maintenance people using their tools, trying to pry open the elevator doors.

After about 15 minutes passed, the doors opened. All of us in the elevator came out with a huge relief in our voices.

That was maybe one of the worst 20 minutes of my life. I'm sure other parents and kids felt the same about being scared. But honestly, it felt like we were stuck in there for an hour.

My parents then said, "How about we just go down to the main level parking, and hope for a close spot. We're not going in that elevator again."

That day was maybe the worst day of my life, from wanting to face my fear, to turning into a huge problem. Ever since that experience of mine I will always take the stairs or just walk a little longer. My brother has a little fear of elevators now because of that situation. For my brother and me, anything is worth it if we don't go into an elevator again. I will never really consider going to face my fear again. Who knows? That same incident could happen again. That elevator being stuck just went down into my elevator history.

THE FOREST

*When a girl gets chosen to deliver a package, she discovers something that she wished to get back for years. In **THE FOREST** by **Clare Birley**, a girl learns to let go of the thing she misses the most.*

Each year in the village I live in, two children between ages 8 and 14 are chosen to deliver a package into the forest. One child is from a poor/working-class family while one child is from a wealthy family. The goal of this delivery is to rid the town of the ghosts and bring peace to the village.

The residents of the village dream that all kinds of far-fetched wonders will occur after a child survives the delivery of the package. My sister used to dream that the village would be blessed with gold and riches. My older brother believed that we would be protected from neighboring villages.

I never thought anything of such sort. My only wish was a little more personal: I hoped *if* someone came back alive, my father would come back, too.

Stories would be told around campfires about the wonders of the forest. Some told creepy tales about wisps of lost souls wandering between the thick tree trunks, trying to find their past lives. Other people told stories of peaceful meadows, tall trees that shot up into the sky, serene crystal waterfalls, and woodland creatures that called the place their home. And then there were those who joked about it being a regular forest dressed up by local folklore. Whether regular forest or not, no one has ever been in the forest and come back out alive.

I live in a small shack with my mom, sister, and two brothers. I am the third-oldest in my family after my mom and 14-year-old brother Liam. After me is my brother John (11 years old) and little sister Delilah (age 9). We live in the part of town where you don't want to leave your silver pocket watch lying around. I have to work two jobs in between school for extra money to pay the rent. Before my dad died we had a bigger house where we didn't have to sleep in the same room.

My typical day starts with me waking up before the crack of dawn to take care of Mrs. Smith's animals before school. After the last task of milking the cows, I shovel down a piece of bread and cheese while combing my disheveled hair. My school day isn't out of the ordinary. Usually I am made fun of for looking like I slept in a barn by my classmates and hit with a ruler by my teacher for not finishing my homework.

Today I was unusually tired from my chores and left with my books at the end of the day. On my way home I stopped to clean Mr. Adison's house, which for five shillings, pays for my family's dinner for one day. Exhausted from the day, I stepped on the porch and picked up the mail. When I saw the package with my name written on it with loopy cursive letters, I almost screamed.

My mom held the package with shaky hands. The ghosts have a rule where only the guardians of the child are to know about the package. The next morning I would sneak away quietly without anyone seeing me except for the other chosen child. (The village doesn't watch when the two children leave; maybe it's the temptation of following them.) Only after the day has ended would people know I was gone.

I ate breakfast the next day at the rugged wooden table in our shabby kitchen. It was dark outside, and the sun showed no hint of coming above the horizon soon. I sat across from my mom. Her eyes were puffy and red like she had been crying. I could see she was trying to stay strong. She tried to give me advice about the woods, but I tuned it out. Whatever she thought she knew about the woods was 99.999 percent wrong. I started to put my coat on before she stopped me and gave me a hug.

"I have something for you." She gave me Dad's compass from the mantle. It had the Irish blessing engraved on the back:

> May the road rise up to meet you.
> May the wind always be at your back.
> May the sun shine warm upon your face,
> And rains fall soft upon your fields.
> And until we meet again,
> May God hold you in the palm of His hand.

Dad once said it would lead me anywhere I wanted to go if I let it.

"Cecilia, dear, I want you to know I will always be proud of you, no matter what." She tucked a piece of golden hair behind my right ear.

I responded with a squeeze and slowly stepped out the door. "Goodbye, Mom, I love you."

With my package in my hand I ran to the edge of the forest boundary with tears streaming down my eyes. I wiped the tears from my face and waited for the other chosen child.

Soon after I arrived, so did Rosalie Williams. As soon as I saw her, I felt a headache coming on. Rosalie is by far the most annoying person on the planet. She gossiped loudly while we walked through the first layer of the forest.

"I wish this forest was less dirty, my boots are getting scuffed!" she whined.

"You wouldn't have anything to complain about if you were already dead in this cursed forest," I shot back at her.

This finally shut her up. She continued to follow me as we got deeper into the thick trees. I followed the compass that mom gave me. I didn't notice before but in the front there were the words "Follow him, he will lead you where you need to go" etched in the glass.

"Stop!" Rosalie whispered. "I hear something." After a moment, I heard the ruffling of tree leaves, too. We looked up, and hundreds of large, human-like creatures looked back down at us. Pieces of bark fell from the tree branches above. They had their bows locked on us, loaded with arrows.

I stood completely still. I felt as though my heart would burst; it was racing so fast. They looked down on us with their beady, black eyes. They wore rags as clothes, and their skin was a bluish color.

Rosalie stepped on a stick to get a better look. The noise triggered the animals to jump down out of the trees and to the ground.

The creatures tied us in rope at their camp. They sat around a fire and spoke in a foreign language. Now that I had a closer look at them, I could see they looked almost crazed. They spoke with the emphasis of a maniac. They had strange hand movements that somehow spoke what they were saying. Their eyes were completely black and empty-looking. It looked as though their souls were trapped in the darkness and trying to get free. They looked at us like they were waiting for something to happen. I had a horrible feeling about what they were going to do with us.

"These are forest elves," I finally said out of the silence.

Rosalie stared at something in the distance. Her eyes had a glazed look.

"My father once told me about them. They dwell in the canopies of trees searching for prey." I looked around my surroundings. I saw a quiver of arrows two feet away from me. I slowly scooched my way over to it. I gently turned around and slowly grabbed an arrow. The forest elves seemed too busy to notice my movements. I sliced the vines that bound my hands. I handed Rosalie the arrow.

We snuck past the elves and grabbed supplies. I found a decent bow on the ground. Rosalie found a knife (how that girl knows how to use a knife, I don't know).

I reached into my pocket and realized they had taken my compass. I stared wide-eyed at Rosalie and mouthed to her what happened. She shook her head. For once, unfortunately, Rosalie was right. I could see the elf that was holding it. He was away from the crowd.

"Maybe I can shoot him," I whispered.

"We'll be noticed," Rosalie whispered back.

"It was my father's."

I loaded an arrow while I could hear Rosalie saying prayers. I put all my concentration on my aim. I let the arrow loose, and I could have sworn that time froze. My heart was beating with the rhythm of a hummingbird's wings.

The arrow hit the elf in the shoulder. He seemed to be unconscious. We snuck over to his hand. I had to pry his fingers off the compass. It seemed undamaged.

"Let's get out of here," I said.

"Best idea I've heard all day," she replied. We raced out of there before you could've said "forest elves."

After we got out of there I realized I had cut my hand. The blood had seeped into the engraving on the glass of the compass.

Rosalie tapped my shoulder urgently. I looked up to see what she wanted my attention for. Complete shock fell over me. I gaped at the figure, but no word could come out. The silvery figure was see-through, and hovered about a foot above the ground. He was six feet tall and looked intently at me.

"Hello, Cecilia" he said with a voice so sad it could make you cry.

"Dad," I whispered so softly you could barely hear me.

"I will show you the way," he said.

"How are you here?" I said, completely forgetting that Rosalie was there, too.

"The compass shows you people that you have lost or loved when your blood touches the engraving. Follow me. I know where you need to go. It's a day's journey from here."

He turned around and headed north. I absentmindedly wiped tears from my eyes. Rosalie put her hand on my shoulder and gave me a hug. "We'll be able to go home, and this will be all over."

We walked through amber meadows and crossed blue streams. The blue sky turned deeper shades of sapphire. The stars looked like pinpricks of light that shone in the night sky. The moon looked like a bowl of milk on a black table. We walked under the shade of the leaves. Patches of ground showed between branches with beams of moonlight. Rosalie sliced branches with her knife. I shivered as I followed my father. The night air was crisp and cold. I could see steam coming from Rosalie's nose.

"Can we make camp?" I asked.

"We're almost there," he said in a daze.

I looked at his outline. I would've done anything to bring him back a few days ago, but he seems distant, almost like he is in a dream.

He stopped suddenly and pointed to the ground. Rosalie and I rushed to where he was pointing. It was a grave. Two names were etched into the stone.

Wilhelm Grimm 1786-1859
Jacob Grimm 1785-1863.

I placed the package on the grave. I looked into Rosalie's emerald green eyes.

"We did it!" I whisper-shouted.

"We can go home!" she said as she hugged me.

My dad dissolved into mist behind me, but I was too happy to care. For once, all was well.

GHOSTS IN THE GRAVEYARD

GHOSTS IN THE GRAVEYARD by *Faith Reeves* is the story of four girls who go into a nearby graveyard to have fun on Halloween night. However, they don't bank on a spooky game going very, very wrong.

"Come on, Alyssa!" an impatient Sophie called as she stared at her friend huddled behind a tree. "You've been hiding there for ages now, and we want to go into the graveyard...now!"

"I don't know, you guys. What about all of the news stories we've heard lately?" Alyssa called back.

"Oh, please!" Julia piped up from behind Sophie. "You really believe that there have been skeletons roaming around at night?" she asked, shaking her head in disbelief.

After a few more minutes of the girls trying to persuade Alyssa to come with them, they gave up and walked into the graveyard. Alyssa wasn't sure what to do other than follow them, so that's what she did. They walked in silence together, all scared, until Sophie turned around. "Okay, so I figured we wouldn't want to be bored. Who wants to play Ghost in the Graveyard? 'Cuz we're in a 'haunted' graveyard, get it?" she asked. The girls agreed and made Alyssa the first "ghost."

"Fity-seven...fifty-eight...fifty-nine...sixty! Ready or not, here I come!" she called out. Despite being terrified at the beginning, all of the girls were starting to have fun and forget their worries. Sophie, Julie, and Harper laughed quietly with each other, thinking that there was no way that Alyssa would find them in their amazing hiding places.

Then they heard Alyssa calling out. "Who's there?" she asked. None of her friends had heard anything, so they stayed hidden, thinking that it was just a trick to get them to come out. Then came Alyssa's small, scared voice again. "I said, 'Who's there?'"

Harper stood up and went over to the patch of land where Alyssa was looking around nervously. "What's wrong?" she asked slowly.

"I heard a noise, like someone walking toward me. It wasn't one of you guys, because you were all over in that patch of land, so I don't know. I think I'm going to go home now. You should, too. This is scary!"

Sophie rolled her eyes. "Just because you thought you heard some footsteps coming toward you doesn't necessarily mean that it was a skeleton. It also doesn't mean that you need to go home!" she said, as if it were the most logical thing in the world.

Alyssa turned and started to walk away. "I'm going home. You can join me if you want to."

Sophie was getting annoyed at all of the fun Alyssa was ruining. "You are such a baby!" she yelled.

Julie and Harper were shocked, but brave. They knew that they were going to be safe. There couldn't really be skeletons walking around haunting people!

Alyssa continued to walk straight toward the exit without looking back at the other three girls. They turned the opposite direction from the exit and walked away from Alyssa.

It was a few minutes later when they heard a scream. It was loud, and terrified. They knew it had to be Alyssa. The girls immediately began to run toward the front gates. None of them had any idea as to what could have happened.

Suddenly Sophie, who was at the front, stopped and gasped. In front of her were footprints. They weren't just any kind of footprints, though. They were skinny, and bony, and almost like a...skeleton! The three girls were so shocked they followed the footprints to a large oak tree, where they stopped. Harper, Sophie, and Julie didn't know what to do. They all stood, with their mouths hanging open, speechless—that is, until a light, wispy hand was placed on Sophie's shoulder, accompanied by the sound of someone breathing deeply. She felt as though someone were watching her. She whipped her head around, and as soon as she saw the pale, gaunt face, she ran.

The remaining girls thought there was no way that the skeleton would ever catch up to her. They could hear Sophie screaming and crying as she went. When she crossed through the front gates it was like a barrier was put up that the skeleton was not able to cross. That didn't stop Sophie, who continued to run all the way down the street.

Harper and Julie started talking. They knew that they should go home. At the same time, they also felt that they should stay and look around for Alyssa. The girls were running on adrenaline at this point. They wanted to find their friend! They decided that they would stay out until midnight because that was the latest their parents had allowed for them.

They looked around all of the patches of gravestones, but Alyssa was nowhere to be found. They finished up just before midnight and knew then that there was nothing else that they could do, so they left without Alyssa.

Thirty Years Later

The three girls that survived the horrific events on that Halloween night went through years of therapy to help them. Alyssa was never found, no matter how hard the police searched for her. The girls all remained with their stories even when everybody doubted them. They never completely figured out what had happened on that terrifying Halloween night.

GUINEA PIG PARK

In a story based on a true event, guinea pigs from a test lab are set free in Central Park. **GUINEA PIG PARK** *by* ***Lily Paul*** *relates events from the pigs' point of view.*

"That's it for today, little guys," the scientist exclaimed with a smile as he peeled off his latex gloves. The scientist picked up the guinea pigs one by one and set them in the cage. The cage door slammed shut, and the lights in the lab flickered off. The only lights still on were the lamp heaters in the turtles' aquarium, which shined through into the guinea pigs' cages.

"What did you test on today, Nico?" asked Lulu as she shuffled out of the wooden guinea pig hut in the corner of the cage.

"The stupid cheese maze thing," Nico replied as she continued to gnaw at her treat stick. She stopped chewing and turned around. "The only good thing about it is the cheese."

Lulu walked over to the dry water bottle and said, "Yeah, they think just because we know how to get through the same maze seven times in a row that we are some sort of prodigies." She looked over into the next cage. "Do you have any water over there?" called Lulu.

Fluffy popped up from the corner of the other cage. "Yeah, why?" Fluffy squeaked.

"They forgot to fill ours," replied Squeaks, popping up from behind Lulu. "Whatever, it doesn't matter. The humans will fill it up tomorrow anyway."

Nico strolled over to the food bowl where Chief, the oldest and most respected guinea pig, was telling a story about his favorite television show. He explained that if you leaned over the wooden hut on a Saturday morning you could see half of the TV from the break room. Nico sat next to Mimi and Greg in the crowd of guinea pigs listening to Chief.

A dark shadow stood in the doorway. The guinea pigs froze. A man walked into the room and started grabbing the guinea pigs one by one, putting them into a duffel bag. The remaining guinea pigs scattered frantically.

"What's happening?" squealed Fluffy. "Is it just another tes—" Fluffy stopped abruptly as the hand reached down for him.

Lulu looked around. The guinea pigs were rapidly getting picked up one after another. "Ted, Greg, Patches, Nico," Lulu counted, "Billy, Fuzzy, Chief, Queenie!" The hand reached down for her, closer and closer. In a blink Lulu was in the bag among the rest of the guinea pigs. The sea of pigs swirled by her.

"Where are we?" Billy screamed.

"Where are we going?" Mimi hollered.

Squeaks squirmed through the bag and up the side where he could just barely see the doors of the laboratory swing open. City air surrounded the pigs. They had been outside many times before in the play pen, but never like this.

Lulu stuck her head out over the top of the bag. The city lights flashed and glimmered. The cool city air blew through her fur. She closed her eyes and took another breath of the cool, brisk air when she was yanked back down into the hot duffle bag. There was a loud thud as they were dropped in the trunk of a car waiting outside the lab. The trunk slammed shut, and the car started moving.

After what seemed like forever the car stopped abruptly. The man pulled open the trunk with a grin on his face. "You guys are gonna be free!" he whispered as he grabbed the bag and threw it over his shoulder.

Chief climbed up over the inside pocket of the bag and looked out over the vast sea of guinea pigs. "Whatever happens out there, we have to stick together!" he said in a booming voice.

The bag started shaking. It got worse and worse! Suddenly the shaking stopped. The zipper opened, and a large man with a ski mask stared down at them with glowing eyes. They ran as fast as they could away from the man. The pigs stuck together in one large mass. They ran and ran until they couldn't see the man anymore.

"Have we lost him?" asked Mimi, panting. There was silence.

"I don't know if we lost him, but we have gotten *ourselves* lost," said Chief, looking around. "Okay, everyone," Chief said, concerned. "It's getting dark and we need to find shelter."

The guinea pigs searched around the park. The park grew darker and darker. The pigs looked high, low, left and right, but a reliable shelter was nowhere to be seen.

"What's that?" yelled Squeaks. In the distance the pigs saw a large structure that somewhat resembled the wooden huts back in the laboratory. The guinea pigs ran as fast as they could toward the structure. With every step, the park got darker and darker, and the pigs got hungrier and hungrier and thirstier and thirstier.

Finally they reached the building. Now closer, they realized it was much bigger and not at all like they imagined. The structure had a large, domed roof and was taller than they had expected. The sign next to this large structure read "CENTRAL PARK BAND SHELL." Chief walked into the massive, domed structure in awe.

"Now that we have shelter I need four pigs to come with me," Chief said. "We are going to get food." Fluffy, Nico, Queenie, and Greg walked forward. "Perfect," Chief said with a small grin. The five guinea pigs set off.

Queenie looked around and said, "Where should—?"

"Shhhh," Chief interrupted. A tall man in a dark green suit with a matching cap and a flashlight stood a good nine yards in front of them.

"What do we do?" Nico whispered softly.

"See those half-eaten hot dogs by the trash can?" Chief asked.

"Yes..." they all replied.

"Good; go get as many of the buns as possible," Chief whispered. "Go!" All the guinea pigs ran toward the garbage bins.

"HEY!" the man yelled as he ran for the pigs. He saw them! They dodged out of the man's flashlight beam. They ran and ran.

"Oh NO!" Queenie squeaked as the bun she held in her mouth rolled out of the wrapper!

"Don't go back for it!" Chief yelled, but it was too late. The man swept up Queenie!

"NO!" squeaked Greg, swerving around and running toward her.

Lulu and Billy looked around, awaiting the arrival of their friends. "There they are!" Billy squealed. As the silhouette of the pigs grew closer and closer, the pigs came to a sad realization.

"We left with five, and we've come back with three," said Chief solemnly. The crowd of pigs looked sadly up at the remaining pigs. Chief, Nico, and Fluffy stared back. "The man was not going to hurt them. He was only trying to bring them back to the lab," Chief said without emotion. He was trying to stay strong and keep a brave face. "We need to find a new home," Chief said. "It's not safe here anymore," he continued. "I found a nice pile of rocks where we can go."

The next morning they set off while it was still dark out and too early for anyone to be watching. "Can't we just go back to the lab?" whined Fuzzy, "I miss the nutri-pellets, and I'm *hungry!*"

"Fine," said Chief with a still, very straight face. "All in favor of going back to the wheel, the cheese maze, the shots, and the tests, say 'Aye.'" The group fell silent. "That's what I thought," Chief said. "You'll see that it's better to be free. After tonight we will look for some sort of fruits or vegetables we can eat." Chief glanced around and continued speaking. "A lot of you don't know this, but I was once a free pig. I lived in the wild, and it was much better than lab life." The pigs all trusted Chief's words and felt confident in their choice to stay free. "All right, it's settled," he said with a small grin. "We leave at dawn."

"Are we there?" Lulu said excitedly as they approached a large pile of rocks similar to the one Chief described.

"WE ARE HERE!" Chief announced to everyone. They all went into the opening in the rock. There was about enough room for a child to sit in. With there being about twenty pigs, they knew they were going to have to expand. Chief climbed up onto a rock and looked out over all of them. "Well..." he said with a grin, "start digging!"

Epilogue

For at least twenty years the pigs have been living happily in the rocks. They have been repopulating, and their group gets larger year after year. Chief is gone, but his kids and grandkids will keep the tribe going for decades to come.

The burrow is now a thriving community with more than fifty pigs. They have expanded deeper into the rock, and have made many underground tunnels. Some people believe if you go to the park at night you just may see the shadows of guinea pigs scurrying around.

IN THE BLINK OF AN EYE

For Billie, a weekend at Aunt Gabriella's is anything but a vacation. **IN THE BLINK OF AN EYE** *by **Vanessa Lohr** tells the story of Billie's strange experience in a mansion that holds a fantastic secret.*

It was 1989, and a young boy named Billie went to his creepy Aunt Gabriella's house. The very first thing Billie saw was this huge, dark, creepy mansion. As he and his family were approaching, he saw a very fat cat tumbling down the windowsill. *Yeah right, cats don't always land on their feet*, Billie thought. "So, why do I have to go here without you? It's not fair. And why is this place called The Unknown Land?" Billie asked.

His mother answered with a sigh. "You've asked me this at home so many times. We're not going to pick you up early. Your sister did it, so stop complaining. It is a Crumbercott's family tradition that when you are 12 years old, you go to your Aunt Gabriella's house. When we asked her, she would always try to change the topic or just say that that is something to discuss later on, so we don't even bother anymore. Your Aunt Gabriella's isn't that bad. She's just a little shy."

Before Billie stepped out of the car his older sister said, "Good luck, you'll need it." Just after Billie got his suitcase out of the trunk, his parents sped off. When Billie turned around, he saw a pale-faced woman watching him from the window.

Billie was about to knock on the door, as a huge lion-faced door knocker caught his eye, when the door opened with a bone-chilling screech. After the cat hissed at Billie, it dragged himself up the stairs. A maid came up to him and said, "That's Devil, the Mistress's cat. The Mistress is awaiting you. Please follow me."

"Hello, Billie, nice to finally meet you. My maid shall take you to your sleeping chamber. Make yourself at home. I hope to make your acquaintance at dinner at eight o'clock," his aunt said.

Billie was brought into his "sleeping chamber." He was stunned, and said, "This is as big as my living room."

At about eight o'clock Billie went to dinner. He started walking down one of the corridors and said. "Where do I go now? This place is huge."

As Billie continued walking down the corridor, he saw a green light shining from under a door. He tried opening the door, but it was locked. He bent down to catch a peek of the inside and saw feet in front of him "What do you think you're doing?" a girl asked.

"Umm, I was looking for the dining room, and as I was passing by I saw this light from under this door. I got curious and tried looking inside," Billie answered.

"Oh, you must be the Mistress's nephew. Follow me. By the way, my name is Alaia."

As she was directing him to the dining room he asked her questions about that locked door and his aunt. Alaia told him, "Your aunt almost never talks to me, but when she does she's always strict. When she sees me trying to see what's behind that door she lashes out and starts screaming at me. But she can't fire me because my dad's the chef and makes such good food she doesn't want to fire us."

They arrive in the dining room right on time. Alaia's father came in and announced that there was going to be French cuisine for dinner. During dinner Billie couldn't stop thinking about that room.

After Billie had eaten so much he was tired. Immediately after dinner he went up to his room, without getting lost again, and went to sleep.

The next morning Billie went to the room and tried to pick the lock without knowing that Alaia was following him. Alaia walked up to him and said, "You're not supposed to be doing that." But it was too late. The door opened with a screech.

In the blink of an eye they were getting sucked into a wormhole. As they were in the wormhole, they noticed that the walls were covered in doors. A wall started sucking all the doors in, but Billie managed to grab a door. He pulled it open while also grabbing Alaia by the feet.

He tried pulling her in, and then someone grabbed him by the hips and helped pull Alaia in, and it seemed like it didn't matter to Billie. All that mattered was getting Alaia back.

After they managed to pull her in, they pushed the door shut. They turned around to see a grown man. He said, "I was wondering when you would finally stop by. Hi, I'm the older you. Welcome to the future. This is my wife Alaia—"

Billie interrupted him as he and the young Alaia stared at each other, saying, "WHAT!"

"You get used to it. These are your seven children: Tobious, Tris, Olivia, Angelina, the twins Jacob and Jessie, and last and not least small Adam," he said. "That's a lot of children, but I have to go now. Bye."

Before they knew it, they were back at Aunt Gabriella's house, where she was waiting for them. "Now have you learned your lesson from snooping around in other people's business? Alaia, why don't you go eat breakfast. I need to talk to Billie.

After Alaia had gone, Aunt Gabriella said, "I didn't want to tell you this because I didn't think you were ready to handle it. But now I have to tell you. The unknown is called The Unknown Land because it is a land of magic. That's why not many people know of this land."

Later that evening Billie visited Alaia's "sleeping chamber" and discussed what had happened that day. They agreed never to talk about it again. And soon, but not that soon, Billie and Alaia got married and had seven children.

KIDS UNLEASHED

Power is something only special people get, and they are chosen unexpectedly. In **KIDS UNLEASHED** *by* **Marisela Elledge**, *maybe those kids are the chosen ones.*

The Viva family has a family of 14, if you include the animals. There is Henry Viva (dad), Eleanor Viva (mom), Duncan, Makenzie, Ethan, Elisa, and Dawn. We have a Rottweiler for each kid. There is Dasiy, Spike, Valentine, Shannon, and Dixy. Oh yeah, I forgot to tell you I live with my grandpa and grandma.

"Mack, come on. We're going to be late!" said Dawn.

"All right, I just want to get my hair done!" Makenzie replied as she walked out of the bathroom.

"Let's go, guys!" I said.

We sprinted down the steps to the bus stop. In fewer than 30 seconds, the bus turned the corner. We were glad we didn't miss the bus because sometimes our parents get a little upset when we ask for a ride because it's cold or we miss the bus. But *nooooo!* The only thing that can make this house any better is the lack of my grandparents. They're alcoholic smokers with no respect at all.

"Man, I seriously miss getting rides to school," said Duncan.

"Yeah, me too," I said.

As we got closer to the school, the louder the bus got. This was typical. But since we were sitting in the same group of seats we usually sit in, it didn't really bother us much.

When we got to school, Fawn didn't wait at all for us to get off the bus and join her, which was unlike her. When we got off the bus she ran back out of the school toward us with bracelets. I don't even know where she got them.

"Just put them on!" Fawn said.

There was something weird about those bracelets from the start; I just didn't know what. When we put them on, something weird happened. I just couldn't take them off. I felt like they were my property now and it was my job to keep it safe.

"Fawn, where'd you get these?" I asked.

"I don't remember," said Fawn. "Anyway, let's get to class."

All day, I couldn't eat a bite. When I tried to, it made me sick. I had this freaky feeling like I wanted to be with my sisters and brothers. I felt depressed whenever I wasn't.

After school, we talked about it. We all had been feeling the same way. We all looked down at our bracelets at the same time. They seemed to be slowly and freakishly moving toward each other. That freaked us out!

We went to the part of the playground where no one went at all and decided to have those bracelets take an eternal dirt nap. We buried them six feet under (well, more like six inches under) and never spoke of those bracelets again.

A LONG DAY

When *Luke Morency* called his story **A LONG DAY**, he wasn't kidding. For Gothalion and Broman, the day will span 200 million years.

Early one quiet summer day, Gothalion and Broman were sitting up in their tree house bored to death, with nothing to do. With the last year of high school starting in fewer than two weeks, the two boys knew this was their last chance for an adventure before classes and homework took over their lives.

Gothalion said to Broman, "I bet you 200,000 dollars that dinosaurs became extinct because they ran out of candy."

Broman, looking skeptical, replied, "There is no way that dinosaurs became extinct because they ran out of candy. If I had to take a guess I would say that dinosaurs must have disappeared from the Earth because of some crazy natural disaster, like a meteor crashing to the Earth."

Gothalion, the younger (by four months!) but often wiser of the two boys, got a sparkle in his eye. The more he thought about dinosaurs, the more he realized that he and Broman needed to solve this puzzle...and he was starting to formulate a plan.

"Well, we'll have to solve this the hard way," said Gothalion. "We will have to go back in time and search and hunt until we find clues that will lead us to the answer."

Broman nodded his head up and down so many times that his dark hair flopped into his face. "YES, YES, YES, let's do this! I am up for the challenge!"

The boys decided they would pool their savings and buy a time-travelling car. These cars were not easy to find and ran on a special kind of fuel, a fuel that could only be found in present times. If they found the car, they would have to make sure to purchase enough fuel to arrive AND return safely from their adventure.

The first thing the boys did was walk to Chuck's Auto Dealership two blocks away. When they got there they found out that there was one more time-traveling car for sale. They counted out their savings and purchased the car and enough fuel to travel back to the Jurassic period, 145 million years ago.

Chuck helped them pour the fuel into a large, fireproof gas can. "Now boys, make sure, no matter what, do not spill this fuel, or you will be stranded in the past. You need every drop of this fuel to return," Chuck said very seriously. "Make sure to check this gas can when you arrive to make sure NONE of it has spilled out." Gothalion and Broman nodded. They understood.

Broman drove them back to his house where they gathered supplies for their adventure. They threw toothpaste, clothes, blankets, pillows, Power Bars, bottles of juice, Little Bite muffins, and a large tent into a huge backpack. The boys jumped back into the time-travelling car and drove until they found a flat open parking lot. It was misty outside, and fog was rolling over the hills.

Broman hit the gas and passed 10, 20, 30, 40, 50, 60, 70, 80, 90 miles per hour...*VOOM!* They were off! It seemed to happen very quickly. All of a sudden the boys were back in the Jurassic period.

Even though the journey seemed to happen in a flash, it was very late when they arrived—very late and very dark. Gothalion put his hand in front of his face and was shocked to realize that he couldn't see his own hand. It was also raining cats and dogs.

They decided to set up the tent as quickly as possible to get shelter from the rain. They were also tired and knew it was time to go to bed. As soon as their heads hit the pillows, they were fast asleep.

When they woke up the next day the sun was so bright it hurt their eyes. It was very warm there, much warmer than at home. They took off their hoodies and were comfortable in t-shirts. They grabbed the Little Bite muffins and juice and had a quick breakfast. After that they started hiking and searching for clues.

Broman was the first to see the candy wrapper under a leaf. He was shocked because he thought Gothalion's theory was ridiculous! They walked for three hours before they found another candy wrapper. Then they hit the mother lode...they found a huge pile of candy wrappers. There had to be hundreds and hundreds of them.

Broman said, "How can this be? I thought we would come to the Jurassic period and it would be demolished by a natural disaster, but there are healthy trees, flowers, and candy wrappers!" There were no dinosaur bites out of the tree leaves but many bites out of the candy wrappers. Gothalion had a huge smile on his face.

But Broman was still not satisfied. He said to Gothalion, "What if these candy wrappers were left here by other human beings? What if they were left here by other people time-travelling like us?" Gothalion didn't *love* this idea, but after much discussion realized that it did make a lot of sense. How could there have been candy back in the Jurassic period when electricity or factories didn't exist yet? How would the candy have been made?

Gothalion and Broman started walking back to where they left their tent and car. By now it was nighttime, and the boys were tired and hungry. They ate their Power Bars, drank more juice, and crawled into the tent to go to sleep for the night.

When the boys woke up they decided it was time to go back home. They laughed about finding the candy wrappers but realized that they may never really know why or how dinosaurs became extinct.

All of a sudden Broman looked frightened. He slowly said, "Gothalion, we forgot to check the gas can when we first arrived. What if some of the fuel spilled out? What if we don't have enough fuel to get home?" The boys ran to the car, threw the door open, and found the gas can. The lid was still on tight. No gas had spilled out, and once again the boys laughed. "PHEW!" they said at the same time.

Broman unscrewed the lid and poured the gas into the car. After that they gathered their supplies, packed up the tent, and put everything in the car.

Just like before, Broman hit the gas and sped up to 10, 20, 30, 40, 50, 60, 70, 80, 90 miles per hour...*VOOM!* They were off! They were home before they knew it, and their lives were back to normal.

The next day Gothalion and Broman were sitting in the tree house. Broman looked over at Gothalion, smiled, and said, "So who won that bet?"

MY FIRST SHOT

In a story that's called **MY FIRST SHOT**, *you travel along* **Adham Elsharnoby**'s *journey to becoming a good basketball player.*

"Come on, Adham, you can do this," I said to myself. It was my idea learning to play basketball because I always wanted to be like my brother Ahmed. Making my first shot was not an easy task. But I accomplished it. I accomplished it by not giving up. It was hard at times and frustrating, but I got through it. And it turns out I'm a good basketball player.

I didn't accomplish this by myself. I had my brother Ahmed by my side. He was good at basketball. He told me to go for a layup, but I didn't know what that was. So he told me what it was and showed me a couple of examples, and I took my first shot. Instead of throwing it vertically I threw it straight up. Even though I was bad my brother kept motivating me and saying, "Good try. That's good for the first try." I was trying to find the ball and before I knew it, it hit me in the head.

After trying for an hour I completely lost hope. It was about 8 p.m., and I was tired, so I went to bed. The dreams I had were about me beating my brother at basketball.

The next day, I woke up, ate breakfast, and started practicing. I was close to making shots. But I never made one.

My little brother Akram kept saying, "How hard it can be?" My other brother kind of lost hope in me. He didn't tell me, but I could just tell by his physical action. But still I didn't give up. I still practiced even though I didn't make one shot. I got better, but I never made the shot.

I got really frustrated and mad. I just shot it, and with my fingers crossed I made the shot!

I ran around the yard. I was happy with myself even though it took two days. Then I kept trying and made one out of every three shots. I showed my friends at school, and they helped me improve.

Now I am actually a good basketball player, and I owe it to my friends and brother. My little brother kept talking about a lucky shot even though I made like ten shots before I had to go in. But then I helped him become a good basketball player.

THE PLANE CRASH

When Valerie and Jackson's plane crashes, the brother and sister are stranded on an island with only their pilot and a little knowledge of survival skills. In **THE PLANE CRASH** *by* **Veronica Szuma**, *the two passengers and pilot must find a way off the island before it's too late.*

I woke up to realize that the plane crash wasn't just a dream. Amy, our pilot, and Jackson were trying to wake me up. Because we were the only people on the plane, I knew that everyone had survived. After I thought that they were done talking, I told them that I was okay.

"Oh, I'm so glad that you're okay, Valerie," Jackson said.

"Let's go to the cockpit and try the radio one more time," Amy said.

After twisting different knobs and trying to speak into something, we all got the notion that there was something wrong with the radio and we were going to have to try something else.

"Anyway, we should probably get out of the plane and explore to see if there is anything that could be used as shelter or food," Amy explained. "Wait a second, if the plane is stable enough, we might be able to use it as shelter."

I thought that Amy seemed extremely optimistic for being in a plane crash. After all, I was freaking out inside, but I knew that I had to be calm for Jackson's sake.

"Okay, how about Valerie and I look for food while you check out the plane," Amy told Jackson. "And remember, *stay here.*" I think that Amy trusted Jackson because we all knew that he had read enough books about planes to know whether the conditions were okay or not.

After Jackson promised not to go anywhere but the plane, Amy and I went out to look for food. To our surprise the island had a plentiful amount of food, like bananas and coconuts, but not any water. While we were walking around, I decided to ask her about how the plane crashed, but she brought it up first.

"Valerie?" Amy asked.

"Yes," I replied.

"If you're wondering how the plane crashed, it was because we took on some bad weather," Amy said.

"Okay, thank you for telling me." Then, we just walked around the island looking for food in silence.

After a while, I started to hear a buzzing noise. "Amy, do you hear that?"

"Yeah, it's almost like a buzzing noise."

When I turned around, there was a swarm of bugs chasing us! They were so different than any other bug that I had ever seen.

"Run!" I screamed. Unfortunately, the bugs attacked Amy, and after that, she had something that was swollen on her face. We ran back to the plane as quick as we could, to find Jackson sitting in the cockpit. "Do you know where a first aid kit is?" I asked.

"In the cabinet, to your right," Amy explained. This obviously wasn't her first swollen face because she knew how to fix it. The only thing that I had to do was pull her brown hair out of her face.

While we were waiting for Amy, Jackson asked, "Do you think we'll get home safely?"

When he asked that question, I started to break down. "I'm honestly not sure, Jackson." I started to sob and realized that Jackson was about to also. "It's okay, everything will be okay," I said. "Let's go and check on Amy and see how she's doing."

After Amy was done nursing her bite, I taught them how to build a fire. Although I hated being in Girl Scouts at the time, I was so glad that I had learned how to build a fire. I told Amy and Jackson that it was best to let the fire burn until it burnt out because we had a better chance of someone finding us that way.

For dinner, we had gourmet bananas with coconut milk. It was still light out and we had no idea what time it was, but we were all tired, so we all decided to take turns taking watch. This was just in case someone came to rescue us. I was about to go get Jackson for his shift when I heard a humming sound. I looked around, and when I looked up, I saw a helicopter! I jumped up and down and waved my hands in the air. When I thought that the helicopter had seen me, I went to wake up Amy and Jackson.

"Wake up, you guys!" I yelled. By the time the helicopter had landed, we were out of the plane and ready to go.

"Does this mean that we won't be able to go see Nana and Papa in Rome?" Jackson asked with a pouty look on his face.

Instead of answering we all laughed, including him.

"How did you find us?" Amy asked the man who was helping us onto the helicopter.

"The missing plane has been all over the news, and when we saw smoke, we decided to take a closer look," he explained. "We came from Venice, in Italy. What about you?"

"Manhattan," Amy and I said.

"Buckle up," he said.

As the pilot flew away, I fell asleep to the humming of the helicopter.

THE TALE OF MANY BEES

A boy finds that there is more in life than good and that evil must be challenged. This is all found in **THE TALE OF MANY BEES,** *by Billy Harvey*.

"AHHH!" I was running for my life from a hive of honeybees that attacked me like a bunch of men cheated in poker. I only accidentally threw a baseball at their hive. While running, one bee hooked onto my leg. I flinched, allowing five more to hook on. From there, every second ten more attached themselves.

The next thing I knew, I was lying on my face in black sludge above the ravine behind my house. I stood up and found that, strangely, all signs of bee existence had been terminated from my body, but surrounding me was a mess of hundreds of dead bees.

Still a little delirious and discombobulated, I fell to the bottom of the ravine. On the bright side, the water from the creek washed away the mud.

The next day at school started similarly to most days. Enzo was annoying people with his science facts, and Bob and Joe were picking on Douglas by the flagpole. Today I had a little more courage and stupidity to say to Bob and Joe, "Leave. Him. Alone." They obviously listened to me, for they changed course for me. I closed my eyes and stiff-armed toward them. The problem with that is I'm terrible at football. I waited and waited for the robust behemoths to attack.

Instead of that I heard an ear-splitting scream come from some girls. I opened my eyes to find that it wasn't girls. Instead it was Bob and Joe. The reason they were screaming was because out of my palm hundreds of honeybees flew. I closed my palm, and it ceased.

Enzo, who happens to be the smartest kid in school, whispered to me, "What...was that!"

I answered curiously, "I don't know. I hoped you would. I mean, all I know is I think I was stung by hundreds of bees last night."

Enzo responded excitedly in his scientific voice. "There is a possibility you were stung by you-know-who's bees. They are loaded with a radioactive plutonium isotope with bee characteristics."

I was so overloaded with information I could only answer, "Oh."

"You-know-who" is the local evil scientist named Professor Arachnid. He has a bounty on his head that's worth around three billion dollars. Once he was good, but now he's trying to rule the world with his mutant spider army. The guy's pure evil.

That night when my parents were out at a dinner, about ten mutant spiders attacked me. That is when I figured out all of my powers. I have wings allowing me to fly and retractable finger stingers and stinger shooters. Bees can come out of my palm, I spit honey, and I have mild super strength. I used all of them in combination to easily take the group out. I left just one to follow back to the Professor.

His lair was crawling with militia spiders, literally. I took them out one by one. I eventually made it to where the Professor was. He saw me and told me, "You may have destroyed my army, but I am much stronger than all of them combined. I see you found my bees. It is impressive considering only a few people on Earth are mentally and physically strong enough to handle the bees."

In seconds it was an all-out war. I sent a foray of bees, which barely made him flinch. Then he stuck my hand to the wall with a web, so I shot a pool of honey at his feet. I cut through the web with my stingers while he tried to use webs to pull himself out. He was half of the way out, so I ran up to him and hit him on the head, rendering him unconscious.

I called the cops. They took the notorious spider to jail and threw away the keys.

TALKING TURTLE

A boy finds a turtle and discovers he can talk in **TALKING TURTLE** *by* **Mandell Newman**. *Then the real adventure begins.*

A boy named Gary went into the woods, walked over to a pond, and saw a turtle. Gary tried to grab the turtle, and the turtle said hi. Gary, never hearing an animal talk, was amazed. Gary picked up the turtle, and that was the start of a new friendship.

"Hey, stop narrating my life!" says Gary.

Fine, have it your way. (I'll just talk quietly.)

Gary and Tim the turtle were going back home when a black van pulled up. A lady stepped out of the van and said, "Give me the turtle," in a harsh way. Gary refused to hand over Tim. The lady asked one more time, and then she pulled out a gun. Gary finally handed over Tim.

Shortly after the black van disappeared, he realized what he had done. Gary remembered that it said "Lexed" on the lady's vest and asked Siri about it. Gary printed out the building layout, got a fake decoy turtle and put it in his pocket, and got on his bike and started for the building.

Gary found the building. He took out a pin he had in his pocket and picked the lock. Gary went through security lasers and found Tim in a cage. Gary took out the pin again and picked the cage lock. Gary swapped Tim with the decoy and put Tim in his pocket. He went back through the lasers, got on his bike, and rode back.

The lady came back and realized that the boy had just swapped the turtles and went for a map of his house.

Gary stayed at his best friend's house, which was across the street from Gary's house. He took a picture of the lady as she approached his house, and he contacted the police. The police came, but the lady had disappeared.

Gary gave the lady's picture to the police. They said the lady was Mrs. Hamper. The police found the Lexed building and laughed at the name. Then they looked inside and found Mr. T with a mini gun. Mr. T unleashed the beast. One man died and three were wounded. A sniper was set up and fired at Mr. T. It was a hit.

The police found the lady and cuffed her. As she was taken away by the police, she swore she would get the turtle one day.

THE TRUE STORY OF RED RIDING HOOD

Have you ever heard the tale of Little Red Riding Hood? Well, in **THE TRUE STORY OF RED RIDING HOOD** *by* **Juliette Hamid***, you'll see what the grandma has to say about it.*

This has been the worst day *ever*! I was just having a normal day skiing, expecting that Red would come two hours after my race. But after I won, I checked on Red with the security cameras that I put on her red cape (she is young, so I have to make sure she is safe), and she was talking to the *big bad* wolf! I can't believe that I forgot to add microphones with the cameras. I couldn't hear what they were talking about.

Now, I have told my granddaughter *many* times *not* to talk to strangers! That big, grey fur ball *cannot* be trusted! I once spoke with his grandmother, and she told me that he has been a troublemaker since he was a cub!

I had to find her fast. Who knew what he might do to my grandchild?

Skiing to Red would take too long; taking my helicopter would take the shortest time. While flying, I couldn't see them. I tried to go lower, but the trees were too tall.

I parked the helicopter and walked toward them. All that was on my mind was Red. You would expect Red to call or something before coming to my house! It's great and all to see my grandchild after a while, but she and her mother both already know that I *hate* surprises! It's just not fun anymore.

Anyway, hiking toward them wasn't a good idea. I had forgotten all about the dangers of the woods. I suddenly heard footsteps approaching. Someone was heavily breathing on me. I turned around, and saw this big blob of muscle and no brain!

It turns out it was Bob from high school. He was the dimwit of the class. "Hey, Bob," I said.

"Hello," he answered back. We both started walking.

"So, what have you been up to all these years?" I asked.

"Nothing much," he said. "But I did become a lumberjack! It was really hard to find a job with that brain of mine. In this job, I don't need any brains. Would you like to see my amazing skills?"

I didn't want to be rude, so I said, "Sure." And he was pretty amazing at cutting trees down. At least he found a job. And for a long time, I watched him cutting down trees.

"Oh my," I said. "I have to go, Bob. I'm trying to save my granddaughter, and for the past 20 minutes or so, I have been watching you cut down trees." And I walked on.

*   *   *

I finally found Red. I saw her talking to the wolf. I hid in the bushes while she was walking toward my house. If he does anything suspicious to my granddaughter, I will use the element of surprise and attack him.

I saw the wolf behind her, quietly sneaking up on her. Red had seen him, and she said, "Oh, hello again. Sheldon, was it?"

"Yeah," he said. "So, um, tell me again: why are you going to your grandma's house?"

"For the past two years, I have been *very* busy with moving into my new house. So I couldn't see my grandmother during that time. Right now, I want to see if she is all right, especially on her birthday," she said.

Oh my gosh! I completely forgot that it's my birthday today, but I couldn't think about that for too long. The only thing that I was thinking about was *Why is he talking to my granddaughter? This must be part of some sort of plan or something.*

"I think I have something in my teeth; can you check, please?" he asked.

I saw his jaw opening, and by instinct, I ran to Red to push her out of the way of the wolf's jaw, but—*SNAP!*—we were both eaten by the wolf.

Sliding down the wolf's throat, Red and I were yelling for our lives. But I realized it was a little too late for that. I guess that "surprise visit" wasn't going to happen.

Surprisingly for a small wolf, he has a big stomach. We both landed in his stomach of bones and goo. I went up to Red to see if she was all right: no bruises, scratches or bites from the wolf. She was fine. Since I am *always* prepared, I waited until the wolf was asleep, and I cut us out of his stomach with my trusty pocket knife.

Red and I were safe at home, and we ate a batch of sweet cookies made by me. But all those silly journalists changed that great adventure into some story called *Red Riding Hood.* And it was all about Red, and they added Bob to it, too! That was so unfair.

WHY THERE ARE TWO JAKES

A boy thinks his grades aren't important—until he gets his report card. He'll learn the hard way that going back in time is not the easy fix he thinks it will be in **WHY THERE ARE TWO JAKES,** *by* ***Larisa Snegourenko.***

There was a 12-year-old boy who had bad grades. His grades were so bad he could've gotten kicked out of school. His name was Jake. His dream was to get better grades. One day at school he got his report card back. He knew his parents would get really mad, because he didn't have a single A or A-.

When he was walking home from school, he decided to go behind the school to an alley. He noticed a business place that wouldn't normally be behind a school. It was a tall, white brick building with clear glass doors. He read a sign that said "Closed for two weeks."

He looked around and then leaned back on the door. He fell straight on the beige carpet inside the building. He wondered why the doors had opened. He then stood up and walked through the hallway. There were people looking at him as if he were doing something dangerous.

He walked into a random room that had something that seemed to be a time machine. He thought if he could travel back in time he could pay attention in class and get better grades. Someone ran to the door, but Jake locked it as soon as that person's hand reached in to pull the door knob. The person started knocking on the door and yelling, "STOP! It's dangerous! No!" To Jake it sounded as if that person was whispering because he could barely hear through the doors.

He got into the time machine. It was unique and fancy. It had a really bright, silver door. The walls were white and shiny. The seat was nice, and it had a very soft cushion. Jake saw a button, and before he pressed it he noticed that it said "Past."

After he pressed the button he felt like the chair was swirling like a smoothie in a blender. The chair was actually in one place. It also felt like there was a screen that was showing everything that happened earlier in his life. He stopped the machine at September. It was really March.

When he walked out of the time machine his destination was outside, maybe because the building hadn't been there six months ago. There was also no snow because it was September again.

He looked at his watch. It was 8:00 A.M. He had five minutes to get to class. He ran through the alley to his school.

In the hallway he saw a boy that looked exactly like him looking for his locker. He walked up to the boy and asked him questions like why he was there and why does he look like a copy of Jake.

Alex, who was a boy Jake met in December, didn't recognize him because technically they hadn't met yet. Alex ran to his and both Jake's first-hour class and asked the teacher why there are two students who look alike in the hallway fighting about a locker.

The teacher came out to the hallway and started asking them when their birthdays are, what type of food they like, and even what company their dad works for. They both answered the same thing to the teacher. The teachers thought it was a coincidence, but when they said they both don't have brothers or any closer family member than a baby cousin, he knew the only solution was to call their parents.

When the principal talked to Jake's mother the whole school found out that there can only be one Jake. Their parents took both Jakes to the hospital. They took DNA and blood testing. The parents knew they had one child even before the DNA results showed that they weren't twins.

The doctor decided to put each boy in a separate room and ask them what they did yesterday. The Jake that took the adventure answered that he got his report card back. The other Jake answered that he went shopping for school supplies. The doctor couldn't even think of anything and then they told their parents what both Jakes said.

"This is impossible, doctor. Today was our son's first day of school. He couldn't get his report card back during vacation," said Jake's mother.

"I don't know what to say. I never had a problem like this in my hospital before," said the doctor.

That second, police officers walked into the room. Both boys got scared.

One of the Jakes said, "It's my fault. I was the one who traveled in time and then skipped school and yelled at this boy. I wasn't meaning to. I need good grades. Can you fix this?"

"Sorry, but we can't leave this. You are like a stranger, but you are a person. Anything in this world can fall apart if you use a time machine," said the policeman

"A time machine?" asked the parents in surprise.

"You care about good grades?" asked the boy from the past.

"Yes, it's a time machine, and yes, I do care about my grades, or at least now I do," he replied

"I want to see my future and be in a time machine," said the past Jake.

Their mother asked, "Jake, are you sure you want to switch places and go to the future?"

"Can you guys get to the point? I have patients," said the doctor.

"Yes, I would give up my past for my future body, I guess," replied past Jake.

A couple of years later after past Jake went to the future and future Jake came to the past, present Jake found a note on his door that said "Hi, myself. This is me. Guess what? In six months you are going to college just like me, or just like you. I mean, just like us. Hope you don't bring a third Jake over if you come to visit. Bye!"

10:15

THE ATTACK
OF THE BIONIC DOGS

THE ATTACK OF THE BIONIC DOGS, *by Snorelle B,* is the story of a girl's world turned upside down. She learns that her parents can't shelter her from all the world's dangers.

My name is Kiera. I am a princess. I live on a planet named Lavetex. I live in a castle with my dad and my mom, the king and queen. Our castle is in Nitira, the capital of Lavetex. My butler Charlie is the one who for the most part takes care of me. When my mom and dad go off somewhere, Charlie looks after me.

Lately there have been a lot of fights and small wars in other countries. As a way to help people with fights and intruders, the different kings and queens of parts of Lavetex got dogs. The dogs aren't regular dogs, though. They're bionic.

The one main power source of all of the dogs is the one named Mauler. He can control all of the dogs by telling them instructions. Mauler is supposed to be locked up because if he got out, there would be danger.

Well, now there is danger in Lavetex. Mauler bit through the metal bars that were holding him away from people. All of the dogs that are under his control are malfunctioning. They're destroying things, and if they don't get stopped, our entire country will be destroyed.

The scientist, Dr. Mayflick, might be arrested if he cannot figure out a way to stop the dogs. Mauler is a dog that feeds on fear. The more people panic, scream, or run away from them, the stronger they get.

I was looking out of my bedroom window when I saw my parents arrive. I got up from my bed and ran down the stairs. I met my parents at the door.

"Mom, Dad, you're back." I embraced them. They hugged me back.

"Hey kiddo, yeah, we're back but not for long," my dad said.

I noticed that my mom had gone to talk to Charlie. I also noticed that she looked a little nervous. She kept glancing at me and my dad. Then Charlie looked over at me and nodded his head. My mom broke away from their little group and said, "What have you been up to?"

"Nothing," I said. "What were you talking about with Charlie?"

She didn't answer me. She just gave my dad a look. He started to say something, but there was a knock on the door. Charlie opened the door.

"Hello, sergeants," my dad said. There were policemen standing on our porch.

"Your Highnesses, I hate to ruin your family time, but we really need your assistance. The bionic dogs are literally up the block from your castle. I came to make sure you are in a safe place."

The other policeman started to talk. "We've waited too long as it is. We have been monitoring their activity, and they haven't stopped. They have crushed houses and buildings, and a couple of people were injured. We can't risk anybody else getting hurt."

I stared out of the window. The policemen were right. I could see Mauler and the other dogs stepping on things and tiny figures running for their lives.

"It looks like we are too late, but I still need your directions. Are we allowed to eliminate them?"

My father had a look of despair in his eyes. "You can if there are no other options."

The policeman looked like he regretted what he was about to say. "I'm sorry, sir, but it's the only choice we really have."

That's when he said something into his wrist and soldiers started dropping out of the sky—well, not exactly out of the sky, but out of helicopters. I saw the police shocking the dogs with electric spheres and crossbows. The dogs still didn't stop walking, though.

Mauler started coming at us. The other dogs followed their master. Mauler was coming closer to the castle. Then I saw it. Mauler's foot was about to come crashing on the left side of our castle.

It felt like it was a half second before his foot slammed into the castle. The left side of our house crumbled into the water below it. Behind me my mom was sobbing into my dad's arms. I almost cried myself.

Then something happened. Someone shot a black arrow at Mauler. It landed in his chest and then exploded. Since all of the dogs were under Mauler's control, they fell, too.

The helicopters dropped a net and picked up the dog scraps. They carried the scraps into the ocean. That is the last I have heard about bionic dogs.

BADLUCK BRIAN

A boy's day starts off poorly and goes downhill from there. In **BADLUCK BRIAN** *by* **Asha Seabron**, *if it weren't for bad luck, Brian wouldn't have any luck at all.*

I wake up in my casual white-sheeted bed and walk downstairs to eat my casual everyday kind of cereal. I pour my one-month-old milk mainly because it never goes bad; at least I don't taste anything bad. Once I finish eating my casual grub, I walk up into my room and switch into my fresh and fancy red buttoned shirt and black dress pants. I grab my bag, get my jacket, and brush my hair with some gel before putting on my poof-ball hipster hat.

I'm your average kid. I'm that brown-haired freckled kid that you probably saw but never talked to in your class. I wait for the bus with everything done for school. It's the second day of being a freshman at Special Kids High.

While I'm waiting, my mother runs out of my house wearing bunny slippers and a pink robe. Her hair looks like an orange afro. What I'm trying to say is that she looks like a complete maniac.

"Brian! Brian! Brian, you left the house without giving Mommy a kiss!" my mother shouts as she kisses my cheek. I turn around to see the bus and all of the other students waiting for me to be finished kissing my mom.

This is the story of me, Brian Badluck, your not-so-average kid in your not-so-average world.

On the way to school the sky starts to pour down, making this day pretty gloomy. My so-called friend Jeremy Popular and I ride the bus together. Jeremy and I get along pretty well, even though I don't fit in his circle of friends.

Once we get to school I get going really fast because we got there pretty late. I run to class through the rain, feeling like I've lost a few pounds. I get to class and sit next to the lovely Brittany Beautiful.

Ms. Bossy walks up to my desk and asks for last night's homework. "Homework, Brian," she says. I open my bag to see that all of my homework and books are gone and probably in the bus parking lot.

There is always that one time when you just freak out and do whatever. You know the feeling, when you just go from calm to insane. I get out of my chair and jump onto Ms. Bossy's desk. To be honest, I almost break it down because of how old it is.

So here I am standing on a desk older than my grandmother, looking at my class full of geeks, hipsters, and whatnot, making a speech on discrimination. Maybe I think this could be my make-up for my homework, or maybe I am just weird. As I am explaining how my dream affects racism and culture, I think, *Why am I doing this? Why am I standing on a grandma-old desk, looking like I'm going to a wedding and giving a speech about my dream which has NOTHING to do with ANYTHING we've been learning in the past day?* But I need to do something.

Once I finish my jaw-dropping speech, I notice Chad Handsome giving me the death stare. He has never liked me, especially since I hang out with his number-one pal, Jeremy Popular. Of course Chad yells out, "Hey, Brian, I didn't hear you. I don't speak dumb."

Then the inner Adele of me says, "Sticks and stones may break my bones, but words will never hurt me."

Out of nowhere three dictionaries are hurled at me.

The next thing I know I'm taken to the nurse's office.

I wake up to see Brittany Beautiful in a waiting seat next to my hospital bed. Brittany realizes that I am awake, and just like that I tell her about everything: everything from the hair gel to the bus parking lot. She listens to me so well it is hard to believe it is *the* Brittany Beautiful. But then something crazy happens.

"You know, Brian, I think you're super-cool and interesting... I think I like y—"

Then I feel the impact of the dictionaries.

Apparently when I got hit upside the head with those books I fell onto the ground and landed on the side of my stomach. I have one-month-old milk rumbling in my stomach like a ticking time bomb about to burst any second.

Then everything goes bad like the milk. I vomit right on Brittany. Since she is in the middle of talking, it lands right in her mouth. I feel like I am sharing: "Oh, hey, Brittany! Here's my saliva."

With anger on the face of the once "Beautiful" Brittany, I leave the clinic. "Badluck" Brian is born.

Around December, I leave Special Kids High and go to a private school called Lamia Scale. I don't want those insults blocking my way for school.

The next year, our two schools merge for a field trip. We go to this theater not far from Special Kids High. The video is related to Special Kids High; it is mainly about bullying. It was done in a way that seems like an apology. I wonder who they're apologizing to....

I still went to Lamia Scale and never talked about SKH again. Maybe I made a bad choice. Maybe I didn't. We never will know that, will we? In this crazy world of ours, a lot of things remain a mystery. So this is the mystery of me, your not-so-average kid, in your not-so-average world.

BROKE DOWN
ON THE SWAHILI SWIRL

One family has a favorite ride at the Kalahari waterpark resort. Come join the funny and wet adventure with Jimmy, Liam, and Dad in **BROKE DOWN ON THE SWAHILI SWIRL** *by **Jim Allen**.*

It was a "fire workin' day" at the Kalahari Water Park. That's what we call a day of anticipated fun and excitement. It's kind of like going to the firework show without the fireworks. Dad, Liam, and I were pumped to go down the Swahili Swirl tube ride. It's our favorite ride in the whole world.

The Swahili Swirl is a majestic, delightfully terrifying waterslide "ride." It is so big it takes up a whole corner of the massive indoor water park. It's a seemingly endless tangle of elevated, curvy fiberglass pipes held up by a web of steel girders and concrete. To "ride" it, you sit on a custom-made, inflated inner tube that holds up to four riders. The tube, full of riders, is pushed off at the top of the slide and glides along inside the water-slicked pipes. The pipes are sometimes dark, and there are a series of sharp corners and drop-offs that scare the daylights out of you. Somewhere in the middle of all that is the bowl that is the "swirl" part of this slide ride. My dad says the bowl is kind of like a toilet bowl— because the tube riders are swirled round and round until finally dropping through the hole in the bottom—which leads to the end of the ride at the splashdown pool.

We raced through the water park to get to the slide before anyone else could get there. The chlorine from the water smelled wonderful to me, having not been there for over a year. As soon as we got to the stairs of the long water slides we stopped to catch our breath.

We quickly ran up the 10 flights of stairs, which Dad said felt like climbing up a skyscraper. At the very top, the air felt thin with a mixture of chlorine. I felt like I had just lost ten pounds going from the bottom to the top of all those stairs.

Liam and I made a deal to not scream so we could freak the lifeguards out. We were all so excited to go down that we couldn't stand still even after climbing up the stairs.

An inner tube came up the inner tube lift for us. The lifeguard got it ready by throwing it into the starting pool. We all sat down in the cold water and were waiting for the light to turn green to slide down. After what felt like an hour the light turned green and the lifeguard pushed us down. The water in the tube splashed us as we turned a sharp corner. Before we entered the bowl itself we entered the drop.

After the first drop, we were in the bowl of the Swahili Swirl going round and round. At that point I noticed the water was stopping like something had happened, and we came to a halt. We all had a look of concern on our faces. We worried what would happen next. Would anyone notice us? Would we be stuck here forever? Would more tubers come crashing into us?

Just as we were about to yell for help, the lifeguards finally realized that the water had stopped and came up the tube with climbing boots and flashlights to rescue us. The lifeguards pulled us down the tube into the landing pool area. We thanked them for rescuing us and then raced back up the tower of stairs to do it again.

COOKY CAHNA AND THE REVENGE OF BLANK

Cooky Cahna is sitting on his couch when—bang!—the R.U.N.s come and take Ralph, Cooky's dog. Read **COOKY CAHNA AND THE REVENGE OF BLANK** *by* **Mason Reynolds** *to find out what it all means.*

Once upon a time, there was a boy named Cooky Cahna who lived in Cookyville. Cooky was watching a scary movie with his dog, Ralph. Then, out of nowhere, robot unicorn ninjas (R.U.N. for short) attacked. Cooky picked up his mega-laser sword and sliced one R.U.N. in half, in an explosion of sparkles. Then another unicorn took off his hand and it turned into a confetti gun. He blew Cooky into a wall. After that, they scanned the room and took Cooky's dog, Ralph. The chase was on.

Cooky ran out of his house and saw the R.U.N.s flying away on their rainbow. Cooky got on his magic Mercedes Benz and drove after them. One of the R.U.N.s saw him chasing them, so he made the call of the unicorn. Out of the woods popped Nyan cats.

When Cooky saw them, he pressed a green button on his dashboard. Out came carrot guns. When the carrots hit their targets, the cats turned into piles of sugar. "Sweet!" said Cooky. But, by then, the R.U.N.s were already gone.

After a while of searching, Cooky remembered about the tracking device he had attached to Ralph. Cooky activated it, and followed the signal to the Mountains of Despair.

Cooky started to climb, when he heard laughter in the mountains. He stopped dead in his tracks. He stayed as quiet as possible, but someone had found him anyway. Cooky turned around and saw Blank's assassin.

"You'll never get to Blank in time!" She lunged, but Cooky was too quick and dodged.

"Oh yeah? Watch me." Then he jumped on the assassin's sword and back-flipped onto the side of the mountain. Cooky pushed off and knocked the assassin off the cliff. "AAAHHHH!" yelled the assassin, as she fell.

Cooky kept on climbing, and when he got to the top he discovered Blank's lair. Cooky was walking around trying to find a way to get in when he saw a hobo wearing a Blank uniform. Cooky walked away slowly. After scouting the whole lair, he decided to just plant a mine on the front door and blow it to smithereens.

When he finally got into the lair, he saw a factory being powered by Ralph on a giant hamster wheel! When Cooky saw his dog he almost called out to him.

Cooky snuck around the lair for a while, planning an escape just in case. All of a sudden he heard *BOOM*! Blank's super awesome gorilla bot 2.0 fell from the sky.

"HAHAHAHA, you fell right into my trap!" It was Blank, of course. "Now, you shall perish once and for all!" Cooky ran for Ralph, but Blank was too quick. "I made some upgrades to my gorilla bot from last time we met," Blank said. "Now surrender or die!"

"Never!" Cooky said, as he kept on running. Blank was right on his tail, but Cooky had one more trick up his sleeve. He pressed the big yellow button on his watch and out came THE SUPER BANANA.

"No," Blank said, "it couldn't be. I have to get away!" But it was too late. Blank's robot came toward the banana, and Cooky shot the banana out of his portable slingshot. He was hoping to destroy the robot, but instead it landed in Cookyville.

"Oh no!" Cooky said, "I shot it toward Cookyville! What should I do?"

Cooky teleported to Cookyville, where the people were in a panic.

"You're too late, Cooky," said Blank. "Your precious little town is now under my control. There's nothing you can do to stop me since your banana is gone." He was right. Cooky's banana was gone, but there had to be another way. Right when Cooky almost gave up, he remembered the spare banana he always kept in the trunk of his car. Cooky jumped to his car and got the spare. He raised it high into the air so the gorilla could see.

"Where do you keep all of these?" Blank asked.

Cooky made a portal to the negative-zone behind Blank. It started to suck Blank in, but it wasn't enough. So Cooky threw the banana into the portal and the gorilla followed. "You'll pay for this, Cooky," Blank yelled, "and your little dog, too!"

After Blank was defeated, Cooky helped rebuild Cookyville with better protection and new homes, so that invaders couldn't take over so easily. When Cooky finished, he walked home and found Ralph watching *How to Make Giant Super Bananas* on the TV.

"Ralph!" Cooky said. "How did you escape? There were tons of guards."

"When you fought Blank, all the guards ran," explained Ralph, "so, I just walked out the front door."

"Oh," said Cooky stupidly.

No one ever saw Blank or any of his minions ever again.

THE DOG

When a young boy decides he wants a dog, he runs into a roadblock: his parents. Read **THE DOG** *by* **Kareem Zamzam** *to find out how a boy does everything he can to get a dog.*

I am at school after we just had a break. I can't concentrate on anything, and I wonder why. I think it's because everyone is sharing their stories and how they had fun with their pets and I wasn't. I start thinking, and when I go home, this happens, because I have wanted a dog forever. At dinner, I ask my mom and dad one more time, "Can I have a dog?"

Mom and Dad look at each other before my dad turns to me in exasperation. "No! For the millionth time, we said you can't have a dog."

I am not ready to give up. "But I want a dog, and I will get one." I will do everything, and I will research and save money and train for it. I will do whatever it takes to get Chase (that is what I will name my dog).

According to this website it says that taking care of a dog is hard work, but if you have the time and the money, then you're fine. That got me thinking: do I have the time with school and all? "Yes, I do." I can make a schedule. I will make time for my homework, free time, and anything else I do during the day. I will also have a chart that has whose turn it is to walk and feed him while I am at school. Luckily for me I don't have to give up anything other than the five minutes that I have to go outside and walk him, which I don't mind at all.

Here's what I came up with in the chart: Monday through Friday whichever parent is home can walk him, and after that at about 12:00 they can feed him and play with him. Saturdays and Sundays I can do all those. The negative about this is that sometimes both of my parents may be out and can't feed, play, or walk him, but I'm sure I can figure something out.

Now it's time to talk to my parents. "Mom, Dad, can I talk to you about something?"

"Sure," they reply.

"I have done research, and if I have the time (including walking, showering, feeding, etc.), and the money (including doctor appointments, food, clothes, etc.) which I do, then I am perfectly capable of having a dog."

"Let us think for a day or two. Then we will answer you."

The next day my mom says, "You can have a dog!"

I now have to go get him and do the paperwork and all of that stuff. I am so excited.

Two days later, I am back home with my new dog. It is so much fun having him around!

THE EVIL CLOCK

THE EVIL CLOCK *by **Anneka Pitera** is about two sisters and their friend who must save their class from an evil clock. Can they succeed before everyone gets eaten?*

Anneka and Serina were best friends. It was a Monday, and they were walking to school. Serina said, "What are you going to be for Halloween?" for that Friday was Halloween.

"I'm going to be a blue bird," said Anneka.

"I'm going to be a blue bird, too," said Sapphire, Anneka's sister.

Once they got to school they went to their first hour, which was Language Arts. When they got there everything was normal, and the calming smiley face clock that always made the three girls happy was smiling down at them. And when the clock's hands moved to 11 and 1, the hands looked like slanting eyebrows. Suddenly the clock started flying around the room, saying, "Who will be my first victim?"

"This has never happened before!" said Sapphire. Everyone screamed and ran around like maniacs, and the teacher looked petrified.

The clock went zooming around the room and finally decided to eat the teacher first. The kids screamed and cried out. The teacher tried to fight the clock, but the clock said, "Trying to fight back is just going to make it worse." So the teacher stopped trying to get away and got eaten. The clock swallowed him whole.

The kids started crying again, and they tried to get to the door. A ghost appeared, locked the door, and threw the key out the window. Everyone screamed even louder.

"Wait! Everyone please calm down!" said Serina.

"But we're scared," said Sophie, another girl in the class.

"I know; I am too," said Anneka, "but we need to try to calm down to think of something that could help us out of this mess. Let's come up with a plan together to try to destroy the clock."

"Right!" said the class together.

"I don't think so," said the clock, and he turned to the nearest kid and swallowed Sophie whole.

The kids tried to get out of the classroom, but the door was locked. Everyone panicked all over again. "Everyone, please calm down!" yelled Sapphire.

Then the ghost reappeared and said, "Everyone, please sit down. You will be here for a while. Now I will introduce myself. My name is Coroline. As you can see, I am a ghost."

"How did you die?" said Ben, a kid in the class.

"That is a story I will never forget," said Coroline. "Years ago, I was in the same situation you are in right now. I tried to destroy the clock. He went crazy, and I was eaten. Then all of my classmates were eaten, too. Except they never came back as a ghost. Only I did."

Ben asked Coroline, "But why are you stopping us from destroying the clock?"

"I am stopping you because the clock said if I did what he wanted me to do, he would bring me back to life and let my friends go. So I obey everything he tells me to do. Many days I try to convince him that I should be brought back to life, and so should my friends. But I just can't convince him. He's just too determined to eat kids and adults."

While Coroline guarded the clock, the clock took a nap. The kids came up with a plan to distract Coroline. While Coroline was distracted, Sapphire went to look for a big book to smash the clock.

Out of the corner of her eye, Coroline saw her coming with the book. Coroline jumped out, which made Sapphire scream, and that freaked everyone out.

"She was trying to smash you, sir," said Coroline.

"Then I shall eat her." And he gobbled her up.

Anneka screamed from terror and got really angry. She said, "If you don't give me back my sister right now I will smash you with all of my might! I won't stop until I get my sister back! Aaaaaaaaargh!" Anneka grabbed a stool, and right when she was about to throw it at the clock Serina grabbed her arm and stopped her.

"Anneka, calm down!" said Serina "I promise we will get your sister back no matter how long it takes, but we will be more destructive if we work together." So Anneka calmed down.

Then the clock ate Ben just because he was hungry. The kids panicked and ran around screaming chaotically. Serina tried to help them all come up with a plan to destroy it.

Coroline said to the clock, "How about you go take another rest. You didn't get that much sleep earlier." So the clock went to sit down and rest.

Once he fell asleep, Coroline said, "I am sorry, guys. I should have known he would never let me go because he said he would let me go three weeks ago. I will let you smash the clock because I think that when you do that I will come back to life and so will your friends, and my friends. I am just taking a guess, but if it doesn't work then I don't know what else to do."

"I want to do the honors of smashing the clock because he ate my sister. I am so mad! So can I?" said Anneka.

"Sure," said Coroline.

Anneka sneaked up behind the clock to smash it, but when she was about to hit it with a chair the clock woke up and said, "Who is trying to smash me? And why aren't you trying to stop them, Coroline?"

"I am done being your slave! I will never again listen to you!" said Coroline. And then Serina came up to the clock and held him down while Anneka smashed the back of the clock with the chair.

When she did that she stood up, looked at the face of the clock, and said, "This clock was always smiling down at me when I walked through the door to this classroom, and he always made me feel better when I was feeling down. I don't want to smash it, but I will for my sister." Anneka smashed all of her body weight on the whole clock, and that smashed it into little pieces.

They waited for everyone to come back, but nothing happened. They waited for an hour, and then Anneka said, "I don't think they are coming back." She cried like crazy.

Just then Coroline began to swirl, and she became a beautiful girl. She said, "It's working!" and everyone cheered as the kids who were eaten came back.

Anneka ran to her sister, and they cried with joy as they hugged. Coroline was so happy her tears made a puddle. "Thank you so much for helping me," said Coroline.

"No problem," said Serina. "We love to help. Don't we, Anneka?"

"Yes we do! We help whenever we can," said Anneka.

All of their classmates thanked the three girls, and so the three girls—Anneka, Serina, and Sapphire—became heroes to their school.

THE HAUNTED OAK

THE HAUNTED OAK, by *Karl Scholar, is the amazing story of a boy who doesn't do as he is told. When he ends up in an unexpected situation, he regrets he didn't pay attention to one particular warning.*

*I*f the rumors are true about where we're going, Patrick thought, how long will we stay there? The Blake family had been driving for about five hours, and Patrick had been thinking the whole time about the rumors he had heard about the village they were moving to.

"It's cursed; don't go there!"

"I'll tell you why it's so cheap: a bunch of kids died there, that's why."

"I have a feeling you won't return from this trip."

As their automobile pulled into the driveway, the first thing Patrick got a peek of was the huge house itself. It was four stories high, made from partly weathered old bricks, and was at least three times bigger than their last one.

While the men his mom hired out of the village moved their furniture inside the house, Patrick and his dad decided to go for a walk with their dog Cookie in the unused cornfields behind the house.

In the middle of the fields stood an old oak, which only blocked part of the crisp winds that so often blew fog from the lake behind the fields. When they reached the old oak, his dad said with excitement, "I have a present for you, Patrick!" and pulled out a golden watch. His dad often bought him presents to strengthen their father-son relationship because he was away so often. Patrick put it on without replying.

He noticed Cookie sniffing at a cavern in the tree. The cavern looked like the kind of hole were rats live: dark and seemingly endlessly long. Abruptly, Cookie threw her head back, howled, and ran back to the house. When Patrick and his dad caught up with him, he was nervously panting at the gate. Unsure what to do, Patrick opened the gate. Cookie bit him and ran toward the village.

Two days later, Patrick wandered through the cornfields again until he suddenly stopped by the old oak. He looked up at the tree. How high it was. Suddenly he felt like climbing it.

After the first few branches he climbed, he noticed something etched in the bark:

Those who climb this tree will perish

He stared at the words, and then laughed nervously. It was an uncertain, almost insane laugh. *What an old joke somebody is playing on me*, he thought. Encouraged, he kept climbing. He was so high now that he could see his house.

Strangely, some objects that shouldn't have been there were hanging on some branches around him. There were books, watches, bracelets, necklaces, toys, and other stuff. "A reward for climbing this high?" Patrick thought.

Abruptly, a voice rustled through the leaves around him: "I gave you a choice, but you did not listen. Now you will perish like all others who tried before you."

Patrick thought he saw something moving. Then he screamed as a huge claw smashed into the bark below him. He desperately climbed higher, but the thing caught up with him quickly. When he couldn't go any higher he stared at the thing. A hideous, beastlike mask had appeared and grinned at him.

His parents found Patrick's corpse at the base of the tree. Next to him was a broken branch. They immediately decided to move out of the house.

No one noticed the golden watch hanging on another branch, gleaming in the sunlight.

THE HOCKEY GAME

THE HOCKEY GAME, *by **Mac Chalem**, is the action-filled story of a group of boys on a hockey team. Read to find out what happens at their championship game.*

The locker room was filled with our team and coaches. Despite a dozen loud boys, it was so silent you could hear a pin drop. We had just finished listening to our coach's pep talk. We were deep in thought, gearing up for our third and final period.

It had been a brutal game so far. We had thirty minutes under our belts, and now the game was tied, 1-1. We had waited so long for this game and to play in this arena. Now, we were here. Many awesome hockey players had skated here before. Now, this ice was ours. This trophy was ours for the taking.

When we heard the Zamboni leave the ice we quickly buckled our helmets and marched toward the ice. Our determination was written all over our faces. Our first line skated out to line up. The music was blasting in the background. We could hear our parents and family cheering for us as the commentators announced our names.

I was at center, my usual position. I was facing a big, tall kid about my age who looked just as determined as me. I wrapped my hands around my stick, positioned myself low to the ground, and with my game face prepared for battle.

It felt like forever until the ref dropped the puck. I watched the puck fall in slow motion. I slapped the black rubber as hard as I could. It went off my stick toward John. John was alone and ready to roll.

He skated up the ice toward the goalie. The rest of our team took off in pursuit of the puck and the goal we so needed. We skated fast. We needed a goal. We wanted to score. I had never seen John skate so fast. It was like he was channeling Tomas Tatar (one of the fastest Red Wings players and a personal favorite of mine). John has a good shot. I felt that he could put us over the top as long as no one caught him.

John stopped on a dime. He lined up and prepared to shoot. The goalie prepared for the destruction. John shot the puck. It was a shot so powerful it was hard to follow. It sailed through the air and hit the glass with such force we thought it would shatter. He had missed the net. Oh no.

The game goes on. We fight one battle after another. Our coach takes a time out. He is fired up. He tries to be calm. He knows we all want to win. He tells us we are skating hard. He says to settle down. "Make good decisions on the ice. Take your time." He sends us back to the ice.

I skate out with my line. I hear my coach yelling. I see his arms waving. He is giving some last minute orders. I can't understand what he is saying. I can only hear the crowd chanting, "LET'S GO VIPERS...LET'S GO VIPERS!" I glance up to the clock. Only 2:00 left!

I line up with the other center. I grab my stick and wait. The puck drops. My stick hits my opponent's stick. I take another shot. This time I strike the puck with a mighty force. The puck goes off toward Will. Will takes it down the ice. He passes to John. John passes to Joe. Joe is stuck with two guys on him. He can't get a shot. He takes it around the net. I hate it when he does this. It makes me nervous. Joe has no choice this time. He shoots.

The puck hits the boards and bounces to me. I shoot. It hits the skate of the kid in front of the goal. It bounces back to me. I have a chance for a rebound. This time I try something different. I decide to fire up my slap shot. I line up and prepare to fire. Off it goes, like a rocket, right into the net. The buzzer rings. We win!

I see my teammates raise their sticks in celebration. I can hear the crowd cheering. I see our coach jumping up and down on the bench. We high-five each other. Our coach runs onto the ice to hug each of us. We fall onto our goalie like a bunch of puppies. It is the best feeling to win. I cannot wipe the smile off of my face even though my cheeks are hurting.

Our coach was right...it was our time! The gold helmet will look great in our showcase!

THE LEAGUE OF RANDOMNESS

Sometimes, the whole world has to rely on the underdog. This is the case when a group of misfit heroes find themselves with the fate of the world in their hands in **THE LEAGUE OF RANDOMNESS** *by Ted Schwartz.*

*B*OOM! Hatman heard a loud explosion. The Hatcave was made of metal that was nearly indestructible. He knew nobody could get inside. But when he turned around his worst enemy was behind him...The Poker. Hatman was ready.

"Hatarang!" Hatman said. It hit Poker in the leg.

"Ha-ha, bulletproof vest!" Poker laughed.

"I hit you in the leg, and that wasn't a bullet," Hatman replied.

"Oh.... AHHHHH!" Poker screamed.

But Poker came with backup. Poker-bots surrounded Hatman. Hatman tried to fight, but he was hopelessly outnumbered. Hatman was so busy fighting the poker-bots that he didn't notice that Jeff, the General of the poker-bots, was sneaking up behind him. Jeff knocked out Hatman with a big piece of metal from the rubble of the Hatcave.

"What should I do with him, boss?" Jeff asked.

"Take him to the hideout, Jeff," Poker said.

Under Woman was meant to take Hatman to the hat rack sale, so she was on her way to pick him up from the Hatcave. When she got there, she saw it was deserted and wrecked. She heard a loud creak; she dived out of the way just as a large amount of rock fell and blocked the doorway. There was a small space above the rock she could easily fly over, but there was also a space to go under. Under Woman loved to fly under stuff. She decided to go under. When she got through, it was still deserted. Hatman was gone.

Hatman was trapped in a small cage made out of steel. Luckily Hatman kept a spare explosive Hatarang in his boot. He got ready to blow the cage, but below him was an army of poker-bots. To his left, he saw a poker-bot guarding his equipment. Instead of blowing the cage, he picked the lock with the tip of the Hatarang and took out the guard with one swift kick. He retrieved his grappling hook, hat, and Hatarangs. He passed over the guards quietly. When he was almost through he heard the Poker's voice.

"Oh Jeff, my trusted poker-bot general, capturing Blooperman will be easy with this Blooponite I stole from the Hatcave!"

"Um, boss, maybe it isn't the best idea to plot our secret plan with the door open...." Unlike most poker-bots, Jeff was part human, with a human head and big bionic arms and a robotic torso.

"Oh nonsense, Jeff, we'll be fine. It's not like anyone is listening to us or anything....."

Hatman continued out of the prison. "I have to warn the others!" Hatman used his randomness phone to signal the League of Randomness. The Lash and the Mean Narrow were the first to respond.

Mean Narrow and Lash were on their way when Mean Narrow threw his Narrow Grenade. It trapped The Lash in a small, inflatable, indestructible box.

"What are you doing, Narrow?"

"Sorry, Larry, but Poker's the one with the money."

"You're mean."

"Well duh, it's in my name."

"Are you seriously a double agent?"

"Hey, I didn't write the script."

Meanwhile at the Hatcave, Hatman and Under Woman struggle to develop a plan. In his time at the prison, Hatman discovered that all of the poker-bots had been powered by the Blooponite, so if they called Blooperman, he would be in danger. They needed to shut down the Blooponite plant. And to accomplish this, they needed The Lash. But The Lash had strangely disappeared....

Lash sat in his cage. He didn't like small spaces. He drifted off to sleep so he wouldn't have to think about his claustrophobia. He woke to the sound of keys jingling. Mean Narrow stood in front of Lash's cage with the keys in his hands.

"Traitor," Lash said.

"Hey, I'm trying to break you out, can't you see?" Mean Narrow responded.

"Wait, you're a triple agent? This is getting too confusing."

"I still don't write the script."

As The Lash and Mean Narrow escaped the prison, they saw a room with the door open. When they looked inside, they saw Blooperman strapped to a chair getting poked by two giant Blooponite fingers!

"Stop it! Stop it, that tickles!" Blooperman said, trying to hold back laughter. Blooperman was very ticklish.

"No! What would be the fun in that?" Poker said.

"Well, it would be more fun for me."

"Huh, I never thought about that. Has what I've been doing all these years been hurting pe—"

That's when Hatman broke through a window. He would have to pay for that later (which could be a problem because under the hat he was broke), but he didn't care. He threw his hat at Poker. It bounced off him harmlessly. "That's it? That's all the mighty Hatman's got?" Then it exploded.

The explosion was so strong it blew off Blooperman's bindings. Released from his prison, Blooperman flew in and punched Poker into the air. While Poker was in the air, Mean Narrow threw his last Narrow Grenade and trapped Poker.

Hatman was getting used to the sound of the gates of Barkham Asylum opening. He brought The Poker into the interrogation room. He was accompanied by Commissioner Fido, and there were two guard dogs outside, so he felt safe.

"Bark bark! Bark bark bark bark!" barked Commissioner Fido.

"Fido, you know I can't understand you when you talk with your mouth full," Hatman responded.

"Oh, sorry. I meant to say nice work out there."

This would be the last time The Poker ever escaped Barkham…at least that's what Hatman hoped.

LIKE FATHER, LIKE SON

In LIKE FATHER, LIKE SON *by Rocco Prindle, Eric is on a mission. He wants to make his famous-athlete father proud of him.*

"Eric!" shouted his mom. "Dad's game is on!

"Okay. Be right down!" Eric exclaimed. Eric lived in a big, four-story house with a pool in the backyard and media room in the basement. Eric raced down as quickly as he could. "I'm here," said Eric. "What did I miss?"

"The coin flip," said his mom. "Did you go down the wrong hall again?" The reason that Eric and his mom were so anxious about everything about the game is because Eric's dad is Luke Kuechly, a middle linebacker for the Carolina Panthers. Eric was proud that his dad had broken records and won so many awards. Trophies lined the shelves in their library.

"Is Dad starting?" Eric asked.

"Yes he is. They are playing the Falcons." There was a pause, and then she said it. "So football tryouts are coming."

"Yes they are. I am trying out for middle linebacker."

"Of course you are. But Cam said you have a good arm." Cam Newton, the Panther's quarterback, is a good family friend.

"I am still trying out for middle linebacker."

"Okay," said his mother with doubt in her voice.

"Mom! Let's just watch the game," screeched Eric. He was not happy with her doubts.

"Okay, okay," said his mom.

The next day at school Eric and his friends Cody, Martin, and Tyler were in the locker room changing for tryouts. "Are you guys excited or what?" asked Eric.

"One hundred percent," said Eric's friend Cody. "I'm going to be the best defensive end ever! Like J.J. Watt, but with better hair," Cody said proudly as he flipped his long blond hair.

"Well, I'm trying out for running back," shouted Tyler. "Running backs get a lot of glory, like Jamaal Charles and Le'Veon Bell. They have those tiny, fast legs like the Flash."

"Okay, well, I'm trying out for wide receiver," said Martin. "Now they get all the glory."

"No they don't," exclaimed Tyler.

"Oh really," said Martin. "Tell that to Golden Tate, Julian Edelman, Antonio Brown…."

"Okay," said Eric. "Don't fight; they both get glory according to my dad, and he would know."

"Come on, boys, let's get changed!" shouted Coach Dixon. "Tryouts start in ten minutes. Let's move!" They all had to hustle to get their gear on because they only had ten minutes to get out on the field.

After the tryouts they were all really tired because they had to do everything in football: pass, tackle, throw, catch, and run. That's when Coach Dixon announced the starters and said the starters could go home. "Wide receivers," Coach Dixon announced. "Jack Quinton, Bret Kale, Martin Brewer, Will Tryen, Casey Dicey, and Daniel Xavi. You are starting wide receivers for Bankwell Middle School."

"Yes! Yes! Yes!" shouted Martin. Everyone gave him "Good jobs" and "Congrats."

"Defensive ends!" Dixon shouted. "Bruce Miller, Cody Hunter, Kyle Rueben, and Asher Dale."

"Yes!" shouted Cody.

"Running back is Tyler Aaron. Good job, kid."

"Yes!" Tyler screeched.

"And now for the quarterback. This person will lead this team to a championship season, and he is—drum roll, please…" — everyone tapped the benches— "…Eric Kuechly." Everyone clapped, and Eric stared in disbelief as the coach handed him his jersey. It was number 12. When he walked home for a celebration with his friends, his dad was there waiting.

"Congrats to all of you guys," said NFL linebacker Luke Kuechly. As all of them showed him their new jerseys, Eric's dad did a funny voice like an announcer and said everyone's name. "Cody Hunter, number 99 on the Bankwell Middle School football team; along with Martin Brewer, number 15; Tyler Aaron, number 26; and my son, Eric Kuechly, number 12."

"Hey, Dad," said Eric. "I wanna be just like you."

LOOSE CHANGE

While scavenging for loose change for college in the mall, Lei finds more than she bargained for—a twin sister. In **LOOSE CHANGE** *by* **Destiny Adams***, these twins may have to re-arrange their plans for college.*

As Lei walks in the mall, she comes across a penny. Not knowing what to do with it, she picks it up and puts it in her pocket. Later in the mall, she comes across a nickel. She does the same thing that she did for the penny and puts it in her pocket. Then she continues walking. A dime appears as she walks and makes a clinking sound as she steps on it.

She is so desperate to get enough money to buy a mini-fridge for her college dorm she'll take a moldy penny and save it.

She slowly picks the dime up and walks away, hoping that nobody saw her pick up a dime off the floor. She scans around looking for a quarter, and then she would have 95 cents, but still not enough to buy a mini-fridge.

She quickly finds one and runs to get it, not noticing a girl who has her eye on the same prize, they collide, not hard, but head first into each other.

Lei looks up at her.

The girl looks up at Lei.

And they scream.

"OMG OMG OMG WE LOOK ALIKE! LIKE TWINS!'" Lei shouts.

Everybody in the mall turns to Lei, and the girl looks astonished.

"I DON'T HAVE A TWIN!" says the girl.

"But now you do..." Lei says, surprised by her calmness about the problem. They're twins, and she is as cool as a sloth.

"I guess...I need to tell my father about this..." the girl says.

"You know what? Not right now; I'm in the mood for some ice cream. Wanna come with? It'll be a great time to talk about this awkward situation," Lei says.

"B-but my dad wants me home by 7:30. He will be picking me up in 30 minutes..." the girl says, stuttering on the first word.

"In the summer? Wow. C'mon, you can text him as we walk," Lei says as she links her arm into the girl's without permission. The girl furiously types on her iPhone even though Lei wants to start a conversation. "I'm Lei, short for Leila," Lei introduces herself.

"I'm Maggie, short for Margret," Maggie introduces herself, still with her eyes glued to the screen.

They enter Mr. Fro-Yo-Yo-Berry's Berry Good Ice-Cream/Fro-Yo shop that is conveniently right across the street from the mall. They both give their orders to the bored-looking employee and sit at the closest booth.

"So...do you even have an idea how any of this happened?" says Maggie. "Aren't you like, 18? Isn't it time to get ready for college?" Lei says as she subtracts 95 cents from the amount a mini-fridge cost, which leaves her the total of $149.05.

"Oh no, I've been prepared. I started my college funding when I was two weeks old," she says with her head up high.

Lei just nods and waits for their parents to barge in and ask for an explanation.

"So, Maggie, what college do you pl—" Lei was interrupted by the familiar jingling of bells when the door opens. Lei's mother and a very unfamiliar man crowd around Lei and Maggie.

Lei's mother walks up to Maggie while Maggie's dad approaches Lei.

"Maggz, it's time to go home, young lady." Maggie's dad hugs Lei tightly.

"Sir, my name is Leila..." Lei mumbles just loud enough so that everybody who is surrounding them can hear.

Maggie's dad looks up and studies Lei. He then looks at Maggie.

"Oh dear," Lei's mother says.

"Twins..." Maggie's father continues Lei's mother's thought.

"This can't be! I was never informed of twins!" says Lei's mother.

"The adoption was closed.... It was a possibility that there was more than one child...or twins," mumbles Maggie's father, who is slowly starting to understand everything.

"Well...I guess it's time to go," Lei says sadly. They may not have had a lot of chitchat, but there's one thing that is keeping Lei from letting her sister leave without hesitation: They're sisters.

"Well, Lei, I guess it's goodbye," Maggie says, leaving out the door, tears brimming in her eyes.

Lei's mother puts her arm around Lei's shoulder and walks with her to the door. "WAIT!" shouts Lei. She slowly writes down the college she is going to attend and the dorm number. "Take this; come visit me when you have a chance."

"Lei, I'm going to this college too!" Maggie screams. She leaps with joy over the fact that if they play their cards right, they may end up in the same dorm.

"Honey, just leave it up to the parents and you guys will be bunking with each other in no time," says Maggie's father.

Lei's mother nods.

The parents start planning, and the kids start chatting.

An hour later, the two sisters left the ice-cream shop with locked arms, arguing about who will get the biggest bedroom in the dorm. They also vowed to always remember that one incident in the mall that could have given them a concussion instead landed them a friendship.

That quarter is still in that mall today.

THE MAGIC WAND!

Three kids find something unusual in the park. It seems harmless, but it will lead them on an extraordinary adventure in **THE MAGIC WAND!** *by* ***Anaya Bracy-Robinson.***

It was just a normal, hot, sunny day in Texas, until three kids decided to change their after-school routine. The three kids' names were Alex, Maria, and Bobby.

When they got out of school they went to the park. Maria was just playing around in the woods and then she tripped over a stick. "Hey, look, you guys," Maria said. "Look at this weird stick."

"So?" Bobby said.

"It just looks odd to me."

Then all of a sudden the stick started vibrating and the ground started shaking! "WHAT'S HAPPENING?" Alex screamed. Out of nowhere, the kids were in Wonderland.

"What is this place?" Bobby said.

"Wonderland," Maria said while she looked at the sign. "I've read about this place in my books, but I never thought it was real."

"Hey guys, look. The stick looks different," Alex said. The stick was blue with sparkles on it, and it was perfectly straight. Also, the tip was silver, and it was shining like the stars at night.

"This place is the opposite of our modern-day world," Alex said. The sky was orange, the road was yellow, and there were no houses—there were just castles for houses. But they a noticed a big, beautiful castle that shined like diamonds. The castle was right in front of them, and when they got closer to the castle there appeared a guard.

The guard was standing at the door of the castle. The guard was huge; he had a bald head and a scar just below his eye. The guard had a uniform on that was all black, and on the corner of his shirt it said "THE GUARD OF KING LUCIFER." They were so scared but somehow got the courage to talk to him. "We are lost and want to go home," Maria said.

The guard replied, "There is only one way to get home. You will need to talk to the King. But I'm not going to let you through unless you can answer this riddle: What animal walks on all fours in the morning, two in the afternoon and three in the evening?"

They discussed among themselves what it could be. Maria cried out, "We are never going home. I don't have a clue of what this could be."

The guard looked at them with no mercy and said, "I guess you guys can plan to be here for eternity because no one gets through me without answering my riddles."

Everyone was so nervous. Bobby whispered to Alex and Maria, "Let's just push the guard and run into the castle."

The guard said, "I can hear you. Now you only have a few minute to answer my riddle, or I will make sure you stay here forever!"

"Oh no," Alex said. "Think, guys. I want to go home. I miss my family. I even miss school!"

But then Maria remembered one of the books she read. The book was about how humans start as babies and then grow up. She also remembered that quote in the book. "Wait, I know it," Maria said. "It's a man since it crawls as a baby, walks as a kid, and then uses a cane when it gets older!"

The guard looked at them and said, "I don't know how you guessed it, but you're correct." However, there was one problem: the kids didn't know it was a trap! "You may enter the castle," the guard said with a smirk.

"Yay!" they all screamed

When they approached the castle, they noticed how beautiful everything was. The grass was really green, the birds were chirping all in tune, and it smelled like a summer day. Bobby said, "I feel like everything is going to be okay." Little did they know it was all a trick.

Finally they entered the castle with hope. They approached the King. "My name is King Lucifer. How may I help?"

Maria stated, "We found this magic stick, and it sent us here. We want to go home, but we are not sure how."

King Lucifer replied, "I can help you, but first I must have the wand."

Maria looked at his eyes. They were reddish and brownish. "Something just doesn't feel right," Maria said.

"Why not?" Bobby asked.

"I don't know why, but something in King Lucifer's eyes isn't right."

Alex yelled at Maria, "I want to go home, so give the wand to him."

"Okay," Maria said, "I'll give it to him, but first let me ask him one question just to see how sincere he really is." She said to King Lucifer, "If I give the wand to you, what are you going to do with it? Are you going to do something wonderful and sweet with it?"

King Lucifer hesitated and said, "Yes, just wait and see."

Maria was so nervous. "I don't understand why you guys don't see that he's evil and can't be trusted."

Alex, Maria, and Bobby began to talk to each other and decided that they were not going to give the wand to King Lucifer. "You're right," Alex said, "something doesn't feel right."

They all ran because King Lucifer began to get angry. All of a sudden his face changed. He became scary-looking. His eyes turned red, smoke came out of his ears, and a horn came out of his head.

They made it out of the castle with the wand. While they were running, Maria had the wand and started chanting, "I want to go home; I want to go home." They just kept running. Lucifer was right behind them.

When Maria was chanting she did not know in Wonderland when you need help an angel will help you. The angel sent a bubble that would send them back home. "Look at this beautiful shiny object," Alex said. For some reason they felt comfort when they looked at it.

Maria, Bobby, and Alex closed their eyes and ran to the bubble. While they were in the bubble they started to have flashbacks of their childhood. Maria remembered being little and playing in her playhouse. Alex and Bobby remembered going on family vacations with their parents. It started to get really bright inside the bubble, like a ray of sunshine and a breath of fresh air. Then they were back home safely.

After they caught their breath, they began to wonder if it was all a crazy dream. Alex said, "Maria, please get rid of that wand."

Maria replied, "I'm going to throw it away right now." She threw it in the trash can, and then they all walked home.

"I hope that never happens again," Alex said.

"Yeah," Bobby and Maria said.

The magic wand turned back into a weird-shaped stick. Hopefully no one will touch it!

THE MUSIC

Everyone in town comes to see the Hollywood California Orchestra play their first concert on what seems to be a normal day. But in **THE MUSIC** *by* **Alaya J. Holmes**, *everything gets out of control when an evil scientist takes over.*

One peaceful day, three kids named Ashley, Mark, and Lisa were about to watch the Hollywood California Orchestra play their first concert. "I can't wait to see the HCO play their instruments!" Ashley said.

"Me neither," said Mark.

As people began to get into their seats, the HCO was warming up. Then, the conductor came out and greeted everyone. "Hello, everyone, and welcome to the Hollywood California Orchestra. We are very excited to be here and perform for you all this evening." Everyone clapped, and the show began.

As they played their first song, it was amazing. The orchestra played together, and the song was very pretty. But there was one flaw. As the song was coming to an end, the HCO's instruments started to glow in a yellow bright light around them, and the instruments started to fly! "What in the world is going on?" Lisa said.

The crowd was murmuring with confusion. And the orchestra was screaming and running all over the stage.

Then, out of the corner of his eye, Mark saw Dr. Chemical, an evil scientist, laughing. "Guys, look! Dr. Chemical!" Mark yelled.

"Let's get him!" Ashley said, as she chased after him.

The kids chased Dr. Chemical all the way to his lab. Dr. Chemical noticed that he was being followed. "Well, well, well. Look who we have here. Nice to see you, Ashley, Mark, and Lisa. How have you been?" Dr. Chemical said.

"Cut the innocent act, Dr. C!" Lisa said. "We don't have time for your mess! Now spill it. We know you did something to the HCO's instruments."

"Oh, that! Some of my best work. I've been testing this potion out for quite some time now. I just never knew when the perfect time to use it was. But using it when almost everyone in Hollywood was in the park was the PERFECT time," Dr. C said, hanging up his lab coat.

"We'll be right over here. We need to talk about something private," Mark said.

"You guys take your time. I'll be over here planning how I'm going to take over Paris. Or maybe keep working on how I'm going to make the squirrels my minions," Dr. Chemical said.

The kids walked over to the corner of the room, where Dr. Chemical couldn't hear what they were saying. "There is one thing I still don't understand. How are we going to get him to talk to us about switching the instruments back to normal?" Lisa said, worried.

"Good point. How *are* we going to get the instruments back to normal?" Ashley agreed.

"I have an idea," Mark said. "We could trick him into telling us."

"But how are we going to do that?" Ashley wondered out loud.

"Just follow my lead," said Mark. "Dr. Chemical, what projects have you been working on lately?" Mark said.

"Well, as you know, I have been working on the HCO and making their instruments fly. But now, I'm working on all of my reversal potions. You know, like how to turn stuff back to normal. I just finished figuring out how to turn the HCO's instruments back to normal. It's right there, on my lab shelf," he said, pointing to the shelf.

"Oh, that's nice," Lisa said.

"Yep. I'll be right back. DON'T TOUCH ANYTHING WHILE I'M GONE," Dr. Chemical yelled at the kids.

As soon as he shut the door to his lab, the kids ran to the shelf and looked up. There were so many potions to choose from.

"We have to be quick; he'll be back any minute," Ashley whispered.

"But which one turns the HCO's instruments back to normal?" Mark said.

"Dude, just look at the labels that Dr. Chemical put on the potion bottles," Ashley said sarcastically.

"Oh, right." Mark laughed.

So they looked at almost every bottle when, "What did I tell you little kids? DON'T TOUCH MY STUFF!" Dr. Chemical rushed into the room yelling.

"Get...the...bottle," Lisa whispered. Mark turned around super-quickly and grabbed the potion bottle. "RUN!" they all yelled.

Dr. C ran after them. But the kids ran just as fast. They ran all the way to the park, and threw the potion on the HCO's instruments as fast as you could say "STOP." And that is what Dr. C yelled from across the park. But it was too late.

The crowd was amused at what they were witnessing that day at the park. "I thought we were here to see a concert!" a lady in the park said, smiling.

"And that is what you are going to see, ma'am," the kids said at the same time.

"I'll get you back for this, you rotten kids!" Dr. Chemical screamed from across the park. As he was leaving, a flock of pigeons came along and pooped right on Dr. C's head. "Really? Curse you, nature!" he said.

The Hollywood California Orchestra got set up again, and played an outstanding concert. "It was just like nothing happened. Like a normal day in the park," Ashley said. "Yep, like nothing you've ever seen."

PERSONAL BEST

When Ray tries out for the school football team, he knows there are many other talented players. His outlook and drive matter most in **PERSONAL BEST** *by* **Nikolas Gjurashaj**.

"Ray, get ready for school," Mom says. As he gets ready for school his mom says, "You are going to be late."

He gets on his clothes and eats one piece of toast and yells, "I love you, Mom."

When he goes to the bus stop he sees the bus driving away. He runs after it and pounds on it. He is also yelling, "Open! Open!" The bus door finally opens.

When he gets on the first step on the bus everyone starts laughing at Ray because he was pounding on the bus. He sits next to his friend Nicole. She says, "You like football, right?"

"Yeah, why?"

"Because I have a sheet for you."

As Ray takes the sheet, he says, "Are you trying out?"

"Girls can not try out," Nicole says.

"Can you at least watch my games and practices?"

"That will be great." Nicole adds, "It will also be great for your dad."

Ray says, "It will be."

After school he has football practice. *There are a lot of good people*, Ray thinks. Coach asks everyone what position they are trying out for, and when he asks Ray, Ray says, "QB."

After practice Coach Simon walks up to Ray and says, "You have great effort for a third-string QB."

Ray says, "Thank you." He wishes he could tell his dad, but his dad is dead.

Once he gets home he tells his mom, and she says, "Dad would be happy."

The biggest bully, Matt, hears Ray is third-string quarterback. He wants to stop that, but it is only getting worse because Ray is doing well.

After practice Coach Simon announces the starting quarterback. "This person has great effort and skills every time he gets the ball,"

Coach Simon says. "The starting QB is Ray." Ray tells his mom, and she feels happy for him.

Coach says "Sorry" to Matt.

Matt mumbles back, "It's fine." Matt says, "See you at practice" to Ray with a weird smile.

The next day at practice, Ray is amazing. After practice Matt grabs Ray and says, "Where you going?" Matt throws a punch, but Ray ducks.

Ray runs inside the school. He tells Coach Simon, and Matt gets banned from the team for trying to hurt Ray.

Overall, Ray took his big dream and protected it, and then it came true.

THE POWER OF
THE ELEMENTAL ORBS

THE POWER OF THE ELEMENTAL ORBS, *by **John Ferguson**, is the story of three boys who find orbs of great power that crash to Earth. The encounter becomes a test of their true selves.*

It was a clear, sunny day in the small coastal town of Happyville, California. Three seventh-grade boys were playing football in the field behind their neighborhood. The boys have been friends since second grade when they were all in Ms. Sunshine's class. While playing football, the boys, Jack, Ty and Robert, saw a meteorite fall from the sky. With a high-pitched crackling sound the meteorite broke into three pieces when it hit a bird in flight. "What the heck just happened?" said Robert.

"You think I know?" said Ty.

"Well, one looked like it landed at the top of Mt. Ferguson, and we all know that Robert is the best climber," said Jack.

"And one looks like it landed in Johnse Ocean, and we know that Ty can out-swim a shark!" said Robert.

"So where is the third one?" asked Jack.

"Look in the forest," said Robert. "I can see smoke coming from over there."

"Fine," said Jack.

Jack was the kindest of the boys. When he got to the forest he looked around and, to his surprise, found the piece of the meteorite he was looking for. It was black. When he got near it, the orb started to talk to him. "Hello, human. I am here to give you the power of light."

"What the crap is happening?" Jack said out loud.

"I am Master Orb. I am here to help you defeat the other orbs, as their mission is to corrupt the people they come in contact with."

"There are more?" questioned Jack.

"Yes, and they are the two other pieces."

"How can I stop the other orbs from corrupting my friends?"

"You have to merge with me."

"And why should I trust an orb that just came down from the sky?"

"Trust me and save your friends, or do *not* trust me, and they die, you die, and this world dies."

Jack's first thought is to panic, but he remembers something his dad likes to say: "The important thing is not to panic. A person never thinks clearly when under the stress of panic."

"Fine. And how do I do that?"

"Just touch me," said the Black Orb in a very creepy voice. So Jack touched the orb, but what Jack didn't know was the orb he found was actually the evil orb. When he touched it he turned black as night.

As he let go of the Black Orb all of the blackness drained from him, and as it drained from Jack the plants and trees around him shriveled up and died. What Jack realized after letting go was his hair was smooth and shiny black like a helmet, he had armor on, and he was holding a long, black samurai sword.

"I am coming for you, Ty and Robert," Jack said in a dark, gruesome voice.

Meanwhile at Johnse Ocean beach, Ty saw the blue orb. It was at least a half mile out to sea, and he had to swim the entire way. When he got there the water rose up around him like a huge platform with water cascading off it like a waterfall. "What the heck is happening to the water? It's solid!" Ty shouted out loud. Then mysteriously a row of weapons appeared in front of him.

"WHAT...? Okay, this is *not* normal, but I want the bow and arrows."

As Ty grabbed the weapon, a giant Poseidon-looking monster with armor that resembled flowing waves said, "I am the guardian of the Water Orb."

"Okay, okay, what is going on here?" Ty thought to himself.

"You have challenged me to a battle!" shouted the water beast.

"I just want the thing that fell from the sky. How do I get it?"

With a trembling voice the water beast replied, "You must defeat me in a battle."

"Pretty sure it's not worth it!" Ty tried to get away, but a wall of water appeared in front of him. "How do I get out?"

"You cannot leave. You have to win or die." After hearing that, Ty felt confused, scared, and frustrated. But he knew he didn't have a choice, so, feeling brave, Ty yelled, "Bring it!"

The guardian got mad and swung his gigantic trident at Ty. Ty dodged the attack and shot hundreds of arrows at the water beast. Ty ran up to it with great force and speed. He jumped and sank two arrows in his eyes. The water creature fell onto the solid water. Ty grabbed the orb and swam to the shore.

Startling Ty, the orb said, "One of the orbs is evil."

This day keeps getting weirder and weirder, Ty thought, but instead said, "Okay. How can I help?"

"You have to merge with me by touching my skin," explained the Blue Orb.

Ty touched the Blue Orb, and his hair turned blue and wavy. His armor of solid waves looked like the waves of the ocean but somehow more fierce and sturdy.

Meanwhile at the top of Mt. Ferguson, Robert saw the last orb. When he went to retrieve the orb, a big rock next to the orb began to move faster as he got closer.

When Robert touched the orb the big rock broke into hundreds of small rocks, and then magically formed into a giant man. "Who is there?" shouted a menacing voice.

"WHAT THE CRAP!" Robert cried. "My name is Robert, and I'm here looking for the meteorite."

"Well, you'll have to go through me!"

Just then a row of weapons appeared in front of Robert. He picked up the giant war hammer because it looked like it would do the most damage.

All of a sudden the giant rock man shot thousands of arrows at him. Terrified, Robert jumped up and dodged most of them. However, an arrow grazed the flesh of his shoulder.

Robert swung his hammer and with a power only given to him by the hammer hit the giant's feet. The giant fell onto the hard, cold, ice mountaintop. Robert saw an opening and jumped up and slammed down his enormous war hammer onto the giant's head. The giant's entire body broke apart into small pieces.

Robert grabbed the orb and sat down. The orb said, "One of the orbs is evil, and *that* orb will corrupt the user and will use him or her as if they were his puppet."

"What does this orb look like?" asked Robert.

"I can't tell you, but you must find the person he corrupted." Then the Orb glowed and turned into armor that looked like a huge boulder.

When the boys got back to the football field Ty and Robert were both thinking, *Who is the evil one?*

"Hey, wow, looking good," said Ty.

"Thanks, you too," said Robert.

"I want to kill you!" said Jack.

"Not going to happen," said Robert.

Jack took out his samurai sword and swung it, which repelled both of them back forty yards. Ty started shooting arrows at Jack. Meanwhile Robert ran up and hit Jack, flinging him up into the air. Ty shot Jack midair, Jack fell, and the evil orb un-merged with him.

"You should have never come here," said Robert, and he smashed the evil orb with his enormous war hammer into millions of pieces.

THE SCHOOL

A boy becomes trapped in school on the coldest day of the year. His predicament shows him how precious life is in **THE SCHOOL***, by* **Liam O'Gorman***.*

"Tyler!" Mom said.

"What?"

"You're going to be late for school!" Oh god, not this again. This happened probably because I stayed up late last night finishing my essay that was conveniently due the next day. I got up, sped down the stairs, and before you could say "tardy," I was on the bus.

I have two really good friends, Samantha and Cooper. On the bus Cooper saved me a seat as always. I sat down next to him. "Hey, Tyler," he said as the bus sped off. We made our regular stops and finally got to our school.

I was on my way to my locker when I looked out of the hallway window, and saw it was snowing like crazy.

In first hour the teacher had us take a test on shifting plates; in second hour, we reviewed punctuation; third hour was all about how to multiply variables; and that was basically my day. But in sixth hour the teacher told us to give him our essays. I looked in my backpack, and—surprise—there was no essay. I must have left it on the counter at my house! I explained to the teacher what happened. He said he totally understood and told me to turn it in later after school.

So, I rode the bus home, and grabbed my essay, and my mom drove me back to school. I didn't think I would need a coat because it would only take several minutes.

I got there and walked to his class. The school seemed empty and abandoned. I put the essay on his desk and started to walk out. It was still snowing like crazy.

Suddenly I heard a crack! A huge tree fell down onto the entryway, covering it completely! I panicked because the power went out, too! I also smelled something that smelled like a gas leak. I know that smell all too well. I went to a safety school and learned about gas leaks.

I was trapped in school with no power and with a gas leak. I was freezing, it was below -10 degrees outside, there was no power inside, and I didn't have a jacket. My body temperature dropped instantly as I was chilled to the bone. I heard my mom screaming and calling 911. Now I had one goal: get out.

I walked around and thought of a way out. The only exit closest to here is the one near the gym on the other side of the school. I was already feeling weak and tired, but I had to keep walking. Since it was the middle of January it got dark fast. And there was no power, so I was walking blindly.

I remembered that there are flashlights in teachers' rooms, and I went to the nearest one. I found that it was unlocked, so I went in. I opened the desk, got the flashlight, and turned it on. Now I could see where I was going.

When I flicked the flashlight on I found that I was in the east wing, right near the gym. By then I couldn't feel my fingers any more or my body. I was weak, but I tried running to get to the door faster, and I tripped and fell. My arms felt like lead. I was too weak to get back up. I couldn't. It was all over, and I was going to die. I'm not sure what made me pass out, the cold or the gas. My head was throbbing. I closed my eyes and heard a noise, a door opening, and people saying, "Go, go, go!" Then I fainted.

I woke up about an hour later feeling...warm. My friends and family surrounded my hospital bed. As I wondered what happened, my friends kept asking if I was all right, and I said yes.

After a ton of paperwork we could finally go home. When we got home I had to go right to bed because it was nearly nine o clock.

The next day we had school, and I was asked a lot of questions by kids and teachers. At sixth hour the teacher said he got my essay, and I got an A+.

SKI SHADOW

*When Jack and his friend John go on a skiing trip, Jack is disturbed by something he sees. In **SKI SHADOW** by **Kaitlin Capinjola**, Jack goes on a crazy adventure to find what he's looking for.*

School had just been canceled because we got about twelve inches of snow the night before. The past few weeks, my new "phase" was going skiing. So, I thought it was a good idea to pack up our gear and head to the mountain.

Lately, Jack and I hadn't been spending a lot of time together. I called him up and told him we were going to the mountain. He was thrilled, and ready to go!

It wasn't much fun getting there; car rides aren't usually. But, after a dreadful trek up to Mount Brighten we were there.

We started to get up the mountain when my eye caught something suspicious. It was a dark shadow at the base of the chairlift. But, it wasn't a shadow of a person; it was more of a creature: it had four legs, and was moving around in a mysterious way. The shadow was hopping around, sort of like a bunny, but more than that. I was confused, and tried not to think about it too much. I looked at it from the ride up the mountain, but I couldn't figure out what it was, or why it was there. *I am probably just paranoid,* I thought. *After all, I just want to ski.*

It had been a while since I saw the shadow, but when Jack and I went down a run by the trees, I thought I saw the same shadow again. I got Jack's attention, and pointed to where I thought I saw the shadow. But, when I recalled where the shadow was, it wasn't there. Jack thought I was crazy, but I swore it was there a few seconds ago. UGH, I was so angry. I hated myself because it felt like it was really there; but then again, I guess I don't really know what I saw. I got it out of my head, until I saw it again.

"There, there it is!" I shouted out to Jack.

"Where?" Jack asked, and when I tried to find it again, it was gone. *We have to find that little thing, whatever it is,* I thought. *Well, it was over by the run "Silversmith," with all the trees.*

I had a mini flashback in my head. The last time I saw the shadow was by other trees as well. "Let's go over here," I said with a hesitant voice. So, Jack and I ventured by the trees.

I was so nervous. First of all, I hated runs with trees, and then again, I didn't even know if this thing was real, or if Jack was right, and I'm just crazy.

Here it goes I started to go down the hill. There were bumps a few inches high, and so many trees! I couldn't even see the snow ahead of me, that's how crowded it was with trees. I got so scared and clenched up. I don't really know what happened next, but I imagined myself getting thrown into the air, because of the bumps. Then, it got even worse. I looked behind me, and I saw the trees come alive.

Now it wasn't just the shadow I had to worry about. It was also the evil trees that had come alive, and were trying to eat me. I saw huge mouths on the trees, and gigantic, super-sharp teeth. The mouths were sticking out of the top of the tree, where the leaves usually are. It was all just a big blur.

When I got to the bottom, I didn't see Jack behind me. I was in total shock. "Jack, did the trees eat you?" I screamed at the top of my lungs.

"What?" he said.

I turned around, and he was standing there with a confused look on his face.

"OH MY GOSH! Did you just see what happened? All the trees were coming alive, and they tried to chase me, and in the middle of it all I saw the shadow, but this time it was gigantic!" I looked at Jack, out of breath, trying to explain what just happened, and he looked even more confused then he was before.

"Are you okay? Did you hit your head on the way down?" Jack said with concern.

"No," I said. "I'm not okay, though. I swear those trees were chasing me!"

After a little bit, Jack calmed me down, and I had some hot chocolate in the lodge. But, I swear I saw that shadow, and I'm positive those trees were chasing me. "Are you sure you went down the same run as me?" I asked Jack. "Because, you were down at the bottom before me, and I went first!"

"Well, yes, I'm pretty sure," Jack said.

"What do you mean you are pretty sure?" I said with confusion. "We have to find out what happened," I said as I was taking off my helmet. Then, as I took a quick glance at my helmet, I saw my

GoPro. "That's it!" I shouted. "My GoPro was on, so we can check it and see what really happened."

My hands were shaking terribly. Jack and I were just about to see what really occurred in the forest. I hooked the GoPro up to a desktop computer that was in the lodge. I scrolled through all the files, and saw the one with today's date on it. "That's it!" I shouted.

My GoPro got a glimpse of the shadow. The next part of the video was me going down the scary run with the trees. But, the trees weren't trying to swallow me whole, or I wasn't flying in the air because of the "huge" bumps.

I was bummed out. I swear on my life everything happened. But, I guess not.

"I told you trees can't come alive," Jack said with confidence in his voice.

"I guess," I sighed.

The rest of the day I was still so confused. But, I guess the day ended happily because I never saw the shadow again.

THE SUMMER IN FLORIDA

Ocean beaches are one reason people love Florida. But danger lurks just off shore in **THE SUMMER IN FLORIDA** *by Heather Malz*.

It was another sunny, beautiful Florida day in 2011 in the middle of a fantastic summer, or so they say. Our family had been sitting on the beach in the bright sun for a while, so we decided to go swimming in the ocean.

The water was cold and refreshing, but the salt water burned our eyes and tasted bad. After a good ten minutes of swimming and having fun, I noticed something big, dark, and , gray out the corner of my eye. It was coming toward shore, dragging red behind it. Then I understood...it was a shark!

The water was filled with tons of people swimming, surfing, and wading. When people noticed it they began to scream louder than thunder, run as if they were in a marathon race, and swim away like a fish. The giant shark was coming toward shore faster than a lightning strike.

Young kids were furiously screaming, crying, and speeding to their parents, trying to get away from the shark. Some people were getting bitten and seriously injured, and others were just lucky to make it out alive.

The ambulances started to arrive at the beach to rush people to the hospital. The beach was almost empty after they took away many on a trip to the hospital, but others were still waiting for a ride. Some people were still in the water trying to get away from the shark. After a couple of minutes people from shore were racing out to help others who were injured out of the water, so that they could get to the hospital.

That night a great, white whale came out of nowhere and scared the shark away. Then everybody enjoyed a long night of fireworks, looking at the red ocean, and a full moon that lit up the sky. And everyone was relieved it was all over and couldn't believe what had happened.

SURGERY GONE WRONG

Life can change in an instant. In **SURGERY GONE WRONG** *by **Talib Davis,** you will learn that surgery does not always go your way.*

David woke up. As he got out of bed to go to the bathroom, he fell out of bed on his lung.

His mom heard the scream of her child and ran upstairs as fast as she could go. She opened the door to find David lying on the ground, crying and yelling. David's mom asked him, "Are you okay, honey?"

"No, I think I collapsed my lung!"

"Okay, David, wait here. I'm going to call 911."

Finally the ambulance came to take David to the hospital. David's mom told the medics to hurry.

When the arrived at the hospital, they quickly rushed him into the surgery room. As the doctors got ready to start the surgery the nurses put him to sleep with a drug. The first incision was made in the chest area, but something went wrong.

One year later, David's mom is still grieving from David's death from the surgery. Since his death, his mother has moved all of his stuff out, has sued the hospital, and has been having suicidal thoughts so that she can be with her son.

THINK TWICE

When a class is assigned a project, it is no surprise that a bullied girl has no partner to work with. However, Aria may have the last laugh in **THINK TWICE**, *by Izzy Parker.*

I walk into Seaford Middle School on a blazing hot California morning. As soon as I walk into the school, the hallways go silent. There are a few whispers and snickers that I hear through the crowd. Do I have something on my face? Am I walking funny?

I speed-walk to my locker and see that someone has written the word "loser" on my locker in black marker. A laugh goes through the crowd as my eyes well up with tears. I'm not too surprised by this, though. I pretty much always get bullied, but I don't have enough confidence to stand up for myself.

I pick out my textbooks and notebooks and slide them into my backpack. The hallway slowly resumes its ordinary noise level of loudness.

I try to run as quickly as I can to my first class before my friends can find me. I don't want to see Emily and Lily give me endless sympathy like they always do. I keep thinking about the locker incident, but my thoughts are quickly interrupted by a voice.

"Here so early?" Mr. Fry asks.

"Yeah, someone   "

Before I can explain what happened, the bell rings and students come piling in. Unfortunately, my class is full of jerks.

"Class, take a seat! Okay, so I have a new project for you guys!" Mr. Fry exclaims. All of the students groan except for me. I don't really mind doing work.

I listen intently for the next 20 minutes about what this project should consist of. We have to make a 12- to 15-slide PowerPoint presentation about an important historical event that inspires us. It needs to contain basic facts, and why it inspires me. This will probably take a long time....

"I know, a lot of work, right? Well, there is an upside to it! Partner up with no more than three people to work on this PowerPoint. You have the rest of the class to work, and it's due this Friday," Mr. Fry states.

Everyone goes wild! Shouting names across the room and fighting over partners is all I can hear. The only person that *doesn't* get up and find a partner is me. I already know that no one in this class wants to partner up with me. I glance around the room. Everyone seems to have found a group, anyway.

Mr. Fry takes notice. "Aria...you may work alone," he whispers to me with an encouraging smile. It's really embarrassing to be left out.

This Monday went by very slowly. Constantly being bullied is *not* very fun. At least Emily and Lily stood up for me as much as they could. Every time an insult came along they would just shout back at how "rude and stupid" the bully is. Of course, the bully would back off only because it was Emily or Lily talking. They are liked by pretty much everybody, and they have major confidence. I'm not even sure why they would want to hang out with a loser like me....These thoughts are stressing me out. All of these bullying problems piling on top of homework is so much stress!

I go home and get right to work on that PowerPoint for Mr. Fry's Social Studies class. It's best for me to work on my hardest and most time-consuming work first, and this is definitely it. I manage to complete an amazing presentation with maximum slides and quality information. It took me a couple of hours, but I'm really proud of myself. The evening goes by with a bit more homework, watching TV, and heading to bed. Let's see how this week goes.

The next four days go as usual. Bullying, class, bullying, class: It all just repeats over and over again. It's Friday now, and I have to present this PowerPoint. You probably know already that I don't have any self-confidence. I'm not sure I'm going to be able to present this in front of the whole class. But of course, I get called *first* to present.

"Aria, how about you start us off with your Inspiring Historical Event Presentation." Mr. Fry gives me yet another encouraging smile.

I get up and feel really shaky as I walk over to the computer. I plug my flash drive into the computer and here it is...my presentation. I think back to last summer when Emily and Lily told me to stop worrying about these bullies and put myself in a happy place. That's what I do. I put myself in a happy place and present my PowerPoint with a grin.

My presentation goes smoothly. It's time to finish it off.

"...And that's why this historical event inspires me," I finish off. I can't believe I just did that. I wasn't nervous or anything! I didn't mess up any words, and I was so confident while doing it.

The class claps. They clapped for me! They look like they actually enjoyed it...I can't believe this!

"Aria...that was one of the best presentations I have ever seen in my whole 23 years of teaching. You guys remember how I promised a pizza party for anyone with an outstanding project at the beginning of the year? Aria, you have earned that party. You may bring two friends with you. Who shall it be?"

The room is absolutely silent. I could even see Joey's jaw almost drop to the floor. Getting a pizza party in middle school is pretty rare. That's an elementary school thing. But this...I earned this.

The room shouts with excitement. I see hands raised up in the air and hear voices shouting, "Pick me! Pick me!" Honestly, I would never pick any of these people to hang out with in my whole entire life. What a bunch of jerks if they think they are going to have a pizza party with me!

"I want my friends Lily and Emily to come to the party, please. They have been supportive and caring through all this bullying that I go through! I know you guys just want the pizza. I'd rather spend my party with people who are true friends to me."   I look over to Mr. Fry to see him with his eyes widened and mouth opened.

"I had no idea that these students were bullying you, Aria. However, I did notice that none of you stepped up and offered to be partners with Aria. I bet you guys are thinking twice about picking your partners, huh? Next time, let's be a little more caring.

"And Aria, you may of course bring Lily and Emily. Ice cream provided." Mr. Fry winks and gives me a smile. It's not the "sympathy encouraging" smile. This time it's the proud kind.

THE UNFORGETTABLE SUMMER

When two girls take a vacation to Vermont, everything seems to be going as planned. Yet things take a turn for the worst in **THE UNFORGETTABLE SUMMER** *by* **Callie Ostrowski**.

One crisp morning near a small cottage in Vergennes, Vermont, two friends awoke to the distant sound of the small waves crashing against the shore. Kristin and Julia were looking to get away for a few days before their parents arrived. It was four hours before their parents arrived and they were looking to go into a nearby town to do some shopping.

"Morning, Jules," whispered Kristin softly.

Julia's eyes squinted at the light peering through the window.

"Ready to do some shopping?" she whispered again. Kristin could tell that Julia was not in the mood to go shopping. Finally, after a shocking 20 minutes, Julia showered and was ready to face the day.

They drove into town looking for a place to eat breakfast. Both Kristin and Julia spotted a local diner that said "fresh hot pancakes." They looked at each other and winked.

By the time both friends were seated, they were ready to order.

"Hello, ladies. My name is James, and I'll be your waiter today. Are you from out of town?"

"Yes! How did you know?" replied Julia.

"Well, we are a pretty small town. Almost everyone knows each other. Where are you guys staying?"

"Oh, just over by the lake in that single cabin."

"Oh, you might want to be careful! I'll be back with some waters."

The two friends exchanged looks and snickered.

"That guy is such a creep! And what the heck was he talking about?" whispered Julia.

"It's probably because we are here all by ourselves. Anyway, let's get out of here! I'm not hungry anyway."

The girls' steps quickened as they headed up the street to a local gift shop. A bell rang as they entered. So far, Kristin and Julia noticed that the town was very unpopulated and empty. The smell of candles and old, reclaimed cedar wood filled the air.

Kristin spotted a postcard that read *Greetings from Vergennes!* "This might be good for our scrapbook!" she said.

"Great idea!"

"So how have you two been?" asked the clerk as she rang up the postcard.

"Wonderful! We just arrived here yesterday from New York!"

"Oh! Where are you staying?"

"In the cabin on Walnut Cove by the lake! It has such a wonderful view!"

The clerk paused a second, and then said, "I'm surprised the owner still lets it rent! That place should have been burned down years ago!"

"What happened?" Julia asked.

"You haven't heard the story? Well, then, I must tell you what happened. Have a seat if you will."

The two friends did as they were told and sat down on creaky wooden stools in the corner of the shop.

"Okay. The story starts with a man who was in his mid-thirties. He was a contractor who built the brand-new cabin. But little did he know that he had built the house over a very old graveyard. Many years passed with no issues. Yet one summer the contractor began renting the cabin. All I know is that the man was killed after one night of being there. The police investigated, but they died also. The story still remains a mystery as to what happened that night."

Julia gulped as her heart pounded.

"I didn't tell you this to scare you, but I told it to so you could be brave young people and prove the others wrong!"

The two friends peered at each other and wondered what this "Haunted Nightmare" talk was all about.

The two friends ran to the car in silence. The drive home was the exact same. Julia's head throbbed. She could not stop thinking about what the clerk had told her. She knew that ghosts were not real, yet she still shivered at the thought of it.

"None of that was true," Kristin said as they stepped in the cabin.

"Hey! Maybe that waiter guy wasn't a creep after all! He could have been signaling to us that there is something wrong!" shouted Julia.

"Nah, I'm pretty sure that guy is just a creep. Besides, he would have told us!"

"Yeah. Let's play a game."

Soon after they started a long game of Monopoly, a low moaning sound began to fill the cabin.

"Eh, don't worry! It's probably just the furnace," Julia whispered.

"But it's seventy degrees outside!" replied Kristin.

"Yeah...I guess you are right."

"I...I will go check out the attic to see if there are any issues."

"Wait! I'll come with you!"

Kristin slowly pulled the ladder down, hoping there weren't any "surprises." On her way up the ladder, she gulped and was thinking, *What in the world am I doing? I mean I know there is—* Thoughts of insanity were soon brushed away when she saw that there was nothing to worry about up in the warm and seemingly cheery attic.

"It's perfectly fine!" Kristin told Julia, who was at the bottom of the ladder.

"Okay..."

As Julia climbed the ladder, she knew her Kristin never lied about anything.

"See! It's perfectly fine!" Kristin said while dancing around on the dusty, oak-wood floors. Kristin pulled two chests from the corner over to the middle of the floor. Both took a seat.

"See, there is nothing to worry about!" shouted Kristin happily.

"Yeah, I guess you were right. That noise was probably the air conditioning or something."

"I bet those people were trying to scare us!"

"Yeah. Let's go tidy up. Our parents are coming soon."

The two friends tugged at the door. It wouldn't open. They stared at each other wide-eyed. But before either friend could open her mouth, the lights went out. They heard loud moaning sounds coming from the corner where the chests had been. The two friends grabbed for each other and screamed.

"It was true! The lady was right!"

They shoved themselves into the far opposite corner of the attic, hoping that they could survive. Once again, Julia kicked at the door. This time, it opened, and both Kristin and Julia's parents appeared.

"Mom! Dad!" they shouted in unison. Both kids ran directly to their room to grab their belongings and run out the door before explaining what had happened that day.

Little did they know that the postcard sailed toward the ground, fluttering back and forth until it hit the ground, gone forever. But Kristin and Julia didn't need a postcard to remember what happened that day.

THE UNLUCKY PENNY

"See a penny, pick it up; all day long, you'll have good luck." Don't tell that to Asha, who experiences just the opposite in **THE UNLUCKY PENNY**, by *Abby Dulio.*

On Wednesday, April 1, 2015, at 3:15, Bella, Asha, Michael, and Sean were walking home from school when Sean and Michael pointed out that there was a penny on the curb of the sidewalk. Asha thought that it was the coolest thing ever when it was just a penny. "Wow! Look at that penny! I call first dibs!" Asha said.

"So, what are you going to wish for, and where are you going to do it?" said Bella.

Michael, Asha's brother, spoke for Asha. "Probably in the Petersons' backyard. They have a tiny little fountain that is just big enough."

"Hey," Sean said, "Michael, did you tell your mom I was coming over so we could work on the science test?"

"Yes I did."

They stopped in front of Bella's house, and Asha walked up to the house with her to say goodbye. "Bye, Bella! See you tomorrow on the bus!"

When Michael, Sean and Asha got home, their parents weren't home from work yet. Michael suggested that Asha go outside to the Petersons' fountain and wish for something. "Are you coming?" Asha asked.

Michael said, "Sean and I have a project to do. Sorry."

"Okay," Asha said.

"Wait, Asha, can you hand me the bag of groceries before you leave?" She handed him the grocery bag and headed out the back door.

When she got to the fountain she wished for it to rain candy gummies, but instead it rained jawbreakers. And she thought, *What the heck! This wasn't supposed to happen!* and looked up to see Michael quickly dashing into his room from the window. She was curious and confused at the same time. She also thought, *Maybe I was just seeing things because a piece of candy hit me in the head too hard. Yes, or maybe Sean and Michael's project materials accidentally fell out of his back window. But then why would they need candy for their project?* And then she was thinking that it was all in her head, shrugged, and went inside to start her homework.

Soon enough her parents were home, and it was dinnertime. Sean had to go, and her parents wanted Michael and Asha to tell them about their day. Michael went first and said he got an A on his math and social studies quizzes. Asha's mom said, "How was your day, sweetie?"

Asha was silent for a second. Then she said, "I found a penny on the curb, and I finished all of my homework." Asha didn't think her news was that great. She wanted to get off of her boring conversation, so she started a new one, "So, what was interesting about your day, Mom and Dad?"

"Well," her father said, "I got a raise from secretary to vice president!"

"Wow!" Asha's mom said. "That is so amazing! And you're not going to believe this...my boss liked my idea for the billboard!"

"Wow! Today is such a great day!" her dad said. "Kids, it is getting kind of late. So you two go upstairs and get ready for bed."

"But, Dad!" Michael said, "It's only 7:30!"

"Yes, I am aware of that. But still you need the rest."

"Fine. Come on, Asha. Let's go."

It was the next day, April 2, 2015, 7:00 A.M. Asha got dressed, brushed her teeth and hair, and headed downstairs. When she got down, her mom asked, "Good morning, Asha! What would you like for breakfast today?"

"Sorry Mom, not hungry."

"Well, you and Michael better get to school or you might be late!"

"Okay, bye, Mom!" Michael was still up in his room, so Asha thought, *Why not try out my penny again?* She was still hungry from not eat eating at breakfast, so she wished for scrambled eggs. You won't even guess what she got: yes, one raw, not scrambled, but one raw egg!

There was not enough time to go inside, so she ran as fast as she could to get to a seat with Bella, but the bus driver stopped her. The bus driver said, "You should clean that mess up right away before it sticks to your hair. Here, I have an old jacket you can borrow to try and clean up whatever that is."

"Thanks!" Asha said.

While she was trying to find Bella in a seat, everyone saw the egg in her hair! But she finally found Bella. As Asha sat down, Bella asked, "What happened?" Bella said it with a chuckle under her breath.

"I was trying out my penny this morning. I wanted scrambled eggs, and I got a raw one!" Asha said.

"Oh. Yeah, you should ask Mrs. Seabron in language arts if you could be excused to go to the gym showers to clean it off."

"That would work! Thanks Bella, great idea!"

"You're welcome, Asha."

When Bella and Asha headed into school, they rushed to their lockers, which were right next to each other. After, they got all of their supplies and headed to language arts. The bell had already rung, but Asha raised her hand. "Mrs. Seabron, can I go to the locker room and get the egg out of my hair?" she asked.

"Oh my, yes, you may," said Mrs. Seabron.

Asha headed to the locker room and started a shower. After her shower, she got all dressed again, and by the time she was done, it was free period. Bella was waiting outside of the locker rooms so that they could walk together. Then it was time for lunch. Bella and Asha sat at their usual table and started eating.

Asha started to talk about her penny and how strange it was. Bella said, "I don't think it was the penny, though. You know that your brother and his friend are really smart and good at tricking you."

"Yes, I was thinking about that because after I got hit with the candy, I saw someone—it was either Sean or Michael that was hitting me with it. It has to be...yes, because yesterday was April 1! Ha! Another one of his tricks!"

Asha got up to go see Michael and Sean with Bella. When she got to his table, she tapped on his shoulder and said, "I know you did it! You are the one who dropped the candy and the egg on me!"

"April fools!" said Michael. "Sorry if you didn't like it, though. I was just trying to make you believe in a penny that would grant your wishes."

"Okay, I won't tell Mom now that you apologized!" said Asha.

UNWELCOME INVADERS

A boy wakes up with mysterious powers never seen before. In **UNWELCOME INVADERS** *by **Dan Oakwood**, his new reality leads him to situations and places he never dreamed of.*

In Detroit, it was a usual morning for most people. John woke up with a strange feeling in his head. Yesterday he started seeing short, red people who gave him things, but it was probably a dream.

"Ugh, my feet hurt. I wish I could just be in the kitchen," John moaned. Suddenly John felt loud noises in his head, and he appeared in the kitchen. "Whoa, what just happened?" John said in alarm. "Maybe I was just dreaming." John had to get ready for school.

John started packing up binders from Mr. Fisher's homework. He ate his breakfast and headed to the bus stop. On the bus he thought, "This bus stinks. I wish I could just be home." John could hear the same loud noises in his head. John appeared in his room. "Ahh! Now I know there is something really wrong." John started to freak out.

"Eww, what's that smell? It seems like it's coming from downstairs. That's weird, because nobody's home today." John crept down the stairs slowly and stealthily. He looked around the corner of the kitchen wall. Then... *splotch!* His face was covered in sticky, slimy, green goo. Not very long later John fainted.

About an hour later John woke up with a loud buzzing in his ear. "Another headache," John groaned painfully.

When John seeped back into his senses he realized he was strapped to a shiny chrome chair. Some tall, green, slimy figures approached him with long needles and weapons, and then one of them said in a raspy voice, "Give us your powers, or we will take them by force." John kicked at the one with the needle. John quickly teleported out of the spaceship and appeared on a dark, green planet dotted with crater holes and plants.

The aliens rushed out of the ship, so John hid. John fell into some slimy and sticky red goo. Now the aliens knew where John was.

The aliens ran toward John, ready to attack him, but then the aliens saw the goo. They started to walk away. John threw some of the red goo at them. They screamed, and shrank until they were about one foot tall.

Suddenly some small red aliens jumped out of the goo and ate the green aliens.

The red aliens weren't harmful to John, and they took him to their city. John stayed there the night. The red aliens talked about the war they were in with the green aliens, far from Earth.

Suddenly the red aliens could hear loud explosions and see bright lasers. The green aliens were looking for John. He went through a pathway in the woods and crawled down a small mining tunnel to an old bomb shelter. There were shouts of both types of aliens, all fighting above him.

Some gooey hands grabbed at John and covered his mouth. He started yelling before he was dragged into a plane back to the green aliens' city.

John woke up in a prison with other aliens. The other aliens were blue and pink, and they said they were travelers who had gotten caught.

John had to make a plan to escape. The room John was in was dark, and the cells were rusty. John teleported to the keys room and took all the keys. He freed all the aliens to help him escape the planet. The freed aliens knocked out all the guards and escaped through an emergency hatch.

The green aliens had some broken ships from the war covering the ground. Some of the freed aliens fixed up a ship. The freed aliens and John all got on a ship and flew away. When John got to Earth everyone was looking for him.

WARNING! FISHING TRIP!

WARNING! FISHING TRIP!, *by* **Abbey Werthmann**, *is a story about two teenaged boys heading out to sea on an average, everyday adventure. When they have an unexpected encounter that has an unusual explanation, will anybody believe them?*

"Okay, let's go over the checklist one last time. Dead tuna fish and amber jacks?" I questioned.

"Check!" Louis said.

"Fishing poles?"

"Check!"

"Bucket, shoes, water, and life jackets?"

"Check!"

"Extra hooks, GoPro on, and last but not least, flashlights?"

"Check, check, and check, Isaac."

Okay, we were ready to head out in the Islamorada, Florida waters during lunchtime around 12:15. We had just eaten our lunch at Salty Sushi. We hopped onto the boat and started the engine. The name of the boat, *Mega Catcher*, glared from the reflection of the water on our way out to sea.

Louis and I decided to anchor our boat eight miles off shore. The waves were big, the flying fish flew through the wind, and dolphins chirped while the seagulls sang. We threw our lines out onto the water and set up all of our belongings. I sat up top on the boat by the second steering wheel, took a handful of Pringles, and took a great, big look at the flock of seagulls flying by. Louis, on the other hand— well, he kind of drank up all the Mountain Dew, the Coca-Cola, and the Orange Crush. He was practically running circles around the boat while I dozed off.

So far we had caught two barracudas, four tarpons, one wahoo, and three snappers. We were having a lucky day on the reef this afternoon.

We decided after about four hours of fishing that we would throw the rest of the baitfish back into the sea because we were done for the day. We were packing up our fish and the rest of our belongings when all of a sudden a big wave hit our boat.

"Probably just the wind picking up," Louis joked. All of a sudden we felt a thump coming from the bottom of the boat. Within a couple of seconds a humongous disoriented shark thing passed under us. Was it a whale? On this creature was a gigantic shark fin, beady red eyes, and a big, flat, white belly. It had features exactly like a megalodon, but was it too good to be true?

The creature made eye contact with me for a long time. With one big grin it splashed and tipped all of our big fish out of the boat, grabbed all our fish we caught that day, and devoured it in one ginormous gulp.

It caught onto our fishing line and jerked us, and then we started traveling farther from shore. As the creature pulled on the line, it seemed to drag us for about a mile and a half. All our baitfish and supplies kept flying everywhere and landing on the surface of the water. We went over all these crazy bumps so fast; we decided to hold onto the boat for our dear lives.

"Quick, Louis, grab something sharp! Hurry, because every two minutes we're dragged a half a mile farther from shore." Louis grabbed his pocketknife and within a couple of seconds a huge "snap" flung our boat. "Ouch!" All that was left of the snapped fishing poles fell on top of me.

We checked for any leaks in the boat or holes, and without finding a single one we scurried back to shore. We hopped off the boat and called Louis's closest friend, Frankie, to tell him what happened. Frankie wouldn't believe us because we didn't have proof. We were still in shock over what just happened.

Louis and I started unpacking the boat to take our minds off of it. Maybe it wasn't real. Maybe we were just in so much shock that our brain tricked us into thinking it was the megalodon. But what would explain the "thing" that dragged us out a whole mile and a half?

"Ouch!" As I went to stand up the GoPro camera bumped the back part of my head, leaving a yellow and purple bruise. This piece of garbage probably didn't even work.

I went to shut the camera off after having a disastrous day when I saw in the bottom right hand corner there were numbers counting up. I looked away, but quickly looked back because at that very moment we realized we had captured something no other person known to man has ever done before. "Do you know what this means?" I rewound the video with Louis and then I saw it: the creature from the deep, the megalodon.

WHEN YOU WISH UPON A BASEBALL

When Gabriella takes a shortcut home through an alleyway, she finds a magic baseball. In the story **WHEN YOU WISH UPON A BASEBALL** *by* **Sarah Johns***, you will go on a journey through the danger of wishing.*

Gabriella dashed out of Tiger Stadium overjoyed with excitement. The Detroit Tigers had just won the 1984 World Series. She slowed down as she approached a dark alley. She knew it was a shortcut home, so she proceeded through it. As she was walking, she tripped.

"Ouch," she exclaimed. She looked back and realized she had tripped over a baseball. She picked up the ball and noticed that the seams were ripped. Gabriella stood up and grabbed the ball. She threw the ball up a couple of times. Suddenly she heard a piercing scream coming from the ball!

"Thanks for waking me up," said the ball.

"Ahhhhhhhhh!" Gabriella screamed, dropping the ball. It rolled around, and she could see that it had two gigantic eyes and a mouth.

"Hi," it said in an annoyed voice. "I grant wishes; be careful what you wish for; blah, blah, blah."

"How are you able to talk?" Gabriella asked in a shaky voice.

"A long time ago a witch found me and decided to put a curse on me for an unknown reason. The curse made me talk and made me grant wishes. Some kids found me and played with me here, in the alley, for a couple of years. But one day, they never came back," explained the ball, sounding very annoyed.

"Cool!" she said excitedly. "I wish I was an MLB player!"

"Your wish is granted," groaned the ball. Before she could blink, she was dressed in a New York Yankees uniform.

"Oh great, I am on the team no one likes," exclaimed Gabriella, sounding very disappointed. She grabbed the ball, sprinted the rest of the way home, and burst through the door.

"Honey, go pack. We leave for New York tomorrow," said her mom.

"Okay," Gabriella said excitedly.

The next day, when they arrived in New York, they headed straight to Yankee Stadium. The team all welcomed her, and they headed into the dugout.

"Well, let's see you pitch," said the coach as he threw a ball and a glove at her.

Just before she left the dugout she grabbed the magic ball and quickly whispered, "I wish I was a good pitcher."

"Your wish is granted," the ball whispered back.

She walked out to the pitcher's mound. She pitched a couple, and her coach ran out to her.

"You are the best pitcher on the team! You will be our starting pitcher for every game of the season," he announced. As she walked back into the dugout, all of her teammates were staring at her. This made Gabriella feel very awkward.

One of the other pitchers came up to her and complained, "Because of you, the rest of the starters will now be traded! Thanks for showing off!"

"I didn't mean to!" Gabriella said.

"Well, now all the team hates you, so why don't you quit the team?" he said meanly. She took the magic ball out once again and wished that her team liked her.

The next day, her whole team came in and started giving her everything from sunflower seeds to World Series trophies. It was a little creepy. She didn't want this much stuff. *How can I fix this?* she thought. *The ball!* She ran over to her bat bag and grabbed the ball.

"I wish everything would go back to normal, and I was back home in Detroit," she said. She heard an unusual chime and ran out to the baseball diamond. She looked around and realized she was not home but still in Yankee Stadium.

"Nothing happened," exclaimed Gabriella.

"Did I forget to mention that you can only make three wishes?" laughed the ball.

She glanced at the ball in her hand and said in a mad voice, "How can I fix this?"

"All you have to do is destroy me, but you wouldn't want to do that to a poor old ball like me, would you?"

"Yes, I would. You did all this to me," said Gabriella. "But how can I trust you? Maybe you just want me to put an end to your strange life, and I'll be stuck with the one I have now."

The ball sighed. "I told you that you have to be careful what you wish for. There is another part to the curse, too. I have to answer everything truthfully."

She dashed out of the stadium and hopped into her mom's car. They drove to their small apartment they had rented in New York, and Gabriella rushed into her room. She rummaged around for her pocket knife that her dad had given her last year for her birthday. She started to cut the leather off the ball.

"Ouch. Stop, stop, stop," cried the ball. "Please, I want to live!"

"No, I don't want this anymore. I want everything to go back to normal," exclaimed Gabriella. She finished cutting it, and before she could blink she was back in the alley near Tiger Stadium. The ball was nowhere to be seen. Gabriella walked home and couldn't have been happier to be there.

THE WONDER OF VOICE

A teenaged girl hopes to compete on a popular televised talent show. In **THE WONDER OF VOICE** by *Alexandra Kochanek*, Adele must perform as well as she ever has in order to help her family and realize her dreams.

A s I wake up in the orange, dewy sunlight, I stare at my alarm clock as it beeps, telling me to wake up. I hit the snooze button like a billion times, but it still won't stop. So I unplug it and hear knocking at my door. "Adele, get dressed and come downstairs to eat," Mom says loudly.

"Okay, Mom," I reply. I run to my closet and grab all of my clothes, place them on my bed, quickly scan through them, and pick out my outfit for the day. It's a red shirt, blue jeans, and a black leather jacket. I think that the judges of the popular TV show *America's Got Talent* will like it, too.

Today is my big day. If I make it and get to the finale, I might win a prize of a million dollars. And that would be really awesome. I would not have to worry about how I am going to pay for my college since Mom lost her job last year and Dad is the only one who supports our family financially.

As I rush downstairs, I notice the smell of Mom's perfume, which is like the ocean's breeze and warm coconut milk. It always makes me feel happy. I walk to the kitchen, and Mom is making her famous blueberry and banana pancakes.

Katy, my little sister, rushes in wearing her panda bear pajamas. "Mom, what's the big wake up call?" she asks, puzzled.

"Today is Adele's big day, remember?" Mom says with a smile. "So let's hurry up, so we won't be late."

As we arrive in front of the Detroit Opera House, where I'm going to sing today, we immediately see the giant crowd of people lining up in hopes of passing the TV celebrities' votes. Even the road is brimming with all kinds of cars and trucks. As Mom, Katy, and I approach the lines, there are immediately hundreds of more people behind us. Where did they come from so fast? Or am I so nervous that I can barely pay attention to what is going on around me? "Well, I suppose we've got to wait now," Mom says tiredly.

After three hours of sitting and walking gradually, we see a camera crew moving toward us. "You mind letting us interview you?" the blond-haired man asks. Mom nudges me, trying to let me know to accept their offer.

"All right, we are on in three, two, one," the blond-haired producer from NBC television loudly says. As the beaming lights shine at me, I say, "My name is Adele, and I'm sixteen years old. I live in Sterling Heights, Michigan with my mom, dad, and my little sister Katy. My dream is to go to the Hollywood University of the Arts to become a professional singer and songwriter. My family has struggled with the economy since my mom lost her job. My dad is the only one who works, and it does not look so bright for me to be able to afford a college. So here I am."

The other producers ask me many question about what I do in my spare time and why I think *America's Got Talent* is going to help me achieve my dream.

After the interview it is almost my turn to perform. The girl in pink hair and leather outfit that was standing in front of me has been gone for a while, so I should be next any minute now.

All of a sudden the host of the show, handsome Chris Lanner, is standing next to me. He smells so good. He must be wearing some expensive cologne. He asks in a gleeful voice, "Hello there, what's your name and how old are you?"

I answer in a serene voice, "I'm Adele, and I'm sixteen."

He says back, "Well, Adele, what are you going to be doing for us today?"

I reply, "I am going to be singing 'Rolling in the Deep.'"

"The judges are waiting out there for you," he says with an upbeat tone.

Here I am standing on the stage of this beautiful opera house. The spotlight beams are shining at my tan skin, making it glow. As I approach center stage, I glance at the celebrity judges of *America's Got Talent*. I can't believe my eyes! Sitting with them is Melanie Brown. She used to sing with the Spice Girls. She still sings, but solo. I love her voice and the way she performs. I'm even more nervous now.

But I need to keep calm if I want to do my best. I close my eyes for just a moment and tell myself, "This is it, go for it." I open my eyes, take a deep breath, and slowly exhale. After greeting them, they ask me about my interests and my backstory.

"Let's hear you then," they say. So I start to sing. I have nothing to lose.

There's a fire starting in my heart,
Reaching a fever pitch and it's bringing me out the
dark.

When I finish my song I feel really good. All the nervousness is gone. When I look at the judges again, I can see all of them standing up, clapping, smiling, and shouting "Bravo," and I just can't believe my eyes! I think I did it. I think I will go to the finale and perform live on TV and maybe even win and not have to worry about paying or getting into the college of my dreams.

I stand under the lights at Radio City Music Hall in New York. This is the final round of *America's Got Talent*. I'm standing here with the other two contestants, a rapper called Champagne and a dance group called Electronics. We are patiently, but nervously, waiting for the results.

"And the results are in," Chris says. "This year's *America's Got Talent* final two are...Electronics and Adele Parker. So can we give them a round of applause?"

The Electronics and I step forward. Chris gets between us and begins, "Now, the winner of *America's Got Talent* is..." There is a moment of silence. I can't believe that a music hall with so many people in it can be so quiet. I can almost hear my heart. "Congratulations to...Adele Parker!"

"Yes!" I shout in my head and give everybody a huge smile. Chris gives me a big hug and a kiss on my cheek. I am so happy and hug him right back and also place a big kiss on his left cheek.

Then I'm trying to find my parents. Everybody is standing up, shouting and clapping, and my eyes can't find them. But I know they are there. It seems as though my dream came true.

WRITE AWAY

Writing has power. In **WRITE AWAY,** *by* **Ryan M. Goodman,** *young Roger McFin discovers he has amazing power and learns what the words "Writing has power" really mean.*

Writing is my favorite class of the school day. When I get to just sit here and write, I feel free and creative. I feel like everything that I write can come alive. I didn't know that this was not so far from the truth.

During class we had a free write, where anyone could write anything. That day I felt like writing about mythical beasts under my command. My pen touched the paper, and I wrote: *Lord Roger McFin, wielder of great magical powers, summoned a warrior dragon to serve and protect him from all who oppose him.*

All of a sudden, I felt light-headed. The paper swirled around my head, and suddenly a tiny dragon seemingly made of blank paper appeared out of nowhere! Then it disappeared! Maybe I had just imagined it? Or maybe it was really there?

As my curiosity got the better of me, I wrote: *A small gold dragon with wings of fire and razor sharp teeth was created with one purpose, to serve Lord Roger McFin.* I felt the light-headedness again, and then a small dragon appeared on my desk! This time it didn't disappear, and it was just as I had described it. I slowly wrote the words *the dragon was dismissed* on my paper, and it disappeared.

As my excitement grew even more I hurriedly wrote: *A large dragon of great power with giant wings, claws that could cut through titanium, and fire breath appeared, screaming, "Serve Lord Roger McFin!"* It appeared immediately this time, in the middle of the classroom. It bellowed, "Serve Lord Roger McFin!"

I yelled, "Freeze!" The dragon stood stock-still, surveying its surroundings. All the students froze, too scared to move or scream—at first. Then all I heard was screaming. One kid even fainted! They were scared. So I said, "Guys, calm down, everything is under control."

Then, Mrs. Laard, my teacher, was looking from me to the dragon; back and forth, back and forth, as if she couldn't believe what she was seeing. So I yelled, "Dismissed!" and the dragon faded away.

She yelled, "What is going on, Roger!" As I turned back toward the front of the room, I saw Mrs. Laard talking on the phone. She then told everyone to stay where they were. So the entire class sat, whispering to each other. I heard people whispering about the dragon, and how I was going to be in trouble. I was starting to get scared. But that was just the beginning of the fright!

Three minutes later, a tank drove up the street with the letters "H.O.U.S.E." on the side. A group of men leaped into the room, yelling, "We are part of the Happenings of Unusual Supernatural Evolution Department." I realized that they had come for me. If I didn't act, they might damage my friends. I had to protect the school—and myself!

The first thing I did was write: *The evil H.O.U.S.E. men were blown through the roof and away from the school by a giant fan.* And of course a huge fan appeared, and they were literally blown through the roof! Next I wrote: *The hero Roger McFin, wearing his chainmail armor that made him invulnerable and was still weightless, his gloves which gave him super strength, and his cape which allowed him to fly, summoned one hundred thousand giant warrior dragons with gold scales and impenetrable armor to serve him and to be his army. He then summoned a red Pegasus with a horn made of titanium and impenetrable armor to ride on during the battle. Next he created laser cannons to fire at the enemies, and summoned an army of futuristic snipers with lasers to protect the school. Last, Roger McFin made the school into a castle surrounded by a moat.* And as I wrote that last period and lifted my pen, the school became a fortress.

After I did that, my two best friends, Selina Stein and Bob Gordo, ran up to me. Out of breath I said, "Guys, we're in for a huge fight." And then the cannon fire began. I had no idea they had cannons! I was about to write something on my paper when I felt a cold hand over my eyes! All I could do before I was grabbed was yell, "Help!"

A few minutes later I was sitting in a chair with a rope around my hands. I saw Mrs. Laard sitting behind the desk. She said, "I can't allow you to escape, Roger; you are dangerous. H.O.U.S.E. will be here any min—Uh!" All of a sudden, Mrs. Laard was on the ground and Bob was standing above her. Selina was standing behind me untying the rope around my hands.

"Thanks, you guys!" I said. I ran to the pen and paper and wrote: *The school was surrounded by a force-field of pure energy.* I ran outside. The H.O.U.S.E. trucks were driving away! We had won!

I knew that I couldn't let people remember that I had these abilities. So I wrote: *Lord Roger McFin used a spell to make everyone except for himself and his trusted allies Bob and Selina forget all about his powers.* And of course, it worked.

Now, every day I think about the power of writing. I test my limits, and do things no one can do. I learned writing has power. And I can control it!

11:15

100 DOLLAR BILL

In **100 DOLLAR BILL** by *Ateeyah Abdulwasi*, *a girl is thrilled when some unexpected money comes her way. But is it really right to keep it?*

When I saw that money, I knew I shouldn't have touched it. I should have just walked away, but instead I was battling myself to walk away. I was too weak, and I took the 100-dollar bill anyway. *What now?* I thought.

Let's go back in time for a minute. It was the same weather, and everyone was wearing the same clothes, but what are you supposed to expect from California? Anyway, I was on my way to entering the Forever 21 store to look at some clothes that I couldn't buy. Just as I was walking into the store, I spotted a 100-dollar bill peeking out from under a car. *What should I do? Should I take it or leave it?* I thought, but I had no time to think, because someone else had also spotted the money. So I quickly said, "That is my money." They then walked away, and I took the money.

All I thought at that moment when the money was in my possession was that I was going to buy my dream dress. I headed inside Forever 21, and since I had the money to buy the dress, I might as well. The price tag read $90. "Perfect," I said.

The cashier, Bobby, asked me for the money, and I handed it to him. Bobby has worked here ever since I first came two years ago. I had never bought anything there before, so that led Bobby to ask, "Where did all the money come from?"

"I...found...it?" I said, and smiled awkwardly. He was surprised; I started to feel guiltier for what I did.

"So you thought just because you found the money it means that it's yours?"

I told him everything. "I feel really bad now," I proclaimed. "What should I do?"

"That's up to you. Look, I wish I could help, but I have to get back to work," Bobby said, and then he rang up my dress and went to the next customer.

I knew what I had to do then and there: I had to raise the money and find whom it belongs to.

After looking for so many jobs, I finally got a job at PacSun. It took about two months or so to get the money back. Then I started to look for the person who owned the money.

One day I was on a tour bus when I finally found her there. She was still looking for her money. I decided to go up to her. I handed her the money and told her what happened.

ALIENS AND CARDBOARD PEOPLE

If aliens make our acquaintance one day, from which direction would you expect them to arrive? **ALIENS AND CARDBOARD PEOPLE** *by* **James D. Morphew** *may keep you from digging a hole ever again.*

Sharkey, Larry, and Bob are 12 years old and have been friends for as long as they can remember. There is something special about these boys, and that is that they each have parents who work at Area 51. This top-secret connection gives these ordinary-looking middle-school boys access to super-advanced technology.

One day the boys were walking to school and talking about the teacher and staff costume competition that students were going to judge today. When the boys approached the school they noticed it was empty-looking. It was silent: no people hanging around, no people going in or out of the doors, no people anywhere.

"Hey! Is this our lucky day?" asked Bob. "No school?"

"Kind of strange that everyone knows except us," said Larry.

Suddenly, they saw something fall out of a second-story window. Something rather large, something rather flat, twirled through the air and crashed into the bushes. "What was that?" they all yelled together. The boys ran to the bushes for a closer inspection. To their surprise, they found themselves looking at a cardboard cutout of their principal Mr. Flopperstopper.

The boys looked up at the open window. Peeking down at them they saw a rather strange-looking figure with a giant head.

"An alien!" Sharkey yelled.

The odd-looking figure said, "No, no, no; I'm just in my costume, and it disguised me from the real aliens that are looking for the humans. The aliens have invaded the school, and turned every person they saw into a cardboard cutout!"

"I don't believe you," said Bob.

"Me neither," said Larry.

Then the alien-looking thing pulled off his mask and said, "It's me, your teacher Mr. Pencilshavings, and it's true! I think my costume kept me from being discovered right away. Boys, we must run away and hide."

Then Mr. Pencilshavings climbed out the window, dangled from the window ledge by his fingertips, and dropped into the bushes.

"Everybody," said Larry, "let's get to our secret hiding spot. Mr. Pencilshavings, follow us."

Their secret hiding spot is actually a giant tree house built in the middle of a stand of 120-foot silver maple trees; they've been building the tree house for the past year. It is made from titanium, with invisible plating that they got from Sharkey's crazy scientist uncle. All that could be seen from the outside were four very large, very tall trees and a rope which looked like it was dangling in midair.

The boys, one by one, climbed the rope, and each boy disappeared as he entered the tree house. Mr. Pencilshavings stared in disbelief.

"Quick, Mr. Pencilshavings, climb up!" exclaimed Bob. Mr. Pencilshavings followed the rope and landed inside the tree house with the boys.

They entered the supersonic elevator to go to Sharkey's room on the 80th floor in the invisible building. The elevator doors opened and everyone screamed in horror at the alien that was looking right at them. Everyone jumped to hit the down button on the elevator, but it was Mr. Pencilshavings's head that actually pushed the button. Down at floor negative 50, the group exited into an underwater cave where a submarine was waiting.

Sharkey led the group into the submarine, "Quickly, everyone!" he shouted. Then Sharkey took the driver's seat as Bob closed the hatch behind them. Sharkey navigated the submarine through an underwater tube that led to his underwater house.

They reached a giant garage door that opened when Sharkey pressed the big red button on the control panel. The submarine coasted into the underwater garage and docked a few feet away from the door to the house. Sharkey pushed another button, and all the water drained from the garage. At the same time, wheels emerged from the submarine so it could stand on the garage floor.

"Can we use that hovercraft that you keep on the roof?" asked Larry.

"Sure," answered Sharkey, "but the elevator is broken, so we will have to put on SCUBA gear and swim up to the roof."

Outfitted in the SCUBA gear, the fearless foursome left the garage and stared swimming upward. Slowly they swam up to the rooftop of the underwater house, which looked like a giant lily pad when viewed from the outdoors.

Sharkey pushed a large green button on the bottom of the lily pad. Silently, a large hole appeared in the lily pad. The four heads popped up from the water to see a shiny, chrome hovercraft rising out of the secret compartment. They all tossed their SCUBA gear onto the lily pad and entered the hovercraft.

"Hey, this is awesome!" said Mr. Pencilshavings. "May I drive?"

"Only if you put the pedal to the metal and fly really fast," answered Sharkey.

So they blasted off the helipad at 1,000 mph. As they zoomed through the sky, they saw a most peculiar sign at an altitude of 35,000 feet. It was a hologram sign with a single word, "Headquarters."

"The only headquarters way up here has to be alien," exclaimed Bob. "Head for it!"

Mr. Pencilshavings made an expert maneuver, bringing the hovercraft in on the alien landing deck. They exited the hovercraft and were immediately attacked. But Larry was prepared with giant plasma swords for all that melted the alien weapons when the activation button was pushed. They won; the humans won!

The fearless foursome checked out the alien base and found a doorway with a sign that said, "General Hipperdipper Private Office." They entered the room and approached the alien general. Suddenly, the general's guards jumped out and attacked them. Once again, the foursome fought with their plasma swords, and once again they won.

Bob asked the general, "Sir, why are you taking the humans?"

The general spent some time thinking and then answered, "To protect our people. We are an underground-dwelling species. We have been exploring the universe, inside the planets, looking for alternate homes. Our home planet was attacked by the Marphonians and exploded! Unfortunately, on Earth, the humans are igniting the natural gas underground, and our homes are burning.

"Stop burning us out of our homes," demanded General Hipperdipper. "This station holds the last of us."

Larry, Bob, Sharkey, and Mr. Pencilshavings huddled and discussed their answer. "We know the Natural Gas Association is burning the underground reserves, but we can't stop them," said Larry.

"No," answered Bob to the general, "we cannot stop the burning."

Suddenly, the foursome was attacked once again, from all sides. The swords clanged, and yelling and screaming filled the air. Larry, Bob, Sharkey, and Mr. Pencilshavings once again emerged victorious! The aliens retreated to their getaway spaceship and flew off to a distant galaxy at 50,000,000,000 miles per nanosecond. In an instant, they were gone.

Back at the school, and all the other locations that had cardboard people, the cutout people were restored to their human bodies. Nobody had any memory of the alien incident except for Bob, Larry, Sharkey, and Mr. Pencilshavings.

The boys restored peace on Earth...or so they thought. There remains to this day a small group of aliens hiding underground in an abandoned mineshaft, and every once in a while a cardboard cutout of a person appears at the mine entrance.

AMESTIA

*On the same day Emily and Olivia discover the kingdom of Amestia, they learn that it is in great danger. In **AMESTIA** by **Aarani Balendran**, two normal girls are sent on a quest to stop Amestia from being destroyed forever.*

All but one of the lights in Amestia were off. In the deepest and darkest part of Amestia lived the evil sorcerer, Antonio. He was in his lab making his invisibility potion. "The last ingredient, a leaf," he said as he gently dropped it in the beaker. When the leaf dissolved, he poured a drop on an apple to test it. Quickly it disappeared, but he could still feel it. "I did it!" he exclaimed. He poured some on himself and started his journey toward the palace.

The palace was the home of the Amethyst. The Amethyst charges all sources of magic. Antonio needed the Amethyst to gain enough power to rule the kingdom. As he walked through the palace with no worry, out of nowhere a purple light started to glow. He entered the hall, and there it was. "It is here." He quickly grabbed it and ran home.

Back in his lab, Antonio took out his spell book. He needed to get the magic from the Amethyst to his wand. When he fully read the page it said he needed ice daisies, goggle berry ferns, and the tallest piece of grass from the tallest peak of Amestia. He would have to melt the stone with the potion and soak his wand in the remains of the stone. To find these things he would have to travel. He would have to leave the stone at home because it would attract too much attention. Finally he left, leaving his house armed with a surprise.

Meanwhile, in the real world, two best friends, Emily and Olivia, couldn't wait until graduation. At International Academy, or IA, graduation was the biggest deal ever. It was a lot of fun, too. There is the ceremony first, and then the school party, and after that many students host parties for almost a whole week. The next week would be filled with college tours. Emily and Olivia were both excited for graduation day, but not for the same reason. Even though they were both extremely intelligent, Olivia was more excited about parties rather than going to college. On the other hand, Emily was very happy about her early acceptance to Harvard.

It was the day before graduation, and the school was buzzing with excited seniors. Emily and Olivia lived two minutes from school, so they usually walked home. At the end of sixth hour the bell finally rang. They both met in the front of the school and started walking home.

About halfway there, Olivia spotted something glowing in the bushes. "What's that?" screamed Emily.

"It looks like a portal," replied Olivia.

"Portals shouldn't exist, and there is no other world but ours for it to go to. It is a scientific fact!" said Emily.

"Let's go in!" said Olivia, and she did not wait for an answer. She hopped right in.

Emily hesitated, but followed. *This might be an interesting adventure*, Emily thought.

Antonio was losing his patience trying to find the ice daisies. They only grew in the coldest part of Amestia. He was so cold that even though he had a ten-pound parka on, he was freezing.

He was climbing up the mountain, and he saw a sparkle behind the bushes. He walked over there and looked behind it. There was a whole garden full! He plucked one from the ground and put it in his bag.

When the girls landed in a different world, they were amazed. The trees were silver, and the lake water was purple. They landed in the forest. The place was beautiful. They kept walking until two soldiers came and surrounded them. Only one thought was in their heads: they were trapped. They had to fight.

Emily took care of one, and Olivia took the other one. Emily punched him in the stomach, and he flew into a tree. Anyone just watching her fight should know that she is a black belt in every type of fighting. Olivia, on the other hand, was new at this. She did really well for a first time. She spun him around and pushed him into a tree.

They started to leave, but in the corner of her eye, Olivia saw one of the soldiers get up. Both girls turned around and went back into fighting position. Instead of attacking, one of the soldiers said, "Congratulations." The girls were very confused.

Not a minute later, a messenger came to say that the queen would like to see them at the palace. They were still confused, but went with him.

Once they got to the palace, the queen explained what Antonio did and that she had tested them with the soldiers to see if they were worthy of getting the quest.

"But why did you need people from our world?" Emily interrupted.

"People in this kingdom have heard stories about Antonio that aren't true. Antonio was described as a horrible monster. Even our bravest knight was scared," said the queen.

"If he already has the stone, then what do you need us for?" asked Olivia.

"He must get the magic into his wand, and he needs a potion to do that. He is currently out of his house, and the stone is in his house. You will also need these." She held out a map and a bag of magic dust. "Good luck."

Antonio had just grabbed the goggle berry ferns from the farm. He had to sneak past the farmer who was very carefully cutting apples. Antonio got by fast and easily to pick the colorful little leaves from the goggle berry tree. He had one more item to go, so he quickly stashed the leaves in his bag and ran to Mt. Figgy, the tallest peak in Amestia. On his way he bought a ruler so he would know exactly which blade of grass was the tallest.

He ran up the mountain and realized that he did not need a ruler. On top of the mountain there was a blade of grass three feet taller than the others. "Come on, that was totally a waste of three gold coins!" he complained to himself.

The girls were following the map to the deepest part of Amestia. They couldn't help but notice that it kept getting darker as they walked forward. When they reached Antonio's house, a robot came out of nowhere. Olivia distracted it as Emily unwired it so it would shut down.

Emily and Olivia saw Antonio running into his house. They had to stop him. They ran into his house, but they could not see him. *He must be using his invisibility*, thought Olivia. She took out the magic dust, and he was revealed.

Antonio was ready to fight. "You will never get out of here without me being the most powerful man in the world!" he said. He was about to pour the potion on the stone.

"Noooool" Olivia rushed over and pushed the beaker out of his hand. It shattered on the floor. As they watched that, Emily grabbed the stone.

"Olivia!" Emily signaled, and they ran to the palace.

Antonio chased after them. "Get back here with my stone!" he screamed as he tried to think of a plan. Then it clicked, and he grabbed his wand and tried to hit them with his freeze ray, but they were moving too quickly.

They arrived at the palace. The guards captured Antonio, and the girls gave the stone to the queen. "Thank you," said the queen.

"We have to go!" said Olivia.

"Our parents must be so worried!" said Emily.

"Do not worry. No time has passed since you got here," said the queen.

It was finally the day. The girls were in their seats. Then they heard their names. As they went up to get their diplomas, they knew they had not had their last encounter with Amestia, knowing something that amazing would never end in one day.

THE BASEBALL TEAM

THE BASEBALL TEAM *by **Scott Rolf** is a story about a kid trying out for a baseball team. He learns you should keep trying even when you lose hope, for there is a chance of anything.*

I had done my homework, and eaten dinner, and I would go to bed in half an hour. Eventually, since I couldn't think of anything to do, I went on the computer.

When I got on the computer, I saw an advertisement for a local baseball team, the Cardinals. I am no superstar, but can hit, field, and throw. I noticed that tryouts were this Saturday and got permission and a ride to tryouts. I thought that if I made the team, it would increase my skills, and it would make me look more athletic.

The next day at school I saw my friend Chris. "Hey, Chris," I said. "Wanna come with me to tryouts for the Cardinals on Saturday? It's a new league since our old one only goes to eighth grade."

"Sure, I'll be there," said Chris. I was nervous he would watch me embarrass myself, but I knew that he couldn't impress the coach that much either.

On Saturday, Chris and I went to the tryouts. The guy running it gave a small speech. "There are four stations, fielding, pitching, hitting and running. Two spots, one's a pitcher, one is not. If you don't pitch then you don't have to complete the challenge."

Fielding was challenge number one. The coach hit us balls as we hopefully recovered them and accurately threw them back. I was looking good and thought I might have a shot.

My hopes decreased when Chris said, "Whoa, who is that because he is amazing."

"That is Steve," I said. "I heard that he has played travel since he was seven."

Pitching was next. The coach called locations, pitches and speeds as the competitors tried to follow the requests. After running this kid I didn't know, Chris, Steve, and I made the cut to hitting.

Chris was first in the cage, hitting three of five and blasting one. The next guy did a little worse than Chris did. I hit four, but none were exactly impressive. I knew that I had done well, but I was nervous because I knew that if Steve did better than or as well as me then he would get the spot. As I feared, Steve put on a show, and not in my favor. It was over with the crack of the bat, and we all knew it.

The other day when I was watching TV, I got a letter from the team's coach. He said that since I didn't make the team but was still really good I could play as a backup. I was excited because I got to go to practices and games, hoping to pinch hit, field or run and possibly make my way to the starting lineup. It would increase my skills and make me better.

It will also help take my mind off of school.

CAPTAIN RYAN VS. JUPITER

The last, best hope for Earthlings is to find another planet where they can make a new home. In **CAPTAIN RYAN VS. JUPITER,** *Benjamin Simmons tells of the encounter that almost ended that mission before it really got started.*

On the way to Jupiter, Captain Ryan saw odd flashing lights in the distance. He also came into close encounters with asteroids. When he was far enough out he could see Earth as a star.

Captain Ryan's mission was to find another planet for humans to live on. They needed another to live on because humans had polluted Earth. Captain Ryan was trying to be a hero by saving humans from the pollution. Ryan was headed to Jupiter first because he could just get it out of the way.

After seven years, Ryan finally made to Jupiter. "Wait, is that land and not gas? Houston, I see land on Jupiter!

Cccccccccccchhchchhhhhhhh. BOOM! Ryan crashed into Jupiter. When Ryan landed he was amazed by the advanced buildings and other structures. He was standing on a planet that was supposed to be a gas ball.

Ryan saw a silhouette, and he walked toward it. He was terrified and interested at the same time. He was thinking about communicating with whatever it is. What else could be crazier than a giant gas ball suddenly becoming a real planet that he could breathe on?

As he moved toward the creature, it got bigger and more detailed. The thing was very tall and muscular and had four arms. It was large with lots of teeth like a shark. The creature hit Ryan and knocked him out and grabbed him.

When he woke up, creatures surrounded him. The leader said, "Why are you here, how did you get here, and are there more of your kind coming?"

Ryan asked, "How do you know English?"

The leader replied, "We studied these things called Humans, a very young inhabitant of Earth. We are the Jupiterainians, and you are not welcome on our planet. I am sorry, but now we must execute you so the word about us doesn't get out."

"Why?" asked Ryan.

The leader replied, "We are afraid of Humans and their destruction."

As the large alien carried Ryan to the prison, Ryan grabbed a knife out of the Jupiterainian's pocket. When he got to the prison he cut the lock with the knife. He ran to his rocket with an army of Jupiterainians chasing him.

All of the Jupiterainians chasing him were trying to stop him. When he got to his ship he took off and was on the run for four years until he lost the Jupiterainians.

While he was away, Earth was not getting any better. There was lots of pollution. When he got back to Earth the humans said to prove what he claimed had happened on Jupiter. He took them back, and they settled agreements with the Jupiterainians.

COPPER

All Morgan wants is a horse. In **COPPER** *by* **Erica White**, *she takes matters into her own hands to get one.*

"Morgan!" my mom yelled. "Come downstairs."

"Okay!" I yelled in reply.

"Why don't you get your brothers while you're at it."

Here is how someone might describe me: Morgan Rodgers is a nice girl who enjoys riding horses. Morgan fits the middle-child role perfectly in almost every way. But something is missing in her life. What is missing is a horse. The horse would make her life complete.

"Tyson, Ash, Fletcher! Mom needs you!" They were out in the field riding their horses. This reminded me about how much I wanted my own horse, too. My mom thinks otherwise. She thinks a proper lady doesn't need a horse, but I am no proper lady by any means. My family owns a farm with much work needing to be done. Since I help, I wear brown embroidered leather boots, a pair of jeans, and a messy shirt. I have brown-colored hair.

I asked my parents if I could get a horse, but they said no. After my parents turned down my horse idea, I decided I would get the horse on my own. My parents were away with my brothers. I took advantage of this, stole a horse, and ran away.

I stayed where no one would find me in the woods. It was a small, old horse stable that nobody went to anymore. I had money saved up from helping on the farm to pay for food. It was warm, so I didn't need much stuff.

When it started to get cooler, it was harder to stay comfortable. I missed my family and farm.

I could not sleep that night. I wanted to go home and see them. I did not know if they would let me keep the horse or not, but I would find out.

The next day I went home. They were mad at me, but happy I was back.

They talked to the owner of the horse and bribed him. When they got to half off the price of food from our farm and some money, he said that we could have the horse.

DEMONS, GODS, AND ALEX ROSS

*This is a story about two best friends who would die for each other—
literally. In* **DEMONS, GODS, AND ALEX ROSS** *by* **Riley Donaldson***, one
of them may just have to do so.*

This is a story of two 12-year-old girls, Madison and Alex, who
are best friends. For starters, Madison's family is from Salem
but moved to Egypt before Madison turned four years old.
She has just lost her mother and grandmother in a fire. She is now
staying with her aunt who lives in Cairo. That was two days ago.
She is heartbroken and is willing to do anything at this point to get
her mother and grandmother back.

Madison's friend Alex looks normal, but on the inside she is
anything but the definition of ordinary. Alex is a demigod: half
human and half god. Alex's mother is an English teacher in Egypt,
and her dad is Osiris, the god of the dead.

Now that I'm done explaining Alex, let me tell you how Madison
and Alex became friends. They first started being friends when
Madison moved to Cairo. There was a force like gravity pulling
them together. When Madison and Alex started kindergarten they
were drawn to each other. They were impossible to separate. So
they stopped fighting the force that pulled them together and just
stayed together mostly all the time. That's how they became best
friends.

Recently, Madison was being taught how to summon gods by
her grandmother. It seemed as if her grandmother was forcing her
to perfect the spell day and night. Madison had to keep practicing
summoning gods. She hated that she couldn't do the spells that she
wanted, but she had to do it. It would crush her grandmother if she
didn't. She knew there was a reason why she had to learn this spell
the day she asked her grandmother, "Why do I have to learn this
spell?"

Her grandmother simply replied, "In due time, child."

Today was the day before spring break and two days after the death of Madison's mom. Madison was shattered. Then she realized what she and her grandmother had been practicing.

She went to her room to summon the only god she knew. She had not learned how to summon other gods before her grandmother passed. She put a magic lock on the door so no one could interrupt her while she was in the middle of her spell. She started to chant, and smoke came off the ground and formed around her in a circle. The circle changed colors from black to red. With the sound of wood breaking, she fell into a hole underneath her. It was about a five-minute fall.

When she reached the bottom she heard an unfamiliar voice. She saw a red shadow and said to herself, "There's a first for everything." Then out of the dark stepped a man.

She bowed and said, "Hello, Hades."

She tried to introduce herself but was cut off when Hades said, "I know who you are, Madison, and I know why you're here. Leave now, or don't leave at all!"

"Let's make a deal," said Madison.

"Fine," said Hades, "what's the deal?"

Madison replied swiftly, "A soul for a soul: my mother is to be brought back from the dead, and I'm to be banished to the land of the dead."

"Deal," said Hades. "Say your goodbyes quickly. You have one day until you are banished to the land of the dead."

Then it was all over. Madison was back at her house in her bed. She was exhausted, so she fell asleep.

The sound of her best friend banging at the door woke her up. She quickly jolted out of bed, took the spell off the door, and tried to say "Come in," but Alex had already walked in and started pulling outfits out of her extra book bag.

Alex asked, "Do you want the gold or the white leggings to go with your dress? Wait, never mind; the gold looks cuter on you." Within an hour the two girls had decided their outfits for the last day before summer break.

Going into school that day, Alex knew it would be a great day, and Madison knew that day would be her last day in the land of the living.

The day went great. The girls said their goodbyes to all their classmates because they would not see them over break, and in Madison's case, EVER!

The two girls just so happened to be the last people to leave the school. Madison started to tremble when she saw black-red smoke rising from the ground, Alex was confused. She knew what the smoke meant; she just didn't know why Hades was here.

Suddenly Hades spoke. "Madison," he said, and the ground beneath them trembled for a while. When it stopped the world was silent, and he spoke again. "Madison, in trade for your mother's soul I will take yours. Is that correct?"

Madison was about to say yes when Alex cut her off. "No, that is not correct, Hades. You will take my soul and my soul only, not me and Madison and not me and Madison's mother. You will also send my soul to Osiris, god of the dead"—also known as Alex Ross's father. "Do you understand?"

Hades replied, "Yes," quietly, but still loud enough to be heard .

"Now, give me me a moment to talk with my friend."

"Please don't do this," said Madison. "It's not safe."

"It's okay. I'm a demigod: half human and half—well, you know, god. I will stay with my father, Osiris. It will be fine," replied Alex.

"No, it's not. You're about to die for me... and how come no one told me there was a god of the dead?"

"I know," replied Alex. "But trust me, Madison. It will be easier for me."

Madison was silent, and then nodded her head. "Thank you. Be safe in the underworld."

Alex smiled. "I'll send someone else to wake you up on time and to pick out your outfits." With that, Alex called out to Hades, "I'm ready," and with a poof of red-black smoke, they were gone.

And that's the story of Madison and Alex.

EDDY'S ASTRO SERVICE

*Those brave men and women who journey beyond Earth don't all work for NASA. In **EDDY'S ASTRO SERVICE** by **Kaden Byrd**, you'll see a different career path to outer space.*

"George, you're going to be late," says my wife, Madelyn, who is an early riser.

"What am I going to be late for, honey?"

"Eddy's Astro Service called, the main astronaut is sick."

I jump out of bed, get dressed, and go downstairs to eat breakfast. I eat an egg sandwich, and the yolk squirts all over my shirt and pants! I go back to the bedroom for my other, and last, uniform. I run back down the stairs, grab my keys, and get in my Jeep.

When I get to the highway, I remember I don't have my wallet. International Code of Aerospace Conduct requires my ID. I go back home to get my wallet and end up in rush hour headed back to Eddy's. This may be my first and last day!

Just then an identical Jeep pulls in front of me with one of those stickers that says "It's a Jeep thing" and reminds me—I have an off-road permit! I go slightly to the side of the cars on the grass, and of course there is litter along the shoulder. I might just make it on time.

Thump, thump, thump, thump—my tire is flat. I have a spare, but it will take me time to switch the tires.

The phone rings, it's my mom, and I haven't talked to her in three months. "Hi Mom, what's up?"

"Hi, Honey, did you find a job yet? You have been looking for a year. How are things going?"

"Actually, funny you should ask—I found a high-paying job. I get to go up into space in a rocket."

"Are you working for NASA?" she asks excitedly.

"Not exactly. Eddy's Astro Service—it's like NASA." I jump out of the Jeep, and I start changing the tire. Mom continues jabbering on, not realizing she is on speaker and I am not responding.

"Oh, do you further the steps for mankind on the moon or fly Apollo 25? That's great, honey; now Madelyn can stay home with Jackson and Emma without worrying about money. And Aidan and

Sophia can keep doing their sport! Honey, I am so proud of you. You are finally going to get things on track. Let's do dinner when you get back from outer space—my treat."

I pause for a few seconds, then say, "About that...I won't be home, I mean I don't know when I will be home." I hadn't even told Madelyn yet that since Eddy's Rocket was not the highest quality aircraft it was probably a one-way trip, and I sure wasn't going to tell my blabbermouth mother. "Mom, I have to go, I have to change a tire."

She gasps. "What? You have a flat tire?"

Stupid me, why did I say anything? "No, an old lady has a flat, I'm going to stop and help her. I'll call you when I get home. Oh, and Mom, I love you." Finally, I'm off the phone, my tire's changed, and traffic is actually moving quickly now.

I have thirty minutes left. I get there with ten minutes to spare. My co-worker is sleeping behind the double doors. "Joe, out partying all night again?"

"Huh? What?"

Just then Fat Al, my boss, comes in. He's five foot, three inches tall and wide. "Joe! George! What are you doing in here?"

I am worried and start to stutter, "I, I, I..."

"You're early! Go get some doughnuts. It's launch day! Let's celebrate!" I relax, and Joe burps.

We go get doughnuts, and I grab the biggest, puffiest, custard doughnut. Wouldn't you know: first bite, and my shirt is covered in custard. Fat Al starts laughing at me. "You can wear one of my shirts."

Concerned and confused I say, "I'm not sure it will fit me. I'm much taller than you," and I whisper to Joe who's sleeping again, "and one-third the width."

Big Al laughs, and his belly jiggles up and down. "George, you are taking trash into outer space. It's not like you are meeting the President of the United States. Heck, if International Code didn't require a shirt, I'd say go without one!"

And that's when it finally hits you: you are a garbage man in a very dangerous vehicle.

FATE VS. WICKED: A FIGHT FOR THE AGES

At Camp Tanuga, War Games is a set day of events once every summer that everyone looks forward to. In **FATE VS. WICKED: A FIGHT FOR THE AGES**, *Grant Blau tells the story of competing against half of the camp to win War Games.*

The winner is...Team Fate! Camp Tanuga War Games 2013 had been decided. My team was victorious against Team Wicked. What an incredible end to an amazing day. All the hard work and dedication had built up to this moment. The excitement was incredible—my team went wild with cheering and yelling. I knew from the minute I saw my teammates we were destined to win.

<u>24 hours earlier</u>

After evening program, during "Friends and Taps," our camp director was reading a story about camp traditions when the Counselors in Training ("CIT") came out and performed a skit signaling the start of War Games. For those of you that do not know, "Friends and Taps" is a song the whole camp sings every day after evening program. Traditionally, War Games is one day during the summer where the camp is divided into two teams that compete to win through Capture the Flag, teams songs, flags, and team spirit. These competitions are judged by "Geneva," a group of counselors and camp administrators who becomes judges for the day.

After the skit, everybody returned to his or her cabin to go to sleep. It was late into the night, sometime around 2:00 in the morning, when I heard footsteps enter our cabin.

"Which bed is Grant Blau's?" whispered one of the CITs.

"The one that is old, rusty...on the top bunk," quickly and quietly responded one of the other CITs.

Then I saw shadows moving across the room toward my bed. I faintly recognized them as the CITs and immediately knew they were distributing t-shirts with team logos to divide the camp in half for the festivities. Going back to sleep was close to impossible. I knew I would toss and turn all night with anticipation. This was always the best day of camp!

We spent the entire next morning meeting with our teams to learn our fast and slow songs and chants and formation for the sprint across the athletic field. This is when we are judged for our team spirit. Afterward, there are people called "wandering warriors" who can work for either team during the War (Capture the Flag).

Before the War begins, we have a silent lunch. Talking means you lose points for your team. I was determined not to be the one who lost points for my team—my mouth was sealed shut! No matter how many times the counselors tried to trick me into talking, I was not making that fatal mistake. After lunch, we still didn't know the score. All the team members returned to team meetings to prepare for the War.

During Capture the Flag, we used sponges with dye to throw at people instead of tagging them. The team is placed in positions around camp to protect their flags and to capture the other team's flags. Each team has two flags—main and outpost.

The campgrounds are divided in half. I was placed on "wandering defense," which was key to our success. I had to make sure our flags were protected at all times and monitor the trails in the woods for the other team. The most important thing was to keep my hands on my sponges, ready to defend our flag if I saw a Team Wicked member.

*Crunch, creak...crunch, crunch...*was it an animal, my own teammates, or Team Wicked members? I put my hand in my bucket and grabbed a sponge—I was ready to attack if needed.

As they grew closer, I could see the "WW" logo on their chest indicating they were wandering warriors with Team Wicked members trailing behind. At that moment, I made the decision to run back to the base to notify my teammates that the enemy was approaching. This turned out to be the right choice.

"Hey guys, Wicked is coming with three wandering warriors!" I screamed.

"Go get the roaming defense as fast as possible," replied one of the CITs.

Team members forming a barrier of sponges in a 10-foot circle protected our base. While we were doing this, our team's offense secured the enemy flags!

We knew we had won the war, and there was only one thing left to judge: the teams' slow songs. This could be the game-changer and determine the winner. The slow songs are songs made by the CITs. This event, like all other events, was judged by Geneva. Team Fate chose "The Scientist" by Coldplay and wrote its own lyrics. Team Wicked wrote lyrics to a song too old for me to know, which is one of the reasons our song won. Geneva always likes classic songs they recognize.

This event is so emotional because this is the CITs' final War Games. Each team sang its heart out, campers and counselors both crying with emotion. Sobbing tears coming down like a waterfall as the songs faded away. Everyone knew camp was coming to a close. No one wanted to say goodbye to summer and their camp friends. The entire day and all of the hard work came down to this one moment.

"The winner is...Team Fate!" Camp Tanuga War Games 2013 had been decided.

FINDING MY FAMILY

A young girl loses her whole family on one day. In **FINDING MY FAMILY** *by* **Caitlin Tabin**, *the locket around her neck could be the key to reuniting with the ones she has lost.*

It was Christmas Eve, and snow was quietly falling as Madeline Jones stared at the stillness, her breath fogging up the window, and her fingers smudging the glass pane. She was fingering her early Christmas present, which she wore around her neck. (It was a heart-shaped locket, made of solid gold, with a picture of her family inside it.) There were flames flickering in the fireplace, and Madeline was nestled between both of her parents on the couch. Her little sister, only five years old, was playing with her dolls on the floor. Everything was just as it should be, if not better.

It stayed like that for five hours, until her mother and father kissed her goodnight. She was very excited for Christmas, and went to bed with a smile on her face. She dreamt wonderful dreams that night, but was forced to wake up because she was so uncomfortably hot. There was a strange glow outside her bedroom door. She soon realized that she awoke to something that would change her life forever.

At just that moment, her door erupted with flames, scaring the life out of poor Madeline. She cried for her parents and screamed for her sister. With the fire finding its way to her bed and no one coming, Madeline jumped out of her window, and fell into a pile of debris, hitting her head. As she watched her house collapse before her own eyes, everything slowly faded away.

Because she was hidden in the pile of debris, the firefighters did not even catch a glimpse of her. Her family looked for hours all over for her, but couldn't find her. They eventually left with heavy hearts and tears streaming down their faces, believing that Madeline had died in the fire.

But Madeline wasn't dead. When she woke up the next morning, she cried out in pain. Her head was throbbing, her back was sore, and above all she was panicked. She hadn't a clue where she was, who she was, or what to do about it. Her teeth were chattering, and she was very scared because, despite escaping the fire, her memory was gone from the blow to her head.

After she cried for about an hour, she finally picked herself up and just started walking. She hoped to encounter someone to help her before she froze to death. She walked for what felt like a week, one step after another. She received a couple of weird glances from people on the sidewalks, but she still found no one to take care of her. Madeline even asked a couple of people out of desperation, but they quickly turned away, thinking that she was a beggar. She raided trash cans for bits of food, and sometimes she could find a half-eaten loaf of bread. After days, she began to feel very dizzy. Her legs gave out, and she collapsed in a snow bank.

Then, a woman appeared. She said something, but Madeline couldn't make out what it was. The woman picked her up, put her in a car, and drove her to a large, white house. The woman carried Madeline up the marble steps into a bedroom, where she laid her down on a mattress. The lady gave Madeline a bowl of soup, and for the first time in a long time she fell asleep with a smile on her face.

The next day, Madeline woke up to the sun beaming on her face. A maid entered a few minutes later and exclaimed, "Oh good, you're awake! When Laura brought you back you were all pale, and your eyes were fluttering, and Laura had to carry you here." The maid gave Madeline some clean clothes to wear, and then told her to walk down to the dining room, where a bowl of oatmeal with berries in it was waiting for her.

Madeline was enjoying the oatmeal when the kind old woman appeared. "Hi, my name is Ms. Lafasi," she said. "I brought you here. I wasn't sure if you were all right, so I hope you aren't afraid. I got scared, and maybe I can help you. Just what on Earth happened for you to walk like that, alone?" The lady then asked Madeline who she was.

Madeline told her, "Well, all of a sudden, I was in a pile of smoky wood, and all I know is this." She took off her golden locket with her name engraved in fancy letters. She opened it up, and showed the lady what she thought was her family. "I don't remember a thing about them," Madeline said. Madeline explained she lost her memory, and the last thing she remembered was waking up in the ruins of a burnt house.

The lady smiled and asked Madeline if she wanted to live with her. Madeline happily agreed. Ms. Lafasi explained, "I always wanted a daughter of my own, and now I finally got my wish."

Eight years went by, and during that time Ms. Lafasi gave Madeline almost everything she could ever want. Ms. Lafasi provided her with only the finest of education, food, and entertainment. Madeline grew up in happiness, and could do anything she could possibly want besides going outside the gate of their house, which Ms. Lafasi forbade. "The real world is too dangerous for you still, Madeline," Ms. Lafasi declared.

Madeline always felt a longing to go outside, though. She missed her real family, even though she didn't remember them at all and even though Ms. Lafasi was very nice, because she wanted to know her real parents. She looked at the picture of them from her locket and tried to remember them every day, but that didn't help at all. Finally, she could bear it no longer. She asked Ms. Lafasi if she could see her family.

Ms. Lafasi suddenly wore a smile on her face, and said she would try to find them. She went on line to look at old newspaper stories of missing girls, and found Madeline's family's names in it. She found their phone number and contacted them. Ms. Lafasi invited them over, but in such haste to get there, her family died in a car accident.

Ms. Lafasi noticed it was taking a while, and when they didn't pick up the phone, she got worried. She decided to wait, but they never came. What she didn't know was on the side of the road were two cars, one of them containing Madeline's dead family, the other car being perfectly fine.

Two days later, there was a knock at the door that would soon change Madeline's life again. When Ms. Lafasi opened the door, an official told her that there was a GPS in a car, and it had her address on it. The officer told Ms. Lafasi that Madeline's family was no longer alive.

In tears, Ms. Lafasi shut the door and told poor Madeline. Madeline collapsed in tears, too, even though she had no idea who they really were. They went to the funeral together, and Madeline finally got to look inside the coffins.

Her memories suddenly came back to her, and her head hurt more than it ever had. She burst into tears, and they drove back in silence. When they reached home, Madeline ran straight to her room and locked her door. She soaked her clothes with tears and cried herself to sleep. She dreamt horrible dreams that night, and forever she will, because she never woke up.

THE FISH STORY LEGEND

In **THE FISH STORY LEGEND** by *Tiana Robinson*, *a man named Fisher seems to be having a lovely day with two mermaids. Yes, he seems to be having a lovely day....*

Prepare yourself for the worst fish story you will ever hear. You will notice that this story has the word "fish" in it a lot. This story is about an old fisherman and two mermaids. It would be best if I told the story from the beginning....

One very foggy morning, an old man named Fisher Fishman woke up with a big stretch and a loud yawn. He got out of bed and slowly crept to the bathroom. He brushed his disgusting teeth full of fish stick pieces and washed his tired face. He packed a small lunch with a tuna fish sandwich, a fish-gut smoothie, and some ice cold fish sticks. He grabbed his ugly yellow rain coat, and went to his old, beat-up truck, which, by the way, smelled like expired fish. He was going to go fishing. He started his truck and drove to the Fish Lake.

Meanwhile, two mermaids were swimming in the Fish Lake. "Oh, Laila, I just can't wait to see the newborn baby fish. Baby fish are *sooo* cute."

"I know, Izzy. I just can't wait." Laila is a blue mermaid with blonde hair and blue eyes. Izzy is a green mermaid with red hair and green eyes. Mermaids are half human and half fish.

Let's get back to Fisher.... *Screech!* Fisher made it to the Fish Lake. He stepped out of his truck and took a big, deep breath.

"Smell the fish. A great day for fishing."

Fisher headed to the back of his truck, singing. "*I is going to catch some fish sticks in the Fish Lake.*" He grabbed his old fish-bone fishing rod made of fish bones and an old, ugly fishing hat with fish ornaments, and he unhooked his old, disgusting, makes-you-want-to-throw-up fishing boat, which, in case you wanted to know, has fish bones glued to it. He put his boat on a wagon so he could roll it to the lake. He sang his stupid fishing song all the way to the docks. He pushed his fish boat in the water, and stepped in.

He row-row-rowed his boat to the middle of the lake. When he got to the middle of the lake, he stopped and cast with his nasty fishing rod in the lake. He sat there for a few minutes.

Meanwhile, Laila and Izzy were swimming past Fisher's boat. "Laila, what is that oval-shaped thing with fish bones glued to it? And how is it staying up there on the water?" Izzy said with a confused look on her face.

"I don't know, Izzy. We should go up to the surface of the Fish Lake to see what is going on," Laila said with a curious thought about the figure casting a dark shadow over them.

Back on the fish-bone boat, as Fisher likes to call it, Fisher was taking a relaxing nap. Then the boat started to shake. Fisher woke up all startled. He looked to the side of the boat. He only saw water. He was relieved.

Then, out of nowhere, Laila and Izzy popped out of the water, scaring Fisher. As he jumped back, Laila and Izzy peeked over the edge of the fish-bone boat.

"Oh. It's only humans. What are you ladies doing swimming in the Fish Lake?"

Laila looked at Fisher, then at Izzy, and then back to Fisher. "We're mermaids, you nincompoop. We are half human and half fish. And the real question is: what are you doing here?"

"Well, I'm doing some old-fashioned fish-stick fishing. I is going to catch at least ten of them," Fisher said, proud of himself.

Laila and Izzy were gawking at him. Then Izzy spoke up. "Why are you fishing for fish sticks at this time of day? It's Sunday morning."

"Why are you up so early?" Fisher questioned.

"I was going to see baby fish..."

"Baby fish sticks?" Fisher interrupted Izzy before she could finish her answer.

"No. Baby *fish*." Izzy had this annoyed look on her face.

"Why would there be baby fish if there is only fish sticks in the Fish Lake?"

"Because fish sticks can't swim. They would probably just float. They are too light to..." Izzy paused for a moment. "Wait, what am I doing? There are no fish sticks in the fish lake, you...you...you nincompoop!"

"Yes, there is!" Fisher yelled.

"No, there isn't!"

"Yes, there is!"

"No, there isn't!"

Izzy and Fisher went on and on about what's in the lake and what isn't. Laila was growing tired of the argument. So she spoke up. "STOP!"

It was quiet for a moment. Then she whispered something into Izzy's ear. Izzy nodded, and they both looked at Fisher.

"So, I decided that you should come have dinner with us, and we can discuss this situation. Is that okay with you?"

Fisher thought about it for a moment, and then said yes.

Izzy and Laila led Fisher to a waterfall. Fisher followed the girls behind the waterfall. There was a small cave. In the cave sat a rock with a flat top that was good enough to be a table.

They all introduced themselves to each other. They told Fisher that they were going to have different types of fish and explain each one of them. They had catfish, tilapia, fried perch fish, large striped bass, whiting, salmon, amberjack, jacks, sword fish, shad, bluefish, mackerels, sardines, tuna, trout, large spotted dogfish, and cobia. For desert they had sushi.

After they ate, Fisher thanked his new friends. He decided he was quite full, so he took a quick nap. While he napped, Laila and Izzy...ate...him.

THE GHOST ON CANTON STREET

It's time for a ghost story. In **THE GHOST ON CANTON STREET** *by Loryn* **Middlebrooks,** *read the tale of how three kids just like you discovered a ghost under their fingertips.*

Do you believe in ghosts? Well, on Canton Street, three special kids did.

It was the Fourth of July. All the kids were playing except for Ronnie, Zoey, and Skylar. They are best friends. They weren't playing because all of the kids were not their age. Zoey, Skylar, and Ronnie were 13 and 14. The other kids were 6 and 7.

Ronnie, Zoey, and Skylar started to get bored, so they played Truth or Dare. "Truth or dare, Skylar," Ronnie said.

"Dare," said Skylar.

"I dare you to go in the spooky house," said Ronnie.

A spooky house sat on the end of the block. Nobody lived in the house. People thought the house was haunted, but nobody knew for sure. The house was very scary and old.

"That house?" Skylar said shakily. The house is gray and white. It has old wood on the floors that are easy to break. The house has stairs that make squeaky noises like two cups getting rubbed together. The house is the biggest on the block. Strangely, it also has a room with the light on.

"Yup, unless you're scared," Ronnie said.

"No!" said Skylar.

"Fine, then we will go with you to make sure you do it," Ronnie said.

"Okay, if that's okay with Zoey," said Skylar.

"Fine, as long as we aren't in there long," said Zoey.

Legend says that a mean old lady named Zequetta had a music box that was magical and some kids stole it from her, so she searched and searched until she died and never got her music box back.

On the next day they met up at the house at midnight so nobody would see them. As they went in they saw the living room. The living room looked like a normal room with carpet and a couch. "Ooh, candy," said Skylar.

"Wait!" Ronnie said.

When Skylar walked up to the table with the candy, she and the carpet fell down a trap that was hidden under the rug in the living room. "HELP!" said Skylar.

"Skylar!" said Ronnie and Zoey.

"We have to save her, Ronnie!" said Zoey.

"Maybe if we follow the trap we will find Skylar," said Ronnie.

They followed Skylar down the trap that was kind of like a slide and saw that it led to the basement. The basement was dark and had lots of creepy stuffed animals. There were board games and clowns, too. "Skylar!" said Ronnie and Zoey as they looked for her.

"Over here!" said Skylar.

They found Skylar. "Skylar, are you okay?" said Zoey.

"Yeah, I'm okay," said Skylar.

They found a door that led to the stairs. The stairs led to another room. As they got closer to the room they saw that it was a bedroom. While they were looking around they saw a woman, and soon realized that it was a ghost. "Ahh, ghost!" they all said together.

"RUN!" Ronnie said, scared. The ghost slammed the door before they could get out.

They almost passed out, but then they realized that the ghost wasn't that scary. The ghost didn't do anything to them. They were able to stop being scared and talk to the ghost. "Why are you haunting all the kids?" said Skylar.

"A group of kids stole my music box," said the ghost. "The box played 'I'm a Little Teapot.'"

"Why do you still live in the house?"

"I can't leave until I get my music box back," said the ghost.

"Is it wooden and pink, and does it have roses on it?" Zoey asked.

"That's it!" the ghost said.

"I have that at home. My mom gave it to me," said Zoey. "My mom said that my grandma found it. She must have been one of the kids to steal it from you. I can get it back if you promise not to haunt any more."

"I promise," said the ghost.

They went to Zoey's house and gave the ghost back her music box. And Skylar, Zoey, and Ronnie never went back into the spooky house again.

GOOD LUCK

When we meet Patrick in **GOOD LUCK** *by* **Madison S.,** *he is not what he used to be. How did he go from being the worst leprechaun in Ireland to the success he is today?*

My name is Patrick, Patrick O'Conner to be exact. I am an amazing, hardworking, and incredible leprechaun who is at the top of the leprechaun chain in Ireland. But I haven't always been this way. In fact, about a year ago, I was the worst leprechaun that ever walked in Ireland! I bet you have no idea how I got to be where I am today. But don't worry, I have just the right amount of time before I have to get back to work to tell you the fascinating tale of me, Patrick, and how I changed my fate.

It was the first Tuesday in February of 1987, and I was preparing for St. Patrick's Day. I was sitting in the St. Patrick's Day prepping room. If you didn't know, it's where leprechauns go to set up plans for making St. Patrick's Day great. For me, it was a room to plan ideas that always fail and ruin St. Patrick's Day. Maybe I would set someone's room on fire or turn all the four-leaf clovers in the world to three-leaf clovers. It was pure torture that I had to sit in the room with happy, perky, and great leprechauns. The planning room was the "happiest place" in the entire leprechaun world. But it was the only place I could go, so I had to live with it. To make matters worse, the most popular leprechaun, Connor O'Hare, came up to me.

"Hey Patrick, I heard that you are going to ruin St. Patrick's day again; but don't worry, the main leprechaun loves me so much as always, he will have me come in and save the day," he smirked.

"Why don't you mind your own business, Connor," I said with my wimpy little voice.

"Why don't you keep your mouth shut or you won't wake up till St. Patrick's Day. Do you hear me?" he yelled for everyone to hear. It didn't help that everyone was staring.

"Okay, Connor," I replied, even wimpier than before.

"That's what I thought," he said mid-chuckle. Soon after that, he left with a pile of leprechaun ladies on him because they thought he was so tough.

Hurting my feelings isn't much of an accomplishment, and the leprechaun Wall of Fame in the room didn't make me feel any better. It made me feel like I didn't belong as a leprechaun. The only reason I am still a leprechaun is because of my great-uncle Patrick. He was one of the most famous leprechauns. If they kicked me out, every one of the leprechauns would be mad at the main leprechaun for kicking the last of my family out of the leprechaun business.

I think it is stupid that the main leprechaun cannot fire me, but to keep even the worst of leprechauns is the leprechaun motto. Instead of a Wall of Fame, they should have a "wall of lame." I would be on it right smack in the middle.

I wish I could just be a good leprechaun like everyone else. Thinking of my failure as a leprechaun made me so mad, I threw my book at the shelves, and hundreds of papers flew everywhere. *Just great,* I thought, *now I have to pick up all of these papers too! I mess everything up, even dumb papers!*

While I was picking up the papers I found a flyer put out by the leprechaun scientist team. It read: "If any leprechauns can find the gold at the end of the rainbow, you will be the luckiest, best, most amazing leprechaun that ever lived." This is the best news I have heard all day. Now I can become the best leprechaun ever! This must have been a sign from the main leprechaun that I should try to be a better leprechaun. It is so weird that the leprechaun scientist team discovered this on the same day I wanted to become a better leprechaun. I never would have guessed they found a way to make everybody be very lucky. I wanted to give the science leprechauns a big hug and to kiss the flyer with all my might.

"Are you okay, Patrick?" asked Liam, one of my fellow leprechauns, when he saw me kissing the paper.

"Perfectly fine, never been better," I happily replied.

"Okay, if you say so," he said while rolling his eyes. But I didn't care one bit. I was too happy to care. Make way, Wall of Fame; Patrick is coming to town!

First of all, I had to come up with a plan, but not just any plan. It had to be the greatest plan Ireland has ever seen

First, I would set up a search room so I could find all the rainbows. Then, I would hire tons of professionals to help track down every possible rainbow. I would have a video camera in every possible place. Next, I would just sit back, and wait for the rainbows to find me.

By February 18, I was totally prepared and ready to go. Oohh, I got my first call for a rainbow. I got all my stuff together and went right away. No surprise, I ended up failing. I thought, "Hey, this is my first time; it's not a big deal." But after a while, it seemed like the failures were piling up. It seemed like the rainbows never ended. When there is no end, there is no gold. What should I do now? I can't do anything but sit in my pile of failures and give up.

I had packed up my stuff and had gone home. I was a failure, and everyone knew it. What was I going to do now?

I looked at my calendar. "Holy cow, it's March 5th! I have barely any time to become the best leprechaun!" I knew right there and then that this would be another year where I would ruin St. Patrick's Day. To make me feel better, I turned on the TV.

It said, "Hello, this is the main leprechaun speaking. If anyone out there would like to be my trusty assistant, I would really appreciate it." That's it! The main leprechaun surely can make me lucky! I could go down there to pretend that I wanted to be his assistant but really ask to be lucky.

I made my way over to the main leprechaun's office feeling very happy. When I saw the main leprechaun, I bolted to him as fast as humanly possible.

"Mr.—Mr.—Mr. Leprechaun," I said out of breath, "can you make me lucky so I can be a good leprechaun?" I said it with a big smile on my face.

"Aren't you supposed to be here to be my assistant?" he said.

"Yeah, but it's almost impossible to talk to you without an excuse, so this was my only chance," I replied.

"Well, since you're here I might as well talk to you," he said.

He looked at me for a while and then after about a minute of silence he said sternly, "First of all, do you believe you are a good leprechaun?"

I replied, "Of course not; I am the worst leprechaun around!"

"That's where the problem is. If you do not believe in yourself, you do not seem lucky. Thinking you are lucky just boosts your confidence and makes you do so much better. But you get most places by working hard," he said.

I replied, "Thank you. I have to go fix something now. Bye!" I ran all the way home as fast as I could. I decided to try really hard!

I worked long hours to make St. Patrick's Day amazing. I made pins with four-leaf clovers on them, and I bought pounds of candy for the kids. It felt like I was working endless hours. I kept messing up on my planning, but I kept trying anyway.

I was getting more credit for my work. Things started looking up for me. Connor would say hello to me, and the main workers would give me compliments. I was pulling out all the stops. I painted rainbows everywhere, organized parties, and a lot more stuff involving St. Patrick's Day. That year, I was the best leprechaun around.

HEROES OF DETROIT

When heroes around Detroit go missing, it's up to the two newest superheroes to save the day. Find out if Detroit will be saved in **HEROES OF DETROIT** *by **Nabyl Edu**.*

In the year 8966, scientists have been experimenting on babies. Their project was to mutate newborns. Eighty percent of people mutated were unaffected, but the other twenty percent had a significant change. The mutation had given them unnatural abilities.

Then things went wrong. Some of these people began to use their abilities to rob banks or enslave Detroit. Luckily heroes rose up and defended Detroit. But even though the conflict was getting worse, scientists would not stop the experiment, allowing more children to be born mutated.

"Heroes have been losing their powers. Scientists believe that this is because their mutation is malfunctioning and/or wearing away," said the news reporter. Just then my mom turned off the TV.

"Skedaddle," said my mom. I raced my sister, Susie, to the backyard. This is not any typical backyard, though. This backyard was made especially to contain our powers and keep them hidden from the outside world. Susie and I have been training all of our lives.

Susie beat me outside, so I was the one to get hit with a blast of fire. Luckily my instincts were able to kick in to counter the fire before it could do any real harm.

"Deflected!" I yelled with joy. Then before I knew it I threw a blast of ice at her foot, tripping her. The fall looked painful, but before she hit the ground she floated up in the air as if she were weightless.

"Hey, that was mean," replied Susie. "I was just messing around." That's when things got real. Imagine an epic dodgeball fight; now replace the balls with all the elements you can think of. If you could see that, then you can see what was going on.

As we battled, Susie flew around, dodging stuff while I ran. This is no ordinary running; I was running at sonic speed. Faster, if I may, but still we almost killed each other. Then Mom came out.

"I leave you out here for three minutes and you almost destroy each other," she said, but she wasn't mad. It looked like something big was about to happen.

"Titanium (me), Moonlight (Susie): the time has come when new heroes are needed in Detroit," Mom was saying. "I have decided that you are ready to save lives and fight crime."

At this moment Susie and I were filled with excitement. We had always wanted to fight crime, and now we would get to do it for real, unaware it was only a matter of time before we realized our family's dark secret. Before our mom could say anything else we were out of sight.

"Come on!" I yelled. "Quick, I want to kick evil butt." Moonlight was flying quicker than the speed of a cheetah while I was running quicker than the speed of sound, so I had to keep going back and forth to keep from leaving her out of all the fun. When she finally made it we discovered that Detroit was being attacked by robots.

"This can only be the work of Dr. Drone," whispered Moonlight. But apparently Susie was too loud, because as soon as she was done with her sentence some robots guarding the perimeter attacked us. I sped around them, creating a mini-tornado, while Moonlight created mini-explosions. In a matter of seconds there was nothing but scraps on the ground.

"That was easy," I said, but the trouble had just begun. Dr. Drone came out of hiding. Immediately Moonlight and I recognized the person and were frozen with surprise. But that was a big mistake. Dr. Drone took this as an advantage.

"Attack the intruders!" he yelled. Then all of a sudden all the robots stopped what they were doing and attacked us. We were outnumbered thirty to one. Then we tried something we had never tried before: we attempted to use our powers as one. The result: an explosion that thankfully wiped out the bots.

"Hey, Dad, get a butt load of this," I called out as I blasted him with water. He toppled over. Moonlight was able to fly close enough to him to grab him by the collar and take him to the top of a satellite tower. I ran up the tower, and as I arrived Dr. Drone was about to jump off the tower.

Moonlight was hurt. It was up to me to get Dr. Drone. Then just as I reached for him, Dr. Drone jumped. I thought he was a goner until he landed with an "Uff!" on the back of a giant mechanical dragonfly. "This isn't last of me," said Dr. Drone.

"We did it! We saved Detroit!" said Moonlight.

"We did for now," I replied. "Let's celebrate a job well done."

When we got home we asked Mom if she knew that Dr. Drone was Dad, and to our surprise she did. "That is not important right now," she said. "What is important is that Detroit is safe."

And that is the story of how Titanium and Moonlight began.

LIVING IN A WAR

Two girls from different sides of the war share their stories as diary entries. In **LIVING IN A WAR** *by* **Monica Inda**, *can they possibly see things from each other's side?*

Dearest Diary,

Today, we bombed the Arabs. I guess that is what we have to do to win this war, but I don't really want it to happen to either of our people…. I overheard my parents talking about the bomb hitting a school. I hope not.

Speaking of school, I went to school today. We were sent home because there was another bomb threat. BLEH. I just wish that we would stop fighting. My people, the Israelites, seem to be upset with the Arabs over Palestine because of some land that we rightfully own, I think….

My parents are not home again today, so I don't have to make dinner. That's good. This has been a long entry, so I am going to stop writing now.

Bye Diary, Maddie

Dear My Diary,

My school got bombed today, and I got hurt, and I was apparently knocked unconscious. I am now in the hospital writing to you. When I woke up from my "sleep" I was told that the Israelites had bombed our school and many students and teachers were injured. I dislike the Israelites, and my parents were worried about me. Mya was also hurt in the bombing. My best friend's parents are worried about her, too. She is probably sleeping by now, and I should be going to bed…Bye.

–Dema

Dearest Diary,

Today, I overheard my parents talking about the bomb that apparently did hit the school. They said that it hurt a lot of kids there. I wished that it would not hurt many kids, but my wish did not come true. I also wish I knew how to stop the bombing and the fighting. My parents also want dinner. I guess I will make salad... that's easy. On the bombing thing, it is so sad that kids almost die because of some stupid war. I really wish I could make it stop, because my parents seem worried all the time.

Bye Diary, Maddie

Dear My Diary,

When I woke up I realized that I had surgery on my leg for two reasons. One- It hurt like crazy, and two- I could not feel my leg. Since I could not walk I shouted for my mom and dad. They both came rushing in while I stared at my leg in disbelief.

My dad was the first to speak. He said that the doctor X-rayed my leg while I was sleeping and saw that I had part of the bomb shell in it, so they had to cut it off. Then the doctor came in and asked for my parents. When they came back in the room, a nurse had medicine in her hand. She gave me some of it. It tasted nasty, and made me tired. I am going to stop here, because I am so sleepy. Bye.

-Dema

Dearest Diary,

When I woke up my parents were gone, so I only had to make myself breakfast. YES! I am not sure where they are, but they left a note saying go to the market at the edge of the border. It is only six blocks away from the house. I had to get some bread and cheese. I like going to the market on Saturdays, because I can see new things on the way.

When I reached the market, there was a big crowd around one girl about my age, but I did not recognize her. I think she was an Arab. When the people moved away, I could see that she was missing a leg. I hope she did not lose it when the school was bombed. I was staring at her for a while till her eyes met mine. I tried to force a smile as she gave an icy glare. After that, I don't remember much, and I hurried home.

Bye Diary, Maddie

Dear My Diary,

My parents and I went to the market today for some meat. I ended up in a wheelchair after the incident. We first went to the Palestine market, but they did not have any meat, so we went to a market right on the border of Palestine and Israel. It was fun, and everybody was nice to me. But then I noticed a girl staring at me. I bet she was a Jew, so I gave her my best evil eye. I wish the Jews would go away more than I wish I had my leg back. The girl staring at me sort of ruined the trip to the market, so I asked my parents to take me home. I hope I never see her again.

-Dema

Dearest Diary,

So, my parents told me to go to the market again today, but I really don't want to. I would rather not meet up with that girl, but.... Down at the market, I saw the crowd of people huddled around the girl. When the girl started to wheel over to me in her wheelchair, I felt like I was going to puke. She told me she was sorry for the evil eye and that her name was Dema. I told her sheepishly that I had never seen someone with a missing leg before and that is why I stared. Then, she asked if I was a Jew, and told me her parents told her that it was not safe talk to Jews because of the war and that. I felt so bad I ran away. My sadness soon turned to anger because I was not the one who hurt the Arabs. I now 100 percent hate this war.

Bye Diary, Maddie

Dear My Diary,

I talked to the girl who was staring at me again today. I don't understand those kinds of people. All I said was that my parents would not want to have me talking to Jews, and she ran away. How does she expect me to tell her to go away? I mean, her people took my leg away from me. Really? Does she think I am going to be her friend? No way. I guess I feel sorry for her. She is as afraid of my people as I am of hers. But I can't let this get the better of me. If I lose hope about the war then things will get worse for me. I cannot keep the cycle going.

–Dema

THE MYSTERY OF THE HYPNOTIST SHOW

Can a 12-year-old detective solve a string of robberies happening in his neighborhood? In **THE MYSTERY OF THE HYPNOTIST SHOW** *by* ***Ryan French****, Matthew Colby will do his best.*

Now open your eyes, and when I snap...you'll be hypnotized! SNAP!

* * *

Hi. I'm Detective Colby, but most people just call me Matthew. That's my real name. I'm 12 years old, and I live with my mom, my dad, my two brothers, and my sister.

It's weird: I have a special birthday, which happens to be the day Sir Arthur Conan Doyle published the mystery *Sherlock Holmes*. Everyone thought my birthday was some ridiculous coincidence and I was going to be some strange detective one day. And guess what? They were right. I run my own detective business and solve mysteries for people who need my help.

Suddenly Mrs. Stirfield came into my office screaming. I asked her what was wrong. She said, "Matthew, please help me. Someone broke into my house!" I asked her when it happened. She said that she had no idea and that she had been gone on vacation for over a week. Then, I asked her if she had any clues in her house that she could identify right away. She had but one clue, and that was a business card she found near broken glass for some hypnotist show that was run by a guy named Jason Ledum.

We went to Mrs. Stirfield's house, and there was Mr. Stirfield with nothing but his suitcase from their vacation in his hand. I asked him if he was all right. He said he was fine and just nervous.

I was looking around, and then I saw it, the perfect clue. This told me so much information, although the clue was nothing but a box. I could tell it was a clue because I saw an address for a house on the box.

I was back in my office saying the label on the box in my head over and over again: "Jason and Jack: a band emerges. Jason and Jack: a band emerges." I saw that there was an address on the box. I thought about that and then looked at the business card. "Jason" was on the business card, but there was no address or phone number.

Suddenly Mr. Finklestein came in and said, "Matthew, get up. I need help right now." Mr. Finklestein was used to yelling at people because he used to be a general in the army.

We went to his house, and instantly I saw the clue I was looking for: on Mr. Finklestein's door there was an information slip for Jason's Hypnotist Show.

I went back to my office and saw all my clues. I had the box, the business card, and the information slip all with the name Jason on them. I looked closely at all of them, and on the box I saw an address for Jack's house. All the information was leading to something because of everything on it.

I asked Mrs. Stirfield and Mr. Finklestein to drive me to Jack's house. After two and a half hours we finally found his house. I saw him playing his guitar outside and walked over to him and asked him what he was doing. He responded saying, "Oh, hi! I'm Jack. And you are...?"

I responded, "Excuse me. I'm Detective Matthew, and these are my friends Mrs. Stirfield and Mr. Finklestein. They had their houses broken into, and we found a clue that had your name on it." (I thought it was kind of weird that I just walked up and he said hi.)

I showed him the box and he said, "Oh, that box." I asked him what was wrong and he said that a couple years ago he and his friend Jason were in a band together. Then one day Jason just flaked out and left for some stupid hypnotist job.

I asked him if he knew where Jason's hypnotist show was and he said, "Yeah, follow me."

We ended up at Jason's place a couple hours later, and we saw him in the window reading a book. We went in and asked Jason to confess. He said he had no idea what we were talking about. I explained to him that we saw his box, his information slip, and his business card. He just stared at me looking clueless. And then I asked him if I could look at the video of his last hypnotist show.

He was showing me the video, and I was looking at all the people that were getting hypnotized, and I saw one person I knew, and that person was Jack! We could tell by his long, shaggy, blond hair and his weird lavender shirt. (Jason didn't notice because he hadn't seen Jack in a very long time).

We all looked at Jack and saw all those business cards in his pocket. "You framed me!" said Jason. Jack didn't say anything. All he did was run and run.

But remember, we had an army soldier on our side. Mr. Finklestein was really fast because he had to do a bunch of running exercises for the army.

After about five minutes of chasing, we caught Jack. We asked why he did it, but he wouldn't talk to us. He just sat there while we called the police.

When the police arrived we told them everything from the burglary to the chase at the end. The police arrested Jack and told us that he'd be in jail for quite a long time. Also everything that was stolen was peacefully returned to their owners. Mrs. Stirfield thanked me for all that I had done. She asked if there was anything she could do to repay me, and all I asked was for her to drive me home as a favor.

When I got home I told my whole family about it. But they were used to hearing stories, so they were just annoyed and bored about it. But I don't care because today I solved a mystery!

THE NEW KID

Jackson moves to a new school, wanting to make new friends and get on a good basketball team. He's got skills and could be the one to save the area travel team from another losing season in **THE NEW KID** by *Jackson Tinsley*.

Jackson Tinsley is dribbling down court. His coach quickly calls timeout. There are ten seconds left in the Midwest Youth Basketball Championship. The Spartans are down two points. The score is 53-55. The Spartans come on the court. Travis Irving passes it in to Jackson Tinsley. He runs down with three seconds to go. He shoots a three from half court to win the game. It goes...

* * *

Jackson Tinsley was a normal boy. He was 12 years old, and was in sixth grade. Jackson had two brothers who were both older. He liked basketball, like any other kids. He wasn't average at basketball; he was amazing. He was the star of the Midwest Wildcats, the best basketball team in the Midwest, until he moved. He moved from Kentucky to Michigan—to East Lansing—where his favorite college was, Michigan State University. Their basketball team was really good. They were top-ranked in the country.

Jackson's parents announced that he would be going to East Lansing Central, where their basketball team was less than average. He wanted to play for a travel team like his old team.

When he went to school on his first day, no one really noticed him. But there was one kid named Travis—he didn't know Travis's last name yet, but he knew that he was good at basketball, judging by him at lunch recreation in the gym. He could cross anyone up and drain the threes. Jackson wanted to be his friend, but was too shy to talk to him.

Jackson went back to school the next day. He met a couple of people, but wouldn't consider them as true friends. He got to know his teachers throughout the week. He really liked his Engineering Tech class. It's the only class he had with Travis. Travis was average height, and had wavy blonde hair. Jackson always saw him across the room, and whenever he did, he would see him look at him, giving Jackson a nice look. It seemed like he wanted to be Jackson's friend, too. He seemed like a popular kid. He had a big group at lunch. They all sat at a table together. They were the popular group.

Finally the week was over, and Jackson could relax over the weekend. The next day his parents had a talk with him about basketball. "We found a travel team in our area. Would you like to try out for them?" his dad asked him.

Jackson immediately answered "Yes!" His dad said that the tryouts were the next weekend, and their team name was the East Lansing Spartans.

The week passed by faster than ever. He thought about how excited he was for his tryout the next day.

Jackson's tryout finally came. He had been waiting for so long. When he went there it was basically the same tryout routine as his old team did. First, there were warm-ups, and then the coaches introduced themselves. He really liked the head coach, who seemed like a nice guy and a good coach.

Finally, the actual tryout began. As he was looking around the gym, he saw Travis. He hadn't known he was trying out.

After a couple of drills, Jackson knew he was one of the best. It was the same with Travis. They were both really good.

He met some kids that went to a different school in his district. They were nice.

The tryout was over in a breeze, and Jackson thought it was way easier than his old team's tryout.

The next day at school something weird happened. Everything else in the day had gone fine until recreation time at lunch. When Jackson was just playing basketball and talking to new people, Travis came up to him. Travis said, "Hey, you looked good at the tryout."

Jackson said, "Thanks, you too." And Travis just walked back to his friends and started talking.

After school Jackson couldn't take his mind off what happened and knew that he and Travis were going to be good friends someday.

The next days of the week in Engineering Tech, he noticed that Travis was moving seats every day closer to Jackson. On Friday, he saw that Travis was three seats away from him. He thought that Travis was trying to be his friend, but Jackson again was too shy to talk to him straight. It was the same thing at lunch rec. He noticed that Travis's group kept on getting closer to where he was playing basketball. He knew this was a sign.

It was finally the weekend. It seemed like this week had been longer than the last one. When he got home his mom told him he made the basketball team. Jackson immediately was very excited. His mom said the first practice was tomorrow.

The next day, Jackson went to the first practice. He saw that all the kids that he imagined would make it had made the team. Jackson was excited to see that Travis made the team.

The next week at practice they announced the starting line-ups. Jackson was the point guard, Travis was the shooting guard, this kid named Bobby was the small forward, another new kid named Frank was the power forward, and a kid named Connor was the center. It was an awesome starting line-up. For the rest of the practice they learned plays and scrimmaged.

In the middle of the week at school, Travis walked over to Jackson. Travis started off by saying, "You look really good at practice."

Jackson said with hesitation, "Ummm, you too." Then they started talking about basketball.

The next day Travis introduced Jackson to his group. He sat with them at lunch, hung out with them at rec, and hung out after school.

Jackson had many practices in the next week. It all led up to their first game against the Auburn Hills Raptors. They lost by five points. Jackson was very mad because he heard that that team was one of their biggest rivals, and he *hates* losing to rivals. Their coach was mad because they didn't run some of their plays correctly.

The next week at practice the coach made them run plays over and over again until they got them right. They had another game the next day. They would be playing the South Hills Bobcats.

They won by thirteen points. Jackson was really happy because the team played awesome! He also enjoyed his first win on his new team.

His team won the next five games. His team was now first in the league, in front of the Raptors by one win.

Their next game was against the Raptors again. This time they won in overtime by three. Everyone was jumping around Jackson because he made the winning three. Their team won their division and was seeded first in the playoffs.

Jackson's team went on to win the first game of the playoffs to go to the semifinals. They won that game, too. Now they would play in the league championship against the Raptors.

As game time approached the team's coach said some inspirational words, and then they went out there. If they won this they would go on to play in the Midwest Championship.

The Spartans were down by two points with two minutes to go. Travis made a three, and they were suddenly in the lead. The Raptors missed, and the Spartans ran the clock down to five seconds. They would have to play solid defense against the Raptors to pull out the win.

The Raptors' point guard took a buzzer beater try and missed it! The Spartans jumped around. They had just won their league and got a huge trophy. They would go on to play in the Midwest Championship, which Jackson later found out was against his old team. They were one of the best teams in the nation.

Jackson had strict and long practices the next week, which all led up to the final game. This game was going to be televised everywhere. It was huge!

They started the game. Jackson's team got the tip. Then, the Midwest Wildcats started a run. The score was 12-2. Jackson's coach called timeout to discuss a game plan.

It didn't help at all. Jackson's team was losing 15-31 at halftime. When his team went into the locker room, his coach was furious. Jackson and Travis had scored all the points. The coach was screaming and yelling at the players, except for Jackson and Travis.

The game started up again. This time his team went on a run. The score at the end of the third quarter was 34-38. Jackson's team would have to play strong to win the game, which they did.

With thirty seconds left, Jackson's team was down by four points. Jackson quickly went in for the layup and made it. Now, their team was down by two points. The Wildcats missed their next shot. Jackson Tinsley was dribbling down court when his coach quickly called timeout. There were ten seconds left in the Midwest Youth Basketball Championship with the Spartans down two points. The score was 53-55.

The Spartans came on the court. Travis Irving passed it in to Jackson Tinsley. He ran down with three seconds to go. He shot a three from half court to win the game. It went right around the rim, and it missed!

The Wildcats started jumping around like they had won. Then suddenly, the Spartans' hope came back. The ref called a foul, which sent Jackson to the line with three shots! The kid who fouled Jackson was now fouled out, and he was their star player!

Jackson went up, missed the first, made the second, and made the third. The Spartans now went to overtime!

In overtime, the Spartans completely demolished the Wildcats in the first few minutes. They were up by eight points. One reason was the Wildcats' star point guard had fouled out after he fouled Jackson on the last play in regulation time.

Then, the Wildcats came back and were only down by two points. There was one minute left in the game. Jackson was taking the ball up the court, when suddenly it bounced off his foot! The other team stole it and scored.

With 30 seconds left, the Spartans had the ball. Their coach called timeout.

Jackson had the ball. He quickly passed it to Travis. Travis then passed back. The Spartans have five seconds to score or there would be another overtime. Jackson broke a kid's ankles, and then took the shot....HE SCORED! The Spartans had won the Midwest Youth Basketball Championship!

The Spartans' bench emptied and jumped on Jackson. Everyone was shouting in the stands and cheering. The Spartans, a complete underdog, had just beaten the best team in the country.

QUANTICOM

Have you ever wondered what life would be like as a technician on Jupiter when everything is going wrong? Well, you can find out in **QUANTICOM** *by* **Ben Crimmins.**

Wayne and Shaun were talking in the car on their way to work when Wayne pointed as they passed a light. "Did you just see that?" Wayne asked in his British accent.

"I couldn't see, I'm focusing on the road," answered Shaun. Then suddenly, the light popped.

"Aw man, do we have to check the Quanticom?" Wayne whined.

"I guess so...."

Once they got about a half a mile away from the Quanticom's turbine field, their car broke down. They simultaneously got out of the car and moaned. "Please tell me we don't have to walk, do we?" Wayne asked.

"Well, how else would we get there?"

"Good point."

They started walking on the rusty highway. "Well, I guess the bright side is that we can bond?" Shaun said as he kicked a rock.

"Yeah, I guess."

"Well, I have always wanted to ask you how old you are."

"337. And you?" Wayne said.

"367."

They paused.

"It still amazes me how humans first invented immortality, and second, how humans made it to Jupiter through interstellar travel, and are harnessing its rather harsh winds and bringing the power back to Earth."

The wind whistled past them.

"Yeah, and also how we invented lights that act as a force field against radiation and the harsh winds."

They both stepped in a green jelly.

"What is that?" Shaun said, disgusted.

"It looks to me like Mrs. Crim's jelly."

"I loved that stuff as a kid."

"Yeah, me too, but what is it doing here?"

"I don't know."

They both reached the outer fence of the Quanticom's turbine field. "What is that noise?" Shaun whined.

"I think the turbines need oiling."

"Yeah, or there are monsters eating them," Shaun joked.

They approached the main gate, and Wayne entered his key card into the slot. When he opened the door, he stood blocking the doorway, frozen. "What?" Shaun asked.

Wayne suddenly and swiftly closed the door and hid behind a rock. "What, did you see a monster?" Shaun teased.

"There – there – there was a monster!"

"Oooookkkaaayyy...." Shaun chuckled.

"Seriously!"

Shaun rolled his eyes and opened the door. He, as well, ran back to the rock. "What is that?" Shaun said, scared to the bone.

"Why do you think I would know?"

Shaun paused and put on his thinking face. "I think I saw Mrs. Crim's jelly on *its* mouth."

"Yeah, me too, and he was also chewing up the turbine's nuclear reactor."

"Well if *it* destroys the reactor, the lights will go off and we will be exposed to the radiation and die."

"Then we have to kill it or lead it away."

They paused.

"I have an idea!" Wayne said

They went around back and opened the back door. When they went in, they hugged the wall and walked to the lounge room. Shaun scavenged through the cabinets and grabbed some peanut butter. He went outside and sneakily walked to the edge of the wall.

Wayne started to scream and jump up and down. The monster became more attracted to the noise than to chewing on the reactor. Once the monster got in sight of Wayne, Wayne opened the peanut butter and said, "Hey, you pig, how can you have jelly without peanut butter and bread? NOW!" yelled Wayne.

Shaun ran at the monster with bread and covered its eyes with the bread. Then Wayne ran at the monster and put the peanut butter in the bread. The monster was startled and stumbled back. Then it took the bread and sniffed it. "Go on, eat it," Shaun said.

The monster ate the bread and ran away. "Well, I guess it was just hungry." Wayne said.

"Yeah, but it will be back."

"As long as we buy PB and J every now and then, he'll be fine."

THE SAD BUT SHORT LIFE OF CASEY

THE SAD BUT SHORT LIFE OF CASEY by *Sean Smith* concerns two friends and a tragic accident. But there is more to the story....

Casey was just a normal kid, until one day his life changed forever. One day when he was young, about six, he watched this science fiction show called *Through the Trip of the Wormhole*. The hostess of the show, Jennet Lang, talked about how she had studied wormholes, and she found evidence that the wormhole only forms when four pieces of a puzzle are put together. Jennet said that the picture formed by the puzzle pieces was unknown. "Whoever has the puzzle pieces...will die. The first one to find a piece was never found again."

Casey was, of course, thinking about how fake that was. He was sadly mistaken. He was going to learn his lesson soon enough.

Ten years later

Casey was about to graduate the 11th grade with a 4.0 GPA and a major case of asthma. The doctor told his parents when he was six that his life wasn't going to last very long, because he had asthma attacks two times a day at least. (The sad part about it is Casey never knew about it.)

Casey was also very unpopular. Some kids even called him a dork and a nerd and punched him and pushed him around. "Hey, you," one of the bullies said to Casey at lunch, "you smell like you just took a dump." Everyone started laughing at him.

The only person that stood up for him was his only friend Philip. "Don't worry about them; they're just jealous of you." Philip always made Casey feel better.

After school, Casey and Philip hung out at the library across the street from both of them. They just brought their computer games from home and played them on the computers there. "Hey, Philip, I'm about to run home and grab some snacks. Want any?" Casey asked.

"Yeah, get me some Oreos, bro," Philip said.

While inside his house, Casey heard loud bells and screaming. He looked out the window and saw the huge burning library building.

Casey ran out of the house and saw people coughing, but he never saw Philip. "Philip!" he screamed.

When he said that, a man came running out, saying, "There—*cough*—is a boy—*cough*—still in there!"

Casey saw Philip in the window screaming, "Help me!" There were tears running down his face.

All of a sudden, the building exploded. Huge pieces of metal went flying through the air, stabbing people in the chest. There were people falling left and right.

Once the fire department came and put out the fire, Philip's parents came rushing through. "Where's Philip?" the mom said, crying.

Casey responded, "He's dead."

Casey was nothing, nothing at school without Philip. He kept getting made fun of and kicked and pushed—the usual.

He was in gym one day, and he was running too fast. All at once, he collapsed on the floor. He couldn't breathe. He had no idea what it was, but when he took his last breath, he looked in his pocket. Then he knew what was happening.

He had four puzzle pieces in his pocket, and he knew at that moment that Jennet Lang didn't lie. "Whoever has the puzzle pieces, will die." Those were his last words, in his head at least.

SEARCHING FOR THE LOST

When everything is in the past, how do you come back to it? In **SEARCHING FOR THE LOST** *by* **Mackenzie Beem,** *a girl learns how to face her fears and find her old life.*

Prologue

The darkness was overwhelming. The air smelled of gunpowder and fear. Thirteen-year-old Mia Zacconi, stuck in a bombing in France, was forced to leave France and go to the USA. Everything she knew turned into nothing. Her family was left behind, and she was left without any clue as to where they were, or if they were alive. Her bravery turned into longing and waiting.

A distant cousin of her mother picked her up from the airport and took care of her, in New York City. When her cousin passed away, Mia felt like she was all alone. All she had left of family were thoughts and memories. Now, being 18, she went to college and owned her deceased cousin's restaurant.

Now

It was just another day, another hope, another dream. She wished her life could be different, normal, with her family. But, just being an ordinary girl, wishes like this were pushed away. All of these thoughts are hidden in the back of the mind, tucked away, hoping to escape but never succeeding.

The busy streets of New York were bursting with their usual business and noises. Crossing the road past the street light, Mia finally caught her breath. She knew this city; she loved this city; she was this city. Not physically, of course, but Mia felt like the city wouldn't be the same without her.

Stopping at the front door of her restaurant she held the door for some customers and walked into the vivid colors and smells. The reds and oranges and greens that made up the restaurant could almost compare to the smells of spaghetti and lasagna. There were a few customers waiting. Walking to the back of the restaurant where the stairs that led to her house were, she thought about her one dream, to find her family.

She wished for home, with vivid colors and loud people, but different, with pretty and loud nature, and native people. Of course, she knew this was impossible, because dreams always stay in the spot, in the back of your mind, hidden and lonely.

Sitting down at her desk, Mia started filing some papers, her mind wandering. She had to get out of this place, just for a little while. She had started getting used to the constant buzz of New York. Her mind was just a blur of paperwork, school, and coffee.

She pushed aside the papers and started on an essay. She wondered how this could've all happened so suddenly. Dozing, she couldn't help but think of her family, and what they would be thinking if they were here. She was going to find some way to get to them, just to see.

Now is finally her time. She had nothing to lose. Booking the flight, she thought, *I'll see them again now.*

Stepping off the plane, Mia had butterflies in her stomach. She was nervous, and she couldn't even imagine what she would do if they weren't here. She had already converted her money into euros. Now she had to call a cab. When she finally got a cab she loaded her bag into the back and sat down.

Looking out the window, it was hard to take in the beauty of the reds and greens and the bright blue of the sky. It was crazy how amazing this was, but something was missing. Suddenly she thinks of what her family would be doing if they were here: her mother with her black hair blowing in the wind, her brothers laughing about some joke they made. The more she thinks, the more she realizes she wants her family to be here; she just wants to be with them again, to be the family they were.

As the cab pulls into the driveway of the hotel, Mia reaches into her pocket to get the money to pay and briskly walks away.

Now in the hotel she puts down her bags and looks around her room and then out the window. Looking at the *boulangeries* and vendors reminds her of her family. She looked out the other window and knew it was time.

Pulling into the driveway she knew too well, the only feeling Mia had was numbness. The aching of anxiety was almost overwhelming. What if they weren't there! She finally pulled out the courage to walk up the familiar sidewalk and ring the doorbell. When the door was answered Mia knew she had made the right decision.

"*Ma mère*, I'm home."

SHARKZILLA

When evil is stirring under the water, will the superhero Fish Face be able to stop the city from being destroyed? In **SHARKZILLA** *by Van Borgquist, will the hero of the land stop the evil Sharkzilla from conquering the world?*

The city was calm, but beneath the water lurked a vicious beast. It was Sharkzilla, The King of the Deep, and he was mad at the people who swam in the ocean hunting other sharks and fish. He was as big as a dinosaur with long legs and short arms, and he had an appetite for sixth-grade English teachers.

Today he took a stand. Today he would be king of two worlds. There was one obstacle in his way: Fish Face, The Superhero of the Land who stopped him every time.

Today Sharkzilla would prevail. He would defeat Fish Face and rule the city. He would make the fishermen pay for what they did to his kind. He would let the fishermen be caught by the sharks. He would reverse the roles of the two classes. That was when it all started for everyone.

In his underwater cave, Fish Face prepared for battle by putting on his armor, strapping his trident onto his back, and putting on his Crown of Atlantis. He was preparing for the invasion that he knew Sharkzilla was planning. After he was prepared, he sat in front of his water screen waiting to see the news that Sharkzilla was on the move.

After ten minutes of waiting, the water screen displayed Sharkzilla walking ashore. Fish Face jumped through the pond in his cave and swam to the surface of the ocean.

As Sharkzilla walked ashore, he wrecked buildings, smashed roads, and shredded cars while people cowered in fear and ran everywhere to get away. Sharkzilla continued to wreak havoc on the city, trying to convince the world they had no choice but to bow down to him, until Fish Face came swimming out of the ocean to stop him. Sharkzilla, as tall as a building, stared down at the small superhero. "You can't defeat me this time," said Sharkzilla as a group of sixth-grade English teachers screamed and fainted.

"I have the Crown of Atlantis, which bestows me great power," Fish Face said, raising the water around him for effect by using only a fraction of the Crown's power. "I also have the Trident of Poseidon," he said as he unstrapped it from his back. "It allows me power over all aquatic animals, water, and storms," he said, bringing a huge wave to the shore and creating a storm.

Sharkzilla charged and stomped on Fish Face, who inflated himself like a balloon. Sharkzilla slashed with his claws, but they bounced off Fish Face's chest. Then Fish Face retreated into a building, and Sharkzilla crashed into it.

While Sharkzilla was stunned, Fish Face jumped on his back and used his trident to control Sharkzilla's mind. He used the trident's power to force Sharkzilla down the Marianas Trench, from which he could not escape.

As Sharkzillla left, Fish Face made the storms and waves stop. It was over, and Fish Face had saved the day.

SMALL BANANAS

Gesseppi attempts to make his life interesting and fun, but things don't go the way he had hoped. Join Gesseppi as he endures his unfortunate adventures with Monkey Man in **SMALL BANANAS**, *by **Amelia Richard**.*

There is an old, faded grey tower. Inside, it looks like a modern apartment. In the tower there lives Gesseppi, his wife Gladice, and his son Noname.

One day, Gesseppi tripped and fell down the stairs. He woke up dazed in a hospital. He then realized how close he had come to losing his life. He thought about his life: wake up, eat, watch TV, eat, sleep, and then start the cycle all over again. He then realized he needed to make his life more interesting, or at least more meaningful.

First, he read the newspaper (something he never did). In one of the fillers, there was an ad: "Hello, Small Banana. Want a cool life? Of course you do! Call me! Because I'm the best! 1-800-999-9999!"

Gesseppi called the number. A grumpy secretary answered the phone. She said the name of the man who placed the ad was "Monkey Man." She sighed. She told him to hold. When she came back she said a payment of 400 dollars was required per trip. Gesseppi agreed. She told him that Monkey Man would be there in about a week.

About a week later, the doorbell rang. When Gesseppi answered, he saw a muscular man in a black jumpsuit. He had on a matching ski mask, and Gesseppi couldn't see his face. Then, out of nowhere, the man in the mask got a cinder block and raised it over his head. He smashed it in Gesseppi's face, and Gesseppi passed out.

Gesseppi woke up dazed. He saw two of everything: two trees, four feet, and six sharks swimming under his four feet. He screeched.

"Hey, you lived! I mean—you woke up!" said Monkey Man.

"Cut me down from this rope!" screamed Gesseppi.

"Okay."

"Wait—!"

"Here you go!" said Monkey Man, cutting the rope around Gesseppi's waist. Gesseppi fell down 43 feet—just missing the sharks—and landed facedown on a rock.

He survived. He couldn't believe it. He also couldn't believe he was in a cardboard box in the back of Monkey Man's Toyota.

After a while they came to a stop. "Here we are!" said Monkey Man, "The Oldish Kitchen!" He came around to lift Gesseppi out of the box. He dragged him inside the restaurant. Inside, there was a skinny, toothless guy with sock puppets. "What can I get you?"

Monkey Man nudged Gesseppi. He looked up at the menu: "Chicken Eyes and Salami Sauce, Johnny Apple-Sauce, Snail Custard, Cream of Elf Vomit..." Gesseppi shrieked and ran out of the restaurant.

Days passed. Monkey Man came knocking on his door. "Ready to play...CUPID?" He was wearing a diaper covered in red and pink heart stickers. He was holding a fake bow and arrow. Gesseppi looked disgusted. "No way am I dressing up in a diaper and going out to shoot people with plastic!"

"But you have to, Midge—I mean, Small Banana! You signed a contract!"

"I'll give you a million bananas."

"Deal!"

Gesseppi slammed the door in the crazy Monkey Man's face. He went to the fridge and got a Dr. Buzz, and sat down to watch TV. And he was happy.

SPACE TRIP

What if an ordinary family one day decided to head to space? It might go something like the story **SPACE TRIP** *by* ***Charles Remenapp.***

In the Brinkley family, almost everybody was heavily sleeping in their own comfortable beds. It was 9 A.M., and their dad, Mark, had just woken up. He said to himself, "I have a brilliant idea." He got out of bed and made a phone call. Then he woke up the whole family and said to meet him in the front yard.

The whole family was there: Sue, Diana, Colin, and him. Mark said to the whole family, "We are going to the moon."

Everybody seemed confused because they were going to the moon early on a nice Saturday morning with no spaceship. Then Mark said, "I have already ordered the parts to make a spaceship, and they are going to arrive right about now." As soon as he stopped talking, the family heard a large truck coming down the road. The truck seemed to be slowing down, and the driver was looking at the houses.

Clang! The truck stopped in the driveway of their house and dumped the parts for the spaceship on the driveway—and I wouldn't say the guy dumped them gently on the driveway, either.

After those parts were dropped off, the whole family began to whine about how they wanted to go to California and they wanted to go back to bed. But as soon as they stopped whining, Mark made them all pitch in on making this spaceship happen.

The family got to work, and it took them a whole week to finish it. All week all the neighbors could hear was *Ping! Ping! Clang! Bang!*

Over the weeks, the Brinkley family was at work getting situated for the trip to the moon. After several weeks they finally got their rocket ship, and now they were able to go to the launch pad and go. The family left the driveway with a 10-ton spaceship on a trailer hitched to the back of their minivan.

They finally got to the launch pad, and they took the ship off the trailer using a gigantic crane. When the crane set down the rocket ship, the family climbed aboard and started the engines. As soon as you know it, they were exiting the atmosphere and on their way to space.

They approached the moon. *Pisshhhh!* They landed on the moon elegantly. The family took out their own spacesuits and put them on.

Their dad was the first person to step out and start setting up the family's space tents.

THE THING FROM OUT OF THE WATER

A hiker encounters something that terrifies him. The narrator is not as impressed in **THE THING FROM OUT OF THE WATER** *by Colton S.*

It was a cold, damp morning with the winds not too high. People were very happy because it was summer. Then one event changed everything.

On this average day, a hiker was hiking (how ironic) and saw something lurking in the shadows. He froze and scanned to see what it was. Silent, the hiker was terrified for his life (and then a monster ate him. The End. Not really).

Well, that's not what he had wished for: a huge, overgrown frog standing seven feet tall (I am picturing a Ninja Turtle; I don't know about you, though). The hiker ran for his life (but unfortunately he got away; I wanted to see some action, but *nooo*, he has to get away).

The next morning the giant frog returned to a lake where it lives, and some people were kicking the mud and laughing like bullies.

THE TOWER OF THE DARK LORD

When evil magic lays the land to waste, the one responsible must pay. Two soldiers embrace the mission of facing down their people's oppressor in **THE TOWER OF THE DARK LORD** *by Lily Heineman.*

Chaz and Drasna had been traveling for a while. The ground around them was hard, grey, and basically dead. The two of them had been sent to slay an evil dark lord. Drasna gripped her magic staff, claws clinking against the metal. Drasna was a lizard, frilled to be exact. Chaz was a dog, more or less a mutt.

"Aye, Drasna, do you think we will be getting there soon? I want to kill that dark lord a million times over!" Chaz said. He looked around at the barren wasteland. His paw gripped the hilt of his sword.

"Yes, we will get there soon. I really want to make that dark lord pay for cursing our kingdom and hurting our people," Drasna said, her claws grinding on her staff.

Chaz sighed. The dark lord had a very selfish reason for cursing the kingdom. She had had powers over color and darkness ever since she was little. People tormented her because of this. She got revenge by sapping the land of color and killing lots of people.

Smoke blocked their vison, making it hard to see. It swirled around in the wind, blocking all hope that they could see the tower of the dark lord.

The two of them walked for a little bit more. When it was starting to feel like they would never get to the dark lord, they reached the tall tower. It was huge, and could easily fit a thousand people in the first floor.

"Why does this person have to be a dark lord anyway? Dark lords are done to death!" Chaz shouted. He looked up at the top of the tower. The tower was surrounded by dark clouds. It looked creepy and would make a weak soul cower in fear and run away.

"Now why would I know?" Drasna snapped. Her sharp teeth were bared, and her frill flared up.

"I'm sorry. Let's just climb the tower and get this over with," Chaz said. He stepped into the tall dark tower. The interior was very prison-like. There were spikes and chains everywhere, the windows were barred, and skeletons dangled from the chains hanging from the ceiling. Chaz looked around nervously.

The two of them climbed the tower. It seemed to go on forever, each floor being almost identical to the last. Drasna had started to give up hope that they would ever get to the top. But finally they got to a floor that was different. It was empty, except for a large hatch in the ceiling.

"This room feels suspicious..." Drasna said. She looked at the hatch. Just then the hatch gave way, and a large wolf-like monster dropped down from above. It had deep, black fur and bright, yellow eyes. It let loose a blood-curdling snarl.

"Drasna, get back!" Chaz shouted, pushing Drasna out of the way as the monster charged.

Drasna waved her staff, and a bunch of rubble flew at the monster. It howled in pain and slashed at Chaz. Chaz parried its swipes with his sword. He then stabbed the monster in the face. The monster melted into black smoke.

"I think the monster was a sign that we are getting close. I think the dark lord is on the next floor," Chaz said. Drasna nodded at this and they walked up the stairs and to the next floor.

The next floor was royally decorated. It looked like it belonged to a king. Sitting on a throne in the back of the room was a black cat, who was dressed in a black dress.

"Hello, now shall we fight? You did interrupt my royal sitting after all!" she said. She took a longsword from a rack on the wall and charged at Chaz and Drasna.

Chaz parried the blow with his own sword. The dark lord encased her sword in shadows and knocked Chaz to the ground.

The dark lord waved her sword, and a shadowy hand grabbed Drasna. Drasna was pinned down by the hand.

Drasna looked at the dark lord and smirked. She waved her wand and a bunch of rocks smothered her. The dark lord gasped for breath but ended up suffocating. A green light pulsed from her body.

The green light engulfed the tower. The tower started turning to grey stone. The ground around the tower turned into a lush, green field. Flowers bloomed, and birds sang. "We did it! We killed the dark lord and saved the kingdom!" Chaz said cheerfully.

The two of them returned to their village. They were revered as heroes, heroes who could do anything.

Chaz continued to be a soldier, while Drasna retreated into the woods, to become a talisman seller. The kingdom lived on in peace, for the threat was gone.

THE UNFORGETTABLE SCHOOL SKI TRIP

Michael, a beginner skier, is going on a school ski trip with his friends and thinks that it's just that. In **THE UNFORGETTABLE SCHOOL SKI TRIP** *by* **Aidan Dwyer**, *Michael will never forget what happened on the ski hill that night....*

There I was, staring at the tallest mountain in Michigan. My mind went blank at the thought of WHY this was a good idea. I was only a beginner skier, and I was thinking about attempting to ski the tallest mountain in Michigan! I thought it would be fun to ski with my classmates, not deadly. Joining the Snow Club was a bad idea.

"Hey, Michael, you've been staring at the mountain for five minutes with your jaw hanging down, and your eyeballs look like they're gonna roll out of your head. Are you chickening out?"

I shook out of the trance that I was in and looked at who said that. It was my friend Bill. He likes to joke around with me.

"Michael, are you coming or what?" said my other friend Jeremy.

I got in line were they were at the ski lift.

Once we were on the ski lift, Bill said, "No way back now, Michael...."

"I'm going to do it! Chill out!" I said. He was right, though; there's no way back now. I can't chicken out now. I have to face it like a man.

As soon as we got off the lift, I skied over to the big billboard that said what the hills were and how hard they were. When I decided which one was for me, I turned around, and they were gone. Bill and Jeremy were gone.

I started to panic. I couldn't be up here alone. I can barely even ski! I tried to calm myself down. "I'll just go down the easiest hill and go find them..." I said to myself.

So I went down the hill. As I was skiing down, I realized that the snow was really icy. Then I passed a sign that said "Warning! You have entered a restricted area. There is no way back now, so take it slow and easy (if you can), and have a nice day." That made me worried. And what scared me even more was that I should have been watching where I was going, because in front of me was a cliff going straight down.

It was too late to stop. I just fell off the cliff and dropped into what seemed like a bottomless pit. I wanted to close my eyes so I didn't have to watch the ground flying up at my feet. But then it hit me: this wasn't the end.

As I was falling, I thought to myself, "Stay flat, land on your feet." And I did. I hit the ground on the bottom of my skis.

As I looked forward, there were what seemed like miles of forest and no other way to go. I knew that my only option was to ski through it. I started to slowly go through the forest, but it was steeper than I thought. All of a sudden, I was flying at full speed. I tried to dodge trees and branches, trying not to get hit.

Then, there was the biggest tree branch I ever saw, and it smacked me in the face. I was flat on my back, probably with a bloody nose, thinking, "Well, at least I'm not dead." I got up and saw I was at the edge of the forest. I was also as still as a statue, because I was staring at a family of five black bears.

My first thought was to ski around them, but when I looked at my feet, I saw I was missing a ski. It was bad enough that I lost it, but when I found where it was, the situation got even worse.

A bear cub was playing with it. I started to shiver. Maybe I won't make it out alive. But I knew that I should try and get my ski. Luckily, all the other bears were asleep, so I would just have to keep quiet.

I slowly walked over to the cub. He looked at me like I was nothing but a succulent filet, and I snatched the ski. As soon as I put it on, the cub grunted, and the bears woke from their deep sleep and glared at me.

I skied away as fast as possible. Faster than I thought, the bears went out of sight, and I was safe. But as soon as I turned around from my victory of not being eaten, I saw two-inch thick wood boards breaking over my face, and then I fell backward.

"Where am I? What are wood boards doing in the middle of the forest?" I said to myself. I turned around and realized that I had smashed into an abandoned mine. As soon as I stood up, rocks on top of the entrance collapsed, blocking the way out.

"No wonder it was boarded up..." I said. I removed my skis and started to wander through the mine. It was really cool. There were old cart rails and minerals to explore. But I remembered my main focus was to get out. So I went to the place that seemed the least dark to find the exit.

When I was too tired to walk any longer, I finally found the exit! I still thought I was doomed, but the exit was at a highway!

I waved for cars at the side of the road. Most of the cars passed by me like I was a speck of dust. After what seemed like hours of waving, a semi-truck stopped right in front of me. The driver rolled down the window and said, "Hey, I'm Alice. You need a ride?"

Man, I need to pay more attention to where Bill and Jeremy are, because then I wouldn't be in this mess. I was not expecting a tomboy in a semi-truck to give me a ride, but it's better than walking.

"Here I go again...who knows what adventure will await me now?" I said to myself.

1:20

THE ADVENTURES OF BATDUDE AND ROBRO

THE ADVENTURES OF BATDUDE AND ROBRO *by Jack Emerick is about two friends who are huge Batman fans. They encounter two other fans of the Joker and Bane, and hilarity ensues.*

It was about 6:30 A.M. in Northbrook, Illinois. The crisp winter air flew through Batdude's window, causing him to jump out of bed. His family still soundly slept while he groggily went downstairs to get a bowl of Lucky Charms. He put on his Batman shirt, pants, socks, and Jordans and walked off to school.

While walking, he saw his nemeses, the Joker and Bae, walking to the back of the school; he got suspicious and followed them. Batdude picked the lock of the tool shed with a paper clip and hid inside as he tossed his "old" iPhone 5 near them while recording so he could hear their plot.

He showed his friend Robro the footage he recorded. The Joker said, "If we dirty up all their other shoes, they'll have to open the collection to put on fresh kicks. Once that's done, you can jump in and snatch their shoes."

The next day was a very frigid Saturday. Batdude and Robro took advantage of this cold weather and took time to make a defense tactic and plan. Batdude explained to Robro, "If this is their legit plan, then we have to prepare for anything. We can't put our Jays at risk."

At around 3:45 in the afternoon, Batdude heard footsteps inside the house. He commanded Robro to prepare the spitball guns if the enemies infiltrated. Batdude got ready with a badminton racket if things got ugly.

All of a sudden, the door burst open. The Joker and Bae stood there with their "gold"- plated Heelys and a humongous can of neon green silly string. Batdude and Robro slid to cover while the Joker fired the silly string.

Robro rushed to the spitball guns to release a barrage of spitballs onto Bae, but he tripped over the maniacal silly string. Batdude tried covering Robro while he wiped the gunk off his expensive shoes. The Joker threw chewed gum on the ground while he dashed toward the collection of Lebrons.

Batdude found a pot on the ground and frantically dug the dirt out of it. He put it into a plastic cup on the floor, and threw it at the Joker. The Joker bellowed with rage as he desperately wiped off his shoes. Robro readied the guns, and hit The Joker right in the face.

Joker's mom called him for supper on his Samsung. He gave up with a red and enraged face as he walked out. It was over. Batdude and Robro had won. They booted the Joker out of their Man-Cave and relocated the high-tops in a more classified location. Robro set up advanced security and traps including marbles, water buckets, rancid milk, banana peels, and flashlights to make sure the Joker never entered the Man-Cave again.

THE ARMS OF A SCIENTIST *T. REX*

THE ARMS OF A SCIENTIST *T. REX* by *Trevor Peterson* *is a short story about a scientist* T. rex *dinosaur who believes life would be better for himself if his arms were bigger so he could clap hands. But something goes horribly wrong!*

There was a scientist *T. rex* dinosaur who thought, "I will make a ray gun that will grow my arms bigger so I can clap my hands." He wanted to clap because when he was in school all the other dinosaurs would tease him. He became a certified scientist so no other *T. rex* would be bullied as a kid.

He went to work in his factory making a ray gun. It took six days. On the seventh day he made the chemicals needed to activate the laser. Later, he tried it on himself. *ZAP.* A flash of lightning jolted out when it hit. But nothing happened. "Maybe my arms will grow overnight."

When he went to bed, his arms grew and grew until they were so big, they broke through the walls. "ARRRRRRRRRRRRRRRRGH! My arms have grown too big! I can't move my arms!"

He rushed to his ray gun, ripping the walls behind him. "Oh no, I put plutonium in the ray gun when I was supposed to use CO_2. Well, I must go on with my day. It's better than sitting in my bed complaining about how bad my arms are."

He went to make some pancakes, but when he grabbed for the mix, the bag ripped, and pancake powder went everywhere. "What a mess." When he went to get in his car to go to the factory, his arms went thought his windshield.

So he hired an assistant, and they went to work for 20 days. On the 21st day the *T. rex* said, "Zap me! Let's see what happens." With a *ZAP* and a flash of lightning, they watched and waited, but nothing happened.

In the morning his arms were back to regular size. He said to his assistant, "I like my arms the way they are, and I don't want to change them."

THE DARKNESS

THE DARKNESS, by *Tim Battle*, is the story of a boy who is afraid of the dark. He goes on a journey where he has to confront his fear.

Johnny's parents always tucked him into bed at night. They used to sing to him and check for monsters under his bed. He sleeps with a nightlight all the time. Now at night his dad sneaks into his room with a mask on and scares him. He always tries to scare him so Johnny won't be scared anymore. "Dad, that doesn't help, so please stop," Johnny says.

One night before dinner his mom asked if Johnny could get the laundry. He went downstairs and saw the laundry room. It was pitch black in there.

"But Mom, I don't want to go in the laundry room. It's too dark!" he yelled.

"You have to go. You need clothes for school tomorrow. Plus the only way to get over your fear is to face it," she called back.

"Okay," he said. When he entered the room he felt a chill up his spine. His eyes went black. He awoke in a dark forest.

There were many creatures in that forest. Johnny didn't know that. He walked aimlessly through the forest. He saw a creature with a stature that was familiar. It looked like his father, so he said, "Dad, Dad, Dad?" He heard a growl and a snarl.

When he got closer he saw a red glow in its eyes and a grin. By that time it was too late. He had to run.

The creature chased him and almost caught him, but it was a rugged and curvy path. There was a big bump in the road. The creature fell. So Johnny was able to get away from him when he turned the corner. Johnny knew now he needed to be more careful with whom he talked to.

As he was running he came across a well. He felt a force trying to push him in the well. Then he fell in. At the last second Johnny was pulled back up by someone named Fatty.

"Thank you," Johnny said.

"You're welcome," Fatty said. "Who are you, strange child?"

"My name is Johnny. Who are you?" Johnny asked.

"I am an imagination in your mind, but call me Fatty," Fatty said. "We must go. *It* is here," Fatty ordered.

"What? Why?" Johnny asked.

"No time to explain," Fatty said.

"Why did we have to run back there?" Johnny asked.

"Did you ever face a creature of pitch black in these dark forests?" Fatty asked.

"Yeah, it chased after me. I thought I lost it. I guess I didn't. I thought it was my father at first. Then it started chasing me," Johnny replied.

They came to the end of the forest. There was a big, bright light. Behind the light was a window. There was a cascade of sparkling stars that enhanced the light around the window. The window was shutting. He wondered why. He saw a giant hand with a glove shutting it. Johnny looked through. He saw his mom cooking dinner.

Fatty told him, "You don't have much time."

He had to get through the window quick. If he didn't, he would be trapped in his mind.

He jumped through the window. The creature tried to follow him. He was blocked by a force. Johnny got through the window.

When Johnny awoke, he was in the laundry room. He grabbed the clothes. He saw his friend Freddy with him. "Dude, are you okay?" Freddy said.

"Yeah. Wait, why are you here?" Johnny said.

"Remember, you invited me over to play video games? Your mom told me you were down here," Freddy said

"Oh yeah. Hey dude, do you want to stay over for dinner?" Johnny said.

"Sure," Freddy said.

They went upstairs, and Johnny had dinner with his mom and Freddy.

This experience made Johnny less afraid of the dark. After Freddy left, he told his mom all the things he experienced. Before Johnny went to bed, he realized that Fatty reminded him of his friend. The way he spoke and the way he acted reminded him of his friend Freddy.

THE FAKE REAL MAGIC HOUDINI

In **THE FAKE REAL MAGIC HOUDINI** by *Ethan DeCosta,* the supposedly non-supernatural Houdini finds his "late" father. However, he's in a place unlike any he's been before.

"Break the glass already! His face is red! He is going to die!"

My lungs burn in agony as I struggle not to breathe.

Blue light, like lightning, suddenly flashes across the whole room with what looks like glass reflectors inside the individual lightning-like streaks.

"Houdini's gone!" Bess, Houdini's partner, shouts over everyone with worry, but everyone cheers and applauds at what they believe to be a trick.

"Okay, everyone, show is over. Leave in an orderly fashion." No one can hear the ushers. It is far too chaotic, but slowly the spectators file out.

* * *

I feel weightless. I soon realize I'm falling from somewhere, yet in an instant I also configure in my brain that I'm not safe. The question I think is, from where? Is there anything I can do to help myself? It's too late.

Out of nowhere, I quickly hit something. I keep falling and then put my hands out while squeezing my eyes firmly shut. I mysteriously freeze. I slowly start to open my eyes, only to be frightened and fall the rest of the way finally to the ground.

When I open my eyes, a strange figure looks at me from the right on a cozy red hammock with a coconut in his hand. I think I may be going crazy. He stares at me while flicking his fingers across the rope of the hammock. Suddenly the coconut beverage he's holding refills on its own.

I try to stand, but the pain is too great. I realize that the amount of pain that I'm feeling in my ankle means it must be broken or dislocated or something. All of a sudden, it starts to heal quickly.

I realize that just as my ankle started to heal, the strange man in the hammock had changed his hand movements. I don't know who he is or what it means, but it seems that somehow in a way I do.

I walk up to him, obviously cautiously. Before I know it he grasps my head in a quick but gentle way. For some strange reason I don't swat his hand away.

"Who are you?" I ask curiously.

After a second look, he drops his hand. "I'm your dad."

I immediately react and punch him for claiming to be my late father.

"I am your dad. I didn't really die. It was just some form of magic I did by accident. No one ever explained to me what sometimes runs through our family."

"Wait just a second. What are you talking about, sometimes runs through the family? Oh, and while we are talking about family, why didn't you ever come back to your family, all of us!"

"Some generations just inherit magic. You and I just happened to. Also, not that I have to tell you since I am still your dad, but I found out everything I could about the same portal that you found and learned enough magic to get to it," he says, loudly and angrily. But he calms down. "I figured that you guys would have given up on, well, seeing me again."

Having real magic makes me a liar for all those magic acts I did when I claimed to be performing tricks, and not using supernatural powers. That doesn't matter, though, for now at least. All I need to do now is get back home to the rest of our family.

I or anybody can see the worry on my father's face about him not wanting me to leave.

Even though I can see that on his face I still ask him, "How do I get back home?" All I can hear is silence, silence, and more silence. The only thing I hear is the worried sound of my heart beating. I'm almost sure that he will say there is no way to get back.

Then he begins opening his mouth. It feels like slow motion to me, but I'm not so sure if that is the worry or the whole magic thing. "Actually, there is in fact a way. There is a way back to the portal that someone can tell you about."

I think I understand what he is saying. Somehow I have a feeling that he already knows where the portal is. I am reluctant to ask him, knowing it might hurt him to tell me. But I have to, so I say, "Do you already know something that you're purposely not telling me?" It then occurs to me that it came off not at all the way I had meant for it to sound.

He lowers his head. "There is a portal on the other side of the world. With how big this world is and without knowing how to use magic, it can take a matter of years to get to it."

I know what I have to do. "Okay then, teach me magic; more specifically traveler's magic," I add.

He says, though, that the only traveler's magic he knows of is no more than 2,500 miles at a time and is a huge power sucker as well. This means that when used it will drain so much energy, it can take up to ten more days for a person's powers to return, and that is for a decent conjurer like himself. The spell simply isn't safe for a newcomer to magic like me.

I begin to explain all the physical training I have already done, but he says any training of that sort will do nothing compared to what is needed. So we train immediately.

Within a matter of six months he proclaims I am ready. I am so happy to see his proud-of-you face. Losing him so early in my life, I never really got a great chance to see that face. I just somehow know that's what this expression means.

Soon after, we start our travels. If we stay in contact with one another, we will be guaranteed to end up in the same place and use half the energy. This means it will then only take half the time to recharge. So I suggest that we go 5000 miles at a time using just as much power as we would separately going 2500 miles. I then take back that offer since I can tell that he just wants more time to see me after so many years away.

Along the way, I question him as subtly as I can, being upset and wanting all the answers before it's time to leave.

Before I know it, we arrive at what I hope is actually close to the end. This time it's not. It's not something that can be solved by magic, at least not where we are now. This is a no-magic zone. For the most part, no magic can be used in the magic barrier of this area. It's an area known as the fogs because everything that happens here happens with no reason and you can't ever really know what's fake or true.

Finally, though, I realize that in this place I've got a skill that no one else has acquired. It is time to use my skills. We need transportation, and we need it quickly because these barriers aren't just against magic. They can trap someone with powers for good.

I scope out everyone in our location with a transportation device. I look over to a young guy who seems gullible enough. I walk over to him and make a bet that he can lock me up in any way and I will get out within exactly fifteen minutes. I promise I will not be flashy in this tough of a circumstance, at least to myself. I don't have that commitment to anyone else.

He locks me up in what is like nothing I've ever seen before. The second I hear the gears as he is opening the device, I know right when he puts one-of-a-kind cuffs on me.

As he opens the locks people are still gathering. The people are crowded by now, making my trick only slightly more difficult for me.

As soon as the unique cuffs are secure I jump over my wrists. In five seconds, not that I counted, I have them off and in his hands. I look over at my dad and again see his impressed face.

We ride out of the town in our newly-won truck, and within an hour we are at the portal probably 25 miles beyond where we were previously. I am about to jump through the portal, but just then I don't. I try to quickly grab hold of my dad. He isn't able to come through. I refuse to leave without him. He just will not go through.

"I refuse to go without you!" I yell as he continues to tell me to go through. When he keeps telling me to go through I scream it at him at the top of my lungs. I then cough. I transport myself accidently.

I'm in an unfamiliar house, or at least I think it's a house. Out of the blue I'm transported again. There is a lady here, and I figure it must be the lady that transported me again bringing me here, considering I'm positive that it just wasn't me. This room bears a very strong resemblance to the previous, leading me to believe I have not yet left this house. I mean I am definitely surprised but also not, considering how many people there must be in the universe plus all the alternate time streams wielding magic. There's plenty of possibilities, but the point is why her who just so happens to be sitting so shadowy?

She is an elderly lady. She turns around and begins to just randomly start explaining about the portal. She is telling me how it works and who gave it those powers and why they made it that way. "There is a time limit on how long you can be through the portal and not go back. You can only be through the portal for a year at a time."

What hit me by the time she is finished and I stop listening is that I am sitting on my own bed. My dad is not here, but I know, though, that I have been there with him—wherever "there" is, because I have what my dad supposedly took to the grave with him...his platinum, silver, and gold dagger with the word "time" inscribed near the top of the hilt. I only now realize that something lies beneath the circular design and inscription. This one-of-a-kind, family heirloom magic dagger holds a rather unique custom timepiece.

FRESH FROM THE DESERT

When Mohamed comes to America, he has trouble adapting. He experiences funny and embarrassing moments adjusting to a new country in **FRESH FROM THE DESERT** *by **Mostafa Ghanem**.*

My name is Mohammed. I moved to New York with my family from Egypt last year. I will admit I was really nervous coming to a new country, and I tried to fit in so hard. Still I faced lots of embarrassing and funny moments.

I have to say the funniest story is the one when my mom packed me a lunch for school. She packed me Egyptian foods with the strongest smell. Really, Mom, come on; were you trying on purpose! Here is what she packed: Tumaya, a really strong garlic paste with pickled turnips, and last but not least a shawarma sandwich. What were you thinking, Mom? This is not Egypt; it's America. The whole cafeteria stayed away from me!

One week later I had an incident with my accent. See, the Arabic language does not have the letter P, so the closest letter is B. I was at Five Guys with my friends where I ordered a burger and "Bebsi." They started dying laughing, so I thought they did not have Pepsi. I said, "Okay, I will have Dr. Bebber." They laughed more, so I got lemonade and a bunch of looks. I don't think I ordered that!

My friends were over at my house one day, and I had forgotten to do my bed. Oh, no, my mom is going to freak. When an Arab mom freaks, she screams like there is a death in the family. So she comes in the room screaming. The reaction on my friends' faces was "These people are crazy! Run!" Their parents actually tell them calmly to make their beds, but not an Arab; oh, no, not an Arab! So now we hang out at their houses.

We got our first car in America. We were so excited. We took it out for a ride, and people in America drive as slow as a turtle. My dad was screaming, "Wake up, wake up!" See, in Egypt people drive much faster, so my dad started to drive like he was driving on the autobahn. The police gave him a ticket so fast that we now use taxis.

Before, I would get embarrassed about these moments, and anyone would, but now I just laugh and know I will never change.

FURIOUS CRIME FIGHTERS

FURIOUS CRIME FIGHTERS by **Will Rogers** *is the story of the Fabulous Five solving crime in their city. When Major Meat is captured, will they save the day?*

One day in the fridge, four superheroes—Pete Pizza, Dougie Doughnut, Pierre Pickle, and Chester Cheese—were watching over the land of Freezerville. Suddenly they heard a loud noise coming from Mayor Meat's town hall. When they went to check it out, they saw a huge hole in the wall. "What happened here?" asked Pete.

"Looks like an attack from Dr. Hamburger again," Chester said.

When they went inside they saw a note: "If you want your mayor back, you'll have to come and get him."

"Dougie, why is Dr. Hamburger always after Mayor Meat?"

"Well," said Dougie, "Mayor Meat and Dr. Hamburger are brothers, and Mayor Meat was always the superior sibling, so after childhood Dr. Hamburger swore to get him back."

"All right, everybody, get onto my back," Pete said with a sigh. Off they flew.

"We're here," exclaimed Pete.

"Wow, that was quick," said Pierre. They blew down the wall with a *bang,* and they all filed in.

"Oh, I see you got the note. But it's too late," said Dr. Hamburger. They all looked over and saw smashed meat chunks.

"Noooo!" said Chester. "Food powers: go!"

All heroes jumped into action. Pete did a flying kick. Dougie used his brainwaves to drop a chair on Hamburger's head. Pierre used his super-strength to obliterate him. Chester hit him with his staff. Together, they took down Dr. Hamburger.

All the superheroes went home. "Where's Mayor Meat?" asked Bob Bacon.

"He is gone now," said Pete.

All the food heroes were sad, and they had a funeral.

"Well, we need a new mayor," said Pete.

They elected a new mayor, and peace was restored.

IFAIL 6

*In **IFAIL 6** by **Kenny Pepper**, Randi's new phone goes insane. Will Randi be able to stop the phone from ruining his life, or will his phone get the best of him?*

"Randi, I got you a new phone!" Randi's dad yelled when he got home from work.

"Sweet, what kind is it, Dad?" Randi shouted as he sprinted to see what it was.

"I don't know," his father replied. "I got it on sale at Bob's Electronics."

"Cool, I will go test it out," Randi said gladly as he walked up to his room. *Let's see here, how do you turn it on?* he thought. Then he found THERE'S NO "ON" BUTTON! *No wonder he got it on sale,* he thought. *You can't turn the stupid thing on. I guess I'll deal with it in the morning.*

Randi woke up, had breakfast, brushed his teeth and hair, got dressed, and walked right out the door. Randi lives really close to his school, so he walks when he can. When he got to school his best friend Spike greeted him like this: "Hey, Randi, how's life without a phone?"

Randi got this huge smirk on his face. "What do you mean?" Randi said as he pulled out his new phone.

"Cool, what is it?" Spiked yelled.

"I don't know, my dad got it on sale," Randi replied. "The only problem I have is that I don't know how to turn it on."

Just then Spike grabbed the phone out of Randi's hand and threw it on the ground. Randi screamed in horror as he picked up his phone, and right when he was about to kill Spike, he could see that his phone was on. "You're welcome," Spike said with a grin on his face.

"What was that for?" Randi yelled at Spike. "You could have broken it."

"I didn't try to break it," Spike said. "I just thought that it might work if I banged it on something." The bell rang, and Randi was still fooling around with his phone.

At the end of the day, Randi did not go home. He sat on a bench in front of his school and tried to figure out his new phone. He turned it on, and tried to slide the screen with his fingers. His screen did not budge. He tried again with the same outcome. He tried moving it with a pencil, paper, and even his tongue! It still did not move.

Randi was blowing the spit off his phone when the screen flipped. He blew again, and it moved again. Then he blew on an app and it opened, but to the wrong thing. "God, this phone stinks!" Randi yelled. "I'm done with you for today," Randi told his phone as he walked home for the day.

The next day when Randi went to his first class (math), he realized that his phone had been making noise, so he pulled it out and looked at it to see if it was on. Not a light lit in the screen. When class started Miss Green asked how everyone's day was going, and Randi's phone blurted out, "Terrible now that you are here." The class looked in astonishment as Miss Green walked over to Randi's desk.

Randi was the first one to speak out of the both of them. "It was not me," he said. "It was my phone."

The whole classed laughed, and then Miss Green spoke. "I'm not sending you to the principal's office because of the rude remark, but because you tried to lie about it," Miss Green said to Randi as she escorted him into the office.

Randi's whole day was like this with the phone and the office. In his next two classes his phone went, "RED ALERT, RED ALERT, BUTTHEAD TEACHING THE CLASS, BUTTHEAD THEACHING THE CLASS." Then in his fourth-hour it said "shut up" any time one of his classmates would speak. Finally in his last two hours it was quiet, but he ended the day in the principal's office anyway.

At the end of the day, Randi got called to the office, and everyone knew what for. He dragged his feet all the way down the hall and into Mrs. Reed's office. When Randi came out Spike was waiting for him. Randi told him all about how she thought that he was being very rude and disrespectful to the staff and how they had worked hard to be where they are so he should treat them with respect. She also said that if this happened again that he would be expelled, and this time he is lucky to only be suspended for two days.

When Randi got home, he could tell that his dad knew what had happened that day. "Sit down," Randi's father said to him when he walked in the door. "Randi, I'm going to just cut to the chase. I am very disappointed in you, and I think that I'm going to have to take your phone away."

When Randi heard that, he almost jumped up and hugged his dad, but he knew if he did, then his dad would take something else away on top of the phone, so he just acted sad. "Okay," he said in sorrow as he handed over the phone.

A couple of weeks later, Randi's dad was ready to give him his phone back, but Randi said that he did not need a phone right now and that he would tell him when he did need one.

After his dad got rid of Randi's phone, he was a straight A student and was liked by many teachers (not including Miss Green). In the end, he realized that a phone just gives you more trouble than you need, and that life is just fine without one.

JACKIE AND HER DAD

JACKIE AND HER DAD *by **Rachel Sample** Is about a sudden death in Jackie's family. She will have to solve another mystery before she can find out what really happened.*

It was a sunny December day and time for Jackie's dad to leave for work. He said goodbye and was out the door. Jackie grabbed her bag and left for school.

Jackie had a great day at school. When she came home she wondered where her dad was. Her mom thought it was strange that he wasn't home also. A few minutes later, she heard a big bang nearby. That surprised Jackie and her mom. They left to see what was going on down the street. When they got there, Jackie saw a dead body. It was her dad.

The police didn't have any clues. They believed it could have been a robbery.

The day of the funeral came, and everyone was very sad. Everybody's eyes had tears. It was so quiet you could hear someone blowing their nose from across the room. When it was Jackie's turn to speak, all she could do was cry.

A man came to the front of the room and spoke for her. After the service she thanked him and asked him how he knew her dad. He said his name was John and that he was her dad's best friend before she was born. He moved and lost contact with her dad but saw the story on the news.

"I think that it may have been my son that killed your father," John said. "I sent my son to go get his brother a birthday present. After we heard a big bang, my son texted me that his friends were invited to go somewhere together. He must have run away so no one would have suspected him. But that is just what I think." John knew the store his son was going to was very near where Jackie's dad was killed. A few minutes later he said that he had to go. "I am really sorry," John said.

Jackie was worried. She didn't know if she should tell the police this information or not. She didn't want to look silly, but at the same time wanted the mystery solved. She decided to sleep on it.

The next day as Jackie was looking through her dad's things she found her dad's diary. The diary told about how her dad had been having arguments with the owner of the corner store and with John's son. The store wasn't far from where her dad was killed. She decided this diary was evidence of who might have killed her father.

She went to the corner store, and she asked some questions. "Who was in this store yesterday around the time my dad was killed? Who bought anything around that time? What did they buy? Did you see anything to solve this mystery?" Jackie was full of questions.

The store owner said he never got along with her dad but didn't hurt him. He thought he saw her dad arguing with John's son about money. She began to worry because John thought it was his son, too.

She called the police. She told them the whole story. The police went to talk to the store owner to find out what happened. The police talked to the storeowner for a long time in the back of the store. He admitted that he did the crime and said he was sorry. He said he was mad and lost his temper and shot him.

As soon as Jackie found out, she was upset. She was happy to know the truth, but also sad knowing her dad was never coming back. Jack said he was sorry, and he apologized to Jackie and her family.

JERRY
THE TIME-TRAVELING DOG

When you see a dog, you think everything is fine, but in Jerry's life it isn't. **JERRY THE TIME TRAVELING DOG** *by* **Jack Darbonne** *is a story about a dog who finds himself in a strange situation.*

In 1995 on a bright, sunny day, right outside Jerry the dog's house, sat Jerry. Jerry was a pit-bull dog and had many things on his mind. Jerry's owner Dave was a genius. Dave knew everything about computers and gadgets.

Dave walked outside and sat down next to Jerry. With a frown on Dave's face he told Jerry about the last dream he had. His dream was about Jerry getting hit by a red car and dying. Intensely, Jerry was listening to Dave as he went on and on about his dream.

Near the end of Dave's story Dave told him that he was afraid his dreams were actually going to happen in the future. Before, Dave had accidentally zapped himself with a device that would make his dreams come true. This device was bad for Dave because he knew all of his dreams would come true. This device was a curse. So Dave decided to keep a close eye on Jerry throughout the rest of the week.

Jerry liked exploring around the house. He went this way and that, but today he found something. He saw a button. The button was behind the couch. It was hidden, but Jerry had a keen eye. Somehow Jerry had not noticed this button before, but it was flashing. Jerry saw this as urgent and thought he should help. Jerry slipped under the couch and pressed the button. Suddenly, Jerry was falling into a black hole.

Thump. Jerry stood up and walked around; he saw all of Dave's gadgets! He was so excited! He went over to the first one and pressed it. The next thing he knew, he was in the same place, but it felt different from before. There were more gadgets than Jerry had seen a moment before. It seemed like he had been somewhere different! Had Jerry just traveled in time?

He climbed his way to the surface of his house and found Dave, older and cooking his favorite meal, eggs. He walked outside and saw an older version of himself walking into the street. He knew what was going to happen.

Jerry had read books about time travel and knew you could not let yourself see yourself. Somehow he had to find a way to save himself, and fast.

All he could find was a long pole resting on the side of the house. It was Dave's pool net pole. He grabbed the pole. He struggled with his paws and managed to scoop Jerry out of the way and save the day. About a second after, the red car came whizzing by just like in Dave's dream.

This was too much for Jerry, and he clicked the button and automatically traveled back to Dave's secret room and went home.

L.B.I.

A girl and her mother realize they have made a bad decision about a hurricane. Find out in **L.B.I.** *by* **Meighan Lindstrom** *if their decision will cost them their lives.*

"Long Beach Island, New Jersey has been ordered to evacuate. Everyone on the Island has to leave by 7:00 P.M. The causeway bridge will be closed at 10:00 P.M.," reported the news anchor from Channel 9.

"I bet it's just another warning, Gracey. Let's just see how it goes for now," Mom said.

"Okay, Mom, but what if it's going to be as bad as they say it will be?" I asked.

"Let's just wait and see. The last couple of times that there were warnings, it never turned into a big storm," she reminded me.

We watched the rest of the broadcast until we heard sirens outside on the street. Police cars were driving around directing everyone to leave the Island. My mom and I went upstairs so the officers would not notice that we chose to stay behind.

We stayed up there for a couple of hours, watching the rain pour. My worry began to grow that this was going to be a serious hurricane. I wanted to tell my mom how worried I was, and that we made a mistake. It was getting dark now and would take too long to get to the bridge if we left anyway.

We were barely able to sleep, listening to the wind and rain. I hoped the storm would quiet down soon, but the storm only got stronger. We woke up around 5:00 in the morning and knew this was not a false warning! "Mom, I think we were wrong," I said. The rain was pounding on our house now. The wind was so strong it blew open one of the windows downstairs. Outside, patio furniture was flying everywhere.

My mom was finally getting it, and yelled, "Yes, we need to leave!"

I ran down the stairs and could see water surging down the street. On the boulevard, there were cars floating, banging into other cars and houses. The boats in the marina were slamming against each other. We ran to our car and tried to start it. The water was too high, and the car stalled out. Mom grabbed our old orange life-jackets from the garage.

"Where do we go?" I yelled.

"The Sea Shell Inn!" she screamed back. "That's where the Coast Guard is staying!"

We tried to run to the old hotel, but we only made it a few houses past our own. There was a strong gas smell in the air that took us by surprise. Siding was blowing off houses and ripping past us. There was no way we were going to make another ten blocks. We had to go back to our house.

The water was almost up to the top porch step. Once inside, we locked the front door and climbed up into the loft. Within minutes, we could see the water rushing in under the front door, spilling into the living room and hallway. Mom opened the loft window. We climbed out onto the roof of the back room.

Immediately, the rain, wind and sand were pounding on us. It felt like millions of needles piercing our skin, as the wind hurled the beach and ocean at us. "How are we going to get out of here? There's water everywhere."

Mom said, "We're going to stay here and hope someone can help us."

It felt like we were on the roof for hours

We were not the only ones who decided to stay and ride out the storm. I knew all the fishermen were planning on staying, as well as the owners of the Sea Shell Inn. I could see the lights of the Inn flickering 10 blocks away.

There was a faint roar in the distance. It was coming closer. Within a few minutes, it was as loud as the storm. A helicopter was heading our way!

We signaled for help, and soon their searchlights were on us. The helicopter circled around, trying to get in the right, steady position. The wind was blowing hard, and the helicopter struggled to keep its place above us. The water sprayed at our house even harder as my mom and I waited. Finally, a Coast Guard rescuer was lowered down on a rope and reached us on the roof.

"I need you both to do exactly as I tell you, and we'll get you both to safety in no time! I'm going to belt you in one at a time, and once you're secure, the rope will slowly lift you up, and you'll be pulled into the helicopter!" he shouted. "Your daughter goes first, while I will stay with you."

We nodded to him that we understood.

The rescuer belted me and signaled to the crew that I was ready to go. Slowly, the rope pulled me up, as I tossed around with each gust.

Within seconds, a crew member pulled me into the helicopter and quickly took off the rope to lower it back down. I was then buckled in and given headphones.

The helicopter continued to rock in the wind. I was terrified that my mom hadn't made it up yet. I couldn't see her from where I was. Each time the wind slammed into the helicopter, I became even more scared.

Finally, my mom and the rescuer were pulled in. We were speechless. We looked down on the island as we flew away, just as the ocean and the bay met.

THE LOCK-UP AUDITIONS

A girl named Jessica learns the true meaning of bravery all because of a summer camp in **THE LOCK-UP AUDITIONS**, *by* ***Courtney M. Young***.

Jessica was nervous, sweating, and couldn't stop going over her music. The ride to the A.S.O. (Amazing Symphony Orchestra) Summer Camp auditions felt like forever when the building was only 25 minutes away.

Jessica's mom, dad, and little brother were coming to see her audition. They were jumping and screaming, but Jessica wasn't. Jessica wasn't jumping around and making a fool of herself because every time she did that she would shake and mess up her music playing. But, when Jessica stepped out of the car, she felt so small compared to the three-story building.

"Don't worry, Jessica, you'll do fine," said Jessica's mom.

Jessica walked in. There was a huge line of people waiting to audition. Jessica grabbed her cello from her mom and got in line. Once Jessica got to the front of the line she saw that Mr. Dan was the person giving everyone their numbers. Everyone on the internet said that Mr. Dan was a very devious person, but Jessica begged to differ.

"Name?" asked Mr. Dan.

"Jessica Bryant," replied Jessica.

"Here you go, number 100. Step in the line to my left and your right," said Mr. Dan.

Jessica got less nervous once she knew her number. She saw some of her friends practicing, but she decided to leave them alone and not worry them.

Jessica found a chair and stand and started practicing her music. She kept messing up and was getting frustrated with herself. Then her friend Callie came over and told her just to relax and play like she never played before. Callie and Jessica were best friends and had played in the orchestra together ever since fifth grade.

Once auditions got started, Jessica felt a little more nervous.

"Number 99!" yelled Mr. Dan.

It was almost Jessica's turn to audition, but she couldn't find her family in the audience. Her family was a family of four. The youngest was her little brother James, and then came Jessica. Her parents were Carol and Carlton. She finally told herself to relax and just go for it.

"Number 100," said Mr. Dan.

Jessica tiptoed onto the stage, got her music set, and started playing. When Jessica played she didn't mess up at all. Once she was done, everyone in the audience clapped and cheered very loudly. Jessica was so happy to finally go home after all of the auditions. Jessica knew that it would take a while to see if she made it into A.S.O.

A couple of weeks after New Year's Day Jessica got her results. Jessica was too scared to open the envelope herself, so she had her mom open it.

"Congratulations! You have made it into A.S.O. We look forward to seeing you this summer. Sincerely, Dan," read Carol.

"Is that it?" asked James.

"Looks like it," answered Carol.

"Well, congratulations, Jessica. We are so proud," said Carlton.

By that time Jessica was screaming and jumping all around the house. Jessica was so thrilled she thought to call Callie and see if she made it.

"Callie? Callie, are you there?" asked Jessica.

"Yeah, right here. We just opened my letter and I got accepted, but my parents will be out of town and I don't know if I'll be able to go," said Callie.

"I'm sure my mom can take you when I go, too!" assumed Jessica.

As the time went by, summer was getting closer and closer. Jessica got so excited and couldn't wait until A.S.O. Summer Camp. Jessica packed early so she wouldn't panic when packing for the trip. Jessica and Callie learned that they could ride together after Carol talked to Callie's parents.

On the day before A.S.O. Summer Camp started, Jessica and Callie couldn't stop talking about it.

"Are you girls ready to go?" asked Jessica's mom.

"Yeah!" replied the girls.

All throughout the car ride the girls fingered their music, and couldn't stop talking about how they thought the overnight experience would go. Jessica was still kind of nervous, but she just let her excitement take over.

Once they were there, the girls said goodbye to Jessica's mom and ran into the meeting room. They were the first people to arrive. Mr. Dan was very eager to see his early arrivals.

"Welcome to A.S.O. Summer Camp," Mr. Dan said to the girls. "Would you to like to bunk in the same room?"

"Uh…yeah, that sounds nice," said Jessica.

Mr. Dan showed them the greatest room in the camp. They agreed to take it, and got settled in. Once more people were at the camp, they had a big meeting about how the camp was going to be. Everyone got the rest of the day to meet and greet other people, get settled, and rest.

In the morning there was a big surprise. No one could get out of their rooms. On a loudspeaker was Mr. Dan's voice.

"Hello, everyone. Get used to your room 'cause you will never come out of these rooms unless someone feels courageous enough to try and unlock everyone," said Mr. Dan.

"Callie, we have to do something about this. I knew something was wrong with that man," said Jessica.

Jessica and Callie tried their hardest to unlock the door, but it wasn't working. So they looked for other ways to get out of their room.

"Jessica, I found an air vent. Maybe we could get out that way," said Callie.

The girls grabbed their phones, broke the vent, and started crawling. The girls traveled through the vent for about 30 minutes until they found the end of it that led to a secret room. They crawled into the room, and there was a lit-up screen on a podium. On the lit-up screen it read: "To unlock all attendees you know that you are never too classic for classical." Also in the room was one of each string instrument. There was a violin, viola, cello, and bass.

"What does that even mean?" asked Jessica.

"Well, let's think. We're at a classical music summer camp, for string instruments only…" thought Callie.

"I got it. We need something that is classical to unlock everyone, like a music note or something," said Jessica.

"So does that mean we need to use one of the instruments?" asked Callie.

"Yeah, I'll play so we can free everyone," said Jessica.

Callie grabbed the cello so Jessica could try and free everyone. Callie and Jessica decided that Jessica should play the hardest note on the cello. Jessica was scared, but then she thought about everyone else out there locked up.

After Jessica played, the words on the podium changed. The podium read: "You are very courageous to save everyone. All doors have been unlocked."

Jessica had Callie call 911 to have them arrest Mr. Dan and his colleagues for their despicable trick. Once Callie got off the phone they were back in their room. They immediately packed their things and headed out. Once again they were the first people out and had a conversation with the police officers. They called Jessica's mom and went back home.

Later that week the police officers said that Mr. Dan and his colleagues would be put on trial for what they did.

"Jessica, Callie. Guess what the police just said," said Carol.

"What?" they asked.

"The officers just said that Mr. Dan and his other workers will be put on trial and you guys are the plaintiffs," answered Carol.

The girls were surprised at what happened, but they knew they needed to do it for the safety of everyone else.

"We are so proud of you guys. How about we invite Callie's family over and have a big celebration dinner?" said Carol.

"I'd love that!" answered Callie.

Later on that year, the girls decided that they would like to run A.S.O. Summer Camp in the future. Their parents agreed to this idea and said that they would help run the business. The girls really appreciated the help of their parents. The girls knew that they would be able to reach this goal once they got out of college.

Many years later, Callie and Jessica held auditions and let almost everyone into the summer camp. They had three meals a day, practiced challenging songs, and had breaks to meet other people. The A.S.O. Summer Camp was featured in a news article in the paper. Their parents were a huge help to this successful goal. Callie and Jessica loved their job.

THE NEW HOUSE

*Kenny and his family move to a new house and discover an unexpected guest already living there. In the story **THE NEW HOUSE** by **Ryan S. Duffy**, a boy and his younger brother learn that moving to a new house can be difficult and even scary.*

"Jordan, run!" I yelled.

"Where is Luke?" asked Jordan in a worried tone.

"I thought he was with you!"

This all started when my younger brother Luke and I moved with our mom and dad to our new house in Harbor Springs, Michigan. "Kenny, stop doing that to your brother. He is only nine, you know."

Yes, I know, Mom.

"Give me back my iPad, Kenny!" yelled Luke. "You are four years older than me. It is not fair when you take my stuff. Hey, Mom, when are we going to be there?" asked Luke.

"Stop being so impatient," I said, perhaps a bit rudely.

"We will be there in 10 minutes," said Mom.

Finally we got there after 10 minutes that felt like an hour because we were not allowed to use any of our electronics. All we could do was look out the windows. All I could see on both sides were trees. I asked, "Dad, are we lost?"

"Of course not. The house is right up there. Do you see it?" said my dad.

"No, all I see is a place that looks like it just survived a hurricane." This place looks like it was built by people who liked big, old, worn down places. I wonder if this place even has paint on it. All I could see was moldy wood and weathered rock. Also, what was up with the broken windows?

"Well, son, I hope you learn to like it because that is our new house," said Dad.

"Let's go inside and check it out," my mom suggested.

The house looked like it was straight out of a horror movie. It had long hallways that led to single rooms with old paintings where the eyes on them seemed to follow you. The house was just as old and worn down on the inside as the outside. But the worst things about the house were the basement and the attic. The basement was dark with one light bulb that would flicker on and off. There were not even windows in this place. I could not see very well down there, which I was a little happy about because who knows what could be down there?

The attic was creepy for a different reason. It was creepy because the floor was creaky, the windows were all broken, and every once in a while I heard this strange moaning sound. In my opinion the house was even creepier inside than out.

My little brother liked it! He thought it was cool.

It was getting late. Because the house was so big, it took forever to look around. Also the house is so far in the woods and away from everyone else, it took forever to get here.

We all went to bed, but I just could not fall asleep because something did not feel right. After a while I got hungry, so I went down the stairs and into the kitchen to get a snack. When I got to the fridge I felt a chill go down by back before I opened it.

I opened the fridge and got out a yogurt. After I finished I walked upstairs, but I remembered that I left the fridge door open. I walked downstairs and walked back into the kitchen to see the fridge door open, but I noticed there was another change. The chair right next to where I had just sat down was pulled out from the table like someone had been sitting next to me. But I just thought it was my mind playing tricks on me because I was tired. I went back to my room to go to sleep.

In the morning Luke and I were walking around the house, and we both heard a loud bang come from the attic. I said, "What was that?" Luke had the idea of checking it out, but I was not so sure about it. But I was the older brother, and I could not act like I was scared.

We both ran up the attic stairs to find the paintings that I called creepy all standing straight up on the floor. Then I saw what made the bang. It was one of the floor boards cracked right in half as if something was standing on it when it snapped. The worst part was no one was up there.

After a long week of these unexplained happenings no one else noticed anything strange or unusual about this house. Luke even invited his friend Jordan over.

It gets worse. My mom and dad left me to babysit them. That was not the bad part. The bad part is they left us alone in this place, and, yes, I said alone. After they left I went upstairs to check on

Luke and Jordan. But I heard a loud thump that came from the kitchen.

I ran to get Luke and Jordan and then grabbed my baseball bat. We walked slowly and quietly to the kitchen. When we got to the kitchen we saw that all the chairs were upside down on the table.

There was obviously a ghost in the house. We decided to find it. We also thought it would be good to turn off all the lights and only use flashlights so we could see the ghost.

I went to the basement because it was the only place I never went to normally. Luke and Jordan thought it would be good to check the attic.

I walked slowly down the basement steps. I was so happy I had the flashlight because I could barely see. I felt the same chill go down my back like when I was in the kitchen. I heard the door lock shut when I got to the bottom of the stairs. I knew it was the ghost that had been haunting the house! I did not know what to do. Then I thought he might be going for Luke and Jordan, so I turned back and busted down the door.

I looked around, but there was no sign of Luke or Jordan. Then I remembered that they were checking the attic. I ran up the first set of stairs and then went down the hallway and saw the ghost creeping up on Jordan. The ghost was the scariest thing I have ever seen. It had ripped up clothes and there was no flesh on his face. It was all bone. "Jordan, run!" I yelled.

Right after I said it, the ghost whipped around and started to chase us.

"Where is Luke?" asked Jordan in a worried tone.

"I thought he was with you!" I said back. We were both sprinting down the hallways with the ghost right behind us.

I told Jordan that I knew a way out, but I told him he was going to have to trust me. He nodded mostly because he was almost out of breath. We ran until I saw the laundry chute.

I told him to follow me. I dove headfirst down it with Jordan right behind me.

After we got to the bottom we saw Luke curled up in a ball in the corner. I grabbed Luke by the shirt and yelled, "Run!" We ran up the basement steps. We ran to the open front door. We were ten feet away when the door slammed shut!

The ghost had finally cornered us. I was frozen in place with shock and fear. My hands were trembling and I was sweating. Then

I heard the car pulling into the driveway. At that moment the ghost disappeared like it was afraid of my parents.

Once they opened the door they looked at us and said, "It looks like you guys saw a ghost."

POWER IN THE TOUCH

POWER IN THE TOUCH *by* **E. L. Robertson** *is the story of 17-year-old Jase Richards. When he visits an engineering center, something strange happens that changes who he is and what he can do.*

Jase Richards is a 17-year-old senior going to Civil Ville High School. He lives with his older cousin Mary Stephens. Mary is 23 years old. Jase has a best friend named Tyson Dickson. Tyson's dad works at an engineering center.

It was senior ditch day at Civil Ville. Mary and Tyson's dad didn't want either of the boys sitting at home all day. Mr. Dickson decided to take Tyson and Jase on a tour of the engineering center.

Jase was bored out of his mind. Something cheered him up, though. During the tour Jase saw an electrical generator. He left the tour to check it out some more. He touched the generator and—*BAM!*—the generator shocked him so hard he flew to the wall with full force.

Jase was knocked out for a few seconds. He wasn't feeling very great. His hands were tingly, he was shaking, and he was seeing two. So Jase called Tyson and told him he was leaving. He didn't want Tyson and his dad to think he just vanished without saying anything.

Jase didn't want to walk home because he thought he was going to walk into a wall or something. Instead he called a taxi. When Jase got home he went straight to sleep.

When Jase woke up he wasn't feeling as weird as he had been the day before. A few minutes later something strange happened. He threw his hand up to yawn, and a blue beam shot out of his hand and cracked his lightbulb. He had no idea what had just happened. Then he swung his hand like he was throwing a baseball, and the beam came out again. This time it came out so hard it hit his television and exploded it. Mary heard the explosion and yelled, "Jase, what was that noise?"

"Nothing, Mare. I just hit the TV with my basketball," Jase replied. Jase didn't want his older cousin to find out because he barely knew what was going on.

His mind just went blank. He decided to skip a full day of school and go back to the engineering center. He went straight to Tyson's dad. He asked a lot of questions. Mr. Dickson ran a lot of tests. He stuck wires to Jase's head and took blood from him.

Mr. Dickson found out that Jase had an electrical ability. Jase was shocked and happy put together. Mr. Dickson was a little bit nervous to let him leave. The thing was that Mr. Dickson didn't have anywhere to keep him. He let Jase leave the center.

Jase wanted to test out his powers some more. He rode his bike to an abandoned warehouse where no one would hear anything. He just threw his arm wildly at the wall.

He was screaming and jumping all over the place. Jase was having a great, great, GREAT time. He was very happy with his new electrical ability.

He told Tyson, and Tyson was thrilled. He thought it was the most awesome thing ever. He also told Mary. Mary was a little happy, but that was all.

Weeks passed, and Jase would go to the engineering center every day after school.

Jase Richards does not want to be considered a superhero. He doesn't want to deal with all of that. He wants to finish high school without all the superhero business in the way. But Jase will always use his powers when someone else is in danger.

THE POWER OUTAGE

It is wartime when the power goes out across Germany. One family makes a brave journey to reset the master switch in **THE POWER OUTAGE** *by* **Chalondra Jewell**.

It was a cold night where you could not see anything. Everybody knew that the war was going on but did not know about the power. Everyone had their power go off in Germany. All of the families had to figure out what happened.

Somehow people thought that it was all part of the war, but did not know. When they woke up, they were on their way to find how to get their lights back on.

It was time to go, but one family knew that they were going to have to leave Dad out of the mess. They went hunting for the switch without him. They would all miss him.

It seemed that the switch was somewhere no one could find it. The people in the world looked and looked forever. Some people figured out where the problem was from, but did not know where to look for the switch.

Somehow that one family figured out where the master switch was. There was a meeting to decide who would go and turn it on. It was decided that the family who found it should go, so they went.

The family found the switch to turn everything back on, but they did not know if it it really worked. They went back home.

It turned out the family did not do anything with the power. But finally someone found out that the master switch was actually right in Germany.

The people knew that the power was all the way back on, but they saved the power like there was no tomorrow.

RICKEY'S PLANE

RICKEY'S PLANE, *by Lundon Harris*, is the story of a rat named Rickey who is accomplishing his life's dream. Through this, he learns not to rely on others for everything.

Rickey, why do we have to be here so early?"

"It's one o'clock, Rinnie. It's the middle of the day! Now, to build my plane," he said to himself. "Pass me that old wood over there!" Rickey shouted.

All the animals had come to the junkyard to help Rickey build his plane. Everyone was there: Rinnie, who is his best friend; the dogs; the birds; and even the sheep. Even all his rat family came to help. And that was hard because most of them got caught in rat traps.

The dogs came to help build the frame. They also came because Rickey offered the biggest bone he could find. The birds helped with the wings, tail, and the rudder. They also got promised worms. The sheep came to help with the seats.

They worked out in the hot, blistering sun all day. They weren't even allowed a bathroom break or a chance to drink any of their ice cold water.

Finally they were finished with the plane. Rickey quickly hopped onto the platform the animals built. He looked around. Everyone was sweaty and looked like they were dipped in a pot of oil and left out in the sun. He took a bow. Everyone was cheering him on.

He started his plane up. Swoosh, swoosh. The rudder was spinning faster than his friend Speedy could run. The plane looked like it was working. Then—vroom!—he was off.

It was very bumpy. He got some air, but he was in line with a tree. He couldn't pull up in time! CRASH. He hit the tree and flew right out. He landed on the other side of the junk yard. "Maybe the propeller wasn't spinning fast enough," he said.

In the distance he could hear Speedy chanting, "I remain the fastest. Wahoo!"

He stood up and walked around in a circle in frustration. He looked up and started to think. At that moment he saw something in the bushes. He slowly walked over, afraid of what it could be. He opened the bushes. Surprisingly he found on an old crank-up car.

At that moment, he had an idea. He rolled the car back to the field they were working in. He went in his own space so it would be a surprise. He took the crank off. He cut down a nearby tree. "Timber!" he shouted. He cut the wood to make thin, long sheets. He nailed them onto the sides of the car and made wings.

Rickey walked over to the crank. It was just an old metal pipe with bends and a handle on it. He slipped the handle right off, and unbent all the bends. Now he had a straight metal rod. He put it in the same hole he pulled it out of. He took the extra wood and made a tail and rudder.

"Finally, it's all finished," he whispered to himself. "My lifelong dream is finally accomplished. I'm glad all of my friends came to help. But, by the way, all the payment won't happen. Sorry."

All the animals stormed off. "We'll get you!" someone shouted.

"Rinnie, do you want a ride?" Rickey suggested.

"Okay," Rinnie replied. She and he quickly scurried in the plane. Vroom! He fired up the plane.

"Hope this ride is better than last time," he told Rinnie. He had a good start, but they hit a bump, and Rickey fell out!

The plane gained altitude. Rinnie tried to steer, but the plane went every way she didn't want it to go. She saw Rickey trying to catch up, but she flew into the street. She was just above all the cars, and if she hit one, the whole plane would collapse.

She tried to dodge all the cars. She then saw Rickey still running after her. It was like she was steering with a blindfold on and the plane was playing tag with Rickey.

"Rinnie, stop!" Rickey shouted.

"I'll try!" she shouted back. She tried all of the buttons. There were two left. She clicked the button that wasn't flashing red and said Do Not Push. She finally slowed down.

Rickey jumped, in hopes that he would land in the back seat safely, but instead he fell face first on the road. He tried again. This time he hopped in the backseat as softly as a pillow.

"Rinnie, we have to switch seats."

"Okay," she replied. They quickly switched seats. But Rinnie's foot hit a lever. They didn't know what it did, or why they had it in there. They both just proceeded to switch seats as fast as they could.

"Aaaaahhh," Rickey sighed in relief. But little did he know that lever that Rinnie pulled was the delay-by-10-seconds ejector seat. He went flying all the way back to the tree.

He thought, "I need to find a way to get Rinnie out of the plane."

He quickly scurried over to one of his relatives. "I need help with something. Are you up to the challenge?" His cousin nodded his head, not knowing what he was getting into.

They ran into the woods. There was a shortcut they followed. "There...the plane!"

They both stood in the plane's path. "What are we doing?" his cousin screamed.

"We need to tie our tails together; we will stand on both sides of the plane and stop it. Or we could die," he quickly added.

They caught the plane with their tails. The plane slowed down, but it was still pushing at their tails. "Hold it!" Rickey cried out. "It's almost stopped!"

It stopped. All the animals cheered. Rinnie jumped out. "That was almost a disaster," Rinnie said.

"Good thing we didn't die!" his cousin oddly stated.

SKYLER'S WIN

Being a good sport is what Skyler does best in **SKYLER'S WIN** *by* ***Allie Brady***. *In this story there are people who do not understand what really matters, but Skyler never loses focus on the important things in her journey to win the gold medal.*

As I step off the ice, I see Missy Gonderson glaring at me about my win against her four years ago. I never really got why she doesn't like me, but I've learned to live with it because it's been going on since we were six years old. Oh, sorry; I forgot to introduce myself. I'm Skyler Jacobs, second consecutive four-time gold medalist. I'm pretty much what you would call an overachiever. My coach, Diana White, is a five-time consecutive gold medalist. She is also one of the hardest coaches in the U.S.A. But her tough teaching pays off on the ice.

The past year I have been getting ready for the Olympics. The last stage to get the gold medal or not is in three weeks, so we are preparing every day and every second. Missy and I are the only ones left to compete for the gold medal. We are forced to practice on the same ice, and it's getting harder to practice because she keeps cutting me off. My coach is talking to her coach, Georgina, right now.

GEORGINA: This is the year my girl is going to win. I can feel it; you better watch out.

DIANNA: Well, I think you're getting a little too cocky because both of our girls have been practicing very hard.

GEORGINA: Missy has been practicing better and I'm sure it will show on the ice more than Skyler.

DIANNA: Think what you want, but it's all up to the judges.

GEORGINA: I guess we'll see.

The two coaches have hated each other ever since Diana beat her coach in 1987. But they have gotten better about how it went down.

There are three more weeks of preparation till the last stage to see if I get the gold medal or Missy does.

These past three weeks have been exhausting. All I have been doing is practice, practice, practice! Tomorrow is finally the day we leave for Russia. While my mom and I were packing, my costume came in the mail. It's beautiful sky blue, and it sparkles like a crystal. Before we leave, I'm going over to Diana's house to check everything out and test the music for the rink.

After a long, stressful flight, we arrive in Sochi. We take a taxi to the hotel. I see Missy walk out of the hotel doors when we drive up. Well, I guess this trip just got a little worse—we are staying at the same hotel.

For the next week, I practiced with Diana in Russia for six hours each day. Now, it's finally February 8—the day of the competition. I step into my locker room to prepare to step on the ice. I'm listening to my routine music and going through the motions. My costume and hair are ready. It's almost time to put on my skates and go on the ice.

Diana says, "Well, here we go." As I step on the ice and Missy steps off, I hear my music, and the stress just floats off like a blanket. I'm saying to myself, *This is what you worked for; this is what you're ready for; it's time; you can do this.*

 I'm done. I did it; I got all my jumps, flips, and spins; my axels were on point; and I did it.

They called us back on the ice for the ceremony to announce the year 2014 gold medalist. I step on the ice with Missy, and...they call my name. I got the gold medal! I am now a five-time consecutive gold medalist.

Missy walks over to me. "Well, you did well, Jacobs; you did well. But next year's my win, I know it."

I reply, "We'll see. You did great, though; love your costume."

"Thanks. Well, maybe I can celebrate with you?"

I respond, "Absolutely."

Missy says, "Last one to the car is a rotten egg!"

SUP PUP SPECIAL

Oreo and his family go on a vacation. Once they get there, everything goes wrong in **SUP PUP SPECIAL** by **Erin Little**.

"Is everybody ready!" my dad yelled.

"Ready!" Mom yelled back.

"Me too!" I shouted.

"Me number after two!" Co-co shouted.

It was time for us to proceed to Florida. I ambled to the car. Co-co's twin, Zo-zo, ran downstairs with his huge suitcase.

"We're only staying for three days," I explained.

"I have to be ready for anything," he hollered. I rolled my eyes, and we advanced to the car.

Eventually, we arrived at a gigantic airport. "Wow!" Co-co exclaimed. "This is awesome!" We walked through the security scan.

I slept in the plane almost the entire time. While I was awake, I noticed how amazing the plane really was. The seats were soft and fluffy. They served you steak and fried shrimp. The floor's cream and pearl color was so cool. But after sitting on the chair, I quickly fell asleep. Zo-zo woke me up when we landed, and we continued our journey.

We were at the hotel, and I went to the bathroom. I heard Mom, and she was really mad.

"How did you lose your wallet?" Mom yelled. "We need money for a room!"

"We could just walk to my Dad's place."

Mom was still annoyed on the way. It was around two o'clock, and the sun's radiation was killing me. Soon, we got there. Co-co was complaining, "We can't do anything."

Grandpa Peanut Butter opened the door. "Hey, kids!" Dad strolled inside with Grandpa. Dad clarified how he dropped his wallet on the plane.

"Grandpa, what can we do?" Co-co complained.

"You can go to my pool," he responded.

Mom went to the guest room. I got on Grandpa's desktop computer, and I looked up some free activities.

"There are free surfing lessons," I said, "at the beach two miles from here." Dad still seemed depressed. I realized that we needed money.

"I could loan you some money," Grandpa suggested. Dad grinned.

"Co-co, Zo-zo, Mocha, it's time to go surfing!"

TWISTED

In the blink of an eye, Allie's world is turned upside down. In **TWISTED** *by* **Mikayla Homer**, *Allie's friends try to convince her that her life will be okay again—but are they right?*

"**A**llie, are you home?" called Mikayla.

"Oh, you're here? Be right down!"

"Allie!" Mikayla, Marley, and Sloane screeched in excitement when they saw her face.

"Hi guys!" cried Allie. "Come on in; we will put your stuff in my room."

The girls ran through the house. They set their stuff down and talked about their plans for the night.

It was settled. The girls would be hosting a party at 3:00 P.M. today.

BEEP!

"Guys! Look at that!" cried Mikayla.

"Oh my gosh!" cried Sloane.

Before them sat Olivia Sparks in her car. The girls hadn't seen her in years. They thought she had died!

"Liv?" asked Sloane, puzzled.

Olivia and Allie have definitely had their fights! They were best friends all through eighth grade. After that they just drifted apart, and Olivia was gone.

Before the girls could say anything else to her, Olivia started to talk. "Hi guys. I know you're super surprised, and I'm so sorry I left so fast. I hope we can start over."

"OMG, Olivia, we missed you so much! Yes, of course we can start fresh!" cried Mikayla

"Let's go, guys!" said Marley, walking away. "We have a party to plan."

Spotted: The four musketeers and Olivia Sparks? Get your popcorn. This is going to be a long show!

* * *

Before they knew it they had everything planned for tonight, and so did I. The girls got back to Allie's room, changed into their new dinner clothes, and left

After dinner and the movies, the girls changed into their pjs and lay on the mattress and talked while braiding each other's hair. A few minutes later, Sloane clicked off the lights, and they stopped talking. Before they knew it they were fast asleep, not knowing that the night was about to fall apart.

Morning came, and the girls saw that Allie was gone. They checked everywhere until they suspected that she had run away in fear. The girls called the cops after two days. She never came back. Allie had been acting weird lately, so they suspected she had run away from all the drama.

Three years went by, and there was still no sign of Allie. Everyone suspected she was dead. They had stopped looking for her about one year after she went missing. She was nowhere! My identity was safe, and so was Allie—well, for now at least.

THE WAR IN THE PACIFIC

THE WAR IN THE PACIFIC *will make you remember the lives lost in World War II. This is author* **Blake Johnson***'s perspective on what may have happened during the battle in the Pacific Ocean.*

P rologue

On December 7, 1941, the Japanese are on the move to bombard the U.S military naval base in Hawaii named Pearl Harbor. The attack on Pearl Harbor is in motion. A soldier sees a bomber plane in the air, and sounds the alarm to alert others of the surprise attack. When the first few bombs hit the base, the battle is the attack on Pearl Harbor. The U.S. fights back with anti-aircraft weapons, but the bombs launch, and they do massive damage to the airfield.

The next few bombs hit the tents. Underneath are well-armed tanks and highly combustible bombs and military guns.

In the harbor there are eight battleships, four destroyers, and four aircraft carriers. The Japanese aim for the ships in the harbor and fire. Ten ships are destroyed by torpedoes.

Pearl Harbor is severely damaged in the fight. The U.S. casualties are two thousand five hundred people dead. Six hundred people survive what looked like mission impossible.

The *USS New Jersey* is in the fight as well, but it is not damaged at all. It is not damaged because the Japanese run out of ammo to shoot at it. Action for the crew of the *USS New Jersey* is just beginning.

* * *

It is 1944. Alpha Team Six, with three battleships, six destroyers and nine destroyer escorts, is on its way to stop the Japanese in the Pacific Ocean. One of these ships is the *USS New Jersey*.

A sailor is running to his post for attack. The captain orders the turrets aimed at the destroyer *Nagato*. The operator turns the turrets at the destroyer. The weapons operator fires the turrets toward the *Nagato*. Only six missiles hit the *Nagato*. When the missiles hit, they do a lot of damage.

The battleship *USS New Jersey* has four decks. The first deck is where the guns are kept. There are at least thirty-six guns on the top deck. There are four sixteen-inch guns, sixteen five-inch guns, ten heavy machine guns, and two rocket launchers. The next deck is where the crewmembers on the battleship have their rooms to sleep. The third deck is where they store the ammo and explosives. The final deck is where the engines are. That is what powers the entire ship. There are at least eight engines.

Another part of the ship is the top tower on the top deck. There are three small decks in the tower. The highest deck is where the ship's lookouts are scouting for enemy ships. The next deck is the bridge, from where the captain steers the ship and controls the speed. The last deck is the operator's room. The operator turns the turrets to the right angle and fires the turrets at enemy ships.

The status of the *New Jersey* is that it sank two ships.

The Japanese have a super-ship called the *Yamato*. It is the biggest battleship in the world. It is the symbol of Japan. When the *Yamato* is present, in the crow's nest, one of the lookouts spots a very big ship in the distance. He sends the urgent message to the officer in the bridge, who commands full speed ahead to the mysterious ship. When they get closer to the ship, they cannot believe what they are seeing. Straight ahead is the *USS New Jersey*. While the *New Jersey* is fighting, they realize a ship is racing toward them. So they go to the ship. It is a very hard ship to beat.

Now is the biggest collision in World War II. Both ships turn to their sides and fire at each other.

Far away from the fight, six American aircraft carriers send five hundred aircraft to the battle. There are two hundred torpedo planes, two hundred machine gun planes, and one hundred bomber planes.

On some islands near the battle, U.S. ground troops try to invade some Japanese bases. The troops find a place to reload their guns. A Japanese soldier saw the troops moving to their base, and fires at the U.S. troops. He gets the attention of the other troops at the base. Next, the fight goes to an air and ground fight.

As they move in closer to the base, the *New Jersey* gets some action. The *New Jersey* fires at the base's anti-aircraft weapons, but a destroyer from the battle at sea came and fired its submachine guns at the *New Jersey*. Then, the *New Jersey* fired its sixteen-inch guns at the destroyer. It was a crucial hit. The destroyer sank into the ocean.

The Japanese knew it was over for them. The U.S. ground troops stormed into the base, and captured the base. They took many troops and officers with them.

From the military naval base in the United States, the *New Jersey* gets a message to help out on the island assault. When the *New Jersey* arrives, it fires its ten heavy machine guns and five-inch guns at the Japanese bases. The guns' accuracy is amazing, helping to provide great damage.

The Japanese respond with anti-aircraft machine gun fire at the United States aircraft. The *USS New Jersey* fires its guns for thirty minutes at the Japanese bases on the island. After so much gunfire at the base, the Japanese know it is the end. The Japanese surrender the fight to the United States. The surrender is signed on the *USS New Jersey*.

After the signing of the surrender, the Axis side lost World War II. Many cities were either destroyed or exploded by a bomb or nuke.

When most cities were attacked, there were usually about sixteen thousand people dead. The devastation for those who survived was great, and they needed to fend for themselves and help to start the city again.

2:20

THE BOY WHO CRIED GHOST

A boy finds out the hard way the trouble with having fun at the expense of others. Will his prank go too far in **THE BOY WHO CRIED GHOST** *by* **Max Tushman**?

There was once a boy named Max who lived in a small village called Huntsville. There were 30 houses in the village. Each house was very different. Altogether, the village had somewhere around 120 people.

One day Max was feeling really bored and took a walk through the woods. Suddenly a clear, white figure that Max guessed to be a ghost popped out unexpectedly and said, "I am the ghost of these woods. Why must you disturb the peace here?"

"I didn't mean to disturb you. I was just really bored and decided to walk in the woods," Max explained.

"Be gone now!" the ghost screamed.

Max ran back into his village, frightened from the ghost, and at the very top of his lungs screamed, "Ghost!"

All the villagers came out and said, "Where?"

Max didn't want to worry the others at first by making them look for the ghost, so he walked into his house all confused and decided to take a little nap. He woke up and found a note from his fellow villagers saying that they could not find the ghost.

Max walked into the village again and sneaked out into the woods a couple of steps. He decided to play a prank on them and pretend the ghost was back because they hadn't listened to him about not looking for the ghost. With his prank in mind, he walked out screaming, "Ghost!"

Max hid as the villagers looked for the ghost Max had told them about. As each moment went on he caught up more and more with the villagers. Eventually, the villagers went home and Max was dead with laughter. The villagers noticed Max laughing and knew that there was no ghost and he had pranked them.

He decided to walk back into the woods again, but was surprised to actually see the ghost. Immediately Max yelled,

"Ghost!"

This time, nobody came. They knew Max was not to be trusted because of his silly prank. The ghost said, "You have been messing around with me lately, so I am going to banish you."

Max disappeared forever without a trace. Even Max's soul went nowhere except to the ghost's chamber with all the other people the ghost had banished. If Max hadn't lied to the villagers, the villagers might have been able to save him. Now nobody knows what really happened to Max, except for the ghost who banished him forever.

BUNNIES, BUNNIES, EVERYWHERE!

BUNNIES, BUNNIES, EVERYWHERE! *by **Jalia Moore** is a story about four friends who discover dangerous bunnies at their baseball diamond. They work on a plan to make them nice, but sometimes one plan is not enough.*

One sunny day, there were softball players playing in the field. One of the players, Amy, went to catch a ball that landed in a bush. She saw a pile of four white, fluffy bunnies by the bush and a sign that read, "Don't touch the bunnies!" She called all the other players over to see the bunnies.

Amy, who never likes to follow directions, decided to touch one of the bunnies anyway. "No, Amy, read the sign!" Jenny said. But Amy moved her hand, the bunny bit her, and the other bunnies jumped on her and began attacking.

"Oh, no! Somebody help her. She is being eaten by the bunnies!" Jenny shouted.

The other players were in shock and couldn't move. James told Ben to help him get Amy, but Ben was just frozen. He couldn't move, so James tried to save her himself. When James reached in to save Amy, one of the bunnies bit him, too! He jumped back, and everyone started running and screaming. James hurried and grabbed Amy, and they ran to the bleachers.

James and Amy sat on the bleachers and saw that more bunnies started to come out of the bushes. Soon they covered the softball field. "Bunnies, bunnies, everywhere!" shouted James. "What a disaster. There are bunnies everywhere!"

"What can we do now?" Jenny asked.

Ben replied, "Maybe we should come up with a plan to make the bunnies friendly and save them?" They all figured that would be a good idea, except for Amy because she was just too afraid to participate.

Amy was bleeding and needed to get some help. First they had to get to James's tree house, which was nearby, so that they could think of what to do about the bunnies and get Band-Aids for Amy.

Ben remembered he had carrots in his lunch bag. "Hey, guys, what if I throw these carrots at the bunnies and see if we can escape to the tree house?" Ben explained. Everyone thought that was a good idea.

Ben threw the carrots on the field, and all bunnies started running to get the carrots. Everyone ran as fast as they could to the tree house.

"Okay, group, let's get to work. We have to do something about the bunnies," said James.

They decided to try different vegetables to see if the bunnies would become friendly. Ben said, "Let's try tomatoes. We will put some in a bowl and take them to the field and see what happens."

"That's awesome!" exclaimed James. Off they went to get some tomatoes and take them to the field.

The rabbits started to eat them and began to turn red. "Ahhh!" screamed Amy. "The bunnies are red! Now they are really going to get me."

Jenny said, "The bunnies are not going to get you, Amy. They are just red!"

"Let's try some celery. Bunnies love celery," James said. They put some celery in the bowl. The bunnies ate it, and then they turned purple. "Oh, no, not purple!" Amy said. "Now they will be meaner."

"Calm down, Amy. You are safe now," explained Jenny.

Then Ben told the gang to try some endive lettuce and see what happens. Endive lettuce has a lot of fiber and helps relieve constipation, so it could bring the evil out of the bunnies and make them happy. "Well, that may work, but I know whatever happens I will always be afraid of bunnies," Amy explained. James went and put the lettuce in the bowl.

Everyone ran to get a closer look. The bunnies ran over to eat the lettuce. "Nothing is happening," said Jenny.

Thirty minutes went by, and the bunnies started to change their color back to white. "It's working, it's working!" everyone shouted.

"How will we know if they are friendly?" asked James.

They got a stuffed animal and tossed it into the crowd of bunnies. "Nothing mean is happening. They like the stuffed animal!" they all shouted.

They all ran to the field except Amy to pet the bunnies, and they were friendly.

"Let's sell the bunnies to kids for twenty dollars and use the money to buy new uniforms and equipment for our softball team," Ben said. Everyone thought that was a great idea.

They gathered up the bunnies and had a bunny sale. Amy went home to get healed from her parents and told them she will never like bunnies again even if they are friendly.

CAPTURED IN THE SEA

When three girls are captured and taken to an island, they realize that it is important to be brave. In **CAPTURED IN THE SEA** *by* **Cool Girl Loves Crystals**, *these three girls will have to come up with an escape plan.*

It was a cool, summer night, and three girls were all surfing at the beach. Kaitlin, Annie, and Leila were all from Michigan, but their parents decided to take them to Florida.

Since the hotel was right across the street from the beach, the parents let them go surfing by themselves. The moon was shining bright, making everything visible to see. The girls were having so much fun trying to catch waves that they didn't even realize that they were going farther and farther out into the ocean.

Before they could ride down another wave, they were all surrounded by boats. There were three boats, each with about five men. One of the men, who looked like the boss, ordered the girls to get into one of the boats. At the bottom of each boat were the words "Black Hawk Organization." The girls looked at each other in confusion and fear. They were too scared to even dare swim away, so they got in one of the boats.

They were taken to an island about three miles from shore. The island was very tiny, making it hard to spot. The only thing on the island was a building that looked like a prison. It was small, box-like, grey, and had very few windows. It looked as if it was abandoned based on the old paint that was chipping off it. The girls were taken inside.

The same man that ordered them into the boat said, "You will stay here and work all day, every day. There are no windows in reach, and doors will remain locked at all times. Don't dare try to escape, or there will be extreme punishment. There are guards everywhere." The girls were all squinting so that they wouldn't burst out crying. They were just 12; they were scared and didn't know what to do.

Day after day went by, and the girls were hungry and in tears. They were forced to make the boss breakfast, lunch, and dinner. After, they would have to do chores and clean. When they failed to accomplish one of Boss's demands, they would get hit. Boss told the girls that they were lucky they didn't have to do chores outside. He said that if they get into enough trouble, they would have to work outside and make items for him with whatever they could find.

That night in their tiny bedroom, the girls were talking about how to escape. "How about we just get in trouble, and when we get sent outside, we can escape!" suggested Annie.

"Yeah, that's a good idea!" agreed Leila.

"I'm just nervous about getting in trouble. I don't want to get hit!" said Kaitlin.

"I know, but we could escape!" argued Leila.

"Okay, fine, let's do it," said Kaitlin.

"All right, good!" Annie said.

The next morning, the girls made Boss an awful breakfast and didn't clean up. They also didn't follow directions and talked rudely (which was difficult for Kaitlin). They were sent outside right away. Boss and the guards, however, forgot about the escape raft outside.

About five minutes after the girls were put outside, they found the raft hidden behind a big bush. The girls quickly climbed in and paddled away as fast as they could. They were so nervous they were going to get caught that they could barely hold onto their paddles. They didn't speak at all because they didn't want any of the men to hear them.

A few hours later, the guards came out to make sure that the girls were working. Not only were they girls gone, there were tons of police boats surrounding the whole island. Boss and all of the guards were arrested and thrown in prison.

The girls were back at the hotel with their parents who had been worried sick for the 12 days that the girls were gone. The next day, they all flew back to Michigan, and everyone was safe.

THE FALSE ALARM

Garvy Ramsbottom *tells the story of Joe, a man who is trying to figure out why his town's emergency alert system has been activated.* **THE FALSE ALARM** *may mean something different than you think.*

It is a dark and stormy night in Bron, Nevada. The night is so quiet that you could hear things that you didn't see.

Suddenly, the alert alarms go off, and everyone on the streets runs for the nearest shelter. Joe Pisano happens to be near the gas station when the alert alarms go off. Lights flicker on and off as Joe races into the gas station.

When Joe enters the gas station, he sees that all the lights are off. Knowing that there is probably no one there, Joe hides under the counter beneath the cash register.

Joe is really concerned about these alarms. It's not every day that the alert alarms go off. The last time the alert alarms went off, there was a jailbreak at the local jail.

Then crazy thoughts start swirling in Joe's head. What if something was really going on? What if someone had fallen out of a window? What if there has been an alien invasion? While all these thoughts are swirling in Joe's head, Joe is completely unaware of the figure approaching the door.

Finally, Joe builds up enough courage to head outside. As he approaches the door, the figure steps out in front of the doorway. "Ahhhhhhhhh! An alien!" says Joe as he races to the doorway.

The figure jumps in front of the door again! Before Joe can run away, the figure shows himself. It turns out to be a police officer! The policeman tells Joe that he is on patrol to tell people that the alert was a false alarm and it is safe to go home.

On the way home, Joe finally feels relieved that nothing is wrong. As he lies in his bed, he realizes that there was something wrong with that policeman. "Eh," he says as he goes to sleep.

Hee, hee, hee! thinks the police officer. *When my fleets of aliens invade Earth, nothing will be able to stop us!*

THE FLIP SIDE

When a girl finds herself in an unfamiliar world, she flips out. In **THE FLIP SIDE***, by* **Sophi Whitman***, Brooke wakes up to an underwater adventure waiting to happen.*

"Hey, over here!" I yell to my brother, Andy. He hears me and throws the tennis ball my way. I get the ball in my grasp, and I throw the ball right back to him. He actually catches the ball for once. Then, he turns around and throws the ball backwards. He totally misses his target, me, and throws the ball in the water.

"Seriously?" I question.

"Sorry, Brooke," he says, but I know he doesn't mean it.

"I'll get it," I say very slowly like it is such a big deal. I run over to the water, and dive right in. It's better to get the pain over with very quickly. When I hit the water it feels like I just jumped into the Arctic Sea. It feels like my whole body is asleep, and is being pricked by pins and needles. When my head surfaces, I swim over to where the ball landed. When I reach to grab the ball something pulls me underwater.

"Woah!" I yell. "Who pulled me down?" I keep thinking underwater. "I bet it was Andy," I surmise.

I surface once again and yell out, "Andy!" When I turn my head to locate my rascal brother I realize that neither Andy nor my parents are on the beach. To be exact, no one I know is on the beach. All I see is a big group of mermaids sitting on a couple of big rocks.

I don't even know what to do or to say. I can't believe my eyes. Where in the world has my family gone? What is going on? I have a million questions flowing through my head right now. I wipe my eyes to see if I was just imagining it, but the sight does not change. "How is this possible?" I say to myself.

I decide to go see if any of the mermaids know what happened. When I start to swim over to where they are located, I notice how weird it is to swim. My feet feel a little odd. When I look down at my legs to see what's wrong I notice something freaky.

"What the heck is that?" I yell. I have a mermaid tail instead of feet. "How do I have a mermaid tail?" I question.

This is so gross! It is a scaly, sparkling turquoise, gross, slimy tail that I don't even know how I got. "Is this a nightmare?" I keep asking myself.

I finally calm myself down, and go over to the mermaids to ask them a few questions. "Hello, my name is Brooke and I was human a minute ago. I was wondering if you know how I got my mermaid tail. If you do know, is there possibly a way I can turn back into a human?" I ask very politely.

After a few seconds of them looking super-confused they all start to laugh. "Sorry, we don't know anything, LOSER!" one mermaid explained.

"Please leave, I hate the smell of human freaks!" another one said.

Once they finish criticizing me and my tail, I swim away as fast as I can.

"I have had enough," I think. "I am going to become human again." I swim around in hopes of finding a helpful sea creature that can give me some advice. I ask hundreds of animals from turtles to dolphins, but no one seems to know a solution to my problem.

When it feels like I simply can't find any other animal that will talk to me, I stumble upon a cave that extends 10 to 20 meters back upon the surface. I decide to go in to see if anyone lives in there. "It can't hurt me; it can only help me," I say to myself.

I swim in toward the back wall of the cave. Once I get pretty far back I start to think maybe no one lives here. It is super-dark and small. Why would anyone live here? I am far back and about to turn around until I see a light and a puffer fish in the distance.

"Come here, Brooke," the puffer fish says in a mysterious tone.

"Why, how do you know my name?" I ask.

"Sweetie, I know everyone's name. Do you have a question you want to ask Rolando the puffer fish?" she questions.

"Do you know a way I can get my legs back? I was playing with my brother one minute and am a mermaid the next," I exclaim.

"Oh, you have a severe case of Mermaidia," she revealed.

"Oh no, is there any possible way you can cure Mermaidia?" I inquire.

"I am not sure. Let me ask the pearl mirror," she replies.

She swims to a huge mirror covered with sparkly pearls. The pearls are smooth, glowing, spherical objects. The light reflects and shows their soft, inner glow. They are hanging all around the perimeter of the oval-shaped mirror. I bet a princess would want this mirror. It looks super-delicate and fragile. Rolando goes up and asks a question.

"Mirror, mirror in the sea, is there even a possibility that there is a cure for Mermaidia?" she questions.

After a few seconds of thinking, the mirror replies.

"There is one and one cure only. It is code 123-mermaid," it replies.

"Oh dear," she states.

"What?" I ask.

"The only cure is to go to the very bottom of the ocean and find a very rare, blue starfish. Then, bring it back to me, but all in one hour. If you don't accomplish your mission then you will permanently become a mermaid."

"Seriously? Why one hour?" I inquire.

"Yes, legend has it that all cures to spells have to be done in less than one hour," she replies. "Here is a necklace that lets you breathe underwater," she says while putting a necklace around my neck.

"Thank you," I say. "Okay, I will do it," I bravely say.

"Good, child. Just remember: one hour," she says.

"Thank you," I say again.

I swim toward the bottom of the sea. Once I reach the bottom I notice right away a blue starfish. This most likely is the rare starfish. I try to pull it off, but I can't. It is like it is glued to the ground. I pull and pull, but can't seem to get it off. I try to get creatures' attention to help me, but no one bothers to even look at me. I keep trying and trying for what feels like forever. I decide to go over by where a dolphin is swimming.

"Do you know how to get the blue starfish off the bottom of the sea?" I ask.

"No, no one has ever been able to pull that off," he states.

"Do you know someone that can help me?" I ask.

"Sorry, no," he says.

"Thanks, anyway," I state.

I swim back down to the starfish to see if I can get it detached. I keep trying to pull the starfish off, but it is impossible. After a while the puffer fish I spoke with before swims down and tells me, "Your hour is up. You are now permanently a mermaid."

I start crying. I will never get to see my family again. I just cry and cry. "Are you sure there isn't another way?" I ask.

"I am sure. I am very sorry," she quietly says. I cry again harder, but you wouldn't be able to see that because I'm underwater.

"Brooke, Brooke," someone says. I open my eyes and find my mom waking me up. "You fainted," she kindly says.

"Wait, I am back on the beach?" I question.

"Sweetie, you never left the beach," she replies.

"Well, in my dream I left," I said with a grin. "I am so happy!" I yell. "So, what actually happened after something pulled me underwater?" I question.

"Well, you didn't actually get pulled down. You fell because you fainted. You passed out from sun poison or the heat, and Andy and I pulled you in to rest," she states.

"Wow! That's crazy," I say. "I am going to go swim again," I proclaim.

"Okay, sweetie," she agrees.

GHOSTS IN THE NIGHT

GHOSTS IN THE NIGHT *by **Emi Dittrich** is the story of Moon, a ghost cat helping to defend her family from a group of vicious city cats that are trying to take over her former home in the forest. Can she save them?*

It was a cool night in the graveyard with a slight breeze. I could see the other ghosts running around. To the mortal eye we are just a swirl of mist, often mistaken as a small patch of fog. "C'mon, Moon, you're such a slow cat!" called Cloud.

"I'm coming!" I yelled. We were on our way to the starry river. We call it that because it always seemed that the stars were trapped in its waters every night.

By the time we got there the moon was high in the sky. I bent down to look in the water. "I wonder if the river will ever stop flowing?" wondered Cloud.

"I don't know," I replied. I poked the white-and-gray she-cat in the side. "It looks like that star is twinkling," I said.

"It does," said Cloud.

As we headed home, I thought I saw a tail weaving through the trees. *It's nothing,* I told myself. I fell asleep in no time because of our long trip to the starry river.

When I woke up I saw that Cloud's spot was empty. I went out to look for her. I followed her scent trail through the gate and past the elderberry bushes. I finally found her in a tree looking at a clearing that had several cats in it. "Moon, they're city cats!" she said.

"Why would they be here?" I asked. They looked like the cats that I fought with moons ago because they wanted to get out of the smelly city and take over the forest. That's when I was killed. "We should attack at moon high," I heard one of them say, "when it's dark enough so they can't see us but not too dark so that we can't see them."

"The forest will be ours!" said another with a torn ear.

They are *the cats that attacked my family!* I thought. "We need to warn them!" I whispered.

"How?" Cloud said.

I ran toward my family's home. When I got there, I could hear paws pounding on the ground. They were all sleeping together. Even though I knew they couldn't see me I knew they could hear me.

I started scratching at trees, and I flung pieces of bark at them. They started to stir. When they were all awake I scratched a message into the dirt. They looked scared, but they stayed where they were.

I sent Cloud back to get other ghosts. When she got back I could hear the city cats creeping through the trees. All of a sudden I heard bloodcurdling yowls and saw other ghosts climbing up the trees. Those were my friends! They jumped down from the trees and landed with their misty claws unsheathed and glinting onto the city cats.

My family jumped on the city cats and fought viciously. The city cats swiped at every little movement and flicker of mist as we dodged nimbly away from their teeth. I felt claws on my shoulder and saw a large city cat clinging to it. I shot under him and pushed him off with my hind paws and saw him land with a thump.

I noticed the city cats were beginning to tire. I heard my sister spit at one of the cats, "Get out, flea pelt, the forest is ours!" I saw one of my friends walk up behind her and fluff up his pelt so he looked huge. The leader cowered in fear when he saw the mist of my friend and the amber glow of his eyes.

The leader yelled for the city cats to retreat. The city cats were battered and their fur was torn as they shot away toward the city through the undergrowth. We had won!

I started to head home when I heard my mother say, "I know you were part of this, Moon. Thank you." I headed home knowing I had done the right thing.

THE GREATEST WAR

Russia and the U.S. are shaking the world with their nuclear attacks on each other. Each side cares only about ruling the world in **THE GREATEST WAR** *by Kyle Coleman.*

The year is 2042. The two strongest countries in the world, the United States and Russia, have battled for two years. It seems like the whole world is shaking and suffering from this war of a century.

Realizing this could end the world, the United States and Russia decided to try to have a peace treaty. The location of this treaty was Hawaii. The U.S. and Russia had just come for a peace treaty that they knew wasn't going to work; little did they know this peace treaty would be part of something much bigger.

Everyone knew that President George Carter and Prime Minister Gegach hated each other. In fact neither leader was actually going to have a peace treaty. They were going to attack each other. That's the reason they both agreed the number of men they should bring was 50,000. This was way too many men just for a treaty, so people already suspected what the outcome would be. Both leaders assumed if they took down the other on live television, nobody would attack their countries. They were hoping their theory was right because they both knew that their armies would be weak after this war.

General Kalis of the American army was flying in America's fastest jet, "SET30." However, he liked to call it "sound" because it didn't make any sound while it was moving. General Kalis felt very strongly that the Russian army would fall after this fight. He made it clear to his soldiers that they would not let a single soldier live. The powerful words he had spoken showed the American soldiers that he meant business. These words were still buzzing in his ears: *Remember, men, we do not forgive and we do not forget. Take no prisoners. The Russian army will fall today.*

"Prime Minister Gegach, what a pleasure."

"Oh, no, the pleasure's all mine."

Both leaders were talking to each other like they were having a friendly conversation. However it was obvious that they hated each other.

"So, Carter, I was—"

Then in mid-sentence, Prime Minister Gegach pulled out a gun. President Carter did as well. They stood there for about five seconds pointing their guns at each other. Then a gunshot was fired. However, it wasn't from either leader. It was from their armies. The war later known as "The Greatest War" had begun.

Bang! Bang! The sounds of gunshots and screams had begun. The whole world was watching. News reporters from every country in the world were filming the epic fight. Fifty thousand of the world's greatest soldiers were fighting in Hawaii. But the fight that most cameras followed was that of the two generals.

The generals were easily the strongest people but seemed to be evenly matched. At first the generals were fighting with their fists. Suddenly the American General Kalis drew out his sword and the Russian general Hablar did the same.

Clang! Clang! They both tried desperately to kill the other. But they couldn't, so they just charged at each other. All you could hear was a ripping noise that was coming from the swords going through both generals' stomachs. They had both stabbed each other in the stomach.

They stood there in shock until an American soldier shot the Russian General in the arm. That seemed to bring Kalis out of his state of shock. As the Russian general was falling, Kalis positioned his sword up and sliced Hablar's heart in two.

Five minutes after the death of General Hablar, Kalis got a rather important call. "Fine," General Kalis said, "if Russia's bringing air forces, then so are we. Call all of our jets. This isn't going to be a ground battle anymore."

"Sir, it will be hard to fight them because they are trying to get to Hawaii, but we'll definitely hold them off and kill as many as possible."

"That's great, Lieutenant, but what are you trying to say?"

"I'm saying that you'll get your ground battle after all."

"If you survive this, Lieutenant Chansmon, I'll definitely make you Captain Chansmon."

There was one big problem with fighting in Hawaii: the volcanoes. About ten minutes after General Hablar was killed, without warning the volcano the armies were fighting next to erupted. This caused both sides to retreat, yet the war was not over. They had long-range fights using tanks to shoot missiles at the other side.

Eventually neither side could afford another casualty, so after three straight days of fighting both sides slowly began to retreat. They were still fighting even while they were retreating. Each side was determined to kill more men on the other side. Eventually both sides broke into a fast retreat.

Even though the war was over, they could not yet relax because the burning magma was close behind them. Eventually the U.S. had to use the rest of its military supply to blow holes in the ground in order to escape the burning magma. However while the U.S. was blowing holes in the ground, the toxic fumes were getting to the soldiers. Some such as General Kalis collapsed.

They were all exhausted from three days of fighting. They didn't have much energy left since they had been ready to die on the battlefield and had given the war everything they had. Some of the people in the tanks didn't see their men falling, so they continued to fire explosives at their fallen comrades.

30 Years Later

"Dr. Silver," General Kalis said, "you had it all along. "

"Yes, Kalis, I did, and get your hands off of me. You know you aren't as strong as you used to be."

"I lost my right leg in that war."

"Then be happy that you didn't lose the other one."

"You had the weapon all along. If you had told us that you found the ninth mystery of the world, that war could have been avoided and we would have wiped out Russia. You're an American doctor who works for the U.S. Army; why would you not tell your superiors?"

"Innocent people would have been killed by the ancient weapon 'Shawl.' It causes three times the amount of damage that a nuclear bomb can create. "

"But you've started the third world war because of that weapon."

"I don't care. I know I made the right decision, and I'd do it again if I had to. Now get out of my face, Kalis!"

"No. You make me sick, scum!"

"Fine. Have it your way, Kalis."

While Silver was pulling out a gun, Kalis saw now-General Chansmon (who'd been there the whole time) pull out his gun, point it at Silver, and wink at Kalis.

Bang! Bang! Dr. Silver shot Kalis right in his heart. There was no pain; he just fell over and died. The last thought that Kalis ever had was "600,422,000." That's how many people died in the war.

However, there was something wrong. Silver had only shot one bullet, but he'd heard two gunshots. Then he felt it. To Silver's surprise, he also collapsed. He couldn't see who had done it because he'd been shot in the neck. He stayed there, barely breathing, for about 30 seconds, squirming around until he could breathe no more and he died.

The last man standing was Chansmon. He looked at the two corpses, picked up his old friend Kalis, and quietly walked away.

HIDDEN

When an average man sets off on a journey to find a lost treasure, things go wrong. In a life-or-death situation, he must find out the truth in **HIDDEN**, *by **Sage Everett**.*

Sam was just your average Joe. He got his degree in college for engineering. After that he spent many years with his loving wife, Abby, and his single child, Emma. But there was something different about Sam. He wasn't satisfied with the life he had. I mean, sure, he had anything anybody could want, but that didn't make him 100 percent happy. There was a hole in his heart that he needed to fill. When Sam took down a burglar who had stolen his Abby's money clip, he discovered that when he was chasing after that man he felt happy. Sam filled the hole in his heart with a bit of adventure. That's just what Sam needed.

Every now and then Sam would be a little bit of an adventurer. He would take a coin and flip it to see where his next adventure would start. When Sam found an ancient tomb in Egypt and made money off his discovery, he started to take his job more seriously. He would go on his ventures more often. He would see his family less and less.

One day his wife and daughter came on one of his trips. It was nothing too bad. Abby and Emma stayed with one of their friends as he tried to uncover something new close by. It worked out just fine. That was their new thing now, going on adventures and catching bad guys, and Sam was happy with it. Everyone was.

Jerusalem
2036
July 26
1:24 P.M.

Sam sliced through the darkness with extreme stealth-like movements. The foe was following close behind as he ran through the dimly-lit cave, and as Sam went farther into the cave the closer he got to the dead end. He was running out of breath, he was exhausted, and it was only a matter of time until he reached the end of the dark, forbidden cave. Sam stumbled to the ground, and the enemy held a sword to his throat. This was the end.

Jerusalem
2036
July 26
9:36 A.M.

Many people have looked for this ancient artifact. Nobody has found it. Sam was going to be the first person to find the Ten Commandments, or at least that's what he had hoped for. His friends who have lived in Jerusalem for a while, Niko and Mia, told him many stories before he went on his trek, but many people had also warned him.

He started with his dig near the Wailing Wall in Jerusalem. If the Ten Commandments were hidden in the temple before it was destroyed, they had to be close to it somewhere. But Sam had no luck digging in the hot sun for hours, until he stumbled upon something. While Sam was digging he opened up a magnificent hole to what looked like a large cave. *Could it be?* Sam was thinking. *Could this really be the one and only cave that held the Ten Commandments for which people have been looking for decades?* But it wasn't. He got all excited for nothing. All that the cave had to offer were some annoying bugs and dirt.

So Sam went back to the Jewish friends, Niko and Mia, for more advice.

"You would maybe have some luck talking to the wise old man down the street," Niko said.

"The wise old man?" Sam said, confused

"He is a man who gives out words of advice to anyone who needs it," Mia chimed in. "Niko is right. You should go give the old man a try. He might just help you."

Sam walked down the street to a little hut that looked worn out and old like the man inside. The man said, "Go to where the grass never grows, where Moses went to pray, and where the Ark was buried many years ago. Go to where lots of people have vanished, and to where the wishes of Moses were granted. And for you, my friend, I give you good blessings, because when you find the Ark you will find more worth possessing."

Sam tried to follow the sage advice that was given to him. It was really hard because he got way too caught up in the whole rhyming thing, but Sam tried to follow what he said. Obviously he had to go to the mountain where Moses had gone to pray the day he got the Ten Commandments from God, but he didn't know what to do from there, so he figured that he could do that later.

After a long climb up Mount Sinai, Sam arrived at the top. He had this feeling that someone was watching him, but he put that feeling aside because right now he had to get to work. Also Sam was confused about what the wise man had meant when he said "You will find more worth possessing."

Sam let his worries slip away from him as he looked for a clue to where the Ark might be. He tried to recall what the man had said, and Sam remembered that he said it was buried. He grabbed his shovel and started to haul dirt from the ground, when suddenly he broke through and fell into another cave. Sam's head banged hard on the ground. His vision got really blurry and dizzy, and everything went black.

Sam awoke with his hands and legs tied up on the floor of the cave. There was another person in the cave with him. He had on a backpack and gear like he was going on some kind of big journey.

"Don't move," the man said. "You're not the only one who wants to find the Ark. Did you really think getting it would be that easy? It's mine now, so don't even bother trying to undo the rope or you will have a much worse fate." Sam assumed that was the person who tied him up, so he stayed quiet. The man looked down the two paths that the cave had to offer. He chose the path on the left side, and he jogged down the cave. Sam watched until he disappeared into the darkness.

Now that Sam was alone in the cave he looked for a way to get untied. He struggled and scooted around on the floor doing whatever he could to get out. Then Sam saw a jagged piece of metal that must've broken off his shovel when he fell into the cave. He grabbed the piece of metal with the back of his tied-up hands. First he cut the rope on his hand. Then he cut the rope on his legs. He stood up and walked down the path that the other man hadn't gone down. Sam walked down the dark, cold cave, not expecting what happened next.

Three weeks ago when Sam had flipped a quarter up into the air he had decided that if it landed on tails he would go to Jerusalem to find the Ark of the Covenant. If it landed on heads he was going to try to find the lost city of Atlantis. The coin landed on heads, but Sam always flipped the coin after he threw it in the air, so it was tails. Jerusalem it was then, and now Sam was so grateful because after he had walked down that cave he discovered the greatest thing mankind will ever find. The Ten Commandments were sitting in the Ark at the end of the cave.

"Stop!" the mysterious man said just as Sam was about to leave. Sam sliced through the darkness with ninja stealth-like movements, but he couldn't hold up for much longer. His chest was about to bust from his heavy breathing. Sam's foot came down upon a rock on the ground. Sam fell to the floor. The enemy caught up and held a sword to his neck. This was the end.

Sam looked back to where the Ark was sitting at the end of the cave. It glowed a bright green.It made a beam of light that headed straight for the villain's face. Sam took one last glance at the Ark, but the lights were gone. He turned his head back to the other man, but he was gone, too, and there was a pile of ashes on the floor were the man had been standing.

Sam approached the Ark with much care. He didn't know what to expect from it after it had put on that amazing light show for him. He opened it so carefully that it took him about a minute to do it. When he looked inside his heart sank to the very bottom of his chest. Inside was a piece of papyrus. Sam's heart rose a little because on the papyrus was a route, and at the end of that route was a big x.

Sam knew his adventure wasn't over yet, so with his treasure map in his hand and his shovel at the ready, Sam set off on another journey.

THE HOUSE AT THE END OF THE STREET

THE HOUSE AT THE END OF THE STREET, *by **Sami Meal**, is the story of a girl whose curiosity with a little doll gets the better of her. It tells us about the importance of caution.*

"Lock the door, quick!" Grandma would always tell me. She was old at the time, constantly having terrors about her horrible childhood. She'd said that we must stay indoors after dark, along with locking all of the windows and doors. I'd ask her every day why we did this, and then she would tell me the stories. Even though I was eight, I still remember the stories (vaguely, that is; my memory has faded lots since).

"This island was a vacation site, until the ferry sank one day. You weren't born yet; your mother was just a baby. Grandpa was there, too, but he didn't survive." She'd always tell these stories with emphasis, waving her arms in the air and rocking back and forth on her chair, the fire waving in response to her movement. I used to think her robe would catch flame. "The first to drown was a little boy, I don't quite remember his name—or, no, was it Peter? Anyway, he was the first to die; then came another, and then another." I would count on my fingers, but couldn't keep up with Grandma's rapid voice. "Only about 15 of us survived; the rest drowned or died from the bitter cold of the water. It was about a mile swim, but we managed to get across. I kept your mother on my shoulders because there weren't any lifeboats! It was horrible! The wind, oh, the wind was bitter and horrible!" Grandma would start to scream and cry.

"It's okay," I'd tell her. "It's over now, you're safe."

"No, Iris, we're not." She'd get close to me and whisper in my ear. "He'll get us, he'll get us in the middle of the night, and trust me, we'll only see a dim, eerie shadow cast upon his face before he kills us!" I never understood Grandma's hallucinations, just that I had to help her regain her surroundings. She'd then tell more stories.

After about an hour of ranting, Grandma would eventually fall asleep, and I'd lie down beside her. In my sleep I'd have recurring dreams of a dark room. Then I'd see a flash of light across a blade and hear a soft whisper, saying, "Goodbye, Iris." I'd always scream when I'd wake up, but after the same dream over and over, it wasn't scary anymore.

About two years later, I heard a thumping noise from my door. I opened the door cautiously and saw a box with my name on it. I brought it inside and looked for Grandma. Since she wasn't there, I got my knife out and cut the box open.

There was another box and a note on top. The note said: "Dear Iris, I found this in my basement and I thought you might like it. Enjoy!" *Hmmm, no signature....* I hesitated to open the box, concerned by the fact that someone knew my name, but did anyway and found a little doll inside.

Later that night, after Grandma fell asleep, I took the doll out and played with it. After a while, I got tired and sat next to Grandma.

I woke up the next morning and found a box of small, sharp sticks next to me. *Oh no, the door!* I realized that I had never locked it. I immediately closed the door and then checked to see if Grandma was okay. She was lying on the ground, with no blood or wounds that I could see. I turned to Grandma and started shaking her.

Grandma sat up quickly and jumped to her feet. She then ran through the wall and down the street. I didn't quite understand why she'd jumped through the wall, but I didn't have time to think about it. I chased after her, but wasn't able to catch up. She ran as though she were a five-year-old. I screamed her name, but she didn't turn around.

I saw her run up to the house at the end of the street that's been vacant for years. I sprinted down the street to the house, but Grandma had beaten me there.

As I stopped to catch my breath, I noticed a shadow on the side of the house. When I neared the house, the shadow got bigger and bigger until I saw what was casting it. It was the doll. He was running up to me with a stick.

I turned to run away, but then felt a pain in my leg that made me go limp. I fell down onto the concrete, and my vision blacked out. My entire body was numb, and I could only hear dreary voices.

"Did you get her?" The voice was small but incredibly powerful. It startled me, but not enough to actually scare me.

"Yes, Master, and I also got her grandmother."

"Good, is there anyone else in that house?" I then realized the voice of the master sounded faintly like a child's voice, perhaps a young boy. I should've made that connection sooner.

"No, I already got her mother. There were no known siblings."

"Well, okay, but what about the father, you idiot!" The boy's voice was growing louder and clearer, as if I were walking toward him.

"There wasn't one, Master; I'm sorry."

"Okay, fine. The plan will still work. She can't hear us, right?"

"Yes, all cannot hear except the gifted, and I'm sure she's not one of them, according to her past. She's unconscious." *What? How am I gifted? Who are these people? What do they want from me? This doesn't make any sense.*

"Good. What other houses can you go to?" The voice of the child became calmer. Even though I'd been listening to their conversation for almost five minutes, I still couldn't identify the voice talking to the doll.

"Well, there's a little girl down the street who hasn't grown out of dolls yet, so I'm sure we could get her."

"Go now, you have nothing else to do anyway." I heard footsteps going my way. "Oh, and Jack," the boy said.

"Yes, Master?"

"Don't call me Master, call me Peter. Oh, and also, can you kill her for me? I'm a bit busy."

The footsteps got louder, and I realized that they were coming toward me. Before I knew it, my horrible nightmares became reality. I saw them come to life before my eyes. I saw the flicker of the light, and I realized that it was only going to get worse. *Wait a minute, the ferry... Wasn't that boy's name... Peter! How is he still alive? Why wasn't I possessed? Oh right, because I'm "gifted." What's going on!*

Before my death, I finally understood the reason for my grandmother's hallucinations, the doll, the dreams, the gifted thing—it all made so much sense.

My pondering stopped soon when my dream, and my life, ended.

I SEE RED

A picky eater might find this story disturbing. Earl C Lucas writes about a tomato hater's worst nightmare in **I SEE RED.**

In my family, getting good grades was something that everyone had done—well, at least everyone but me. This fall I was determined to excel higher than anyone ever could. It was all worth it when I got the grades. All my friends and I had a huge party. Finally everything was looking up, until after I got the grades and was then treated to the most petrifying experience.

When what seemed like a never-ending school year ended, my grades were off the charts. They were all A+'s! As an reward my parents decided to take me to a hotel that had five-star reviews and that was next to a restaurant with the same reviews. When I found out about this I was pumped up. Just when it seemed as if nothing could go wrong, everything became a complete nightmare.

When we entered the building, everything was red. There was also a terrible smell, which gave me a sense of déjà vu and some really terrible vibes. When seated I could finally make out what I was smelling, and I hated it. It was the smell of my most hated vegetable, the tomato.

Now I know that if I were to throw a tantrum, not only would I embarrass myself, I would also embarrass my parents, making them think even less of me. However, I wouldn't have to eat any of those despicable tomatoes. But, thanks to my conscience, I acted selflessly and stayed at the table.

The waitress we had was very peculiar about me. Every time I looked at her, she would stare right back at me like she could see the fact I despised this place. Looking through the menu, I saw a bunch of different things that had nothing to do with tomatoes at all, which bugged me. *What kind of restaurant smells like it was conquered by the kingdom of tomatoes and doesn't have any dish that has to do with a single tomato!* I thought. Then when the waitress finally asked me for what I wanted, this time she didn't even look at me; talk about creepy and rude!

I decided to play it safe and asked for a cheeseburger with fries. Thanks to my observational skills, I just knew that my meal was going to be the best in the world—until it came. I didn't think it was possible, but my meal was made entirely out of tomatoes! The buns, lettuce, cheese, and the meat were really tomatoes! Even the fries were made out of them. My parents weren't concerned at all. They were only focused on two things: the check and their food, which surprisingly they devoured in 10 seconds.

While watching them eat I got hungrier and hungrier, and I finally decided to give in and eat. I made a huge mistake. Uncontrollably, fluids came gushing out of my mouth and kept constantly stopping then going, stopping then going, and stopping then going. My parents, not having any idea what was going on, freaked out and immediately called an ambulance.

My whole life was flashing straight in front of my eyes. The lights from the ambulance were making me feel even sicker, and my heart was pounding my chest like it wanted out and was for its life—my life. My eyes got heavier and heavier, and I decided to give in.

It was hard for me to regain consciousness, but when I did I felt a lot of splashing and sloshing around. I also felt something sharp on me, but I couldn't exactly put my finger on it. I was then lifted and placed on something warm and meaty. The next thing I heard was someone saying, "Here is your meal, sir."

Finally I can see a light. When my eyes get adjusted to it, I realize I'm in the restaurant where I had the accident. I still smell that same nasty smell, but this time it's stronger than before. A man looks at me from above and says, "Excuse me; I asked for no tomatoes!"

And that's when I realized I was the tomato.

LOST IN THE NEW YEAR

LOST IN THE NEW YEAR by *Scooby Doo Girl* is about the Wilde family's crazy road trip to Minnesota. The experience should strengthen their family bond—if they can survive a major snowstorm.

Griffin and Blake bickered in the back seat. They were fighting over a baseball card. "Shut up!" Haley shouted.

"Haley, don't tell you brothers to shut up," Mrs. Wilde said, "and boys, please stop fighting and settle down. You're being really loud." Haley sighed. The boys calmed down, and the baseball card fell into one of the cracks between the back seats and was long forgotten once the boys found a squishy football to fight over.

"Don't worry, kids, we're only two hours away," Mr. Wilde said with a smile on his face. Everyone groaned, even Mrs. Wilde. Two hours wasn't anything to complain about considering that the Wilde family had just spent fifteen hours driving to Minnesota. Haley was staring at the snow outside of the window, fascinated by how tall it piled up. Coming from Rhode Island, snow wasn't something Haley was very familiar with.

The car turned into a gas station. Mr. Wilde opened his car door. "I heard a storm was coming. I hope we can make it in time for the party." Mr. Wilde was clearly the only one who was excited for his brother's legendary New Year's Eve party. Mrs. Wilde wasn't very convinced.

In a few minutes, they headed back on the road for another "fun" car ride.

As one hour passed, the storm started to settle in. It became colder and windier, and everything was covered in snow. It was nearly 6:00 P.M., and the roads were getting worse. Mr. Wilde was fearful of the roads and the storm's timing. Mrs. Wilde was getting worried, too, but didn't want to scare the kids.

Only one of the two lanes on the road was open. The whole road would have been closed if it weren't for the slight car tracks. Mr. Wilde was going to have to pull over soon. It was getting harder to see where they were going. *EEEEEEEEESSHHHHHHH!* The car spun out in the middle of the road and into the deep snow in the lane next to them. The Wilde family was screaming in fear and amusement.

When Mr. Wilde stepped out of the car he checked the tires. The car could not move when he started it. *Where are the snowplows?* he thought. Mrs. Wilde immediately stepped outside the car to see if her kids were okay.

Mr. Wilde went straight for help. Haley, Griffin, and Blake were all safe. After everyone calmed down, Mr. Wilde still wasn't back. Mrs. Wilde started to get worried. It was 7:30 P.M. Mrs. Wilde went to go look for him.

Mrs. Wilde walked for what seemed like miles. She thought she heard people, but she also couldn't tell if it was just the wind. "Shane! Are you out there?" Mrs. Wilde called.

"Jennifer?" Mr. Wilde called. "I'm over here."

"Where are you? I can't see you."

"I'm behind the snowplow. Nobody is around here. Where are the kids?"

"I left them in the car; we need to get back soon." Mr. Wilde agreed.

Haley knew something was wrong; even the boys were quiet. "Come on, boys," Haley said, "let's go." Griffin and Blake looked confused.

"Where are we going?" Blake asked.

"To go find Mom and Dad. It's already 9:00." Griffin started to look queasy.

The kids headed off into the storm. Haley was nervous, and the boys were freezing. It was getting closer to midnight, closer to the party. Haley knew her dad was looking forward to his brother's party. Haley, Griffin, and Blake were all worried about their parents. Haley looked for a path to follow, in hopes of finding her mother's footprints.

Mr. and Mrs. Wilde slowly traveled through the snow hoping to make it back to their kids. Mr. Wilde didn't care about the New Year's party anymore. All he wanted was to find his family and be warm. Mrs. Wilde was deathly worried for her children, only hoping she would see them soon. It was so hard to see when the snow was blowing everywhere. Shockingly, it was 10:30 P.M. Mrs. Wilde tried to remember where the car was. Mr. Wilde led the way he thought was correct. They both knew that the kids would be scared.

Griffin and Blake stomped around in the snow after Haley. Haley followed some tracks in the snow that she thought looked right, though she wasn't sure if they were going in the right direction. As the parents traveled toward the car, the kids traveled to where they once were.

Forty-five minutes had passed, and there was still no sign of their parents. The snowstorm was luckily dying down.

The roads were finally plowed, making it easier to walk. Mr. and Mrs. Wilde were still looking for their kids. "Finally!" Mrs. Wilde yelled, "The car! The car!" Both of them could tell that the car now had space to move!

Mr. and Mrs. Wilde opened their car doors to find the car empty. Mrs. Wilde's face turned red. "Get in the car, Shane! We're going to find them!"

Haley, Griffin, and Blake could finally see where they were going. At 11:40 P.M., Haley started to lose hope. Griffin and Blake were tagging along, pretty clueless about what was happening. Haley heard a car but couldn't see one. The hope started to appear again.

"I'll look for them and you drive," Mr. Wilde said. He could see things move in the window. It was 11:52 P.M. Mrs. Wilde knew that they were getting closer.

Haley saw headlights far away. The vehicle was moving slowly, but it was moving. Haley wondered why she never crossed her parents when they were walking, but it turns out that there were two different roads that led from their car.

Griffin and Blake were tired of walking, and so was Haley.

The car was coming closer and closer. It passed them! Haley's gut dropped as she heard fireworks go off in celebration of the New Year. She knew they had taken the wrong path. The kids suddenly heard a car honk behind them!

"Hey, kids!" Mr. Wilde said. "I haven't seen you since last year." Griffin and Blake's faces lit up. Mrs. Wilde ran out of the car and hugged all of her children. Haley was so relieved. The Wilde family was finally reunited.

Even though Mr. Wilde had missed his party, everything was okay, and the Wilde family was probably more relieved than ever.

A MESSAGE TO THE FUTURE

A MESSAGE TO THE FUTURE by *Alexandre Guellec* *is about a young boy named Thomas who finds an artifact that could affect his country. He is trying to find his way until the war begins.*

On August 1, 1903 in northern France, it was Thomas's fifth birthday. He was digging in his backyard for fun when he found something shiny and ancient. Thomas was wondering what it was, so he went to call his dad to help dig it out. When they finished digging it out they realized it was a small, brown, and rusted chest.

He and his father brought it in quickly. They were anxious to open it. After realizing it was empty, their disappointment was devastating. Thomas decided just to keep it for safekeeping.

Early in the morning eleven years later, Thomas was examining the inside of the chest. What he found inside after all these years was a letter hidden in a compartment. The note was flaky and dusty, and it crumpled easily in his hands. Then he read it aloud. It said: "Bloodshed is coming soon. It will be devastating. A world war is coming." It was written and signed by the famous fortuneteller Marc Guy. There was a date written: 1914, August 8. That date was just one week later.

"Thomas," his father said, "go to the national newspaper in Paris. Tell them about this note, and show them proof of the upcoming war."

Later that day Thomas arrived in Paris. He went into the newspaper office and asked to meet with the director of the company, saying he had urgent news. He was accepted right away and flew up the stairs of the building.

He entered the man's office. His name was Edward Du Pont. Thomas explained what he had and what the letter was predicting. "This needs to be announced immediately to the people of this nation," Thomas explained. "If you want me to show you proof, I shall."

Edward disagreed. "Why should I believe you? For all I know this is you imagining what you want to prevent happening."

"I do not understand why you don't believe me," Thomas replied. "I don't have much imagination myself. Common sense is my strength. That is why you have my word." After that, Edward felt differently, and he looked to see that this boy was right: the signature of the famous fortuneteller was there.

Edward had been aware this event was being talked of around the country and people around the world were having dreams and visions about this topic. "This message will be transferred immediately to the president," informed Du Pont. "I will ask him to warn the people of the terror that lies in our future."

The next day people were leaving on boats and on trains to other, "safer" countries. The country was chaotic and out of control. The police were posting notices that explained every man aged 16 years and older who was strong enough to fight needed to participate in the world war. Thomas had turned 16 the day before and would be forced to fight in the war.

War preparations had begun and were affecting a large part of the country. After the first 14 hours of that day, over half the country had fled. Later that week some people were saying that they had started to see German troops arriving.

By August 8th, France had fought well and hard but in the end was conquered by Germany who had been prepared many months earlier.

The world war had started. And a year later, Thomas continued to fight in the rebellion with the great Charles de Gaulle.

MORE THAN ONE BEST FRIEND

Jealousy and drama can sometimes test friendships, but true friendship will last forever. **MORE THAN ONE BEST FRIEND**, *by* **Melodie Willis**, *is a story about friendship drama.*

It was the first day of school at Harper Woods Middle School in Springfield, Illinois. To my left sat a girl always possessing a very bright smile. Her smile compelled me to want to meet her. I went up to her and said, "Hello, my name is Harmony. What is your name?"

She replied, "Adabel." Then she smiled. I couldn't help but smile back.

We talked and hit it off right away. We were "Best Friends Forever." We got each other's phone numbers and began to text, to Skype, to FaceTime, to Snapchat, and to email each other. We were in contact with each other after school as much as we were during school. We ate lunch together, we did our class assignments together, and we even rode the school bus home together. We were inseparable.

Two weeks before Christmas, a new girl came to Harper Woods Middle School and was put in our classroom. "Class, we have a new student. Her name is Brianna Johnson," our teacher, Mrs. Jackson, said. "Make her feel welcomed and introduce yourself to her when you can."

"Let's go meet her, Adabel. She seems like a nice girl."

"Hello, my name is Harmony, and this is Adabel, my BFF. Welcome to our school, the coolest school in the world."

"No, no, in the universe," Adabel interjected. We laughed. "Do you want to eat lunch with us? You can sit with us if you like."

"Sure, I have extra licorice I can share with you."

From that day on, she began to hang out with us.

One Saturday afternoon, when Adabel was away all day for a dance competition, Brianna came over to play with me. We had so much fun. We asked if she could spend the night. To our delight, our parents said it was fine, so she slept over. We painted our nails, prank-called people, danced, ran around, and baked desserts.

The following weekend I wanted to get together with my friends again. I called Adabel. She was not home, so I called Brianna again, and she asked if I could come over her house to visit. We played together and like always we had a lot of fun. Then Brianna asked if I could spend the night. I said, "I don't know, but I'll call my mom." When Mom picked up the phone I said, "Mom, can I spend the night?"

"Is your homework done?" she asked.

"Yes, Mom, I finished it yesterday."

"Okay, let me ask your dad. I'll be right back.... Your dad says it's okay. I'll stop by and bring your toothbrush and an extra change of clothes. Let me speak to Brianna's mother." I took the phone to Mrs. Johnson. She spoke with my mom to make arrangements.

We had so much fun that night. We didn't go to sleep till two o'clock in the morning.

The following Monday at school we told Adabel about the fun we had. She smiled, but I could tell there was something wrong.

At lunch Adabel sat at a different table. "Adabel, why aren't you sitting with us at lunch today?"

"I just wanted to be alone today."

"Why, is something bothering you?" I said.

"No, Harmony, I just thought since you have a new BFF, I will have to find a new BFF."

"What do you mean, Adabel? You are still my BFF."

"Well, it doesn't seem that way. You are always talking with Brianna. To make things worse, you guys have sleepovers and don't invite me!"

"Oh, Adabel, don't feel that way. Just because I have a new friend doesn't mean I like you any less."

"Well, it seems that way."

"Adabel, I'm not trying to destroy your friendship with Harmony. I just want to have friends, too," said Brianna.

"Adabel, we don't have to limit our best friend to one person. We can all be BFFs," I said. "Surely if one BFF is good, then two BFFs are better. We will just have to always include each other. Come sit with us. We can call ourselves the Sister-Sister-Sister Clique. For short we can call it SSS. We can be more than best friends. We can be like sisters. What do you think about that?"

"Well, I like that. It sounds cool."

She then came to our table, and we all shouted, "Sister-Sister-Sister for life!"

THE MYSTERIES OF KABBOT ISLAND

*Go for a ride with Harvey Williams and his family as they search for their missing uncle. In **THE MYSTERIES OF KABBOT ISLAND** by **Joseph Da Silva**, the journey becomes an adventure as they encounter one mystery after another that leads them to the greatest treasure of all.*

CRASH! BOOM! As we hit the ground, all I was hearing was ringing through my ears and pounding in my head. The sound was so loud that I only slowly started to feel the agonizing pain in my twisted ankle.

My dad, my cousins, and I had set out in a seaplane to try to find my grandfather. I was looking through the smoke to see if I could see my dad and my cousin and see if they were okay. Looking left and right, I struggled to get up, but I could hardly stand on my leg. There was a blazing fire in my eyes, and I was thinking I was close to death.

Finally getting up limping, I looked around for them, not knowing what was going to happen next. Out of the corner of my eye I saw footprints on the sandy shore, telling me that maybe one of them was okay. Frozen with fear, I waited for someone to see me.

Before we get any more into that, my name is Harvey Williams, and I am 16 years old. I'm the nephew of the famous present-day treasure hunter and explorer, Henry J. Williams. He went missing just a few years ago in Kabbot Island, known for one of the greatest treasures in the history of all time. My uncle tried to get there by taking a cargo plane and has been missing ever since. Our entire family has been worried. This trip was my dad's and cousin's plan to go to Kabbot Island to find him.

Let me tell you what happened. My dad and my two cousins, Charlie and David, and I were on our way flying over the beautiful islands of Hawaii, and then out of nowhere came this huge, booming, loud storm. It hit the wing of the seaplane and sent us crashing down to the water close to the beach. I remember my dad holding my hand tightly and telling me to brace myself against the door and the dashboard control panel.

When we hit, we bounced on the water and jerked around, but surprisingly, there was only medium damage to the plane. There was so much smoke and my leg hurt so badly that I couldn't see or find anyone. I was so worried because I couldn't make out any signs that anyone was okay, until I saw the footprints in the sand. Even though there was a throbbing pain going through my whole body, I knew I needed to find out if anyone else was hurt.

I yelled their names. "Dad, David, Charlie! Are you guys O.K.?" Nervously, I waited for an answer.

Finally, my hope got up a little when I heard the familiar voice of David saying, "Over here!"

He was outside of the plane on the beach. David was on the ground with a large piece of metal trapping his arm. "Do you remember how that happened?" I said.

"The jagged jerking turns threw me out of the plane before we hit the shore. I landed in this grassy sand, but I think part of the plane landed on me." I leaned over and with all my strength pushed the metal off him, finding out there was a very bad bruise on his arm.

Then I spotted Dad and Charlie lying further down the beach. Charlie had a pretty bad stomach bruise. Dad was knocked out, so we had to wake him. Slowly he came to, and recognized us all. There was slight moment of relief, until the reality of our situation hit me. We were stranded and without much of anything to protect us. After being through a crash like that, all we could think about was how lucky we all were to be alive.

We knew we had to set up camp on the beach, to rest and figure out our plan before night would come upon us. Out in the middle of nowhere, with injuries and needing food and rest—who knows what this place is like and what could happen at night?

We worked as fast as we could without causing more damage to our injuries. As we huddled and started to gather sticks and branches to make a shelter, no one spoke. It was so quiet that all I could hear was the water and all I could feel was the worry of not knowing what was ahead or what was going to happen.

I needed to find something to support my leg in some kind of way so the pain wouldn't drag on or slow us down during the whole adventure of looking for my uncle. As we collected branches for a shelter, I asked, "Do any of you guys see any branches that could support my leg? If you see one, can you save it for me?" They said that they found some by a coconut tree. And trust me, I was very relieved to find something there, even though I knew it would slow me down a little. But as long as I had something to support my leg, I knew that I could do more to help everyone out and figure out how we were going to get out of this mess.

We took the rest of the branches and leaned them against a few trees to make a shelter for my dad and us to lie in. I had the branches that I could use for crutches to help me take the weight off my ankle, and this made it easier to get around. We used palm tree leaves to tie some of the branches together, and by sunset we had a small space to protect us from the night that was falling.

Quickly before dark we had to figure out if there was a source of food. We all went together as a group for protection in case there was anything bad on the island. Luckily there were coconuts, and shaking a tree as hard as we could got us a total of a dozen. We went back to our shelter, and while it was not the best, it looked pretty good for a place to sleep for the first night.

As I tried to fall asleep, I couldn't relax. The pain in my leg came back in the night, and after all that went on today I couldn't sleep. Still feeling pain in my leg, I could see that David and Charlie were feeling way better, and thankfully so was Dad.

The next day, everyone was up before me. It was really nice of them because they were already at work looking for more supplies and wood for the shelter. I wanted to help and figure out a way to take part in the work any way I could, so I sharpened a stick to make a spear to see if I could catch any kind of food in the water. I managed to find some branches and sharpened one with a sharp rock on the beach.

I had never seen such exotic and beautiful fish before in my life, and I couldn't believe my eyes. They were so pretty, I almost hated to spear them, but I knew I had to look past their beauty and do something to help us all survive.

When I got back to the shelter, the guys were surprised to see the fish that I caught. I have to admit I was a little surprised, too. "Do any of you guys mind starting a fire?

Luckily there was a flint in the rescue and survival box in the plane. I knew David could do the job, and almost immediately, David said, "I'm right on it!" Just as I predicted, he got that fire started in less than ten minutes.

We each took a stick, and once the fire was hot, we managed to cook the fish that night. I'm going to be honest, that was some of the best fish I have ever had. My dad, David, and Charlie all agreed with me.

That night by the fire, we talked about what we were going to do the next day. Since we were feeling stronger, we knew we could probably start looking for my uncle. We all went to bed that night with full stomachs, and for a short moment it did not seem so bad. We were feeling better and figuring out what we needed to do.

As we started to drift into sleep, I heard sticks breaking on my side of the shelter. I can't explain the adrenaline going through my body right then. Our eyes all popped open, but no one said a word. I forgot all about my leg and the throbbing pain. We could hear something out there breathing slow and steady. For a second I thought, *Could it be?* Then I quickly erased my thought of what it could be, and the next second, it hit me. Before I could say the words to myself, I looked out, and it was standing on its hind legs reaching the top of the palm tree. It was a dinosaur.

Stunned and frozen with fright, we all held our breath. As the dinosaur moved farther away we whispered to each other that it was time to see what was going on.

When we got out of the shelter, our movement caught the dinosaur's attention. It was taller than a huge skyscraper, but moved so gracefully on the beach. It was the biggest animal and the scariest animal I had ever seen. It had big teeth and eyes and smooth skin. It almost looked friendly, but we knew it was not, and when it found us with its huge eyes, all we could do was run.

I ran so fast I was running blind through the palm trees, seeing if the rest were by me, and thankfully they were. We tried to stick together and keep everyone in sight. My leg was pounding, but I had to keep up with my family. We didn't look back once, but we could hear the thumping and feel the vibrations in the ground. We knew we had to find a safe place. Trees were coming down behind us as the dinosaur moved through the jungle.

About a half mile later we found a somewhat small cave to give us a little place to hide. We all moved into the cave and held our breath as the dinosaur moved toward the opening. The nose of the dinosaur pushed its way into the opening of the cave. It snorted loudly, and stinky air swished into the cave. It was a good thing we were holding our breath. Before we knew it, the dinosaur gave up and slowly moved away.

The intense feeling of relief brought tears to our eyes. I am not sure if that or the plane crash was the scariest moment in my life. Thank goodness we were all able to move fast and outsmart the dinosaur. Once we caught our breath, my dad said, "It's time to rest here a bit and see if we can figure out where we might begin to hunt for our uncle."

All of a sudden, we became aware of an extra person or animal by us. Afraid that it might be another animal that could hurt us, Charlie, David and I stood in silence. Dad was brave enough to ask, "Who's there?"

An older voice said, "Boys, is that you?" All at once, we smiled because we all knew it was my uncle.

David and Charlie said, "Dad, is that you?" but in a softer voice so we wouldn't put ourselves in any more danger.

I asked, "Do you know what's out there?"

Our uncle said, "You have no idea. I've been here for almost a month."

"How did you survive?" we whispered.

"I have some supplies with me." He listed them as we went closer to him and the boys reached out to hug their dad. He kept listing, "A bowie knife, matches, water, and cans of meat." As he was going through supplies he had that helped him survive, the one that caught my attention was the flare gun. I could think of a lot of ways to use that right now.

"Why didn't you use the flare gun?" I interrupted.

"Oh, my boy, I needed to save that for when I really knew that I would have a chance. Now that you are all here and I know that there may be a chance to get us all off this island together, let's figure out the best plan and how to use it. Now is the time to get some rest, boys, and we will try in the morning."

As I drifted off to sleep this night, I had more strength than pain, lying next to my dad. Charlie and David were finally back with their dad, and I dreamt of our next day while hoping that our time on this island was coming close to an end.

When the birds started to chirp, they woke me up. Everyone else was just starting to get up, too. All we could think about was when and how we were going to use the flare gun. So, my uncle and

Charlie went out to investigate the area and find a good place to fire the gun. They returned with their plan.

We moved out to a clear area and set off the flares. The area was not too far from the cave so we could be safe and see if there was any response to the flare.

Not even two hours later, three helicopters could be seen, and we ran out to the clearing. One of the helicopters landed and rescued us from the island. But my uncle was not going to let us go without going to another small cave. Before us were the ancient artifacts of gold and silver that gave him the reason to come here in the first place and start this journey. He handed many of them to each of us, and took his sacks he had filled and ready in hopes he would be rescued alive to tell his story of discovering these treasures.

The whole way home, my uncle told us about what he did when he set out to explore Kabbot Island. You could tell he was happy to be on his way home with his family, but he spoke of every detail like it had happened yesterday. Even though he was happy and grateful to be alive, we all could feel how excited he was to tell us what happened and knew that his next adventure was probably not too far away.

THE NEW WAY TO TELEVISION

Television has a way of sucking in its viewers. That becomes the bizarre and literal truth for two friends in **THE NEW WAY TO TELEVISION** *by **Luke Gregory Anderson**.*

"Hey," I said as I walked into David's house.

"Oh, hey," he said. I walked into his living room and sat on the couch. "What's up, Sam?" David said.

"Nothing much."

We started watching TV when his mom walked in. "Hi, Sam," she said.

"Hello, Mrs. Arnold," I replied. We talked a little more until she made her way into the kitchen.

David and I were watching a documentary on monkeys. The monkeys were messing around picking through each other's hair. Then, I started to feel a little dizzy. "Uh, David, I don't feel very good."

"Actually? Neither do I," David said. And being kids we didn't do anything about it because it was a Saturday and we didn't want to spend the day in bed.

As we went on watching the same old show I started to feel worse and worse. My palms were getting damp and sweaty, and my forehead started burning up. I was about to say something to David when I blanked out. And in what felt like a millisecond later I awoke lying down and hearing bird chirps.

"Sam?" I looked over and saw David standing up.

"David? Where are we?" I asked.

"Where have you been?" David said.

"What? What do you mean?" I replied.

"Really, dude, I've been here for four and a half hours alone in the dark. It just lightened up," he said.

"What? We were just on the couch like three seconds ago." David looked at me like I was an idiot. We were just about to discuss it when we heard rustling in the trees. "What was that?" I said.

"Do you expect me to know?" David said.

"Well, I'm not the one who has apparently been here for four hours."

"Four and a half, for your information!" David screamed. We looked up and saw three monkeys glaring down at us. "Hey, does any of this look familiar?"

I looked around and saw that we were in a huge jungle. "I think we are in the channel we were watching," I said.

"What? That is imposs...OUCH!"

I looked over and saw David rubbing his head and a banana lying on the ground next to him. Then another banana hit me. "OUCH!" I said. We looked up to see that all of the monkeys had bananas in their hands ready to throw. "Run!" we both screamed.

We both ran and ran until we reached a kind of glitchy black, grey, and white wall. "Isn't this the screen that you see when your TV isn't working?" David said.

I said, "Yeah, I think so." We looked down and saw that the wall was never-ending. We were trapped. The monkeys were getting closer. "What should we do?" I said.

"I don't know!" David said. As they got closer and closer, David started to panic. He tripped and fell straight through the wall like it was thin air.

"David!" I stood there, thinking I had no other options, and jumped straight through the wall.

I appeared to be in a factory. David was standing there when he said, "Dude, stop doing that! I think I have been in here so long I have watched ever single *How It's Made* episode! It's not fun."

I started laughing and said, "So whenever we go through one of those walls we appear on a different channel?"

"I think so," David replied.

"So maybe if we keep on going through them we can get out of your TV?"

"Yeah, probably."

"Then let's go," I said. We started making our way to the other side of the factory where the wall was. "Well, I hope this is a cool episode," I said.

Then a voice blared through the speakers on the ceiling. "And now, HOW IT'S MADE FOR.... NAILS!"

"Oh, God!" I pouted. "Let's get out of here!" I said. I think once we heard that it was on nails, it took us about thirty-two seconds to get to the other side.

Once we got there, David said, "You can go first." I laughed and jumped in.

Once I got through, David appeared a second later. "How long was it?" David said.

"How long was what?" I said.

"The wait before I got here."

"I don't know, one second?"

David looked at me and said, "I'm not talking to you." I cracked up until I heard a *BANG*. We looked around and heard another *BANG*. It was a gunshot.

We climbed out of the closet that we had appeared in and snuck out of an old house. Everything was in black and white. "I think we are in an old movie," I said.

"Yeah, I think so."

We crawled outside and saw a gunfight going on. The men were trash-talking back and forth like they were both afraid to actually shoot at each other. I was watching when I felt a hand on my neck. Someone picked up David and me and dragged us into a room. I turned around and saw a man.

"You two shouldn't be out there...wait, who are you guys?" We were afraid, but for some reason we told him our names. "You guys aren't from around here, are you?"

"No, sir," I said.

"Let me guess: you were watching TV and you appeared in here. Am I correct?"

"Yes! How did you know?" we screamed.

"When I was a young man the same thing happened to me."

"Well, do you know how to get out?" I said.

"There is only one way. You need the remote."

"What do you mean? The remote is on David's couch!"

"No, that is not the original remote. The TV did not come with the original remote," David said.

"Then how are we going to get out?" I asked

The man walked over to a table that had a drawer in it. "What are you doing?" David asked. He pulled open the drawer and pulled out a remote. "Wait, is that the original?"

"Yes," he said.

"Then why didn't you get out?"

"I met someone and got married," he said with a grin. "Okay, no more questions. You two need to get out of here."

"How do we use it?" I asked.

"You need to press the power button off and on VERY fast," the man said.

"Okay, we can do it," David said.

We both held onto the remote, and before the man could even say "Safe travels," we pressed the power button very fast two times like he said.

We reappeared back on the couch at David's house. David looked at me and said, "We cannot tell anyone about this. They will think we are crazy." I agreed.

David's mom walked in like we had never been gone. "So, do you kids want any popcorn?" she asked.

David then said something I will never forget. "Can we get a new TV instead?"

THE REVENGE

In **THE REVENGE** by *Carlos McIntyre*, a boy does his best to protect his father from Death. The boy is fearless, but does he stand a chance against the power of Death?

Ryan's father was dying. Ryan's first thought was to stop Death from getting to him. Ryan had already lost his mother to Death. He didn't want to lose any more people he loved. Ryan told his dad that they should move around to many places in the world to keep him from death. So they moved to many places and finally decided to settle down in a village by a forest.

Ryan went to the blacksmith in the village and paid the blacksmith 6,000 galleons to make a sword to kill Death himself. The blacksmith told Ryan, "It is impossible to kill Death," but Ryan got mad, and had the blacksmith make it anyway.

Death is a skeleton that kills people once his timer for them runs out. Well, he doesn't actually kill them. He just takes their souls from their bodies. Their bodies stops working, and they turn into ghosts. He does this with a special scythe that passes straight through people's bodies. Their bodies wither away in stone, and then they turn into ghosts.

Death was coming for Ryan's dad because his timer had run out. However, Ryan's dad just kept disappearing, and Death knew why. Death knew Ryan was behind this problem. Death had to keep balance in the world and take Ryan's dad's soul. Death knew people thought he killed them. But he took their souls to keep the world from getting too crowded.

Ryan returned to the blacksmith for the sword. It had a diamond tip on the blade that glowed, and the blade was made of titanium. Ryan went to the eldest man in the village and asked where he could find Death to kill him. The man said, "Go into the heart of the forest right next to the village. It's a bad idea to stay here with your dad, because Death lives close by."

Ryan got back to the inn where he was staying with his dad. There he saw Death standing over his dad's motionless body, with his scythe in his hand, and then Death disappeared. Ryan shouted up to the sky, "I will get you!" and then he started crying, not with sadness but with anger.

Ryan made his way to the center of the forest. While he was walking he heard the cracking of sticks and saw the moving vegetation begin to close up his way out. He believed he could easily cut his way out with his sword. He continued on toward the center of the forest.

He then saw a bunch of blackened bones and saw a BEWARE OF DRAGON sign but continued on. A blast of scorching fire came toward him. He could feel the intense heat as he ducked. He ran and saw a cave with a dead knight with a shield. He picked up the shield. He ran and hid behind a rock and waited.

The dragon climbed up on the rock. Ryan let the dragon blow fire at the shield. The fire hit back at the dragon's eyes, blinding it. Ryan stabbed the dragon in the underbelly, and the dragon exploded into a pool of magma. Ryan was barely able to block the magma with his shield.

Ryan continued through the forest and came upon an ogre sleeping. It wore a necklace made of human skulls. Ryan slowly walked past the ogre. Ryan was just about to get away from the ogre when he accidently stepped on a bloody rib and the rib snapped. The ogre chased Ryan. Ryan ran off with the ogre close behind. Ryan saw a giant spider and web up ahead and slid under it. The ogre then accidently got stuck in the web.

Later Ryan saw a pack of skeleton dogs. At first he thought the dogs were friendly. Then they chased him, so he climbed into a tree. When the dogs were about to give up he jumped out because a giant evil-looking bird came toward him. The dogs chased him again. Then Ryan came upon a plaque attached to a black metal fence that said "The Death Estate." Ryan climbed the fence, and the dogs wouldn't follow and ran off.

Once inside the estate Ryan saw everything was in black and white including the fire in the house. He saw Death already waiting for him, sharpening a sword with a skull handle and a very dark, black blade. Death approached Ryan and said, "You put this upon yourself!" He swung at Ryan. Ryan blocked with his sword. Death's sword became chipped. Death pulled back his sword from the attack and it reformed itself where it had gotten chipped. Ryan stepped back.

Death said, "I know you think I kill people! But I just remove their souls when the time is right."

Ryan screamed at him, "That's killing people!"

Death replied, "No, it is not. It is not even painful. The world would get crowded if I did not do this, and even if you attack me, you can't kill Death." Death let Ryan slice at him to prove his point. The titanium sword went straight through Death, but Death wasn't affected at all.

Death said, "Attack me one more time if you still want to kill me." Ryan charged without his weapon, and took Death's sword and swung. Death dodged and said, "Do not do this, foolish boy. Do not take a weapon of Death!" Death made his scythe form in his hand from a cloud of dark, black smoke. Death touched Ryan with his scythe, and Ryan saw his body right in front of him turn to stone and then wither away.

Right before he completely withered away he threw Death's sword. He never saw what happened next.

SAM SHIFT

A young boy discovers that he has a special power. He learns that life doesn't have to be boring in **SAM SHIFT** *by Dominick Stoops.*

I wake up in a puddle of sweat. I'm in my room. I'm in my bed, but it's not me. I feel different. I walk out of my room and notice I'm the only one home. That's strange. Where are my dad and brothers? I run to the closest mirror. WHAT! HOW? *Thump.* I hit the floor hard.

I can feel the hot sun blazing through the window. It must be morning. I must have had an awful dream. No, a nightmare! I'm extra-relieved because I can't explain what happened last night. I guess I don't have to because it's Monday and I'm hungry. I find a note in the kitchen:

> Dear Sam,
>
> Happy Monday. Went to work early. See you tonight.
>
> Love, Dad

An annoying sound comes echoing down the hallway. "Good morning, Samster. Make sure not to eat all the food. You're not the only one hungry around here." It sounds like a hyena or nails scratching the blackboard, but it's neither. It's my stepmother, Gina.

"Yes, ma'am," I respond and run out the door.

I get to school just in time for the warning bell. I have to find Maddy. Maddy and I have been best friends since I can remember. If anyone will help me, it's her. After second hour I finally see Maddy.

"Maddy, I can't take it anymore. I have to find my real mom," I say.

Maddy stares at me for a long minute. "I'm in. When do we start?" she says.

"I found a letter she wrote my dad a long time ago. Come over after school and I will show you," I say.

After school, I show Maddy the letter.

Dear David,

Leaving is the hardest thing I will ever have to do. If anyone were to find out who I am, it will put you and Sam in terrible danger. Please tell Sam I love him. Do not tell him who he is.

Love Always,
Monica

P.S. Kula Maui, Hawaii. I work down at the beach. It's okay.

Maddy and I decide to go searching for my mother. We pack a few things: flashlights, a couple of pairs of clothes, money, rope, and Sour Patch Kids. Before we catch the first train out of this town, we realize we need water and food. It looks like we will have to stop at 7Eleven on our way.

I wonder if I should tell Maddy about the nightmare I had last night.

When we get to the 7Eleven, Maddy notices two men in green suits staring our way. Why would they be looking our way? That was super weird.

I am grabbing a couple of bottles of water when I feel someone put me in a chokehold. I can barely breathe. Suddenly, Maddy comes from who-knows-where and hits the man over the head with a coffee pot. She screams, "RUNNNN!"

I can feel it happening. I'm sweaty again. I feel strange.

I can't be dreaming. Not this time.

I shape-shift into a cheetah. I growl, "Maddy, hop on." Maddy jumps on my back, and we escape.

By the time we get to the train station, I have shifted back to myself. Who were those guys? What did they want?

Maddy doesn't say much. She stares at me.

Finally she says, "WOW, that was AMAZING! SAM, how did you do that?"

"I don't know, I respond."

"Before you turned into a cheetah, I saw that man who put the chokehold on you slip something in your pocket." I reach into my pocket to find a note:

> We know who you are. We can help. If
> you want to know where your mother
> is contact Agent Smalls and Agent
> Brothers from SIC (Supernatural
> Investigation Center).

As Maddy and I think about that, we have no idea how interested those guys really are in us. Looking back, I can imagine their conversation going something like this:

"We shouldn't have let him go," said Agent Smalls as they walk away from 7Eleven.

"Don't worry. We will have other chances," said Agent Brothers. "I know where they are going."

"How?" said Agent Smalls.

"I put a note in the boy's pocket, and at the same time I took out their receipt for the train to California," said Agent Brothers.

"So what did you say in the note?" said Agent Smalls.

"I said in the note that we are going to help him," said Agent Brothers.

"But aren't we supposed to capture him?" said Agent Smalls.

"We are going to trick him. Duh," said Agent Brothers. "We can't let this one go like Monica."

"Wait, wasn't Monica that shape-shifting freak like that boy?" said Agent Smalls.

"Yes," said Agent Brothers. "The boss won't be happy if we can't capture this one."

Maddy and I find seats on the train. "So..." says Maddy.

"I know this is kind of all going so fast," I say. "I have something to tell you. I had this dream that I was in my bed, but it wasn't me. And the more I think about it, I feel it wasn't a dream."

"That makes sense," says Maddy. "I mean, you changed into a cheetah. I think that so-called dream wasn't a dream, either. Wait—did this just happen recently?"

"Yes, so?" I answer.

"You're 13, so isn't that like the big 16 for guys?" says Maddy.

"Yes, so?" I say again.

"Your powers must just kick in because you're 13," says Maddy.

"Oh, so this is the age for boys like me for their powers to kick in," I say.

Maddy pulls out two tickets for Hawaii.

"What about those guys?" I say.

"Oh, don't worry. They don't know where or when we are going," says Maddy.

"Good. Those guys really scared me."

At the exit, the two men are waiting, but Maddy and I don't see them. "Where is everyone?" I say.

"I don't know," says Maddy.

As Maddy and I walk farther, I see the two men again. They're holding stun guns. Agent Smalls yells, "Don't move, or else!"

I have the feeling again I'm changing. Maddy yells, "Sam, turn into a tiger!"

I do. This time I can change on my command. I growl so loud probably the whole world hears it. I body-slam them, and they fall to the ground.

I feel cooler. Then I look at myself, and I'm back to human. I quickly grab the stun guns and stun them.

The police are here in a blink. Maddy and I get out of there as fast as we can. On the plane Maddy yells at the flight attendants, and the next thing I know we're in first class.

In Hawaii I ask around for my mom. People say she is at the beach. We go there, and I finally reunite with my mom—you know, a lot of hugging and crying, but it all goes well.

I thought this would be the departure of Sam and Maddy, the best friends for life. But it turns out she has an aunt who lives in

Hawaii, so Maddy can stay in Hawaii and we can go to school together.

I get so many letters from my dad. It turns out that my step-mom and my dad are getting divorced. So it's a win-win for me. I get to live in Hawaii with my mom and my best friend. Plus I didn't die from those agents!

Meanwhile at the prison, the two agents are counting the days until they get out. They shouldn't be counting. They're in there for life.

SHINE

SHINE by **Kate Potocsky** *is about a young dancer who is suddenly placed in the spotlight. She learns to stay confident even when the world surrounds her with hate.*

It all started in first grade when I was the superstar student for one day. A superstar student is whoever scores the highest on a test. A girl named Annie was always the superstar student until I scored higher than her, once! I screeched with joy thinking my class would too. I was wrong.

Annie had always been very popular. She was not happy I had ruined her winning streak. That same day, she told all her friends that I made up nasty rumors about them all. It was a lie! From that day on, they all hated me. Now I'm in seventh grade and suffer through the hate mostly every day of my life.

"You're ugly, you're stupid, and you're dumb. You look like a chicken. *Buck Buck. Buck Buck.* Go back to the pre-school!"

I thought about everyone tormenting me. I'm just a person exactly like them, and they don't seem to see it. They crush my dreams. They bully me for the silliest things. I don't understand. I used to try my hardest not to let the haters get to my head. Obviously, I failed. The negative words took over my confidence and completely outraged my happy thoughts. I don't wear designer clothes and I don't live in a mansion and I don't act snobby. Nothing makes sense to me. Society needs a makeover.

That is when I'm not dancing, though. When I dance I feel powerful, like I can pretend to be whoever I want to be and no one will care.

I was wrong. Everyone cares. They look at me in horror like I just killed somebody. When I dance I block out the criticism and glaring faces. The second the music dies, my spirit goes along with it.

I sit in bed thinking about the horrible things people say. But every once in a while, I have a good day.

Today was a good day—well, that was in the beginning. My day started great and then went downhill from there until after school.

My mom had a day off work and could drive me to school in her minivan. I was so thankful that I didn't have to take the bus. The bus is terrible. Against all odds, my sworn enemy for life Annie is on my bus. Normally when I take the bus I sit alone in the back listening to her scream, "Macie, why do you always sit alone? Oh wait, I already know!' Everyone laughs.

That wasn't happening today because my loving mom was right by my side. I was sitting in the passenger seat of my mom's minivan trying to block out the terrible visions of Annie.

My mom knows how to make me feel good about myself. "Honey, you look so pretty today! I love your new shirt! Have a great day at school, sweetie. I love you!"

I sprinted to the front doors where I always meet my best and only friend Kelsey. People often say how much we look alike. We both have long brunette hair and pale blue eyes. We both have light brown freckles scattered along our noses. We walked to our first hour together.

I was so happy when I received my math test. I got my first 100 percent this year! I was thrilled. Second-hour Spanish was fine and the same with third-hour language arts. During fourth hour social studies, my day changed.

Annie accused me of cheating off of her test. I didn't do it. Mr. Brown obviously believed her because she is the biggest teacher's pet ever. I could tell by the look on his face, too. He didn't fail me, though, but only because he didn't have any evidence of the cheating.

Worst of all, I sat alone at lunch! Kelsey got a lunch detention. Once again, I was all by myself. I unpacked my peanut butter and jelly sandwich, apple, and water bottle. I sat quietly for the rest of lunch. When lunch was over, I went to the library during recess to look for a new book.

The rest of the school day wasn't horrible, but it wasn't great either. It went by annoyingly slowly. There was one point in science when Mrs. Dawn called on me and I wasn't paying attention. It was super embarrassing. I saw Annie whisper to her friends and laugh.

After school at 4:30, I left for dance class. The icy snow caused tons of traffic, so I was seven minutes late to my class. It was a Wednesday afternoon. On Wednesdays, I have ballet class.

I hated ballet class! My bun is always too tight, my leotard is too loose, and my itchy pink tights are ripped.

We rehearsed our dance several times. I was in the back row behind Annie who was front and center. By the fifth time we did the dance, I was worn out. Annie was still full of energy. In fact, she was full of too much energy. She jumped as high as she could to do a perfect split leap. She landed on her right leg! Just watching her fall to the ground made me cringe. Tears plopped onto the shiny dance floor while everyone was rushing to help her up.

With a moment of hesitation, I ran over to help also. I realized that not helping her would not make me any stronger. Making fun of her would not make me any better. Just because she's not my best friend doesn't make it okay for her to lie on the ground in pain.

My dance teacher Rachel hurried to the phone and speedily called 911 and then Annie's mom. Her mom sped over to the studio. Around two minutes after she arrived, an ambulance lifted Annie onto a stretcher and hurried to the hospital. In horror, everyone watched as the flashing lights took Annie away.

Rachel swears she saw Annie's leg twist. She could tell that Annie would be benched for the rest of the season. In panic, Rachel cried, "The show must go on."

Rachel quickly told me to take Annie's spot in the dance. I was seriously scared that I would make a fool of myself. Rachel's actions made me think of an old quote:

"You're only as strong as your weakest player."

I was the weakest player. If Rachel never gave me a chance to shine, then I never would.

After class, Rachel asked to see me. I was nervous she would tell me she made a mistake by putting me in Annie's place. It was no mistake! Rachel whispered that I was really improving and that she wanted to give me a chance.

I, Macie Abigal Williams, was going to be front and center. I ran to the car to tell my mom about the good news. I went home and practiced every step in the whole entire routine until my legs hurt. The recital was only two weeks away.

Those two weeks went by a lot faster than I thought they would.

Throughout the weeks, my dance classmates made fun of me. They told me how much I didn't deserve the lead role. Annie's posse (almost the whole class) treated me the worst. They thought she made a mistake, too.

"If Annie can't be the lead, then someone else should! Not you! I don't even understand why Rachel chose you! She must have been confused and in shock when Annie fell. I bet it was all a mistake and she didn't have the heart to tell you!"

It was Wednesday, June 23. My knees were shaking. My hands were clammy and cold. My stomach was filled with butterflies. I felt as if I would vomit all over the place.

We had just finished my jazz number. Of course, I was in the back for it. I didn't mind being in the back row because I know I can't be the star of everything. I had two numbers in between jazz and ballet. I hurried to the dressing rooms and threw on my gorgeous, shimmering, blue ballet dress. Rhinestones decorated the corset top while different shades of snowy-looking tulle surrounded the waist, drooping out into an amazing tutu. My hair was secured in a bun with a million bobby pins and half a bottle of hairspray. Everything was perfect.

As I watched the next dance finish, I fixed my makeup. I applied wintery colors on my eyes to match the beautiful costume. I took a fluffy brush and swiped on some more coral blush. I smoothly smeared creamy red lipstick and a matching gloss over my lips. I was ready to rock and roll.

I gracefully danced onto the stage, being careful not to trip. I leaped, jumped, and turned wonderfully throughout the whole dance. Then came the big split leap. I almost changed the choreography and didn't do it because Annie was doing that exact move when she broke her leg, but I didn't! I leaped as high as I could and stunned the audience. Loud cheers and claps filled the theater.

As I was posing to conclude the dance, I caught a glimpse of Annie clapping slowly in a wheelchair with a broken leg and a mean grudge on her face. The grudge didn't bother me. I was so shocked that she was clapping at all! I excitedly walked off stage to get ready for the ending speech and scholarships.

There were around four dances after my big performance. After every number presented, all students entered the stage. Rachel was announcing the scholarship winners: "Nancy Smith, Karen Lancaster, Lenah Free..." and so on.

I sat on stage waiting to go hug my mom and dad. I decided to never listen to the winners because I was never one. Suddenly, my name was announced! I wasn't paying attention, but I did hear my name. I was shocked! I froze on stage for a second. It was such a surreal moment. My parents and siblings cheered as I strutted down the stage to receive my prize and give Rachel a hug.

My dance career had just begun.

SWEET, SWEET REVENGE

Revenge means everything to Jade. See where revenge takes her in **SWEET, SWEET REVENGE** *by RJ Danielson.*

"How could they exile me? I am the princess. A sorceress princess," I whine to Ann, my sorcery teacher.

I look at her. She just rolls her eyes at me. She has heard the story over a hundred times the past three years. Ann and I could be sisters, if it wasn't for our eyes. Both of us have long, raven black hair and pale skin, and are about five and a half feet tall. I have bright, jade green eyes, while Ann has the most spectacular dark-as-midnight eyes. "I think it may be the fact that you tried to kill your sister, the soon-to-be queen," says Ann.

She knows I don't like to talk about my insolent sister, Shade. She always brings her up. Sometimes I think Ann likes Shade more than me. But that really makes no sense. She doesn't even know Shade. "Ann?"

"Yes?"

"I was wondering—"

"That's dangerous."

"First, that is just rude. And second, do you like Sh-Sh-Shade more than me?" I stutter fearful of the answer.

"Why do you think I would like her more than you?" asked Ann.

"Oh, nothing, I was just wondering."

Well, I feel better after I get that off my chest. When Ann isn't looking I let out a breath. I didn't even realize I was holding it. I can't believe I actually thought she liked Shade more than me. I must be going crazy.

The next day Ann says she has big news and to get ready for breakfast quick. I got down to breakfast. I was surprised. We usually only have oatmeal for breakfast, except on special days. But for some reason today we have bacon, eggs, orange juice, and pancakes. Hmmm, I wonder what the occasion is. I'm a little nervous.

It's past eight o'clock, and I am stuffed. I'm starting to think that whatever Ann has to tell me isn't going to be good. She knows that I'm very gullible when I am stuffed with food. Oh no, what if she is planning to leave? What if she thinks that I can't be taught anything useful? What if, what if...? Ugh.

Ann coughs. By the time I raise my head she is staring right at me. "So, Jade. What I wanted to talk to you about is..." Oh no, what could it be? Here it comes. Ann surprises me with what she says next. "I think it's time for you to avenge yourself."

For a few moments I just stare at her in disbelief. "Phew, here I was thinking you were going to leave me or something. That is so much better. When did you start thinking I was ready?"

"Oh, for about a few weeks now."

"Really? I didn't think I was that close."

"Yeah, I didn't think that you would be ready for a while, but your magic has grown rapidly," expressed Ann with a smile.

I am so proud. She believes in me. I guess it is time to pack. I'm ready. I know what I need to do.

The next morning I begin my journey. I am returning to the place where I grew up, the Kingdom of Tranquility. Oh, how I loved it there. I began to get lost in my own memories.

I was eighteen years old. It was cold for a summer day but not too cold. In the morning I woke up and was told to go down to breakfast right away. There was a surprise.

When I got to breakfast my whole royal family was there: my mother, the queen; my father, the king; and my sister, Shade.

Shade is four years older than me. We could easily be mistaken for twins. It didn't take long to find out the news. I sat down, and my mother sprang it on me. "In a few weeks Shade will become queen."

Everyone was silent. It felt like forever. But Shade couldn't hold in her excitement. "What? I can't believe it! I thought it would be later," Shade said.

"What!" I couldn't understand that decision. "I am the greater princess! I am a sorceress!"

"Jade," my mother said intently. I didn't hear the rest of it. I didn't want to hear the rest of it. I was already out the door. I was planning my revenge. This couldn't be happening. I just couldn't stop myself.

The next night, I was caught trying to assassinate my sister. My parents exiled me for the attempted murder.

I must have replayed that story ten times before I realize I am standing just outside the castle wall. I am going to get into the castle the next night. But for now I will camp out in the woods near the kingdom.

I am curious the next morning. I can't help it. I go into the kingdom to see how everyone is doing. I need food, too. I buy two loaves of bread and three muffins. I am nearly seen by two old friends, and suspiciously looked at by four knights. I think it may be this hood I am wearing. The hood is as dark as midnight, covers my face, and may seem like something odd to wear in the middle of a summer day.

Night falls, and I go to the castle. No one is outside. I know how to get in the castle. When I was a child, I found a hole in the west wing of the castle. I could get in and out without anyone knowing it. I get inside easily. I begin to use the magic I perfected while exiled. I make myself float high above anyone who may walk by.

I know exactly where to go. But when I get there the door is locked. There is one more spell to use. I just need to touch it with my dragon ring. *ZAP!* The door swings open.

I am going to use my magic dagger. All I have to do is scratch her neck with it. It is so easy. And next I go to my parents' room. They would never expect this. But it is my revenge, and I do the same thing to them. I slip out silently and make my way back to my camp in the woods.

I am awakened by a scream. I know it was all the way from the castle. I am safely a half mile away. I can't wait until I can tell Ann. She will be so proud of me. I start my journey back to Ann. Once again I am happy.

THE SWORD OF DEMOS

Three demi-god friends go on vacation, only to discover that an army of monsters is trying to find an ancient weapon to destroy the world. It is up to the friends to stop them in **THE SWORD OF DEMOS,** *by Bryan Tran.*

Don't *you just hate when your friends abuse your godly powers? I do.*

"Stop being such a baby, Trey!" Cyrus said as he was forcefully pushing my head underwater. Cyrus was a son of Artemis. Being a son of Artemis was really rare considering Artemis only wants girls in her group of hunters. Cyrus was a normal American-looking guy with brown hair.

To be honest, I would have to agree with Cyrus. I can breathe underwater and re-energize from it.

"Why are you even struggling? We know you can't die from this," Sofia said as she laughed her head off. Sofia was a daughter of Athena. Athena was said to be smart and amazing in coming up with battle strategies. Sofia's only power was the battle strategy part; she was as smart as a normal mortal. Sofia was like Cyrus, a brown-headed American with a swimsuit on. I wish I could blast them with water-controlling powers, but mortals would freak out. I found this out when I was in training. My trainer, Nathan, told me that I should never use my powers or my weapon in front of mortals because they could see what we see.

After a while, they finally stopped trying to drown me.

After a whole day of fun at the beach and pool, Cyrus, Sophia, and I decided to go back to the hotel. As we were walking back, I heard two people talking in Greek. I heard the words "meeting at beach," and "Sword of Demos." I instantly knew that something bad was going to happen. The Sword of Demos was a sword with horrific powers used by the demon lord, Demos, to overthrow the Gods of Olympus. Luckily, he failed. Demos almost overthrew Olympus until Zeus finally allowed the demigods to help defeat Demos and his army.

After the two people walked away, I told Cyrus and Sofia what I had heard. "Guys, wait up. I just heard two demigods talking about the Sword of Demos. They said they were meeting at the beach for something."

"And what's your point?" Cyrus asked. "People at the fort have been talking about it. They could just be here for vacation."

"But why would people be meeting at the beach? Wouldn't they be meeting inside their hotel rooms?

"True. Let's take a shower and grab our gear," Cyrus said.

"If there really is a group of Demos's followers, we should ask gods for assistance," Sofia said.

An hour later, all three of us went to the beach. We saw what seemed like a mini-sized army with black dogs scattered about.

"Whoa. There are Hellhounds everywhere. There shouldn't be that many dogs in one area. This is definitely a group of Demos's followers," Sofia said.

Once we confirmed the information about Demos's sword, we prayed to our parents. I asked for some of Poseiden's troops and a wall of fog to cover the beach, Sofia asked for some of Athena's troops, and Cyrus asked for Artemis's wolves. Just in case people were still out, I also asked for Poseidon to raise some fog over the pool area and hotel. The sun was setting, so we were expecting people to be in their rooms.

It took about 30 minutes for our prayers to arrive. Our numbers were only half theirs, but we were more skilled than they were.

"All right," Sofia said. "Trey and Cyrus, attack the front, and I'll attack from the back. Archers are in the back. I think my wolves and I can take them."

"Sounds like a plan," I said. Once Sofia got behind them, I mouthed "3, 2, 1," and yelled, "CHARG-." I suddenly felt all of my energy draining out of my knee. Someone had shot me with a magic arrow in the knee. My teammates and I were stunned. "GO!" I told Cyrus and my troops. They went into battle.

I pulled out the arrow, wrapped the wound with a bandage, and made it to the water. As I submerged, I heard screams and howling. The reason I submerged was because one of my godly powers was to re-energize from any type of water. It took me about five minutes of re-energizing to the point where I could go into battle again. I rose from the water, took out my clam shell, and willed it to turn into a sword. I rushed into battle.

None of our troops were dead except for some of Cyrus's troops. The rest of us were holding up well. As I slashed three Cyclops at once, I tried to think of a plan to escape the battle and destroy the army. I scanned the battlefield for any advantages and saw that my Atlantic troops were next to me. Because I was distracted, a Hellhound jumped on me and tackled me to the ground. The Hound's jaws were gigantic with razor-sharp teeth.

Just as he was about to bite my face off, the Atlantian stabbed the Hellhound in the back and was disintegrated into sand. As I was saying thanks, he disintegrated into a million pieces of dust. A vampire-like creature killed him with one bite to the neck. I kicked it in the stomach and stabbed it.

Standing up, I saw it was Sofia, Cyrus, most of mine and Sofia's troops, very little of Cyrus's troops, and me against what seemed like 150 monsters. We were greatly outnumbered. As I got punched in the gut, I thought of the perfect plan that would destroy the monsters. I think. I sliced the monster in half and yelled, "GUYS, RUN TO THE CLIFF!" Cyrus, Sofia, and our troops understood what I was about to do and ran.

I then tried to focus and willed a wave to form out of the water. The wave was the size of a monster truck. I myself was amazed. I then forced it to crash only on the monsters. I watched as the monsters were washed into the sea and drowned. After I let go of the water, everything went black.

I woke up to my friends feeding me nectar, a godly food that could heal mortal injuries.

"Are you okay?" Sofia asked.

"I'm fine. I'm just really tired."

"I think that's enough fun for this vacation. Let's head back to the fort," Cyrus said. We walked back to our hotel room and packed up. We sat at the beach as we waited for our boat to bring us back to Pennsylvania.

THE TRUE MEANING OF HER LIFE

In **THE TRUE MEANING OF HER LIFE** by *Ainsley Stearns*, living is the only thing that is on Vironica Blu's mind. To a ten-year-old girl with cancer and a family that she loves so much, dying is not a possibility.

"Vironica has cancer," the doctor said. Vironica (Roni) Blu's parents were at the doctor's office getting the results back from her MRI. "She has cancer. It looks as though she may not survive," the doctor said.

"What!" her mother said as she slumped into the chair numbly. Her father stood there frozen in fear, not able to say a word.

Once they recovered enough to talk, her father was the first to speak. "What? She can't, though. That can't be right."

"There has to be some mistake," her mother wailed.

"How long do you think she will live?" her father asked matter-of-factly.

"About a year. She will have to start chemotherapy treatments, though," said the doctor.

At home Vironica's parents called her over to the couch. "Vironica, we need to talk to you. We got the results back from your MRI at the doctor's, and you have cancer. We will need to start chemotherapy this Monday."

"What! That's so not fair! Why is this happening? What's chemo? How long will I live? Will I even live? This is so not fair!" she repeated as she burst into tears. Her mom came over and hugged her until she calmed down.

"Chemo is a medicine that will hopefully fight off your cancer. The doctors estimated about another year or so that you will live," said her parents. She started to cry again.

"I'm so sorry this is happening, Roni. If we could do something more we would. You know that," said her parents.

"But what about Sam, and Will, and Anna, and Vikki? Do they already know?" said Roni.

"Of course your brothers and sisters know," said her parents.

"But Vikki and I are twins. I don't want to leave her especially," said Roni.

"Don't start saying that, Roni. You're going to get through this, and you're not gonna die," her twin sister Vikki said, walking in the room and then hugging her tightly for a long time.

On Sunday they all went to church. Vironica sat next to Viktoria like usual, but this time being extra clingy to her especially. Her parents told the pastor the news, and he prayed for her and her family. She listened to everything the pastor suggested and did it all, with a little extra. She continued to do it all and went to church in the following weeks. In those weeks, the Blu family was reminded of the true Healer, Jesus.

Roni began to hear of the ways she might be healed. She was so excited!

At her next appointment, her parents figured out that her cancer was spreading fast. "She may only live about two months," the doctors informed her family.

Her parents told Roni and Vikki first. They cried together.

"I am certain that we are going to stay together and that you are not going to die no matter what," said Vikki.

When the rest of her siblings were told they all cried and prayed for her. Even little Sam said a prayer. Being only two, though, it was short.

As the days went on, Vikki tried to comfort Roni, but was not successful. Roni began to feel worse and worse. On the day she felt the worst, the doctors told her she was dying, and fast! Roni and Vikki prayed through their tears with everyone by her side. She prayed one more time that Jesus would heal her.

Vironica Blu was in the hospital dying with her closest sibling, Vikki, by Roni's side.

The pastor came and prayed over her and her family that Jesus would show her and everyone else a miracle and heal her.

It seemed as though the hours and minutes flew by faster than ever before, in a terrible way. As Roni lay in her bed she hoped and prayed the feeling of slowly dying would not take her from this world for good.

One by one her family came in to ask if she needed anything. Every time someone would come in, she would start crying. She was not holding up very well at all. One minute she would be fine and the next sobbing. Once, the nurses had to bring in Vikki because they couldn't calm her down!

The doctors felt her last hope was an emergency operation. But Roni was certain she would live. Her friends and family came in one last time to hug her and say goodbye. It was the hardest thing any of them had ever done, especially Vikki. They spent almost ten minutes together crying and hugging until the nurse took her down to prep her for surgery.

An hour later she went in for an operation to remove the cancer. Her sister, Vikki, broke down and cried, praying that her sister would come out alive. Her other siblings and her parents prayed long and hard for Jesus to show them a miracle.

At that moment, Vironica Blu believed with all her heart that God would heal her. God showed them a miracle. The surgery was successful, and she was sent to the recovery room. Vikki had to be held back from attacking her with hugs.

"Let me see her," Vikki said.

"Let me see her! Can I see her yet?" Vikki and her siblings would impatiently ask the front desk.

"No, not yet," the nurse would repeat.

In the time it took for the nurses to take Roni to a recovery room, Vikki had asked to see her more than ten times!

When she was finally moved to a room, all of her family took turns praying with her and hugging her. They had all prayed and asked God and Jesus to show them a miracle, and He did. The cancer that she was not supposed to heal from was healed by having faith in God and Jesus, with the help of her family.

Roni and Vikki went on to tell her amazing story, along with the rest of her family.

ZOMBIE ATTACK

What would you do if you woke up one day and found your world taken over by zombies? Find out what one man does when he has to save his family in **ZOMBIE ATTACK**, *a heart-pounding story written by* ***Dilan Daniels***.

It was Saturday, June 1, 2016, a day that I will never forget. When I woke up that morning, my household was in its usual chaotic mode. My kids, Eli and Mia, were running around while my wife was in the kitchen making breakfast.

"Good morning," I said, pouring myself a cup of coffee. "So, what plans do you have to do today?"

"Well, the kids have swimming in an hour. After that I was going to go over to my sister's house, then come home. What about you?"

"I have some work to finish. How about we do pizza and a movie tonight?"

"That sounds good," my wife said, putting my plate of food in front of me.

An hour later my house was quiet. I turned on the news just to have some sound in the house. Just as I was getting into the project that I brought home from work, a breaking headline came on: "Hello, I'm Carmen Harlan reporting. A chemical outbreak has occurred in West Norfolk, Virginia. We have heard that the outbreak is spreading, because individuals along the East Coast are becoming infected by the second. The Department of Homeland security is asking that everyone stay in their house or some safe location in case this is airborne. More news will be coming."

Immediately, I picked up my cell phone to dial my wife. All that I received was a busy signal. I ran to grab my house phone and attempted to call again, but had no dial tone. I decided to grab my keys to my car in hopes that I could drive up to the YMCA on Lincoln Street in Birmingham and meet up with my family and get them back home. When I went back into the kitchen to get my keys off of the counter, another breaking news story was taking place.

"Hello, this is Carmen Harlan reporting again. The outbreak has spread to the Detroit area. It is important that everyone remain in their homes. We do not know the effects of the outbreak. Viewers have reported seeing zombie-like individuals walking in streets and terrorizing others. Please, stay safe." And then the television and electricity went out. I started to panic. My family was out there, and I needed to get them back home and keep them safe.

I grabbed my keys and opened my front door and was shocked at what I saw. It was like the walking dead in my neighborhood. People were walking down the street in a trance with half-peeled skin and bloodshot eyes. When I looked directly across the street, I saw my neighbor, Ms. Wright, with the same facial expression that I had. She began to scream hysterically at the zombies. I could tell that she was petrified. When she screamed, they stopped and turned toward her door. She tried to shut her door, but they overpowered her.

I looked on in horror as I watched them bite and eat her. For a split second I wondered if there was anything that I could have done to help her, but I realized that my decision to watch the horror from across the street was best. Ms. Wright was an older woman, and she would have slowed me down at some point on my mission to save my family.

After the zombies finished eating the flesh of Ms. Wright, they then got up and began to walk away in a trance-like state. I looked closer at the zombies. Shock ran through my body when I saw Mrs. Smith. Mrs. Smith was Ms. Wright's neighbor that lived two houses down. I remember she would wave to me each morning while gardening in her yard when I went to work. The sweet, old lady had turned into a flesh-eating zombie. For a split second I wondered what happened to her husband. I looked at their house, pondering the whereabouts of Mr. Smith, but I knew he was probably no longer alive.

Slowly, I closed my door, because I did not want to attract their attention. I ran to my sink and threw up. My wife and kids were somewhere out there, and in order to reach them, I had to go through the zombies.

I washed my face and thought. I did remember from television shows that as long as you did not make any sounds, zombies would not bother you. I did not know if that was true, but that was all that I had to get out of my current situation. However, before I left my house I needed to make some weapons. What happened to Ms. Wright could not happen to me.

Quickly, I looked through the kitchen drawers and grabbed spoons, forks, and knives. I took tape and wrapped it around the knives and forks. Before I closed the kitchen drawer I saw a meat cleaver and quickly grabbed it. I figured that since a zombie's body is decaying, a meat cleaver could protect me better. I grabbed the cutting board to act as my shield if need be. I opened the cabinet under the sink and took out the Lysol spray bottle. Lastly, I grabbed a lighter. Before walking to the door, I said a prayer that I would find my family.

Before opening my front door, I peeked out of the curtains to see if there were any zombies. There were none. I slowly opened my door, trying to be as quiet as possible. *I only have to make it about ten feet, and then I am at my car*, I thought. Once I got into my car, I didn't care about making any noises, because I would be able to run them over.

As soon as I stepped onto my porch, to the right of me I saw a zombie! A low gasp left my lips. Unfortunately, it was not low enough. The zombie turned toward me.

Thankfully, I had the lighter and Lysol in my hand. I lit the lighter and sprayed the Lysol. Fire came out. I then took my knife and cut its head off.

After the zombie lay on the porch, I looked up to see if any others heard us. No one had.

I chirped my alarm as I ran to my car. Immediately all of the zombies on the street turned my way. I quickly got in and tried to turn my car on. It did not turn on. It seemed like the walking speed of the zombies quickened. I closed my eyes and prayed for my car to cut on. Just as a zombie was outside of my window and raising his hand, my car cut on. I quickly put my Mustang in reverse and hit a few zombies on my way out of the driveway.

Luckily, when I got on Southfield Road, there were not many zombies in my way. But I did run over a few just because.

I finally made my way to the YMCA on Lincoln. When I turned into the parking lot, I saw that two zombies had broken the glass and were trying to get in. They turned to face me when they heard the car. As they turned and began to walk toward me, I saw my wife and kids peek through the window. They were alive!

I knew that I had to act quickly and quietly so I would not attract any other zombies to the area. I got as close to the door and the zombies as possible. I grabbed the cutting board and my meat cleaver. I kept the car running as I exited the door.

"Run to the car while I fight them off!" I yelled to my wife.

I ran to one zombie and hit him on the head with the cutting board. I quickly took out the meat cleaver and cut his arms off. If the zombie had no arms, he could not grab me. Before the other zombie could touch me, I kicked him to the ground and cut his head off. I noticed out of the corner of my eye that my family was in the car. I also noticed other zombies on their way to the parking lot.

I got in the car and locked the doors.

"I can't believe this!" my wife cried. "Everyone inside is dead. We only survived by hiding."

"It's going to be okay," I said, hoping that I had calmed her down.

As I backed out of the parking lot, I was happy that my wife had told me to fill up my tank the night before.

Since this outbreak took place on the East Coast, I thought that by driving west, we might be able to survive. As we drove down Southfield Road, I noticed all of the bodies lying on the ground. I said a quiet good-bye to my hometown of Southfield as I drove to safety on the West Coast with my family.

ISOLATED FROM THE INSIDE

ISOLATED FROM THE INSIDE, *by **Damon Muegge**, is the story of a middle-school student who is trapped in the chaos of a viral outbreak that was started at his school. With only two friends by his side, the question is: will they make it out alive?*

I was quickly walking through the twisted school. I could feel my heart pounding like a drum throughout my body. I came across two doors. "Do I go left or right?" I asked myself.

I decided to take the left door. I then very slowly and cautiously wrapped my cold, shaking hand around the doorknob. As I pushed the door open, I could hear my conscience telling me not to continue, but I proceeded anyway.

Once the creaking of the door stopped, I slipped my body through the crack and into the room. I was walking deeper and deeper into the pitch-black room, when I suddenly felt a cold, pale hand grab hold of my shoulder! I quickly turned around, smacking the hand away from me.

"Wait, it's okay!" said a panicky voice. As the figure moved closer, I could slowly start to make out his face and recognize who it was.

"Joe?" I asked.

"Yes, it's me. I've been looking everywhere for you!"

Then out of the darkness another face became recognizable. It was Ellis. I knew they weren't zombies because both of them could actually speak, and zombies cannot.

As my eyes adjusted to the darkness, I realized what room of the school I was in. It was the room that started it all. Here's what happened.

A class full of students was doing a science project on a virus. No one is quite sure of what really happened, due to the fact that zombies are hunting every last one of us down. But I think what happened was one of the students was studying a highly-contagious virus called selenium. It's a radioactive substance that automatically shuts down the body and reboots it to follow its first instinct: to eat.

Nobody knew the virus was spreading until the first victim. All I know is that it was a complete accident, and only a couple of people are still alive. Once the government was updated about the virus, they locked everyone inside the school so that the virus wouldn't spread even more. Luckily the virus wears off, leaving the victim of it no longer alive, but at least it cannot infect anyone after. Sadly, it takes about three to four hours until it wears off.

CRASH! The crushing sound of glass filled the halls of the school, echoing everywhere.

"What was that!?" cried Joe.

"I don't know; how 'bout you two go check it out?" said Ellis. And as stupid as we were...we did.

As soon as Joe and I stepped foot into the hall, Ellis slammed the door behind us, locking us out!

"Ellis!" I yelled. "Let us back in!"

"I'm sorry, I just can't risk my life. I have to use you two as bait so that I can get myself out of here."

Suddenly the screeching voice of the undead filled the room that Ellis was in! It filled my ears with fury, making me jump so high I thought I could blast through the ceiling! As its pale skin became visible behind Ellis, my eyes widened with horror. Its cold hand wrapped around him and pulled him into the darkness!

"That was the safest room in the building!" I mumbled.

A sudden beam of light burned my eyes as a police officer flashed a light at us. "I got two over here!" he yelled. "It's okay, you two are safe now...I'm gonna get you two outta here."

"Thank you," I said. I shook his hand, and we started to leave.

He cleared the way, taking us out into the sunlight where a ton of police and doctors were, but only a couple of survivors. As soon as we got out, a surgeon came over to us and started checking our eyes and stuff. She got us some water, but I didn't drink it because I thought I'd throw up after all the things I saw. One person yelled over to us and told us to get in an ambulance truck so that they could take us to the hospital.

As I was walking to the truck I felt a slight, wet trickle of blood run down my hand. I looked down at it and saw a small gash with white bubbles fizzing out of it. "I wonder what this is?" I asked myself.

Oh, yeah: It was the first symptom of the virus!

Index of Authors and Titles

Made in the USA
Charleston, SC
09 August 2015